D1228438

VOODOO VENGEANCE
AND OTHER STORIES
BY JOHNNY CRAIG

Publisher and Executive Editor: GARY GROTH
Senior Editor: J. MICHAEL CATRON
Series Designer: JACOB COVEY
Volume Designer: MICHAEL HECK
Production: PRESTON WHITE
Associate Publisher: ERIC REYNOLDS

Fantagraphics Books, Inc.
7563 Lake City Way NE
Seattle, WA 98115
(800) 657-1100
Fantagraphics.com. • Twitter: @fantagraphics • facebook.com/fantagraphics.

Special thanks to Cathy Gaines Mifsud, Dorothy Crouch, John Benson, Marie Severin.

First Fantagraphics Books edition: December 2016
ISBN 978-1-60699-965-3
Library of Congress Control Number: 2016908697
Printed in China

First Appearances

Guided by EC historian John Benson's research on EC release dates, we present the stories in this book in the order in which they originally appeared:

VOODOO VENGEANCE

AND OTHER STORIES

BY JOHNNY CRAIG
WITH JACK DAVIS

FANTAGRAPHICS BOOKS

Seattle

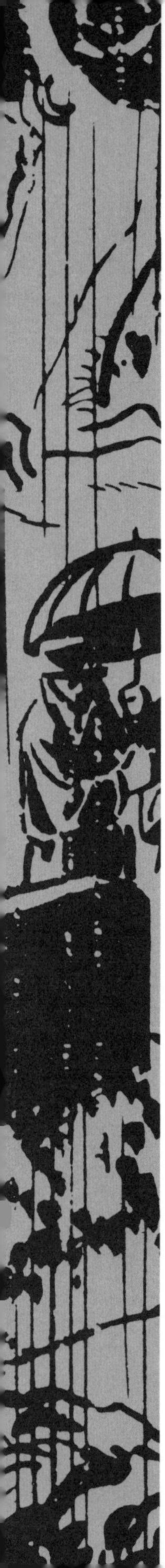

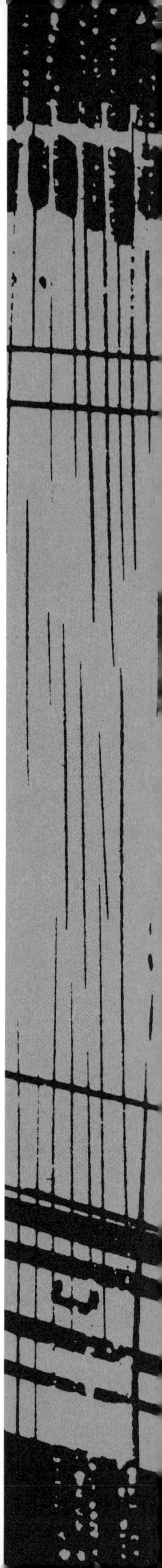

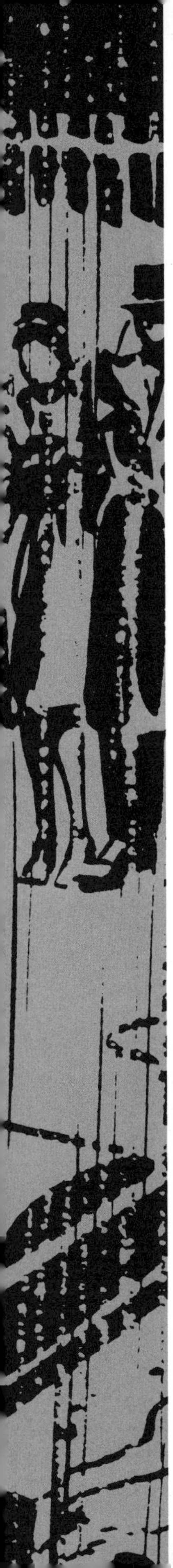

EC Comics did not publish writer credits and its master records no longer exist. Based on the best information available, we believe the creator credits above to be accurate. We welcome any corrections.

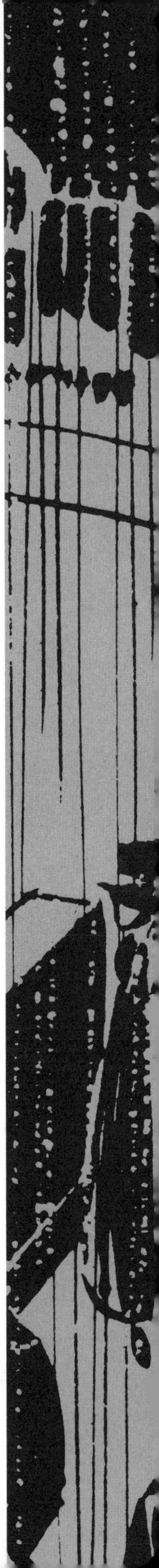

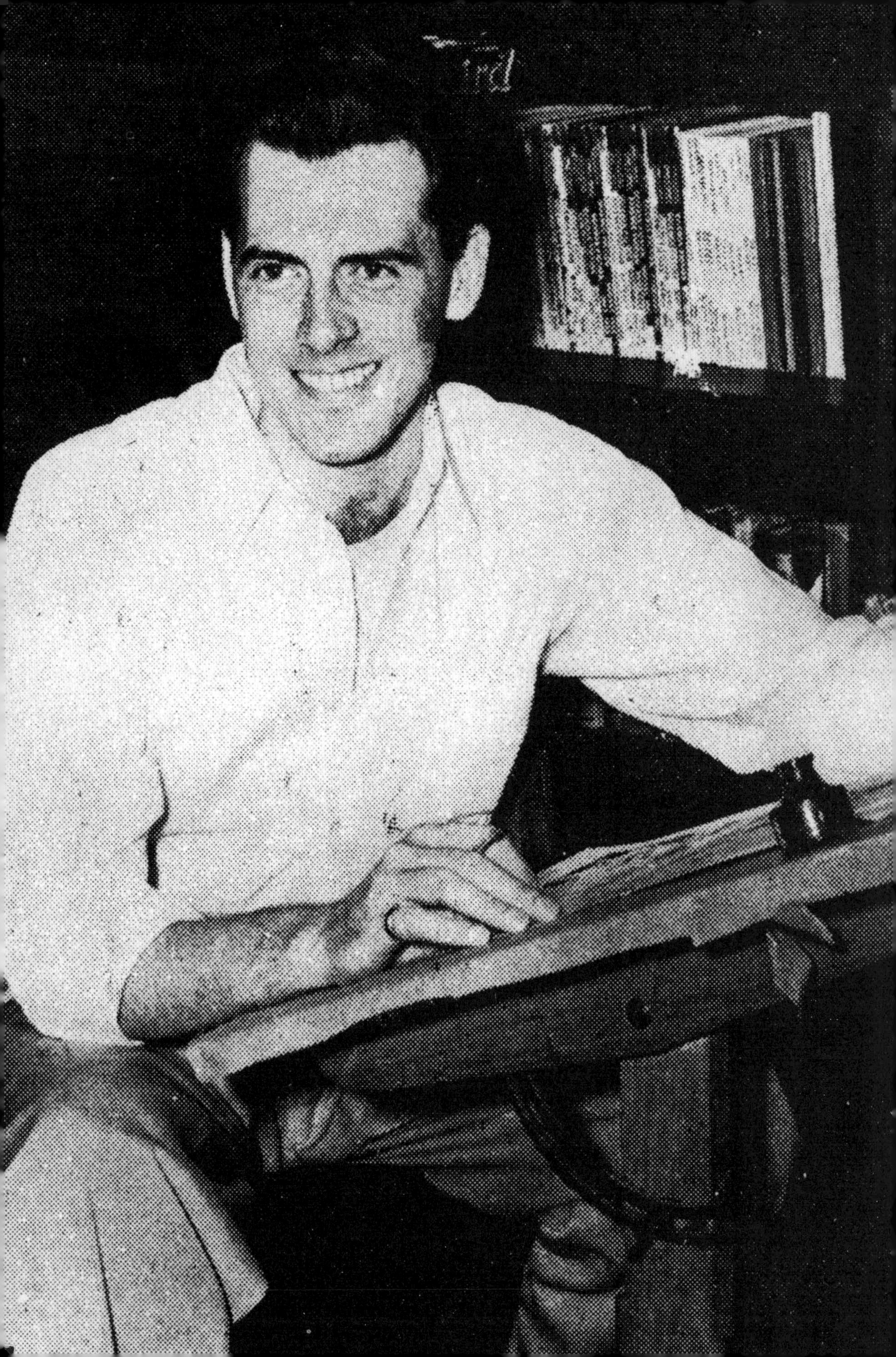

LARRY STARK

JOHNNY CRAIG, STORYTELLER

Johnny Craig had the cleanest line of all the EC artists —
but he was also the slowest worker on that history-making
creative team.

In the EC house ads that featured thumbnail caricatures of all the artists, Craig was usually sleeping, or relaxed into something soft. Because he took his time, Craig produced fewer stories than his fellow EC artists of similar tenure, so it's easy to think of him as "just another great EC artist." Craig was initially hired by M.C. Gaines — Bill's father — and he was still there, working on Picto-Fiction projects, when Bill decided to cancel all his other titles and publish only *Mad* magazine. So Johnny Craig worked for EC Comics longer even than his publisher.

Johnny Craig and Graham Ingels — whose styles were perhaps the furthest apart of all the EC artists — started at EC within a year of each other, doing covers. Over the years, Ingels drew 29 covers, most for *The Haunt of Fear*, but Craig's EC career cover count comes to 102 — if you include the single cover he and Al Feldstein did together as "Aljon" (*Modern Love* #2, August-September 1949) — making him far and away the most prolific EC cover artist. EC's next most prolific cover artist was Feldstein himself, with 73, counting the cover he inked over Al Williamson (*Weird Fantasy* #18, March-April 1953) and the Aljon cover.

The careful work Craig put into his covers — and in the splash panels beginning each story — made them standalone works of art.

When he worked on stories, Craig had one advantage over other artists at EC: with few exceptions, he wrote all the stories he drew, so words and pictures developed together in his mind. In both, there's a kind of quiet craftsmanship in Craig's work — so it might be best to think of him as a writer. However, he had a few artistic clichés (in the best sense of the phrase) that marked his drawing style.

About here would be a good idea to switch from artist Johnny Craig to writer, or better yet, *storyteller* Craig.

As a general rule, Craig's stories started with an event or a narrator telling the reader he had an experience to relate. What followed was often a twisty tale that ended in quite a different place than expected. Craig's writing is fluid, measured, and verbally alive and inventive, with a lot of deliberate detail. Sometimes his endings were so subtle the Vault-Keeper had to explain them in his final paragraphs.

Let's dip into this grab bag and see what's here:

"Voodoo Vengeance!" (p. 1) was loosely suggested by a short story by John Collier in which a seller of spells and poisons suggests that people who bought love potions almost always came back for poisons later. Collier left the matter there, but here Craig fills in the revisit — this time to the shop of a voodoo practitioner

OPPOSITE: This 1951 photo accompanied Johnny Craig's "Artist of the Issue" feature that ran in EC Comics in early 1952.

selling carefully prepared dolls. And of course elderly, mustachioed Caleb Standish arrived home early to discover his young, gorgeous wife has a lover, and Q.E.D., he goes back for a doll. The exchange, "Please! You loved me once ..." "Hah! I only married you for your money!" shows up, with minor variations, in many EC crimes of passion.

Now there is a detail about the ending I must talk about, but it will spoil your enjoyment, so go read the story first. It starts on page 1.

Really. Stick your thumb or finger on this page, and go read "Voodoo Vengeance!". Then come back here, and continue reading with the next paragraph. ...

... Notice how the story ends: a disaster for wife Sally is briefly described, after which the penultimate panel shows Caleb, his face distorted in horror, staring out at the unspeakable. Then it's the joke-filled final monologue by the Vault-Keeper that deals with what storyteller Craig *didn't* show.

(By the way, the introductory speeches by the Vault-Keeper in Craig's stories are never joke-ridden, as they almost invariably are in Feldstein's intros. Craig saved his — usually feeble — jokes for his endings. Maybe Craig didn't have much of a sense of humor, or didn't relish puns as much as Feldstein obviously did?)

The moral of "Vampire!" (p. 9) is "Make sure you shove your wooden stake through the right heart!" — and variations of it were an EC house plot. It's set in Marsh Island, Louisiana, where "the blazing, sweltering heat of day changes to the moist, sticky uncomfortable heat of night." Craig uses beads of sweat and clouds of mosquitoes on his New York City characters — but in comics, sweat is a cliché for nerves, and the tiny insects look more like butterflies.

On page 10 panel 3, the handsome young doctor/hero is shown full face. His is a long oblong countenance, with a high straight forehead above prominent brows, and a jaw square at the base with 45-degree angled jawlines. It is Johnny Craig's face, identifiable from photographs, and it appears in almost all of his work. Doctor Reed argues with a fat, cigar-chewing detective (anticipating *In the Heat of The Night* perhaps?) over a series of bloodless corpses, then disastrously tries solving the crimes himself.

On page 12 panel 5 and page 13 panel 2, Craig tries something only Graham Ingels excelled at: the newel posts of the staircase are topped with round, *fanged* faces. The prose in captions is excellent, the plot development unhurried — but one thing about the EC house plots: they're so predictable!

The opening panel of "Murder May Boomerang" (p. 17), and the last panel of the story on page 24 are identical, suggesting the hero's story is recycling through his mind again and again as he aimlessly drives around. Craig spends two pages outlining the love-bond between the motherless hero and his father, then switches to present tense in which, off camera, Dad is beaten by an escaped convict. An enraged hero taking him to a hospital is eager for revenge and sees an opportunity. This is an excellently crafted story building genuine emotions to a surprising conclusion.

"Impending Doom!" (p. 25) is a shameless steal of a classic story. The title escapes me, but I heard it several times on a radio program called *Escape!* — where evocative music and the voice of William Conrad transported me every time.[1] In that version, an artist does a quick-sketch portrait of a man in court but with no idea who or why. On his vacation hike he comes upon a gravestone carver finishing a sample that has the *artist's* name on it with that very day as the date of his death. It is the man in his portrait. They decide to wait for midnight to set things right — and the story ended with the rasp of the carver ominously sharpening his chisel.

But Craig introduces a third character — the artist's old flame, now the carver's unhappy wife.

Craig tells this story in two-panel tiers nearly every page and hardly any narrative boxes, and many panels have little or no backgrounds. This gives Craig plenty of room and time to tell the story; but I bet you can tell which version I prefer.

So let me digress here and talk about the women of the 1950s — eloquently displayed in the three center panels of page 6. She is buxom but tightly brassiere'ed, and eight or nine heads tall in heels, without an ounce of extra fat. Her wasp waist can't be much more than 22 inches around, and her long legs go on forever. The 1950s was a good time for boys growing toward manhood, weren't they?

The hero in "Horror House!" (p. 32) writes stories for horror comics — when his couple-of-dozen friends don't take over his apartment for endless parties.

So he buys a suburban house — cheap, because it's haunted. But peace is short-lived. His friends try to boomerang the house with sound effects, which seem to work until … but, aah, that would be telling, wouldn't it?

Two panels of crowded friends give Craig an opportunity to show off a variety of faces. Like most comics artists, he preferred faces in profile, as in the first (p. 33 panel 2), but varies them in the second (panel 3).

Late in the story is a personal cliché — people are shown staring in horror out of the panel at something Craig never draws. I think this is a more effective approach than, say, Jack Davis's joy in rotting flesh.

---

1 *Tales of Terror*, the authoritative index to EC Comics by Fred Von Bernewitz and Grant Geisman (Fantagraphics Books and Gemstone Publishing, 2000) cites the short story "August Heat" by W.F. Harvey, as Craig's inspiration.

In "Mutiny" (p. 39), three thieves replace the crew of a sailing vessel because its captain just got paid with a fat bag of diamonds. The problem is making him tell where they're hidden — and maybe this Captain Cutter isn't as helpless as he looks. The story gives Craig a great opportunity to indulge in rock-'em-sock-'em fisticuffs for a change. The best example is the second panel of the last page (p. 45), showing one sock. On a totally black background, the two figures are in furious action — but shown an instant *after* the punch. One figure is caught in mid-air, flying over the rail; the other twisted by the follow-through of the punch. The dynamism in both figures defines what has and what will happen.

"Nightmare!" (p. 46) is one of the second-person narrative stories that Bill Gaines and Al Feldstein were discussing when I first visited the EC offices. Some people thought it drew the reader in when the disembodied narrator begins "One of *your* employees has fallen to his death from a scaffold!" It never did pull me in — but then, I identify not with the protagonist but with the writer when I read a story.

In this rain-soaked tale, "you" are a construction engineer so exhausted with overwork that "you" keep dreaming about

being buried alive. But when dangerous reality imitates "your" dreams ...

The splash panel taking up three quarters of page 1 (p. 46) is drawn from the point-of-view of a person viewing a funeral from down in the grave — a gimmick Craig used more than once.

But one glaring detail here is an unexplained inside joke: when the psychiatrist asks "your" name, "you" answer, "My name is John Severin!" At the time, Severin's name was not known to EC readers, as he was about four months away from his EC debut. But Severin did share a studio with Harvey Kurtzman, who was already working at EC, and Craig may have met him through the Kurtzman connection.

"Dead-Ringer" begins with an amazing splash page (p. 54), one of the few full-page splashes in EC Comics. Except for the bottom inch or two, it is the black night sky, pricked out by a few tiny dots of stars. The bottom edge is the brow of a grassy embankment behind which a disheveled figure kneels, pleading to three figures in suits and fedoras "Don't kill me! Listen to my story!"

His story, neatly told, is of his trying to pass himself off as a wealthy businessman, his identical double. But his new identity is hated to extinction. (It's almost *It's A Wonderful Life* in reverse!)

The top five panels of page 4 (p. 57) demonstrate Craig's use of lighting and shadows — even though the wood in which he buries the body, in the next two, looks quite sunlit!

I see "Werewolf Concerto!" (p. 62) as a peculiarly unsuccessful story — and saying it's set in Hungary doesn't help. Readers are asked for six pages to empathize with someone who suddenly reverses direction — but until then he seems to do nothing to help the situation except cry. It may seem thin ("He must find a victim!" the writer says to himself!) because the cute ending-gimmick takes so much time in set-ups, and predictable details are heavily underlined. But then, comics were for *kids*, right? So they needed to be led, step by careful step — nah! I don't buy it.

The opening splash (p. 62) features two "disembodied faces" — a personal storytelling technique Craig used often.

The war Johnny Craig served in had been over for six years when "Flight From Danger!" (p. 70) was written, but though it's set in the Soviet sector of occupied Berlin, all the heroic clichés are rigorously in place. (Except the hero is "only wounding" Soviet soldiers — in old *German* helmets — with his pistol!) A scientist and his daughter "developed the hydrogen bomb" but want only Americans to have it. (An act of treason when Julius and Ethel Rosenberg tried to do the reverse.)

Several panels here have no background detail. I don't know whether that was to save drawing time or to concentrate attention on the action — but it happens a lot in Craig's stories. By the way, that's again Johnny Craig's own face on the hero (page 72, panel 6). He gets emotion by what he does to those eyebrows!

"Poison!" (p. 76) — an early Crime SuspenStory — is a neatly crafted, subtle story of murder, blackmail, and of cleverness upset by plausibly unforeseen circumstances. There is a mood in the murderer's mind that neither character states, yet both of them know what's going on.

The housekeeper-villain has a long pointed face, and instead of the flowing locks of a love interest, she wears a tight round bun — and she smokes!

Curses create atmosphere, and at EC they always come true. In the costume epic "The Curse of The Arnold Clan!" (page 84), a murdered brother lays his dying curse on the future of his murderer brother — a weird curse, one that works only once every 50 years. That's enough, though, to let the current eldest Arnold family denizen ignore it — the curse goes down originally in 1750, and supposedly, he's almost lived through the last day of 1950. The details here are clever, but people in EC horror stories are usually tripped up by unpredictable accidents.

England was always terribly foggy in 1950. (It wasn't in 1970, when I got there.) So foggy, in "Terror On The Moors!" (p. 91), as to make an American tourist abandon his car and ask shelter of an old, eccentric lord and his short, bald, toothless butler. The mansion ends up demolished like the house of Usher (by fire, not water), but before that there's catalepsy and

premature burial and ominous screams and movements in a locked room. The relationships are subtle, but Poe hovers in the background. And, after waiting a whole day for rain to stop and learning the bizarre story, once a fatal fire has snuffed out anyone who might tell it, our American gets back in his car, and slowly motors away ...

"Seeds Of Death!" (p. 99) is classic Craig. He takes six panels for a full-page preamble, then explains how a disembodied human hand ended up in a trash fill. It's a typical romantic triangle with a murderous jealous husband, but beyond that, nothing is predictable. A bittersweet final twist only adds spice to the story. It should be read, not commented upon.

On pages 4 and 5 (p. 102 and 103), Craig departs from the standard comics format of three tiers of panels — something he rarely did.

That splash page (p. 99) reminds me of this quote, from another of Craig's stories: The Crypt Keeper cracks: "So come in and relax. We can *hold hands*! Heh! Heh! I have a whole *casket* full of them!"

I find the details of the telling of "Backlash!" (p. 106) much more interesting than the story itself. It tells of a writer driven mad by rejection slips. And I can personally vouch for its plausibility — only two magazines ever published the dozens of stories I sent around. Craig's writer invents a foolproof locked-room mystery, writes it into a story — and keeps getting it back, unread. Of course, Craig never divulges the secret, but the protagonist uses that secret to become a locked-room serial killer. Odd — but the frustrated writer in me finds that believable!

Notice the faces here. On five of them, there is an odd line across the bridge of the nose. I think, since Craig is famous for his use of lighting and shadows, that these were signals to colorist Marie Severin of where she should lay in a shadow — for instance under the brim of a hat.

The third panel of page 5 (p. 110) is full of the "disembodied faces" of a city terrified by the killings. That's one of Craig's artistic clichés; another is the total absence of any backgrounds in the opening splash panel on page 1 (p. 106).

But oddest of all are the first three panels on page 6 (p. 111), which show the hero in a bar, a close-up of his listening face to the right, and in varied depth background, four other men discussing the locked-room killer. There are two dialogue balloons in each of the three panels, in

which different words appear — but each of the three panels is identical! Probably readers familiar with EC (like me!) would absorb the words and notice none of the drawing. I wonder, though, if Craig was loafing here, or trying for an effect.

When revisiting the world of voodoo, Craig joins two legends about Haiti — the doll and the zombie — in unusual new ways. In "Voodoo Vengeance!" (page 1) what happened to the doll happened to the victim, as the standard cliché has it. In "Voodoo Death!" (p. 114), however, a doll pursues its victim holding a needle like a rapier. And instead of a zombie's traditional mindless, soulless shamble, this one looks and acts and talks just like a live human being.

In several panels there are no details, but the background is solid black. On the top tier of page 120, panel 1 is in bright white light, while the next is all in deep shadowed blackness — even though the lamp at the center remains lit! All in all, this is a very peculiar story indeed.

"Sink-Hole!" (p. 121) starts with a preamble, and tells the story of a pretty young airhead who makes every mistake possible, including marrying a crotchety old farmer on the strength of his fifteen-year-old photo mailed to her lonely hearts club address. There are indeed sinkholes in the limestone plains of Iowa that could swallow whole towns, not just a mere tractor, and underground rivers might wash a body into a deep well — but only at EC would a tale of empty marriage and wrong choices end up as this one does.

Here in "The Sewer!" (p. 129), the splash panel's close shot of a sewer entrance could be a blown-up detail from a *Spirit* splash page by Will Eisner, who taught the entire comics industry how to draw water.

The narration begins in the midst — near the end, actually — of the story, which for three quick pages is an ordinary romantic triangle murder tale. But then there's a fascinating twist, when the murder suddenly drives the lady insane. The murderer flees, hides in the sewer during a heavy rainstorm and ...

It's a neat and well-told story; but right here I'd like to pause to talk about "The anatomy of the *sock*!" I mean the action panel next to last on page 131. The two figures are shown, not at the point of fatal contact, but in the *result* of the punch. The husband is flying back into the panel, the hero is twisted violently to the left with the follow-through of his blow — and the point of contact is marked by a starburst. There aren't even any background details to distract the eye from the event.

Compare this with the action panels on pages 44 and 45 of "Mutiny"; the final panel in "Seeds Of Death!" (p. 103); page 148 panel 6 in "Southern Hospitality!;" and the first panel of the final page in "Hatchet-Killer!" (p. 181). Each of these is unique, but the technique is the same.

"Midnight Snack!" (p. 182) is, for me, the weirdest story in the bunch. The hero keeps waking up from blackouts and finding himself in odd places doing peculiar things. The one constant is that he's ravenously hungry, even though the smell of food makes him nauseous. He learns eventually what's happened to him, but the reader is never told how or why. The only clue seems to be his midnight reading of a collection of horror stories. Maybe you'd better not read *this* book late at night!

"*My* money? I don't have any money! I thought *you* had money!" So screams a Northern gigolo, stuck in the tangle of Southern heritage and history called "Southern Hospitality!" (p. 143). Georgian pride meets naked greed as he hopes to live selling heirlooms out of the mansion's dusty attic — and he might have gotten away with that, if not for the vengeful portrait of a Confederate general. In EC stories, it usually turns out that way.

Apparently, you've got to be a member of the clan before you can hear the family banshee heralding death — so, in "The Howling Banshee!" (p. 153), when an ex-bookie's past begins to catch up with him, it's his wife who hears the call. 'Tis a pity his second chance gets cut so short, and it's a pity these two young lovers can find only the one thing to talk — no, to argue about. A very thin story indeed, but with a twist.

The twist to this romantic triangle — "A Toast ... To Death!" (p. 158) — is indeed clever, and it's inevitable that a girl named Sherry would marry a guy more in love with his grapevines than his much younger wife. And yet, in a sense it's those grapes that eventually avenge their vintner-owner's murder!

It's interesting that the once-beautiful heroine of "About Face!" (p. 166) spends four of the story's eight pages with a black silk bag tied around her head, looking through volumes of witchcraft and voodoo, hoping to find a cure. The one she finds is contrived — but not much more than the several twists in the plot themselves. For the ending to work, she must actually *be* ugly, and Craig opens the story with her shoving that lovely face into the mouth of one of her tamed lions. The three parts of this story are each quite well told, though they fit uncomfortably together. And, how odd: an EC horror story with a happy *and* shocking ending!

EC characters are very high-strung, and they jump easily to wrong assumptions. The flavor of building tension in "Hatchet-Killer!" (p. 174) is a little like the way Arch Oboler wrote it into radio plays on the *Suspense* or *Inner Sanctum* programs. Just as with comics, these radio dramas got only 30 minutes — less

commercials — to scare the wits out of boys like me.

The prose here is lovely: "... the raindrops sound like a million softly falling footsteps that herald the approach of death!" Where in a *Superman* story could you find anything to match that? This is one of Johnny Craig's best performances.

Half of the opening splash for "The Vamp!" (p. 182) shows the disembodied faces of the three protagonists — the blonde wife in a tightly upswept ponytail, the Hungarian vixen with her dark hair caressing her ears and neck, and between them, the perplexed eyebrows of our hero. The story has two Americans on a whirlwind European tour for three panels, but while "getting some air" in Budapest our hero runs into a woman, and it's apparently lust at first sight. There is of course a very odd twist, everything happens a little too quickly, and the Vault-Keeper explains the ending.

But plot pales to the fact that the artwork is signed "Craig & Davis" and it's fun to guess where fast-and-scruffy Jack Davis took on the inking of Johnny Craig's careful pencils. I can't quite tell, but by page 5 (p. 186) or certainly page 6 (p. 187) there are more blacks (and more wrinkles) — and the top-center panel of page 187 is a pure Jack Davis figure, seen from the back, hunched, and supposedly running. See if *you* can separate one artist from the other.

LARRY STARK (b. August 4, 1932, New Brunswick, New Jersey) "gave up reading comic books forever" in his freshman year of high school when "true" romance comics took over from "true" crime comics.

But four years later, he discovered EC Comics. While attending Rutgers University, he faithfully wrote a letter commenting on each new EC comic book. Bill Gaines proclaimed Larry to be "EC's Number One Fan," and awarded him "a free lifetime subscription to everything I publish."

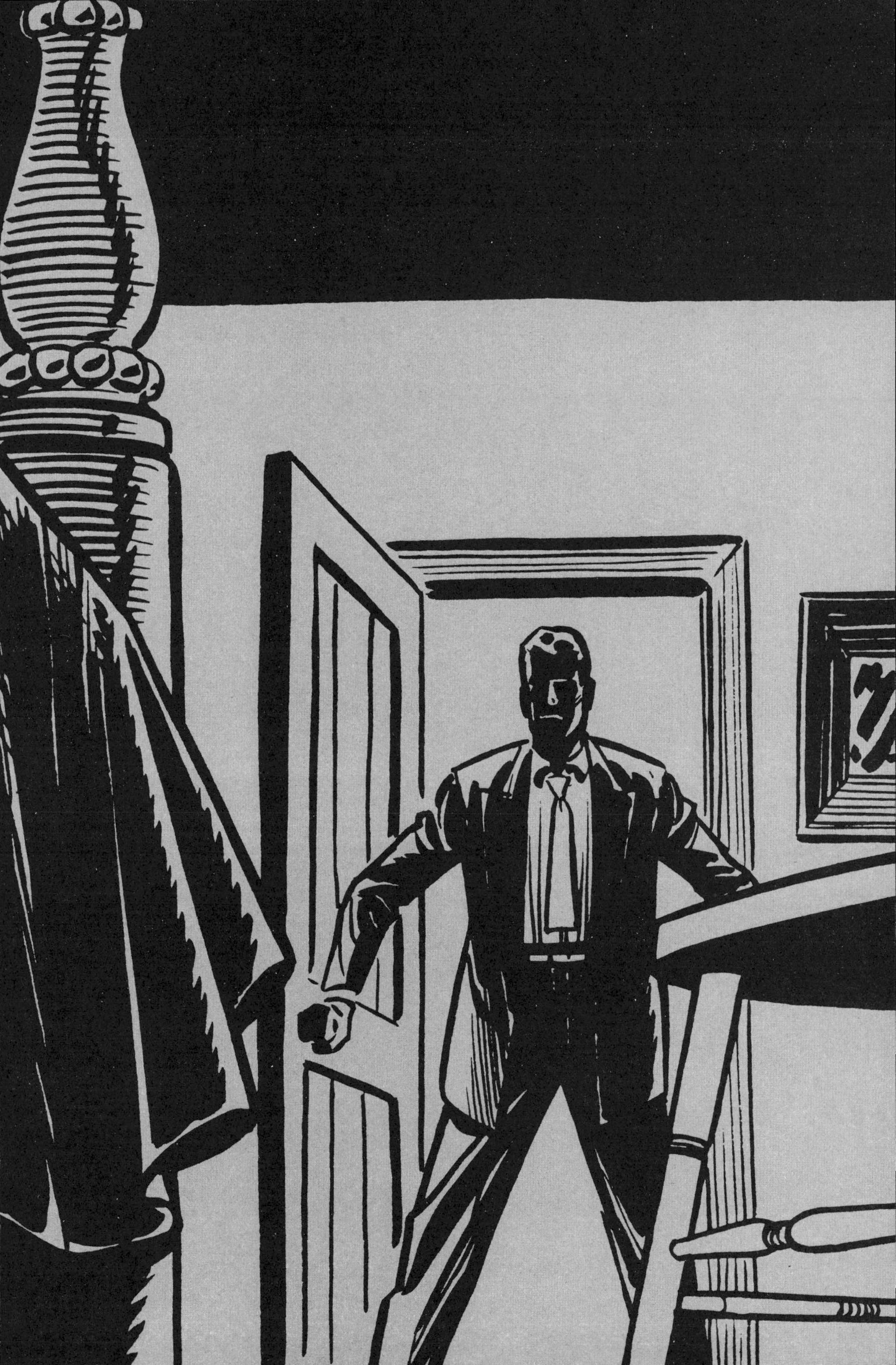

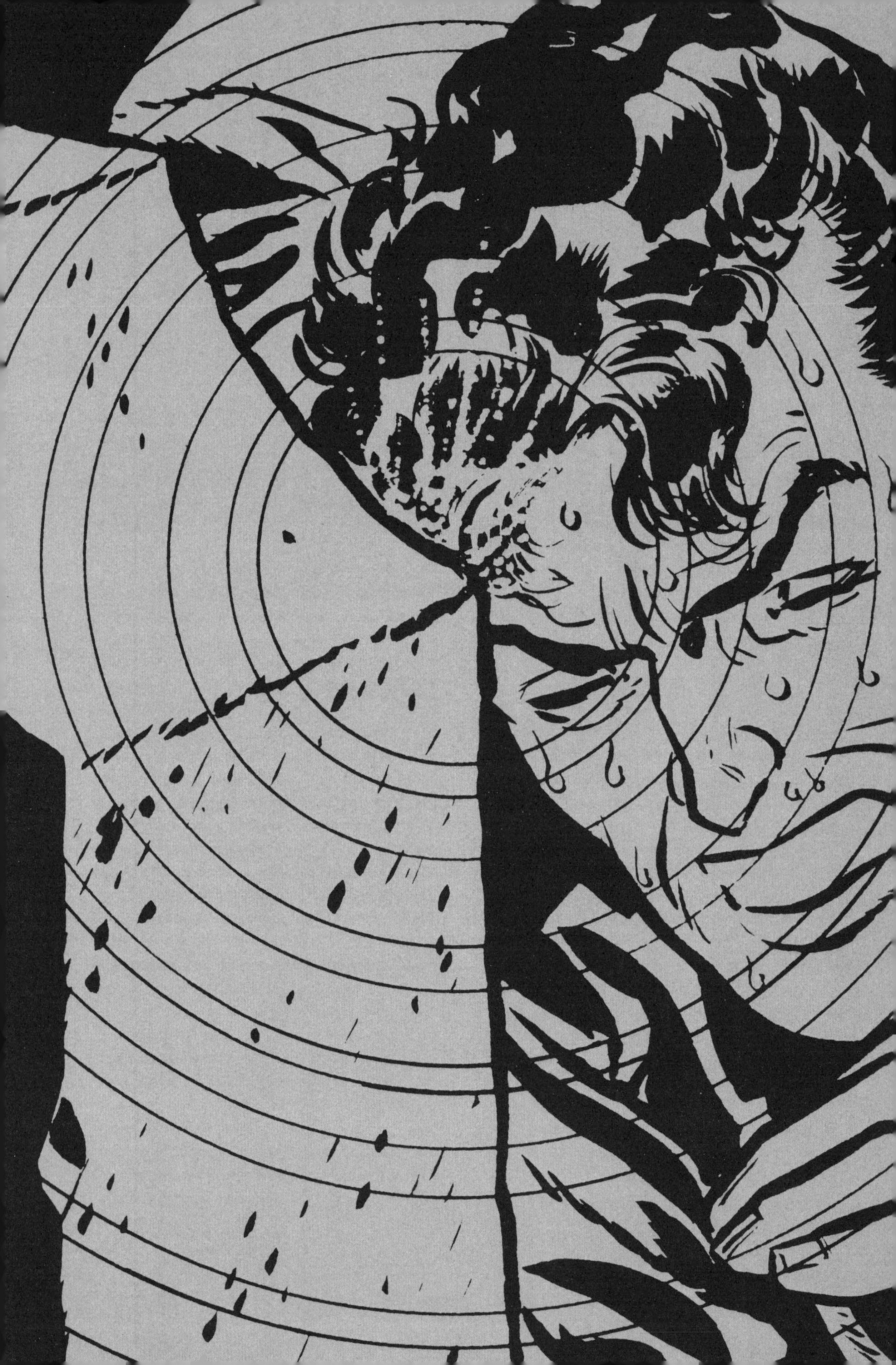

THE VAULT OF HORROR!

WELCOME, ONCE AGAIN, TO THE VAULT OF HORROR! I SEE WE HAVE MANY *NEW* READERS WITH US THIS TIME! HEH, HEH! I TRUST YOU HAVE PROPERLY PREPARED YOURSELVES! BY THAT I MEAN YOU *HAVE* MADE SURE *ALL* THE DOORS AND WINDOWS ARE LOCKED, HAVEN'T YOU? FOR THE TALE I AM ABOUT TO UNFOLD WILL TRULY BE AN INITIATION FOR YOU! YOU OTHER READERS WHO HAVE BEEN HERE BEFORE... READY? HEH, HEH, HEH! GOOD! NOW, LIE BACK IN YOUR GRAVE AND GET A GOOD GRIP ON YOUR NERVES BECAUSE WE ARE ABOUT TO BEGIN THE STORY I CALL:

VOODOO VENGEANCE!

FOR THE PAST THIRTEEN YEARS, CALEB STANDISH HAD LEFT HIS PALATIAL SUITE OF OFFICES AT PRECISELY FIVE P.M. AND HAD WALKED ONE BLOCK TO THE GARAGE WHERE HE ALWAYS PARKED HIS CAR, BUT *THIS* DAY, HE LEFT *EARLY*...

NOW THAT'S STRANGE! I'D SWEAR THIS SHOP WASN'T HERE BEFORE! I PASS HERE AT LEAST TWICE A DAY! FUNNY HOW I NEVER NOTICED IT!

HMM... ANTIQUES... ODDITIES! SOME NICE THINGS IN THE WINDOW! I THINK I'LL GO IN... MIGHT BE ABLE TO PICK UP SOMETHING NICE FOR SALLY!

I'M LOOKING FOR A GIFT TO GIVE MY WIFE, BUT IT'S SO DARK IN HERE I CAN'T SEE YOUR WARES! COULDN'T WE HAVE A BIT MORE LIGHT?

THE POWERS OF THE DARKNESS, SIR, ARE INFINITE! FRET NOT, FOR I HAVE THAT WHICH YOU SEEK!

HERE, SIR! I THINK YOU WILL BE INTERESTED IN THIS... THIS... *DOLL!*

A *DOLL*? NO! I'M AFRAID THAT'S NOT WHAT I HAD IN MIND! MAYBE YOU COULD SHOW ME SOMETHING ELSE!

IF YOU DO NOT CARE FOR *THIS* DOLL, SIR, PERHAPS YOU WOULD BE INTERESTED IN ONE NOT SO *ORDINARY!* PERHAPS... A *VOODOO DOLL!* HMMM?

A *VOODOO DOLL*? WHAT THE DEVIL ARE YOU TALKING ABOUT?

A WAX DOLL THAT WILL BE THE EXACT DUPLICATE OF ANYONE YOU *NAME!* ONLY, OVER THIS DOLL I SHALL CAST A *VOODOO SPELL!* AND WHATSOEVER HAPPENS TO THE DOLL, SO SHALL IT ALSO HAPPEN TO THE PERSON IN WHOSE LIKENESS THE DOLL IS MADE!

ROT!

HINGS OF THE CCULT

DEATH AND THE BEYOND

2

HEH! YOU DISBELIEVE! BUT IT'S *TRUE!* IN THE PAST I HAVE MADE MANY SUCH DOLLS...FOR THOSE WHO MIGHT WISH... AH... HARM TO ANOTHER!

I... I DON'T BELIEVE YOU! I... I THINK I'LL... I'LL LEAVE!

BEFORE YOU GO, REMEMBER THIS! IF EVER YOU WISH TO DO SOMEONE HARM... OR TO *KILL* SOMEONE... COME TO ME! MY VOODOO DOLLS...

ST...*STOP!* T...TAKE YOUR HANDS FROM ME!

HEH! HEH! HEH! HEH! REMEMBER WELL MY WORDS, SIR! *REMEMBER WELL!* HEH! HEH! HEH! HEH! HEH! HEH!

HEH! HEH! OLD CALEB CERTAINLY LEFT *THERE* IN A HURRY! HE HAD BEEN GREATLY FRIGHTENED AND ALL THE WAY HOME THE WEIRD SHOPKEEPER'S WORDS ECHOED AND RE-ECHOED THROUGH HIS MIND! HEH! HEH! HEH!

CALEB ENTERED HIS HOUSE... AND AS HE QUIETLY CLOSED THE DOOR, HE HEARD HIS WIFE'S VOICE...

SOUNDS LIKE SALLY IS TALKING TO SOMEONE! SHE DOESN'T EXPECT ME HOME THIS EARLY... I'LL SNEAK IN AND SURPRISE THE SWEET YOUNG THING!

BUT, SALLY, HOW MUCH LONGER DO WE HAVE TO WAIT?

DARLING, DON'T BE SO IMPATIENT! FOR ALL THE MONEY HE'LL LEAVE ME WHEN HE DIES, I CAN AFFORD TO BE NICE TO THE OL' GOAT! ...GIMME A KISS...

3

OH, NO... SALLY... NOT YOU! HOW... HOW *COULD* YOU, SALLY? HOW COULD YOU *DO* THIS TO ME? SOB

WITH HIS EYES BRIMMING WITH TEARS, THE BROKEN-HEARTED OLD GOAT... ER... OLD MAN LEFT THE HOUSE AND DROVE BACK TO HIS OFFICE!

IT ISN'T RIGHT FOR HER TO HURT ME THIS WAY! IT ISN'T RIGHT! SOB; I WISH I COULD HURT *HER* SOMEHOW! BUT... I CAN'T... I... I STILL *LOVE* HER!

SOMETIME LATER HE PARKED HIS CAR AND WALKED TOWARD HIS OFFICE. SUDDENLY, HE STOPPED...

"IF EVER YOU WISH TO DO SOME-ONE HARM, COME TO ME!"

HEH! HEH! I KNEW YOU WOULD RETURN! YOU WISH ME TO MAKE YOU A *VOODOO DOLL,* DON'T YOU? HEH! WHO IS IT TO BE, SIR? WHO IS IT TO BE?

MY... MY WIFE!

THE NEXT MORNING, CALEB BROUGHT THE SHOPKEEPER PHOTOGRAPHS OF SALLY AND WAS TOLD TO RETURN AT MID-NIGHT! AFTER A NERVE-WRACK-ING DAY, HE RETURNED TO THE SHOP AND WAS USHERED DOWN INTO THE CELLAR...

SIT THERE, SIR! YOU MUST BE PRESENT WHILE I PER-FORM THE *BLACK MAGIC* RITUAL WHICH WILL CHANGE THIS WAX FIGURE INTO A *VOODOO DOLL!*

YES... YES, OF COURSE! P... PLEASE HURRY, WON'T YOU... I... I FEEL QUITE... NERVOUS!

THE SHOPKEEPER BEGAN THE BLACK MAGIC RITUAL. HE CHANTED WEIRD INCANTATIONS AND DANCED BEFORE THE DOLL... AND CALEB SAT WATCHING...

4

FOR WHAT SEEMED LIKE HOURS, THE RITUAL CONTINUED! AS THE SHOPKEEPER BECAME MORE AND MORE FRENZIED, CALEB GREW MORE AND MORE FRIGHTENED. HIS CLOTHES WERE WET WITH PERSPIRATION AND HIS MIND WAS IN TURMOIL...

SUDDENLY, IT WAS OVER...

HERE, SIR, IS YOUR DOLL! REMEMBER...WHATSOEVER HAPPENS TO THIS DOLL, SO SHALL IT ALSO HAPPEN TO THE PERSON IN WHOSE LIKENESS THE DOLL WAS MADE!

I...I UNDERSTAND! HERE...HERE IS YOUR FEE! I...I... I WANT... T-TO GO H-HOME NOW!

CALEB LEFT THE ANTIQUE SHOP AND WENT HOME. HE SLEPT FITFULLY, BUT NEXT DAY HE AWOKE RESTED AND COMPOSED...

I MUST HAVE BEEN MAD! I...I CAN HARDLY BELIEVE IT REALLY HAPPENED! BUT THERE IS THE WAX DOLL TO PROVE IT! I...I WONDER IF WHAT HE SAID ABOUT IT IS TRUE! I...I MUST FIND OUT!

GOOD MORNING, CALEB! OH... WHAT A BEAUTIFUL STATUE! AND... WHY, IT'S A...A STATUE OF ME!

DON'T TOUCH THAT!

WHY, CALEB! THAT IS A STATUE OF ME, ISN'T IT?

ER... AH...YES! YES, I HAD IT MADE! BUT... I DON'T WANT YOU TO TOUCH IT! IT...IT'S VERY...DELICATE! YES, DELICATE! PROMISE YOU WON'T TOUCH IT!

OF COURSE, CALEB, YOU DEAR! IF IT WILL MAKE YOU HAPPY, I PROMISE NOT TO GO NEAR IT! YOU SWEET DARLING! YOU'RE NOT ANGRY WITH LI'L OL' ME...ARE YOU, DEAR?

OH, SALLY...SALLY, HOW CAN YOU SAY THOSE THINGS WHEN YOU DON'T MEAN THEM? HOW CAN YOU LIE TO ME LIKE THAT?

NO...NO, SALLY...I'M... NOT ANGRY...

THAT'S GOOD! OH!... THERE'S THE PHONE! I'LL GET IT!

ALL RIGHT, SALLY! I'LL JUST PUT THE STATUE UP HERE ON THE SHELF... OUT OF HARM'S WAY!

5

DARLING, YOU CAN'T COME TODAY! MY HUSBAND'S HOME! ...YES, I'LL MEET YOU TONIGHT! SAME PLACE...YES!...YES, OF COURSE I LOVE YOU... NOW, GOOD-BYE...

THE CHEAT! THE LIAR! IF SHE THINKS SHE'S GOING TO MEET HER LOVER TONIGHT, SHE'S MISTAKEN! I'LL STOP HER... BUT HOW? HOW...WAIT! THE *VOODOO DOLL!*

WILL IT WORK? I WONDER!...BUT IT'S THE ONLY WAY I CAN STOP HER! I'LL...I'LL TRY IT! I'LL...I'LL JUST...

...SCRATCH THE STATUE'S ARM... *LIKE THIS!*

THE SCREAM SHOCKED CALEB INTO ACTION! QUICKLY PUTTING THE DOLL BACK ON ITS SHELF, HE RAN TO THE KITCHEN...

SALLY! SALLY, WHAT'S THE MATTER?

CALEB! DO SOMETHING! CALL THE DOCTOR! I JUST CUT MY ARM WITH THIS BUTCHER KNIFE! IT'S BLEEDING TERRIBLY! *DO SOMETHING!*

CUT YOURSELF?... *GOOD HEAVENS!* HE WAS RIGHT! IT... *IT WORKS!*

DON'T JUST STAND THERE, YOU IDIOT! CAN'T YOU SEE I'M BLEEDING! GET A DOCTOR!

AFTER THE DOCTOR HAD BANDAGED SALLY'S ARM, HE GAVE HER A SLEEPING PILL AND LEFT. NATURALLY, SHE DIDN'T MEET HER BOY-FRIEND THAT NIGHT, BUT CALEB WASN'T AS HAPPY AS YOU AS MIGHT EXPECT!

IT'S AMAZING! WITH THIS DOLL I HOLD SALLY'S LIFE IN MY HANDS! IT'S...IT'S WEIRD! I'M ALMOST AFRAID OF IT!

6

POOR CALEB! HE DISLIKED HURTING SALLY BECAUSE HE STILL LOVED HER! BUT HE *WAS* JEALOUS, AND IF THAT WAS THE ONLY WAY HE COULD KEEP HER, THAT WAS HOW IT WOULD BE! WELL, FIENDS, SALLY RECOVERED RAPIDLY... AND ONE NIGHT...

CALEB, I'M GOING TO VISIT AN OLD GIRL FRIEND! I...AH... MAY BE A LITTLE LATE SO DON'T WAIT UP FOR ME!

HA! SHE DOESN'T FOOL ME! I HEARD HER MAKE A DATE WITH HER LOVER!

SHE MUST THINK I'M A *FOOL!* WELL, I'LL SHOW HER HOW *FOOLISH* I AM! I'LL JUST BREAK THE DOLL'S LEG THIS TIME! *THERE!*

CRACK!

SALLY! SALLY! ARE YOU HURT? WH...WHAT HAPPENED?

CALEB! HELP ME! I FELL! MY...MY LEG! I...I THINK IT'S BROKEN!

ONCE AGAIN THE DOCTOR WAS SUMMONED. SALLY'S LEG *HAD* BEEN BROKEN AND SHE HAD TO REMAIN IN BED FOR A LONG WHILE. HEH, HEH! CALEB WAS *VERY HAPPY!* BUT IT DIDN'T LAST FOREVER! SALLY BECAME WELL...

OH, DARLING, I KNOW IT'S BEEN SUCH A LONG TIME! BUT I COULDN'T HELP IT! CALEB WOULDN'T LEAVE ME FOR A MINUTE! HE'S SUCH A PEST...YES, DON... I'LL MEET YOU TONIGHT! GOOD-BYE, DARLING...

SALLY...

CALEB! WHA...? WH...I...I THOUGHT YOU WERE OUT!

DON'T PRETEND, DEAR! I KNOW WHAT'S BEEN GOING ON, BUT...BUT I CAN'T BE ANGRY WITH YOU! SALLY, PLEASE...I LOVE YOU...

WHY, YOU OLD *FOOL!* YOU BEEN *SPYING* ON ME, THAT'S WHAT! *SPYING* ON ME!

SALLY, PLEASE...DON'T! I'VE GIVEN YOU EVERYTHING! I BEG OF YOU... LEAVE THAT MAN! I CAN'T STAND IT ANY LONGER! PLEASE, DARLING, *PLEASE!* YOU LOVED ME ONCE...

HIS FACE CONTORTED IN STARK TERROR, CALEB COULD ONLY WATCH HELPLESSLY AS THE WAX IMAGE OF SALLY SAILED OVERHEAD AND STRUCK THE INNER WALL OF THE FIREPLACE...

THE PIECES FELL ON THE BURNING LOGS...THE LICKING FLAMES LEAPED AROUND THEM... AND THEY BEGAN TO MELT...

WELL, DEAR READERS, THAT WAS A *SMASHING* CLIMAX, WASN'T IT? TOO BAD SALLY WAS SUCH A *HOT*-HEAD! SHE REALLY *WENT TO PIECES* OVER HER *SHATTERED* ROMANCE! HEH! HEH! HEH! NOW THE POOR THING IS ALL *BROKEN UP!* YEP...OLD CALEB FINALLY *MELTED* SALLY'S COLD HEART IN ONE *SOUL-SEARING* SCENE, DIDN'T HE? HEH! HEH! HEH! NOW THAT YOU'RE *WARMED UP* TO MY TALES, *PULL* YOURSELF *TO-GETHER* AND READ ON... HEH! HEH! READ ON!

THE END

8

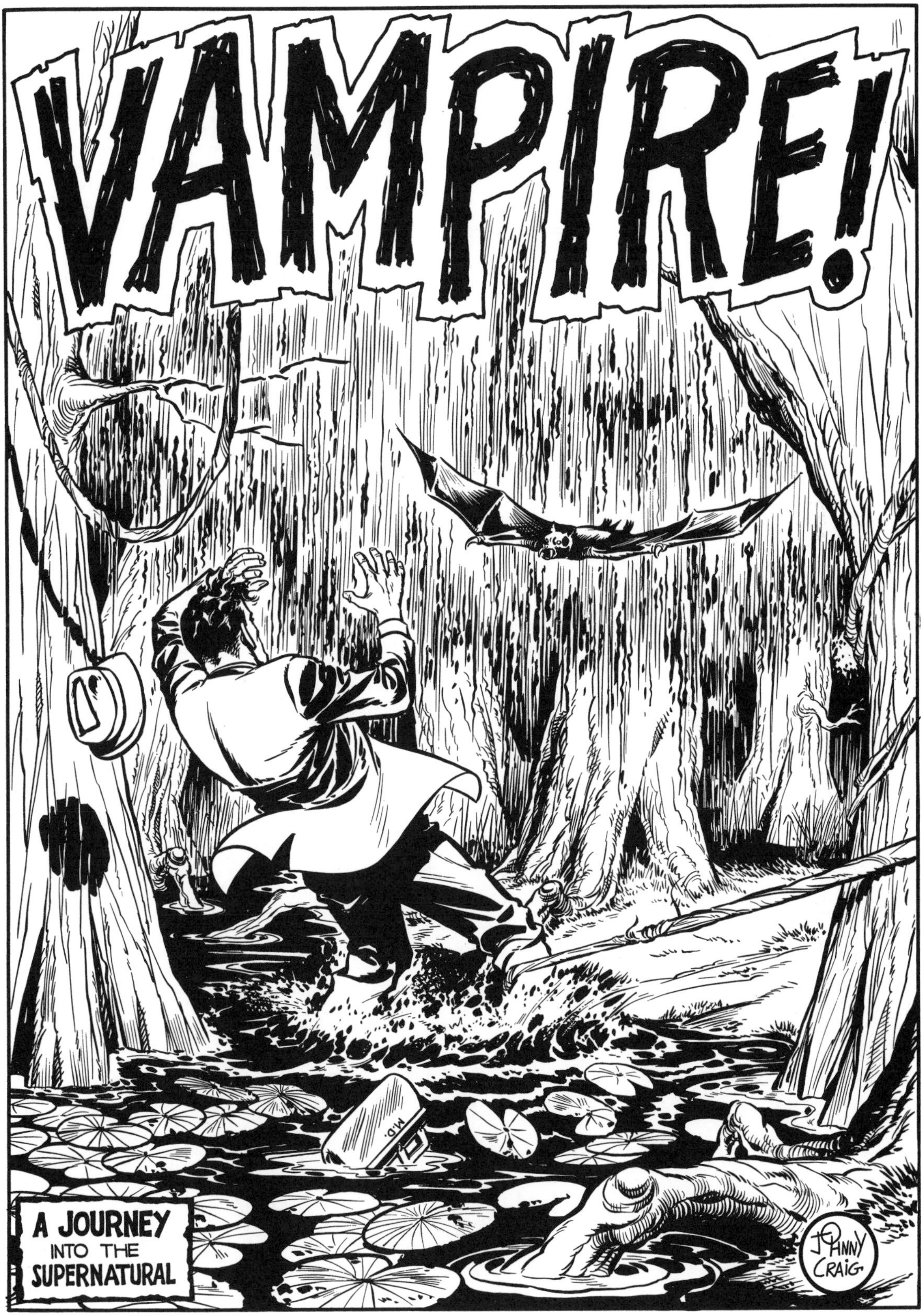

VAMPIRE!
A JOURNEY INTO THE SUPERNATURAL
M.D.
JOHNNY CRAIG

MARSH ISLAND... A PATCH OF LAND OFF THE COAST OF LOUISIANA, INFESTED WITH SWAMPS, QUAGMIRES AND MALARIA-CARRYING MOSQUITOS, WHERE THE ONLY CHANGE FOR THE FEW INHABITANTS FROM THE BLAZING, SWELTERING, HEAT OF DAY IS THE MOIST, STICKY, UNCOMFORTABLE HEAT OF NIGHT, AND WHERE BIZARRE AND MYSTERIOUS SETTINGS MIGHT VERY WELL FORM A PERFECT BACKDROP FOR...

VAMPIRES!? ARE YOU CRAZY, DOC? EVERYONE KNOWS THERE ARE NO SUCH THINGS!

IT'S THE ONLY ANSWER, CHIEF HUGHES! I STUDIED MEDICINE IN HUNGARY... AND I'VE SEEN MANY CASES LIKE THIS OVER THERE!

JIM REED M.D
MARSH ISLAND CORONER

CONFOUND IT! I CAN'T TURN IN A REPORT THAT SAYS THAT! JUST SAY "CAUSE OF DEATH... UNKNOWN!"

BUT I KNOW HOW SHE DIED! LOOK, CHIEF... LET'S START ALL OVER...

EARLY THIS MORNING, THE BODY OF LAURA BATES WAS FOUND IN THE BAYOU, SEVERAL MILES FROM THE HOUSE WHERE SHE LIVED AND WORKED AS A MAID! RIGHT?

RIGHT...

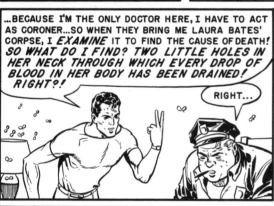

...BECAUSE I'M THE ONLY DOCTOR HERE, I HAVE TO ACT AS CORONER... SO WHEN THEY BRING ME LAURA BATES' CORPSE, I EXAMINE IT TO FIND THE CAUSE OF DEATH! SO WHAT DO I FIND? TWO LITTLE HOLES IN HER NECK THROUGH WHICH EVERY DROP OF BLOOD IN HER BODY HAS BEEN DRAINED! RIGHT?!

RIGHT...

...BUT IF YOU SAY THAT LAURA BATES WAS KILLED BY A VAMPIRE, YOU'RE GONNA HAVE A HEAP O' PEOPLE IN THIS HERE TOWN LAUGHIN' AT YOU... AND DON'T YOU FORGET THAT!

I KNOW, I KNOW!

... BUT I STILL SAY SHE WAS KILLED BY A VAMPIRE...

ALL RIGHT! IT'S TOO BLASTED HOT TO ARGUE! ...BUT I THINK YOU'RE NUTS!

YOUNG DR. JIM REED SIGNED THE DEATH CERTIFICATE, AND IN THE FOLLOWING DAYS, POLICE CHIEF HUGHES' WARNING BECAME A REALITY...

HA! HA! LOOK! THERE GOES "BAT" MAN!

2

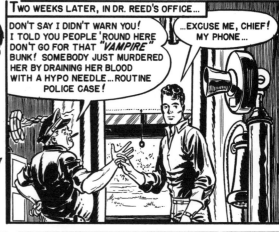

TWO WEEKS LATER, IN DR. REED'S OFFICE...

DON'T SAY I DIDN'T WARN YOU! I TOLD YOU PEOPLE 'ROUND HERE DON'T GO FOR THAT "VAMPIRE" BUNK! SOMEBODY JUST MURDERED HER BY DRAINING HER BLOOD WITH A HYPO NEEDLE...ROUTINE POLICE CASE!

...EXCUSE ME, CHIEF! MY PHONE...

HELLO...YES, THIS IS DR. REED! WHAT?... YES, OF COURSE...I'LL BE THERE AS SOON AS POSSIBLE...GOODBYE, MR. WINSLOW...

DID YOU SAY "GOODBYE, MR. WINSLOW?"

YES... WHY?

OH, NOTHING...EXCEPT THAT LAURA BATES WORKED FOR HIM AS A MAID... BEFORE SHE WAS KILLED!

OH...

JONATHAN WINSLOW LIVED DEEP IN THE TANGLED SECLUSION OF THE MURKY SWAMP. HE SELDOM CAME TO TOWN AND MOST PEOPLE HAD NEVER SEEN HIM OR HIS DAUGHTER AT ALL. THE MOON WAS HIGH IN THE HEAVENS WHEN DR. REED FINALLY EMERGED FROM THE TREACHEROUS PATHS OF THE BAYOU AND RAPPED ON THE AGED WOODEN DOOR...

GOOD EVENING, DR. REED... COME IN, PLEASE...

THANK YOU, MR. WINSLOW! WHAT'S THE TROUBLE?

IT'S NELDA, MY DAUGHTER... SHE'S NOT BEEN WELL LATELY! SHE FEELS WEAK AND LISTLESS... I WANTED YOU TO HAVE A LOOK AT HER!

CERTAINLY, MR. WINSLOW... JUST LEAD THE WAY!

BLAZES... HOW CAN HE WEAR THAT TUX IN THIS STIFLING HEAT?

3

11

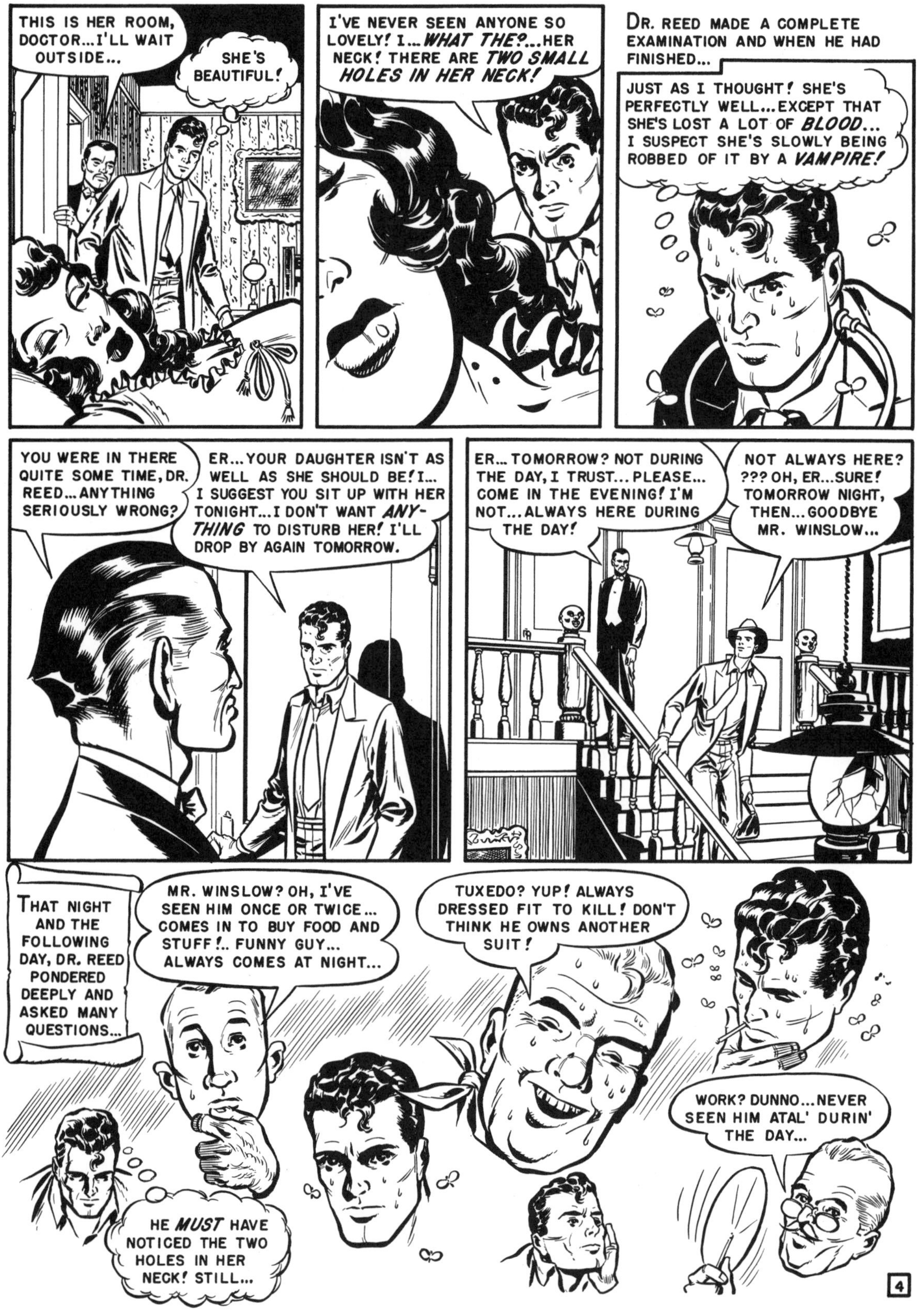
THIS IS HER ROOM, DOCTOR...I'LL WAIT OUTSIDE...
SHE'S BEAUTIFUL!
I'VE NEVER SEEN ANYONE SO LOVELY! I... *WHAT THE?*...HER NECK! THERE ARE *TWO SMALL HOLES IN HER NECK!*
DR. REED MADE A COMPLETE EXAMINATION AND WHEN HE HAD FINISHED...
JUST AS I THOUGHT! SHE'S PERFECTLY WELL...EXCEPT THAT SHE'S LOST A LOT OF *BLOOD*... I SUSPECT SHE'S SLOWLY BEING ROBBED OF IT BY A *VAMPIRE!*
YOU WERE IN THERE QUITE SOME TIME, DR. REED...ANYTHING SERIOUSLY WRONG?
ER...YOUR DAUGHTER ISN'T AS WELL AS SHE SHOULD BE! I... I SUGGEST YOU SIT UP WITH HER TONIGHT...I DON'T WANT *ANYTHING* TO DISTURB HER! I'LL DROP BY AGAIN TOMORROW.
ER... TOMORROW? NOT DURING THE DAY, I TRUST... PLEASE... COME IN THE EVENING! I'M NOT...ALWAYS HERE DURING THE DAY!
NOT ALWAYS HERE? ??? OH, ER...SURE! TOMORROW NIGHT, THEN...GOODBYE MR. WINSLOW...
THAT NIGHT AND THE FOLLOWING DAY, DR. REED PONDERED DEEPLY AND ASKED MANY QUESTIONS...
MR. WINSLOW? OH, I'VE SEEN HIM ONCE OR TWICE... COMES IN TO BUY FOOD AND STUFF!.. FUNNY GUY... ALWAYS COMES AT NIGHT...
TUXEDO? YUP! ALWAYS DRESSED FIT TO KILL! DON'T THINK HE OWNS ANOTHER SUIT!
WORK? DUNNO...NEVER SEEN HIM ATAL' DURIN' THE DAY...
HE *MUST* HAVE NOTICED THE TWO HOLES IN HER NECK! STILL...
4

DR. REED WENT TO THE OLD HOUSE AGAIN THE NEXT NIGHT AND WAS LED TO NELDA'S ROOM BY MR. WINSLOW. THE YOUNG DOCTOR MADE ANOTHER EXAMINATION...

GREAT SCOTT! SHE'S WORSE! SHE SHOULD BE *STRONGER* TONIGHT! UNLESS THE VAMPIRE AGAIN... *NO...* MR. WINSLOW WAS SUPPOSED TO STAY WITH HER *ALL NIGHT!* BUT YET...

MR. WINSLOW! WHERE ARE YOU?... STRANGE... HE'S NOT HERE! PERHAPS DOWNSTAIRS...

THE YOUNG DOCTOR SEARCHED, BUT OLD MR. WINSLOW WAS NOT TO BE FOUND. IT WASN'T TILL MUCH LATER THAT HE THOUGHT OF...

THE CELLAR... I HAVEN'T LOOKED DOWN HERE! MAYBE SOMETHING HAPPENED TO... *SAY,* WHAT'S THAT OVER THERE?...

A--A COFFIN! *WITH DIRT IN IT!* *BLAZES!* WHAT A FOOL I'VE BEEN! IT'S ALL CLEAR NOW! *MR. WINSLOW IS THE VAMPIRE!*

MR. WINSLOW WANTED ME OUT HERE TO KEEP AN EYE ON ME! BECAUSE *I'M* THE ONLY PERSON ON MARSH ISLAND WHO KNOWS HIS MAID WAS KILLED BY A *VAMPIRE!* ... AND NOW *MY* LIFE IS IN DANGER! ... AND NELDA... WHAT ABOUT NELDA?

THERE! I'VE LOCKED HER IN HER ROOM! BEST I CAN DO NOW! I'LL HURRY TO TOWN... COME BACK TOMORROW...

WHA...? OH... IT'S IT'S YOU, MR... I... I... DIDN'T HEAR YOU COME IN...

JUST CAME BACK FROM A WALK, DR. REED... HOW IS NELDA?

OH, ER... SHE'S... FEELING BETTER! BUT I DON'T WANT HER DISTURBED... JUST... JUST LET HER REST...

OF COURSE, DOCTOR! GOOD NIGHT...

5

LORD, I HOPE I'M DOING RIGHT! WINSLOW EXPECTS ME TOMORROW NIGHT, BUT I WANT TO BE THERE DURING THE *DAY!* VAMPIRES ONLY PROWL AT NIGHT! DURING THE DAY THEY SLEEP IN THEIR COFFINS!®!/XW THESE MOSQUITOS!... I'LL BRING A CROSS... AND A WOODEN STAKE TO DRIVE THROUGH HIS HEART...THE ONLY WAY TO KILL...A *VAMPIRE!*

THE FOLLOWING DAY WAS A HECTIC ONE... AND DR. REED'S ATTEMPTS TO GET TO THE HOUSE BEFORE SUNDOWN SEEMED DOOMED TO FAILURE...

OKAY! OKAY! SO IT'S ANOTHER BLOODLESS CORPSE WITH TWO HOLES IN ITS NECK! BUT IF YOU START RAVING ABOUT *VAMPIRES* AGAIN, I'LL LOCK YOU UP! NOW GET BUSY! I WANT A COMPLETE AUTOPSY REPORT BEFORE YOU LEAVE!

BUT CHIEF... IT'S SO LATE...

HOURS LATER...

I THOUGHT I'D NEVER GET HERE! *WHA...!* THE DOOR'S OPEN! I'M TOO LATE! *HE'S GONE!*

NELDA! IF HE'S HARMED HER, I'LL...

NELDA! YOU... YOU'RE SITTING UP! YOU'RE... YOU'RE FEELING BETTER!???

I FEEL FINE TONIGHT, DOCTOR! BUT WHY ARE YOU SO EXCITED?

NELDA, LISTEN TO ME! YOUR FATHER IS THE CAUSE OF YOUR ILLNESS! LITTLE BY LITTLE, HE'S BEEN DRAINING YOU OF YOUR BLOOD TO FEED HIMSELF! THAT'S WHY YOU KEPT GETTING WEAKER! YOU FEEL STRONGER TONIGHT BECAUSE *LAST* NIGHT HE CAUGHT SOMEONE ELSE! PLEASE! BELIEVE ME! IT SOUNDS HORRIBLE, BUT IT'S TRUE! YOUR FATHER IS A *VAMPIRE!*

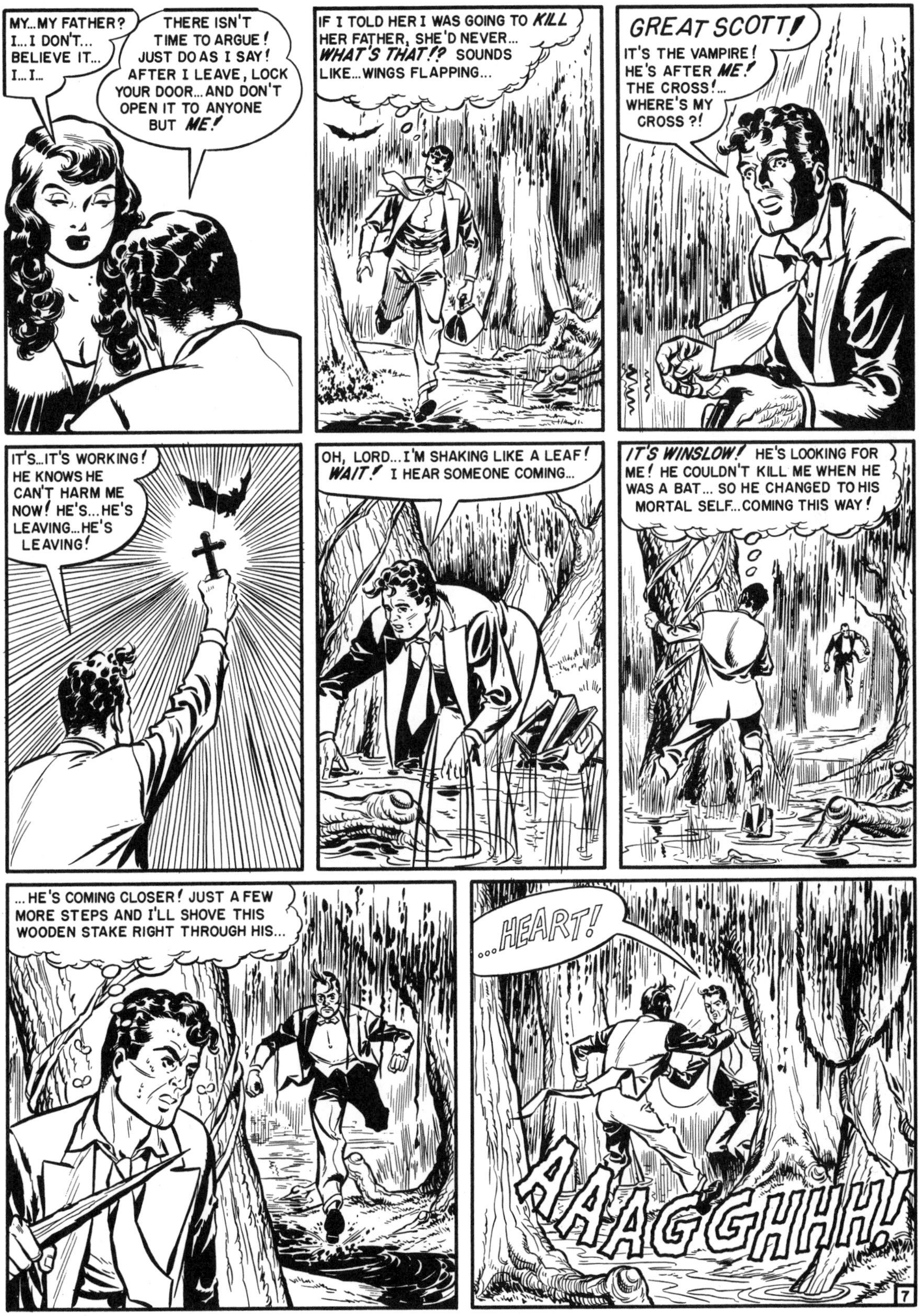
MY...MY FATHER? I...I DON'T... BELIEVE IT... I...I...
THERE ISN'T TIME TO ARGUE! JUST DO AS I SAY! AFTER I LEAVE, LOCK YOUR DOOR...AND DON'T OPEN IT TO ANYONE BUT ME!
IF I TOLD HER I WAS GOING TO KILL HER FATHER, SHE'D NEVER... WHAT'S THAT!? SOUNDS LIKE...WINGS FLAPPING...
GREAT SCOTT!
IT'S THE VAMPIRE! HE'S AFTER ME! THE CROSS!... WHERE'S MY CROSS?!
IT'S...IT'S WORKING! HE KNOWS HE CAN'T HARM ME NOW! HE'S...HE'S LEAVING...HE'S LEAVING!
OH, LORD...I'M SHAKING LIKE A LEAF! WAIT! I HEAR SOMEONE COMING...
IT'S WINSLOW! HE'S LOOKING FOR ME! HE COULDN'T KILL ME WHEN HE WAS A BAT... SO HE CHANGED TO HIS MORTAL SELF...COMING THIS WAY!
...HE'S COMING CLOSER! JUST A FEW MORE STEPS AND I'LL SHOVE THIS WOODEN STAKE RIGHT THROUGH HIS...
...HEART!
AAAGGHHH!
7

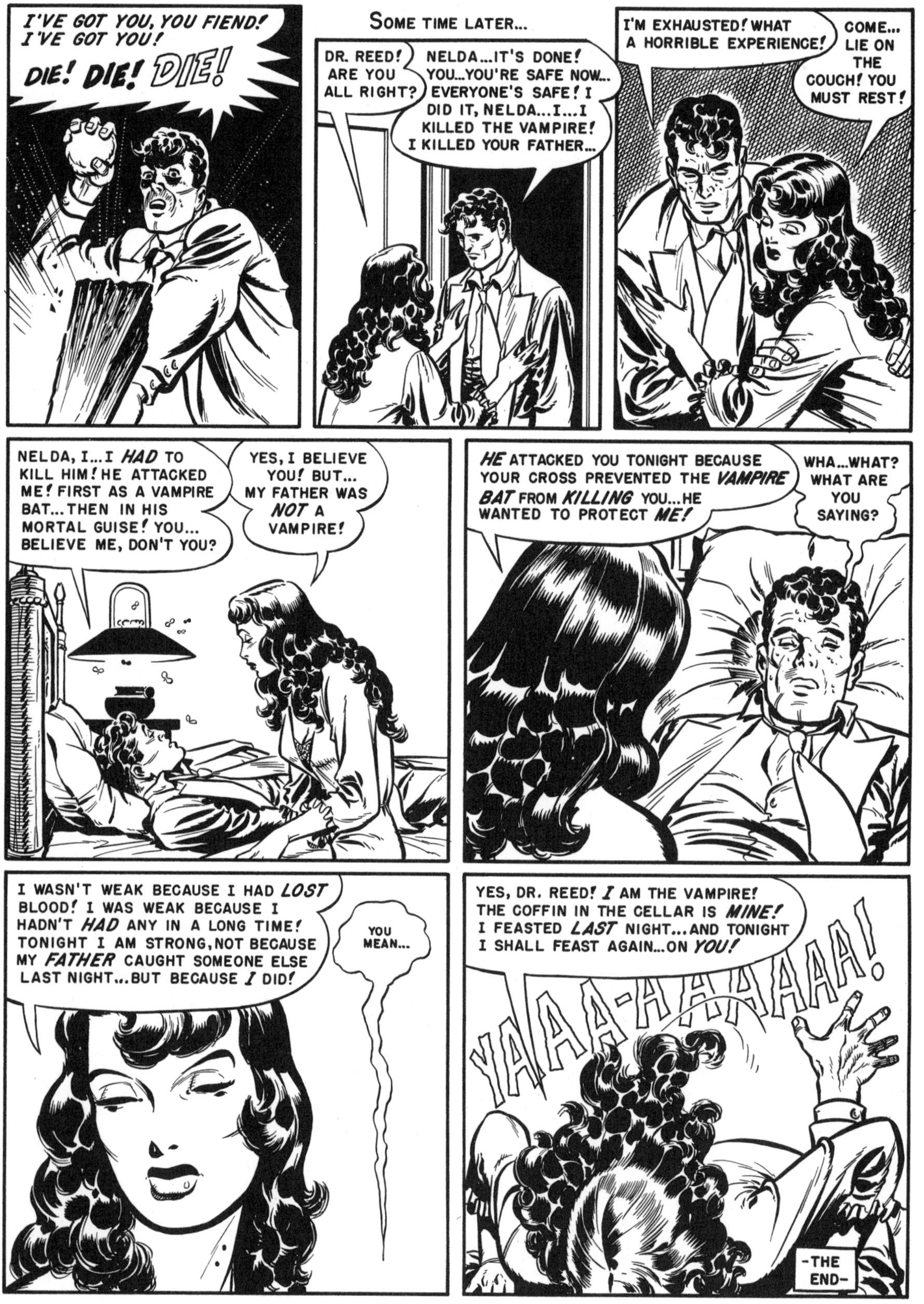
I'VE GOT YOU, YOU FIEND! I'VE GOT YOU!
DIE! DIE! DIE!
SOME TIME LATER...
DR. REED! ARE YOU ALL RIGHT?
NELDA...IT'S DONE! YOU...YOU'RE SAFE NOW... EVERYONE'S SAFE! I DID IT, NELDA...I...I KILLED THE VAMPIRE! I KILLED YOUR FATHER...
I'M EXHAUSTED! WHAT A HORRIBLE EXPERIENCE!
COME... LIE ON THE COUCH! YOU MUST REST!
NELDA, I...I HAD TO KILL HIM! HE ATTACKED ME! FIRST AS A VAMPIRE BAT...THEN IN HIS MORTAL GUISE! YOU... BELIEVE ME, DON'T YOU?
YES, I BELIEVE YOU! BUT... MY FATHER WAS NOT A VAMPIRE!
HE ATTACKED YOU TONIGHT BECAUSE YOUR CROSS PREVENTED THE VAMPIRE BAT FROM KILLING YOU...HE WANTED TO PROTECT ME!
WHA...WHAT? WHAT ARE YOU SAYING?
I WASN'T WEAK BECAUSE I HAD LOST BLOOD! I WAS WEAK BECAUSE I HADN'T HAD ANY IN A LONG TIME! TONIGHT I AM STRONG, NOT BECAUSE MY FATHER CAUGHT SOMEONE ELSE LAST NIGHT...BUT BECAUSE I DID!
YOU MEAN...
YES, DR. REED! I AM THE VAMPIRE! THE COFFIN IN THE CELLAR IS MINE! I FEASTED LAST NIGHT...AND TONIGHT I SHALL FEAST AGAIN...ON YOU!
YAAA-AAAAAA!
-THE END-

MURDER MAY BOOMERANG

WE HAD BEEN DRIVING FOR HOURS. THE STEADY HUM OF THE MOTOR AND THE SWISH-SWISHING OF THE WINDSHIELD WIPERS HAD DEADENED MY BRAIN UNTIL I DROVE WITHOUT THINKING. ON AND ON... NEVER STOPPING, NEVER WANTING TO STOP, *AFRAID* TO STOP. AND AS OUR CAR TRAVELED THE ENDLESS MILES OF HIGHWAY, MY MIND DRIFTED BACK THROUGH TIME... THROUGH THE PAST WEEKS... MONTHS... YEARS... AND I WAS A YOUNG BOY AGAIN...

AFTER MY MOTHER HAD PASSED AWAY, MY FATHER AND I HAD BECOME CLOSER TO EACH OTHER THAN EVER. ALL THE LOVE WE SHARED FOR MOM WAS NOW GIVEN TO ONE ANOTHER...

GEE, DAD... IT SURE IS DIFFERENT AROUND THE HOUSE NOW THAT... MOM'S NOT HERE...

I KNOW, SON! BUT WE HAVE TO MAKE THE BEST OF IT. YOUR MOTHER WOULD WANT US BOTH TO BE STRONG.

DAD DIDN'T HAVE A WELL-PAYING JOB AND HE HAD TO WORK HARD. I WAS GOING TO GRAMMAR SCHOOL AND I REMEMBER HOW HE WOULD COME HOME AT NIGHT... SO EXHAUSTED!

HERE, DAD, SIT DOWN! I FIXED DINNER FOR YOU...

THANKS, LAD! YOU'RE A GOOD BOY... A GOOD BOY!

OH, WE HAD OUR GOOD TIMES. WE WENT TO THE CIRCUS AND WE SAW A COUPLE OF BALL GAMES... EVEN WHEN WE REALLY COULDN'T AFFORD IT...

HEY, DAD, LOOK! A HOMER!

HOW ABOUT THAT?

...OF COURSE, WE HAD TROUBLES TOO! I ALWAYS TRIED TO HELP...

QUIT SCHOOL AND GO TO WORK? NO, SON... WE DON'T NEED THE MONEY THAT BADLY. YOU GO TO SCHOOL... THAT'S MORE IMPORTANT! AND I WANT YOU TO PROMISE NEVER TO THINK ABOUT QUIT-ING SCHOOL AGAIN!

O.K., DAD... IF YOU SAY SO! I... I JUST DON'T LIKE TO SEE YOU WORKING SO HARD...

WHEN I GRADUATED FROM HIGH SCHOOL, I WANTED TO LOOK FOR A JOB! BUT...

MY BOY, YOU HAVE TO STUDY HARD TO BE A CHEMICAL ENGINEER! A COLLEGE EDUCATION IS A MUST! AND DON'T YOU WORRY ABOUT ME... I'LL BE ALL RIGHT!

AND SO I WENT TO COLLEGE. IT WAS THE FIRST TIME DAD AND I HAD BEEN SEPARATED, AND I MISSED HIM AND WORRIED ABOUT HIM SOMETHING FIERCE! THEN...

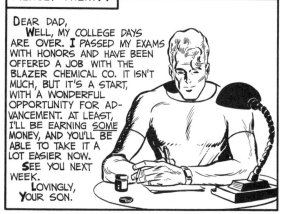

DEAR DAD,
WELL, MY COLLEGE DAYS ARE OVER. I PASSED MY EXAMS WITH HONORS AND HAVE BEEN OFFERED A JOB WITH THE BLAZER CHEMICAL CO. IT ISN'T MUCH, BUT IT'S A START, WITH A WONDERFUL OPPORTUNITY FOR AD-VANCEMENT. AT LEAST, I'LL BE EARNING SOME MONEY, AND YOU'LL BE ABLE TO TAKE IT A LOT EASIER NOW.
SEE YOU NEXT WEEK.
LOVINGLY,
YOUR SON.

DAD MET ME AT THE TRAIN. I WAS SHOCKED TO SEE HOW ILL HE WAS... GAUNT... AND OH, SO TIRED!

DAD, DAD! GEE, IT'S SWELL TO SEE YOU AGAIN!

MY BOY! MY BOY! (SOB!) I'M... I'M SO PROUD OF YOU!

DAD DIDN'T HAVE TO WORK SO HARD NOW THAT I HAD A JOB. AND THEN ABOUT SIX MONTHS LATER...

WHA...WHAT? SON! WHAT'S THE MATTER!

DAD! DAD! IT'S HAPPENED! I MADE IT! I FINALLY MADE IT! *I'VE BEEN PROMOTED!*

WHY SON, THAT'S *WONDERFUL!*

DON'T YOU REALIZE WHAT THIS *MEANS*, DAD? I'LL BE EARNING *PLENTY* OF MONEY NOW! YOU CAN STOP WORKING!

STOP? STOP WORKING? BUT, SON...

NOW DON'T ARGUE, DAD! YOU'VE WORKED LONG ENOUGH! YOU NEED REST! I'M GOING TO TAKE CARE OF YOU, DAD! I'M GOING TO TAKE CARE OF YOU!

OH, SON! I'M...SO PROUD OF YOU... SO HAPPY!

DAD! MY DAD...

I HAD BEEN GIVEN A VACATION WITH MY HUGE INCREASE IN PAY, SO WE RENTED A HUNTING LODGE IN THE MOUNTAINS. THIS WAS DAD'S FIRST VACATION IN YEARS, AND HE WAS LIKE A GREAT BIG KID...

THIS FRESH AIR IS GOOD FOR YOU, DAD! YOU LOOK BETTER ALREADY!

FEEL BETTER, TOO, SON! I'M SO HAPPY I COULD CRY!

YES, DAD WAS FEELING BETTER! AS THE DAYS WENT BY, COLOR RETURNED TO HIS CHEEKS, LIFE TO HIS EYES. HE GAINED WEIGHT AND I FELT WONDERFUL TO SEE HIM SO HAPPY.

SAY, SON...LOOK OVER THERE! I NEVER NOTICED THAT BEFORE!

OH, THAT'S STATE PENITENTIARY! GRIM-LOOKING ISN'T IT?

BR-R-R! WHEN I THINK OF ALL THE CRIMINALS THAT ARE COOPED UP IN THAT PLACE, IT GIVES ME THE SHIVERS!

C'MON, DAD! LET'S HEAD BACK TO THE LODGE! IT'S GETTING LATE!

YES, DAD AND I REALLY HAD OURSELVES A TIME! THERE WASN'T ANYTHING WE DIDN'T DO!

ONE DAY I HAD TO DRIVE TO TOWN TO PICK UP MORE SUPPLIES.

...LONG DRIVE! I'M GLAD I HAVE THE CAR RADIO TO KEEP ME COMPANY!

WE INTERRUPT THIS BROADCAST TO BRING YOU A NEWS BULLETIN! THREE ARMED AND DANGEROUS CONVICTS HAVE ESCAPED FROM STATE PENITENTIARY!...

STATE PENITENTIARY? SAY, THAT'S NOT VERY FAR FROM THE LODGE!

NEARBY RESIDENTS ARE WARNED TO STAY INDOORS, ALTHOUGH POLICE OFFICIALS EXPECT THE TRIO TO BE APPREHENDED SHORTLY! WE RETURN YOU NOW TO OUR STUDIO...

GEE, I HOPE DAD'LL BE ALL RIGHT! MAYBE I OUGHT TO TURN BACK!...NO... I GUESS HE'LL BE SAFE!

PURCHASING THE SUPPLIES TOOK LONGER THAN I EXPECTED. WHEN I FINISHED, I DECIDED TO HAVE A CUP OF COFFEE...

WE INTERRUPT THIS BROADCAST TO BRING YOU A SPECIAL NEWS BULLETIN! TWO OF THE THREE ESCAPEES FROM STATE PENITENTIARY HAVE BEEN CAUGHT! HOWEVER, THE THIRD, ALVIN CARCAS, IS STILL AT LARGE!

ALVIN CARCAS, CONVICTED OF KILLING THREE PERSONS, AND RESPONSIBLE FOR THE DEATH OF TWO POLICE OFFICERS THIS AFTERNOON, IS BELIEVED HIDING IN THE VICINITY OF PINE LAKE! HE IS THE MOST VICIOUS OF THE THREE WHO ESCAPED, AND WILL KILL ON THE SLIGHTEST PROVOCATION...

PINE LAKE! THAT'S WHERE THE LODGE IS! AND DAD'S ALL ALONE!

4

I SPED BACK TOWARDS THE LODGE! I WAS FRIGHTENED NOW... AFRAID THAT SOMETHING HAD HAPPENED TO DAD!

THE MILES FLEW BY BENEATH THE WHEELS! I HAD TO HURRY! I HAD BEEN CRAZY TO LEAVE DAD ALONE IN THE FIRST PLACE...

IT WAS AN ENDLESS DRIVE AND IT SEEMED LIKE AN ETERNITY BEFORE I SCREECHED TO A STOP IN FRONT OF THE LODGE...

EVERYTHING SEEMS OKAY! MAYBE I WAS WORRIED OVER NOTHING!

HEY, DAD! DAD, I'M BACK!

HEY, DAD! I SAID I'M BACK! WHERE ARE YOU!

HE'S NOT HERE!

DAD! WHERE ARE YOU!? ...SAY...WHAT'S THAT BUNDLE OVER THERE IN THE CORNER???

WHY, IT'S CLOTHES! PANTS AND SHIRT! AND WHAT'S THIS OVER THE SHIRT POCKET? WHA..! IT'S A SERIAL NUMBER! A PRISONER'S SERIAL NUMBER!

60914362

THE ESCAPED CONVICT'S BEEN HERE! DAD! DAD! WHAT'S HE DONE TO YOU? WHERE ARE YOU???

5

21

DAD!

OH, DAD! DAD! ARE YOU ALL RIGHT? WHAT HAPPENED?

...CONVICT...CAME HERE... CHANGED CLOTHES...TOOK... YOUR HUNTING CLOTHES... BEAT ME...LEFT ME FOR DEAD...

DAD WASN'T HURT BADLY, AND WHILE I PATCHED HIS CUTS AND BRUISES, HE LAPSED INTO SILENCE... A GLASSY, DAZED LOOK ON HIS FACE!

THE DIRTY YELLOW KILLER! I SHOULD HAVE BEEN HERE WITH YOU! BUT I'LL GET HIM FOR YOU, DAD! I'LL GET HIM! AND WHEN I DO... *I'LL KILL HIM!*

I HELPED HIM OUT TO THE CAR AND SAT HIM NEXT TO ME. HE KNEW WHAT I WAS GOING TO DO! AND I WAS GLAD THAT HE DIDN'T PROTEST...

WE'RE GOING TO LOOK FOR HIM, DAD! YOU'VE GOT TO POINT HIM OUT TO ME!

WE DROVE FOR A LONG WHILE. NIGHT WAS SETTING IN AND IT BEGAN TO DRIZZLE. WE DROVE SLOWLY, OVER ALL THE DESERTED BACK-WOODS ROADS... SEARCHING FOR THE MAN I WAS TO *KILL!*

6

EVERY SO OFTEN I GLANCED AT DAD! HE SAT THERE SILENTLY, STARING DAZEDLY OUT THE CAR WINDOW. HE WAS SUFFERING FROM SHOCK BUT HE WANTED TO FIND THE CONVICT ALMOST AS MUCH AS I DID!

IT WAS GETTING DARKER NOW AND THE RAIN WAS COMING DOWN HEAVIER THAN BEFORE. THE LONGER IT TOOK TO SPOT THE KILLER, THE ANGRIER I BECAME! I WAS IMPATIENT TO WREAK MY REVENGE ON THE FILTHY SKUNK! I WANTED TO SEE HIM *DEAD!*

SUDDENLY, THE HEADLIGHTS PICKED OUT A FIGURE TRUDGING THE ROAD AHEAD OF US... A FIGURE WEARING HUNTING CLOTHES!

SON! THERE! HE'S THE ONE! HE'S THE ONE!

ALL THE HATRED I HELD FOR THAT ONE MAN ROSE WITHIN ME, CROWDING EVERY- THING ELSE FROM MY MIND! NOTHING ELSE MATTERED! I STEPPED ON THE ACCELERATOR.

MY ENTIRE BODY WAS TIGHTENED INTO A KNOT! DROPLETS OF SWEAT BURST OUT ON MY BROW AND THE MOTOR ROARED A DEATH CALL! BUT I HEARD NOTHING... I FELT NOTHING! EVERYTHING IN THE WORLD FADED... EXCEPT FOR THE LONE FIG- URE IN THE ROAD.

SOMEHOW WE SKIDDED TO A STOP! I STEPPED OUT... TO MAKE CERTAIN I HAD DONE THE JOB WELL! AND WHEN I SAW THE BODY SPRAWLED GRO- TESQUELY ON THE MUDDY ROAD... I KNEW HE WAS DEAD!

7

ALL THE FURIOUS HATRED HAD LEFT ME NOW THAT IT WAS ALL OVER. I...I FELT EMPTY.. LIKE THERE WAS NOTHING INSIDE OF ME...LIKE MY BODY WAS ONLY A SHELL. AND I WAS SHAKING...

I...I GOT HIM FOR YOU, DAD! I GOT HIM FOR YOU. YOU'RE OKAY, NOW... EVERYTHING'S OKAY! WE...WE'LL GO BACK TO TOWN NOW...

SOMETIME LATER, WE STOPPED IN FRONT OF THE SHERIFF'S OFFICE. AS I SHUT OFF THE IGNITION, I SAW A MAN WAVING GOOD-NIGHT TO THE SHERIFF...PROBABLY A DEPUTY GOING OFF DUTY... AND HE WAS WEARING HUNTING CLOTHES...

SON! THERE! HE'S THE ONE! HE'S THE ONE!

SUDDENLY, I REALIZED WHAT A HORRIBLE MISTAKE I HAD MADE! DAD WAS OUT OF HIS MIND! HE *DIDN'T KNOW* WHO HAD BEATEN HIM...HE ONLY KNEW THE MAN WORE HUNTING CLOTHES!

I KNEW THEN I HAD KILLED AN INNOCENT MAN... AND THAT FOR THE REST OF HIS LIFE, DAD WOULD POINT TO EVERY MAN HE SAW WEARING HUNTING CLOTHES AND WHISPER "SON! THERE! HE'S THE ONE! HE'S THE ONE!" IN A DAZE, I PULLED AWAY FROM THE CURB AND DROVE OUT OF TOWN...

WE HAVE BEEN DRIVING FOR HOURS. THE STEADY HUM OF THE MOTOR AND THE SWISH-SWISHING OF THE WINDSHIELD WIPERS HAS DEADENED MY BRAIN UNTIL I DRIVE WITHOUT THINKING...ON AND ON...NEVER STOPPING...NEVER WANTING TO STOP...*AFRAID* TO STOP! AND AS OUR CAR TRAVELS THE ENDLESS MILES OF HIGHWAY, MY MIND DRIFTS BACK THROUGH TIME...THROUGH THE PAST WEEKS ...MONTHS...YEARS... AND I AM A YOUNG BOY AGAIN...

THE END...

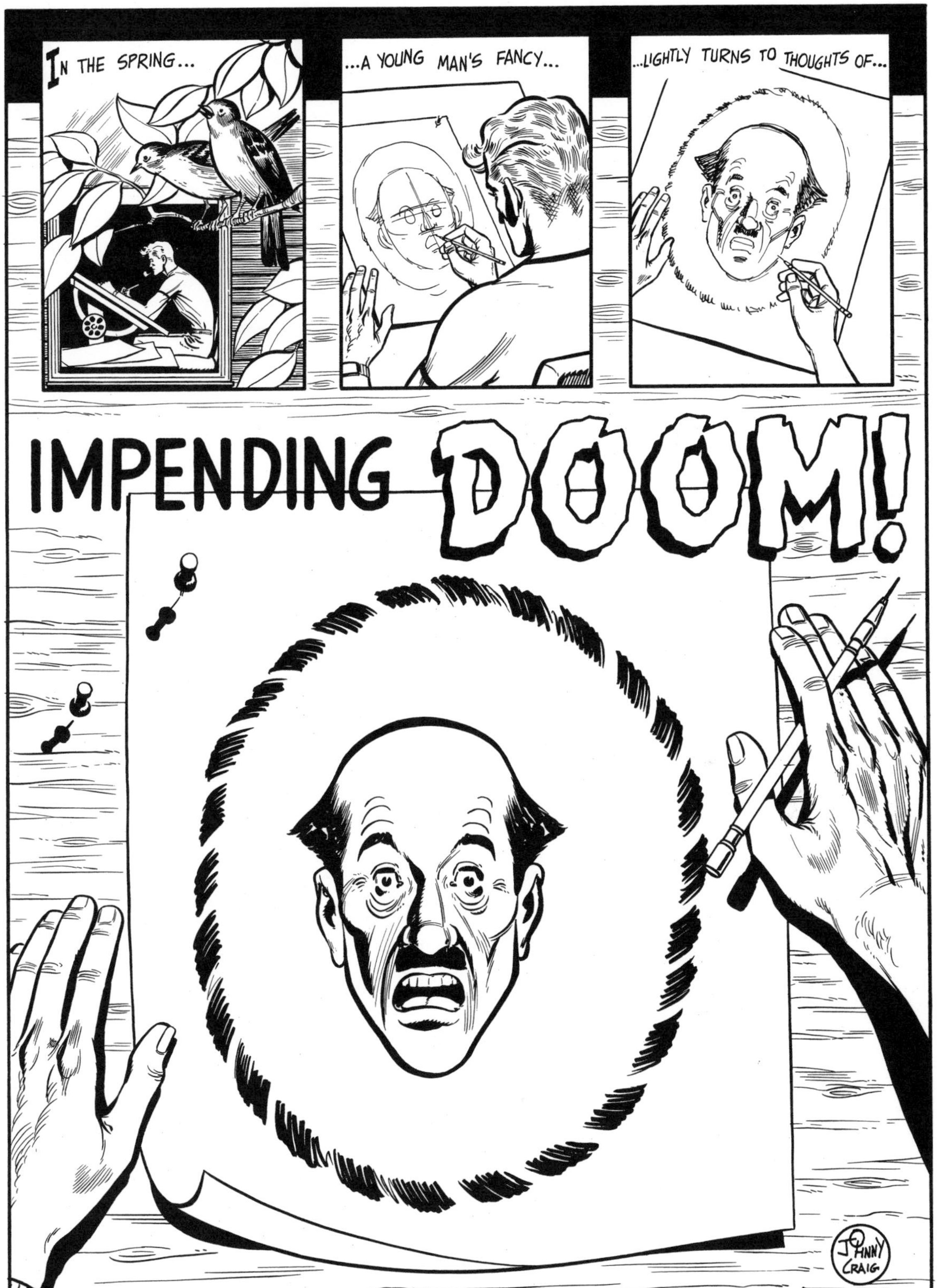
IN THE SPRING...
...A YOUNG MAN'S FANCY...
...LIGHTLY TURNS TO THOUGHTS OF...
IMPENDING DOOM!
JOHNNY CRAIG

LUVVA MIKE! WILL YOU LOOK AT THIS! WHY IN THE WORLD DID I DRAW THIS FACE? I DIDN'T EVEN REALIZE I WAS DOING IT! FUNNY... THE EXPRESSION IS ONE OF EXTREME... *FEAR!*

SURE IS STRANGE! MUST HAVE BEEN DAYDREAMING! MY MIND WAS A MILLION MILES AWAY! BUT WHY, ON SUCH A *LOVELY* DAY, WOULD I DRAW SUCH A... A *HORRIFIED* FACE?

OH, WELL... NO USE WORRYING ABOUT IT! GOSH, IT'S A SWELL DAY! TOO NICE A DAY TO WORK! THINK I'LL TAKE A WALK!

SOMETIME LATER...

... DOES A PERSON GOOD TO GET SOME CLEAN, FRESH AIR... SUNSHINE! I'VE WALKED A GOOD FIVE MILES AND I DON'T FEEL A BIT TIRED!

YES, SIR! NOTHING LIKE THE GREAT OUTDOORS! NATURE SURE IS WONDERFUL... YOU DON'T HAVE TO BE AN ARTIST TO APPRECIATE IT! SAY... WHAT'S THAT NOISE?

SOUNDS LIKE SOMEONE BANGING... OR HAMMERING ON SOMETHING! OH... OVER THERE... A HOUSE!

HMMM...ALEX KORDOVA...GRAVE-STONES! NICE CHEERFUL OCCUPATION! SOUNDS LIKE THAT NOISE IS COMING FROM AROUND IN BACK!

CLANK! CLANK!

UNIQUE STONECUTTING GRAVESTONES
ALEX KORDOVA PROP.

YES, I WAS RIGHT! THERE HE IS WORKING ON A GRAVESTONE! THESE MUST BE SAMPLES OF HIS WORK! NICE DESIGN!

HE'S MAKING SO MUCH NOISE, HE DOESN'T KNOW I'M HERE! WELL, THE MAN KNOWS HIS STUFF... HE'S GOOD! WHAT'S HE WORKING ON NOW?

CLANK

HMM...LET'S SEE! "HERE LIES THEODORE J. WARREN"!??? WHY, THAT'S MY NAME! "BORN APRIL 25, 1922..." HOLY SMOKE! I WANT A CLOSER LOOK AT THAT GRAVESTONE!

"BORN APRIL 25, 1922... DIED JUNE 9, 1950!.."

HEY!

BORN APRIL 25, 1922
DIED JUNE 9, 1950

3

27

GOOD LORD! THIS IS FANTASTIC! YOUR FACE! *YOU* ARE THE MAN I DREW! WHAT'S GOING ON? *AM I DREAMING*?

CALM DOWN, MISTER! TAKE IT EASY! WHAT'S THE MATTER?

THAT HEADSTONE! THAT'S *MY* NAME AND *MY* DATE OF BIRTH! WHAT MADE YOU PUT *MY* NAME AND BIRTHDATE ON THAT THING?

YOUR NAME? HMM... THAT'S QUITE A COINCIDENCE! BUT DON'T WORRY, MISTER... THIS IS JUST A SAMPLE I'M DOING! YOU KNOW, TO SHOW PEOPLE WHAT KIND OF WORK I DO!

MAYBE SO, BUT YOU HAVE MY *DATE OF DEATH* AS JUNE 9, 1950! THAT'S... *THAT'S TODAY!* AND THEN THERE'S THAT PICTURE I DREW...

THERE ISN'T ANYTHING TO GET EXCITED ABOUT! I JUST PUT TODAY'S DATE BECAUSE I'M GOING TO FINISH IT TODAY! LIKE AN ARTIST DATES HIS CANVAS WHEN HE FINISHES A PAINTING! ... WHAT'S THAT YOU SAID ABOUT A PICTURE?

HERE! LOOK AT THIS! IS THIS A DRAWING OF YOU, OR ISN'T IT?

WELL, I'LL BE DARNED! SURE IS *ME*, ALL RIGHT! YOU DIDN'T MAKE ME LOOK ANY TOO HAPPY, DID YOU?

THERE'S MORE TO THIS THAN JUST *COINCIDENCE!* I... I DON'T KNOW WHAT IT MEANS, BUT IT'S... IT'S LIKE AN *OMEN* OR SOMETHING!

BOSH! I'LL ADMIT IT'S ODD, ALL RIGHT! BUT I DON'T BELIEVE IN SUCH A THING AS *FATE* OR ANYTHING LIKE IT! SAY, COME ON IN THE HOUSE! MY WIFE WOULD LIKE TO SEE THIS PICTURE!

THE ODDEST THING JUST HAPPENED, DEAR! I WAS...

TED!

WHA...? *ELLEN!*

4

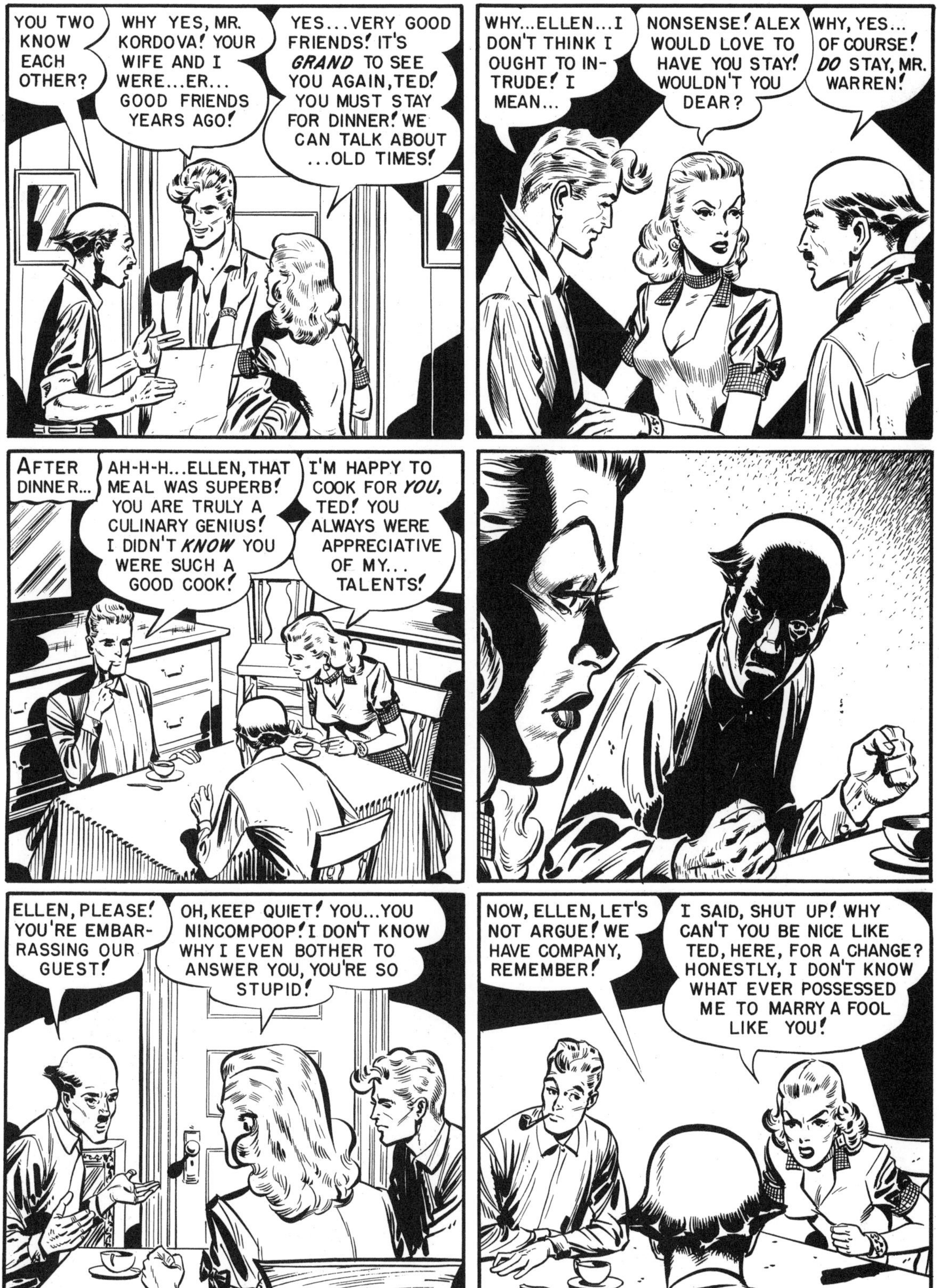
YOU TWO KNOW EACH OTHER?
WHY YES, MR. KORDOVA! YOUR WIFE AND I WERE...ER... GOOD FRIENDS YEARS AGO!
YES...VERY GOOD FRIENDS! IT'S GRAND TO SEE YOU AGAIN, TED! YOU MUST STAY FOR DINNER! WE CAN TALK ABOUT ...OLD TIMES!
WHY...ELLEN...I DON'T THINK I OUGHT TO INTRUDE! I MEAN...
NONSENSE! ALEX WOULD LOVE TO HAVE YOU STAY! WOULDN'T YOU DEAR?
WHY, YES... OF COURSE! DO STAY, MR. WARREN!
AFTER DINNER...
AH-H-H...ELLEN, THAT MEAL WAS SUPERB! YOU ARE TRULY A CULINARY GENIUS! I DIDN'T KNOW YOU WERE SUCH A GOOD COOK!
I'M HAPPY TO COOK FOR YOU, TED! YOU ALWAYS WERE APPRECIATIVE OF MY... TALENTS!
ELLEN, PLEASE! YOU'RE EMBARRASSING OUR GUEST!
OH, KEEP QUIET! YOU...YOU NINCOMPOOP! I DON'T KNOW WHY I EVEN BOTHER TO ANSWER YOU, YOU'RE SO STUPID!
NOW, ELLEN, LET'S NOT ARGUE! WE HAVE COMPANY, REMEMBER!
I SAID, SHUT UP! WHY CAN'T YOU BE NICE LIKE TED, HERE, FOR A CHANGE? HONESTLY, I DON'T KNOW WHAT EVER POSSESSED ME TO MARRY A FOOL LIKE YOU!
5

NOW, SEE HERE! I'VE HAD JUST ABOUT ALL I CAN TAKE...

LOOK AT YOU! A MISERABLE *WRETCH!* YOU'LL NEVER BE ANYTHING BUT WHAT YOU ARE! A DUMB GRAVESTONE CUTTER! TED'S A *SUCCESS!* HE HAS MONEY! HE'S YOUNG, HANDSOME, *EXCITING!* YOU'RE *NONE* OF THOSE THINGS!

I'VE HAD *ENOUGH!* I'M GOING OUT TO MY WORK-SHOP! THERE ARE SOME THINGS I WANT TO DO!

GO AHEAD, RUN, YOU SPINELESS SIMPLETON! FOR ALL I CARE YOU CAN GO OUT AND *NEVER* COME BACK!

OH-H, THAT MAN! HE AGGRAVATES ME TO DEATH! I CAN'T *STAND* HIM ANY MORE! ESPECIALLY... SINCE I'VE MET *YOU* AGAIN... TEDDY...

AH... ELLEN... PERHAPS I'D BETTER LEAVE...

NO, TED... DON'T GO! ALEX WON'T BE BACK FOR HOURS! AND WE... WE HAVE TO TALK ABOUT... OLD TIMES! REMEMBER?

YES... BUT...

OH, THERE'S NO USE KIDDING MYSELF, ELLEN. I *AM* GLAD TO SEE YOU AGAIN! BUT YOU'RE *MARRIED*..

FORGET ABOUT ALEX, TED! JUST THINK OF *YOU*... AND *ME!* IT'S BEEN A LONG TIME... BUT YOU HAVEN'T FORGOTTEN, HAVE YOU, TED? YOU COULDN'T FORGET *ME!*

NO... NO, I HAVEN'T FORGOTTEN! THOSE NIGHTS... YOUR KISSES...

I WAS CRAZY TO MARRY ALEX! I'VE KNOWN ALL ALONG THAT IT WAS *YOU* I WANTED! AND *YOU* WANT *ME*, TOO! I CAN SEE IT IN YOUR EYES! IT'S NOT TOO LATE... WE CAN STILL BE TOGETHER! KISS ME, TED! KISS ME *HARD!*

ELLEN... I... IT'S NOT RIGHT! YOUR HUSBAND...

KISS ME!

I... I... OH, ELLEN... ELLEN...

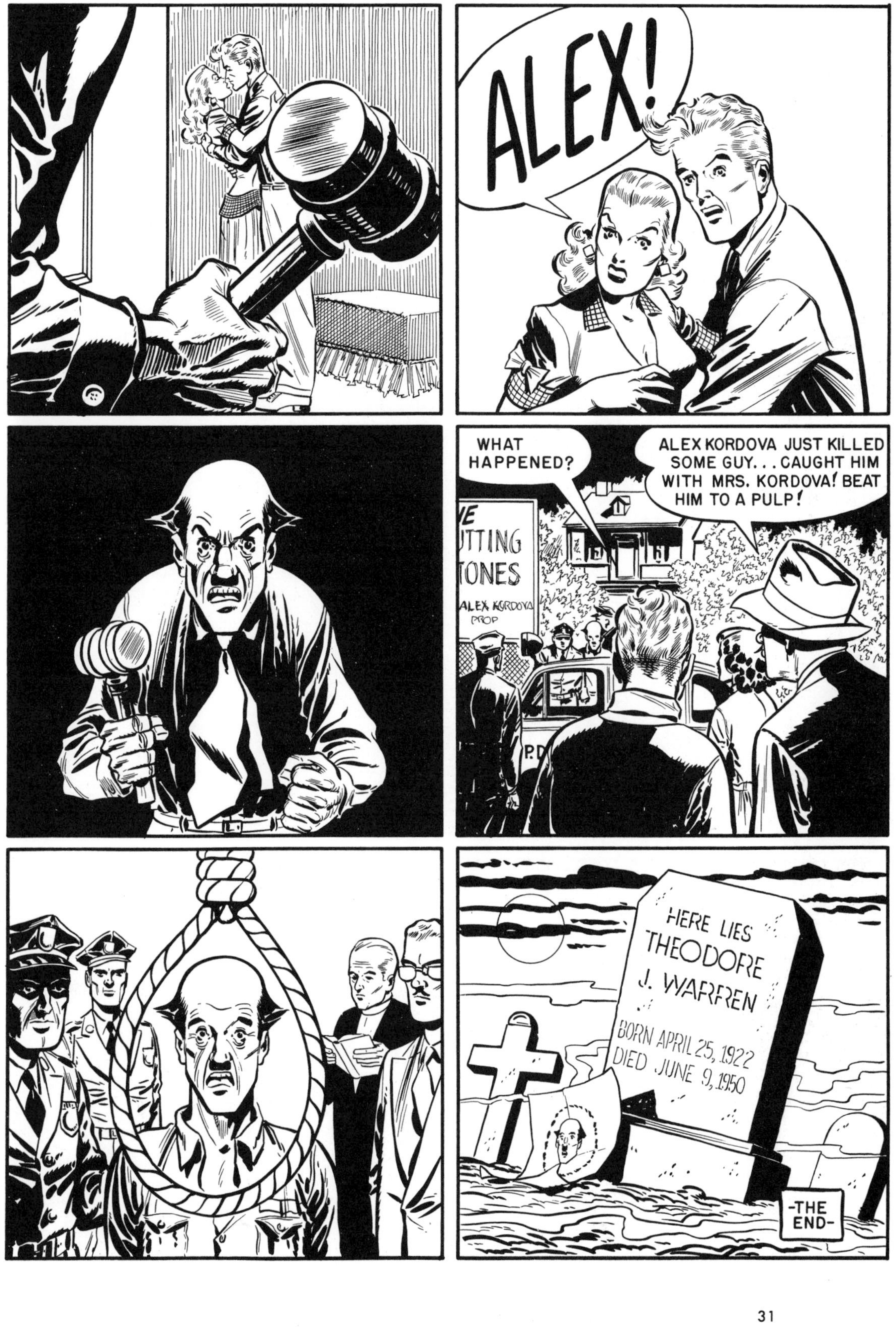
ALEX!
WHAT HAPPENED?
ALEX KORDOVA JUST KILLED SOME GUY. . . CAUGHT HIM WITH MRS. KORDOVA! BEAT HIM TO A PULP!
ALEX KORDOVA
PROP
HERE LIES THEODORE J. WARREN
BORN APRIL 25, 1922
DIED JUNE 9, 1950
-THE END-

THE VAULT OF HORROR!

WELCOME, READERS... WELCOME TO THE *VAULT OF HORROR!* THIS TIME I HAVE A TALE FOR YOU THAT EVEN PUZZLES *ME!* STRETCH OUT COMFORTABLY, NOW... AND COVER YOURSELVES WITH DEEP BLACK DIRT TO KEEP *WARM!* I WOULDN'T WANT YOU TO CATCH *COLD* FROM THIS *CHILLER* I CALL ......

HORROR HOUSE!

NOW LISTEN, HENRY! EITHER YOU GET YOUR STORIES IN ON TIME OR YOU LOOK FOR ANOTHER PUBLISHER! THIS BUSINESS OF BEING LATE HAS GOT TO *STOP!*

OKAY, BOSS! *OKAY*, YOU'RE *RIGHT!* BUT IT'S NOT MY FAULT! FRIENDS ARE ALWAYS BARGING IN ON ME... THROWING PARTIES... *IN MY APARTMENT!* I CAN'T GET *RID* OF THEM!

WELL, EITHER *YOU* GET RID OF *THEM*...OR *I'LL* GET RID OF *YOU!*

OKAY, BOSS! I PROMISE. I WON'T BE LATE AGAIN. I'LL OUTWIT THEM... SOMEHOW!

HORROR

GOREY MYSTERIES

EDITOR

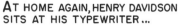 AT HOME AGAIN, HENRY DAVIDSON SITS AT HIS TYPEWRITER...

 I HAVE A TERRIFIC PLOT FOR THIS NEXT HORROR STORY! IF ONLY I'M NOT INTERRUPTED—HANG IT ALL! THERE'S THE DOORBELL!

RING! RING!

 HIYA, HENRY, OLD BOY! THOUGHT I'D BRING THE GANG OVER! HAVEN'T SEEN YOU IN A COUPLE OF DAYS!

OH, NO!

DON'T LET US BOTHER YOU, HENRY, IF YOU'RE BUSY! YOU GO RIGHT AHEAD AND WORK, DAHLING!

 HEY! WHERE'S YOUR LIQUOR, HENRY?

OH, I BET YOU SAY THAT TO ALL THE GIRLS...

THROW BACK THE RUG! I FEEL LIKE DANCING!

HENRY! YOU OLD MEANY! WHY HAVEN'T I SEEN MORE OF YOU?

LOOK, HENRY! I GOT A TERRIFIC STORY FOR YOU! THERE'S THIS GUY, SEE...

 WELL, THAT DOES IT! I CAN'T TAKE ANYMORE OF THIS! IF THEY LIKE MY APARTMENT SO MUCH, THEY CAN HAVE IT! I'LL JUST PACK UP MY CLOTHES AND TYPEWRITER...AND LEAVE!

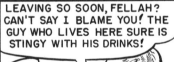  LEAVING SO SOON, FELLAH? CAN'T SAY I BLAME YOU! THE GUY WHO LIVES HERE SURE IS STINGY WITH HIS DRINKS!

SOME HOURS LATER...

I SHOULD HAVE DONE THIS LONG AGO! I'LL FIND SOME QUIET PLACE HERE IN THE COUNTRY WHERE I WON'T BE DISTURBED AND...HEY...

THAT HOUSE! IT'S PERFECT! JUST WHAT I NEED! WHY, I BET I COULD WRITE SENSATIONAL HORROR STORIES WITH ALL THAT MOOD AND ATMOSPHERE! I'LL BUY IT!

2

LATER, AT A REAL ESTATE AGENT'S OFFICE IN TOWN..

YOU...YOU WANT TO BUY *MILLFORD MANOR?* BUT... *NOBODY* WANTS TO BUY *THAT* HOUSE! IT'S... IT'S *HAUNTED!*

HAUNTED! HA! HA! WHAT NONSENSE! THERE'S NO SUCH THING AS HOUSES REALLY BEING *HAUNTED!* I'LL BUY IT RIGHT NOW!

...AND AT THE GENERAL STORE WHILE BUYING FOOD...

MILLFORD MANOR? GLORY BE, STRANGER! ARE YE *DAFT?* DON'T YE KNOW THAT PLACE IS *HAUNTED?*

DON'T TELL ME *YOU* BELIEVE THOSE OLD WIVES' TALES. *HA! HA!* WELL, I MAY *WRITE* GHOST AND HORROR STORIES, BUT I DON'T HAVE TO *BELIEVE* 'EM!

AH... I'M ALL SET! PLENTY OF FOOD, TYPE-WRITER RIBBON, PAPER!.. THIS IS GOING TO BE *GREAT!* I CAN'T *WAIT* TO BEGIN WRITING!

BY CANDLELIGHT, HENRY WORKS ON HIS LATEST STORY. HARDLY DOES HE TAKE TIME OUT TO EAT AND SLEEP, SO EN-THUSED IS HE..! THE DAYS PASS.....

FINISHED! AND IN RECORD TIME, TOO! AH! I *KNEW* THIS PLACE WAS PERFECT FOR ME, THE MINUTE I SAW IT!

THIS IS THE BEST STORY I'VE EVER WRITTEN! BOY! WON'T MY BOSS BE SURPRISED? WHA... SOMEONE AT THE DOOR...

HIYA, HENRY, OLD BOY!

THOUGHT YOU'D LOSE US BY HIBERNATING, EH?

YOU NAUGHTY BOY! HOW COULD YOU DESERT US LIKE THAT? YOU MUST COME BACK TO THE CITY, HENRY! YOU SIMPLY *MUST!*

RETURN TO THE CITY? NOT ON YOUR LIFE! I'VE FOUND A HOME HERE, AND *HERE I STAY!*

BUT... BUT HOW CAN ANYONE *LIVE* IN A GLOOMY OLD PLACE LIKE THIS? IT'S... IT'S *AWFUL!*

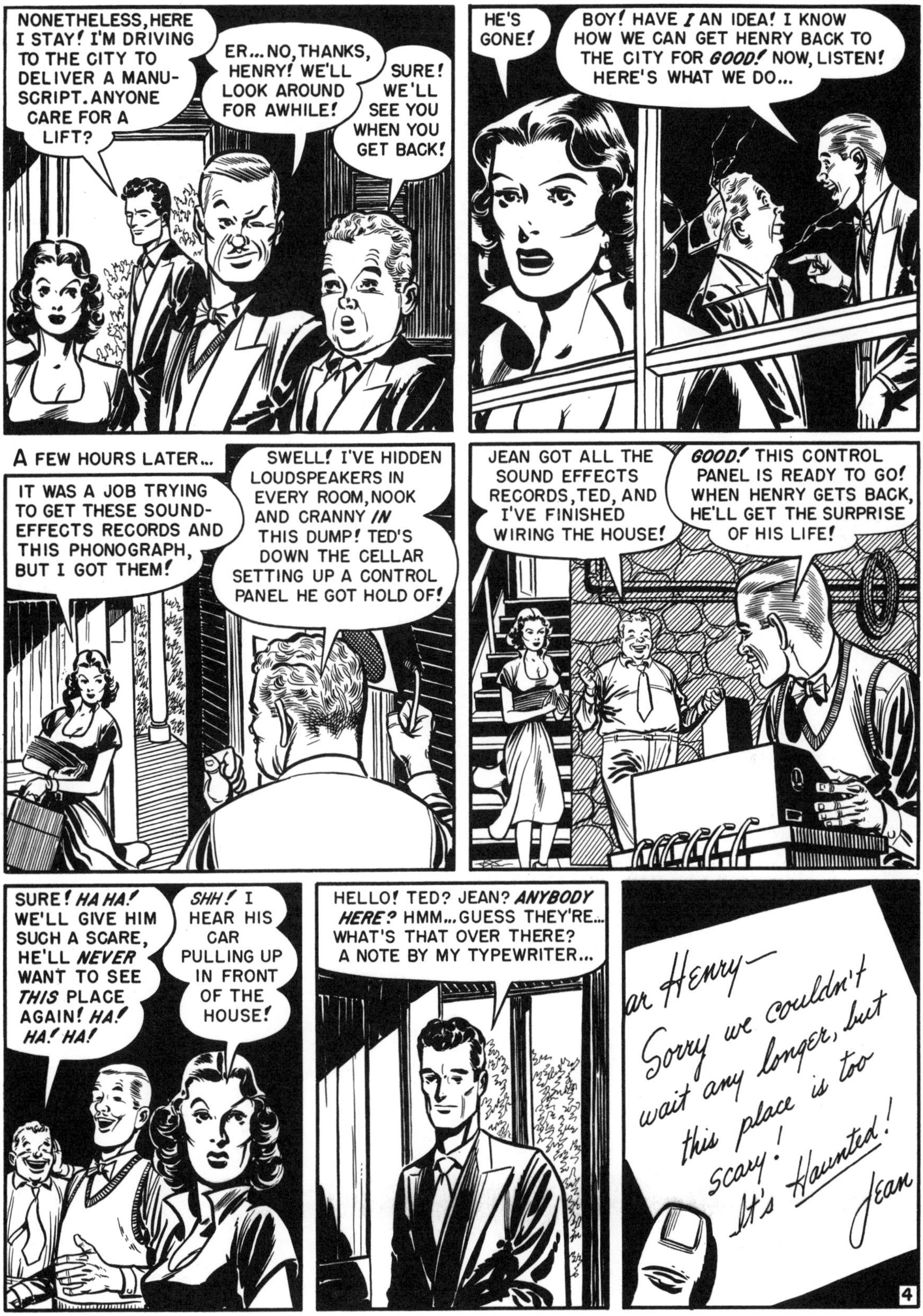
NONETHELESS, HERE I STAY! I'M DRIVING TO THE CITY TO DELIVER A MANUSCRIPT. ANYONE CARE FOR A LIFT?
ER... NO, THANKS, HENRY! WE'LL LOOK AROUND FOR AWHILE!
SURE! WE'LL SEE YOU WHEN YOU GET BACK!
HE'S GONE!
BOY! HAVE *I* AN IDEA! I KNOW HOW WE CAN GET HENRY BACK TO THE CITY FOR *GOOD!* NOW, LISTEN! HERE'S WHAT WE DO...
A FEW HOURS LATER...
IT WAS A JOB TRYING TO GET THESE SOUND-EFFECTS RECORDS AND THIS PHONOGRAPH, BUT I GOT THEM!
SWELL! I'VE HIDDEN LOUDSPEAKERS IN EVERY ROOM, NOOK AND CRANNY *IN* THIS DUMP! TED'S DOWN THE CELLAR SETTING UP A CONTROL PANEL HE GOT HOLD OF!
JEAN GOT ALL THE SOUND EFFECTS RECORDS, TED, AND I'VE FINISHED WIRING THE HOUSE!
GOOD! THIS CONTROL PANEL IS READY TO GO! WHEN HENRY GETS BACK, HE'LL GET THE SURPRISE OF HIS LIFE!
SURE! *HA HA!* WE'LL GIVE HIM SUCH A SCARE, HE'LL *NEVER* WANT TO SEE *THIS* PLACE AGAIN! *HA! HA! HA!*
SHH! I HEAR HIS CAR PULLING UP IN FRONT OF THE HOUSE!
HELLO! TED? JEAN? *ANYBODY HERE?* HMM... GUESS THEY'RE... WHAT'S THAT OVER THERE? A NOTE BY MY TYPEWRITER...
ar Henry—
Sorry we couldn't wait any longer, but this place is too scary! It's Haunted!
Jean
4

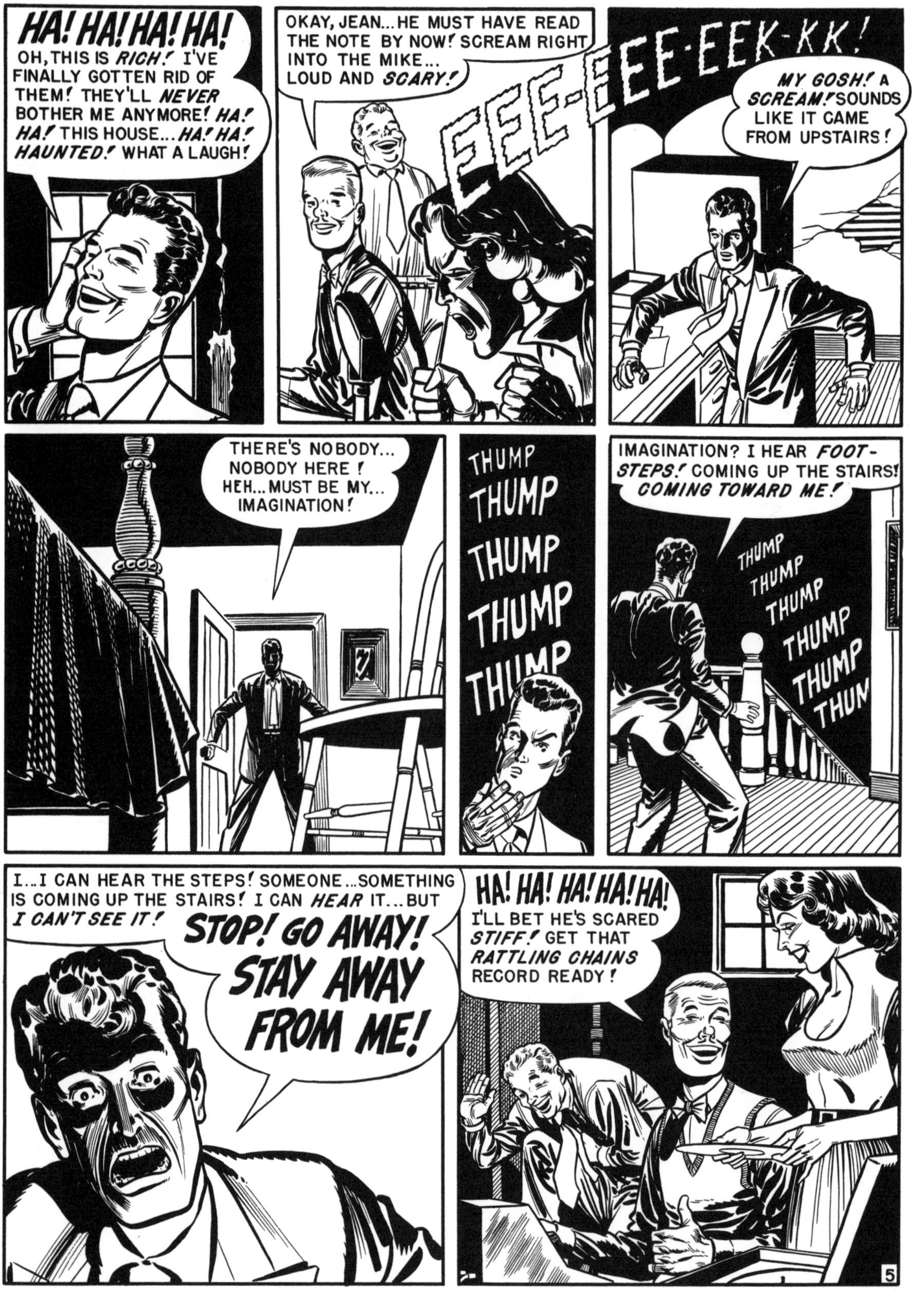
HA! HA! HA! HA! OH, THIS IS RICH! I'VE FINALLY GOTTEN RID OF THEM! THEY'LL NEVER BOTHER ME ANYMORE! HA! HA! THIS HOUSE... HA! HA! HAUNTED! WHAT A LAUGH!
OKAY, JEAN... HE MUST HAVE READ THE NOTE BY NOW! SCREAM RIGHT INTO THE MIKE... LOUD AND SCARY!
EEE-EEE-EEE-EEK-KK!
MY GOSH! A SCREAM! SOUNDS LIKE IT CAME FROM UPSTAIRS!
THERE'S NOBODY... NOBODY HERE! HEH... MUST BE MY... IMAGINATION!
THUMP THUMP THUMP THUMP THUMP
IMAGINATION? I HEAR FOOT-STEPS! COMING UP THE STAIRS! COMING TOWARD ME!
THUMP THUMP THUMP THUMP THUMP THUM
I... I CAN HEAR THE STEPS! SOMEONE... SOMETHING IS COMING UP THE STAIRS! I CAN HEAR IT... BUT I CAN'T SEE IT!
STOP! GO AWAY! STAY AWAY FROM ME!
HA! HA! HA! HA! HA! I'LL BET HE'S SCARED STIFF! GET THAT RATTLING CHAINS RECORD READY!
5

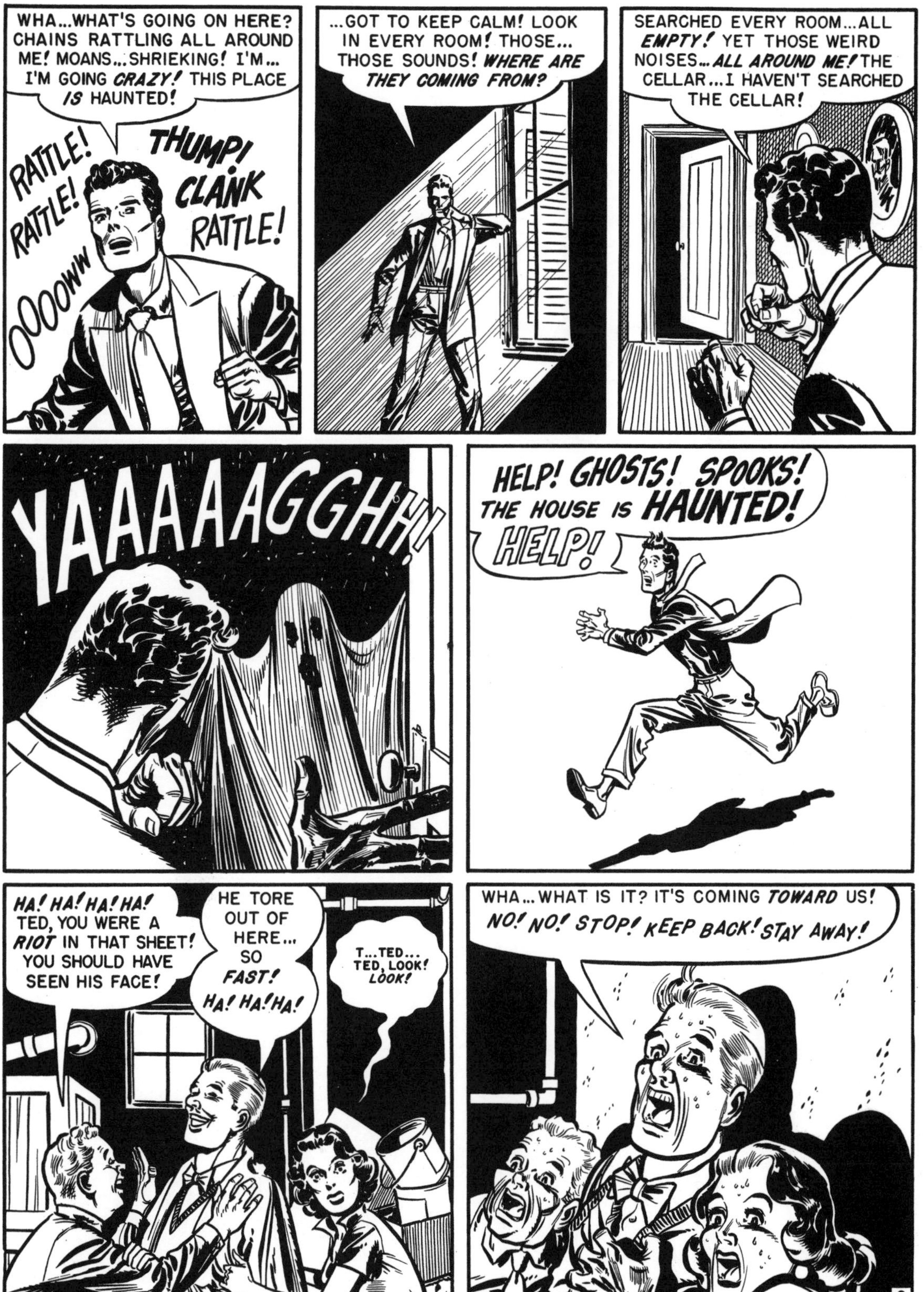
WHA...WHAT'S GOING ON HERE? CHAINS RATTLING ALL AROUND ME! MOANS...SHRIEKING! I'M... I'M GOING CRAZY! THIS PLACE IS HAUNTED!
RATTLE! RATTLE!
THUMP! CLANK RATTLE!
OOOOWW
...GOT TO KEEP CALM! LOOK IN EVERY ROOM! THOSE... THOSE SOUNDS! WHERE ARE THEY COMING FROM?
SEARCHED EVERY ROOM...ALL EMPTY! YET THOSE WEIRD NOISES...ALL AROUND ME! THE CELLAR...I HAVEN'T SEARCHED THE CELLAR!
YAAAAAGGHH!
HELP! GHOSTS! SPOOKS! THE HOUSE IS HAUNTED! HELP!
HA! HA! HA! HA! TED, YOU WERE A RIOT IN THAT SHEET! YOU SHOULD HAVE SEEN HIS FACE!
HE TORE OUT OF HERE... SO FAST! HA! HA! HA!
T...TED... TED, LOOK! LOOK!
WHA...WHAT IS IT? IT'S COMING TOWARD US! NO! NO! STOP! KEEP BACK! STAY AWAY!
6

A FEW HOURS LATER, HENRY RETURNS...WITH THE CONSTABLE AND HIS DEPUTIES...

CONFOUND IT! EVERYONE *TOLD* YOU THE PLACE WAS *HAUNTED!*

OKAY! *OKAY!* JUST HELP ME GET MY TYPEWRITER AND CLOTHES! I'LL GO AND...*SAY!* WHAT'S THAT IN THE DRIVEWAY?

GOOD LORD! IT'S A *MAN!* BUT... HIS *FACE!* LOOK AT HIS *FACE!*

IT...IT HAS NO... NO *FLESH!* LIKE SOMETHING HAS *EATEN...* *CONSTABLE! COME INSIDE! QUICK!*

WE FOUND HIM...JUST LIKE THAT!

TED! IT'S TED! THE ONE OUTSIDE MUST BE *ROGER!* BUT WHERE'S JEAN?

LISTEN! SOMEONE *LAUGHING!* SOUNDS HYSTERICAL!

...COMING FROM THE CELLAR! *C'MON!*

HA! HA! HA! HA! HA! HA! HA! HA! HA! HA! HA! HA! H HA HA

JEAN!

GREAT SCOTT! SHE'S AGED TWENTY YEARS! SHE MUST HAVE SEEN SOMETHING *HORRIBLE BEYOND WORDS* TO MAKE HER THE BABBLING LUNATIC WE SEE!

HMPF! CONTROL PANEL...SOUND EFFECTS RECORDS! THEY TRIED TO SCARE ME INTO RETURNING TO THE CITY!

...ONLY THEIR LITTLE PLAN BACKFIRED! JUST WHAT *DID* HAPPEN, WE'LL PROBABLY NEVER KNOW!

HENRY RETURNS TO THE CITY WHERE THE GANG STILL WHOOP IT UP! ONLY *NOW* HENRY ENJOYS IT...HE DOESN'T *LIKE* BEING ALONE ANYMORE!

HEH, HEH, HEH! WELL, READERS, DID YOU LIKE MY AMUSING LITTLE TALE? I HOPE SO! TO THIS DAY NO ONE KNOWS WHAT EVIL IS POSSESSED BY THAT *HORROR HOUSE!* HEH! BUT IF YOU WANT ANOTHER STORY... HEH! JUST READ ON!

MUTINY

OUR STORY OPENS IN A SLEAZY BAR NEAR THE WATERFRONT... WHERE THIEVES, MURDERERS, AND CAREFREE SEAMEN MINGLE IN AN EFFORT TO FORGET THE MONOTONY OF LIVING! FOR THIS IS PORT ELIZABETH, SOUTH AFRICA...

...AND WHEN THE CAP'N GOT PAID A FORTUNE IN DIAMONDS, HE GAVE US A *BONUS!* GOOD MAN, THAT CAP'N... NICE LAD!

YOU'VE HAD ENOUGH, HAWKINS!—C'MON, NOW... CAP'N WANTS TO SHOVE OFF BY MIDNIGHT! WE GOTTA GET ABOARD!

THE TRIO LEAVE THE NOISY BAR AND WALK DESERTED, SWELTERING ALLEYS...UNAWARE THAT THEY ARE BEING FOLLOWED...

...YESSIR, A *FORTUNE* IN DIAMONDS!

CLOSE YOUR HATCH! YOU OUGHT TO KNOW BETTER THAN TO SHOOT OFF YOUR MOUTH AROUND *HERE!*

THE BATTLE WAS SHORT... AND BITTER...

SEARCH THEIR CLOTHES! SOME IDENTIFICATION WILL TELL US WHAT SHIP THEY'RE OFF. THE CAP'N WILL NEED THREE NEW MEN, AND AFTER WE'RE ABOARD AND OUT TO SEA...

HA! HA! HA! I GET IT, HOOK! THEN WE GO AFTER THE BAG OF DIAMONDS!

SOMETIME LATER, CAPTAIN STEVE CUTTER, SKIPPER OF THE *SHARK*, FACES THREE MEN WHO HAVE JUST COME ABOARD...

LOOKING FOR WORK, EH? WELL, I *DO* NEED A CREW...CAN'T WAIT ANY LONGER FOR THE MEN I HAD. OKAY...I'LL SIGN YOU ON!

AND SO CAPTAIN CUTTER PUTS TO SEA, ALONE WITH THREE VICIOUS MEN WHO COVET HIS FABULOUS BAG OF DIAMONDS!

THREE DAYS OUT FINDS THE *SHARK* ON COURSE WITH MUTINY IN THE HEARTS OF ITS CREW...

NOW'S THE TIME! LASH THE WHEEL, SKEEVER! WE'LL OVERPOWER CAP'N CUTTER AND MAKE HIM TELL WHERE THE DIAMONDS ARE!

THERE! I'VE MADE THE LOG ENTRY...OH... SOMEONE AT THE DOOR!

HEY!

GRAB HIM, MATES!

HOLD HIM, YOU IDJITS! *THIS'LL* TAKE THE FIGHT OUT OF HIM!

HE'LL TELL WHERE THE DIAMONDS ARE... AND *QUICK!*

HOOK, YOU BEEN BEATING HIM FOR TWO HOURS! IF HE HASN'T TALKED BY NOW, HE *NEVER* WILL!

BLAST YOU, CUTTER! TELL US WHERE THE DIAMONDS ARE! YOU'VE *HIDDEN* THEM SOMEWHERE ABOARD SHIP! FOR THE LAST TIME, *TELL US WHERE!*

AWRIGHT! MAKE READY A LIFEBOAT! WE'LL SEE HOW THIS FOOL LIKES BEING SET ADRIFT WITHOUT PROVISIONS! THEN WE'LL SEARCH THIS TUB FROM STEM TO STERN!

THAT'LL TEACH THE BLASTED NUMBSKULL! BUT TO SHOW I GOT A GOOD HEART, I'LL LET HIM HAVE SOME FOOD! *HA!* *SKEEVER!* GET A SACK OF *FLOUR* FROM THE GALLEY!

FLOUR TASTES GOOD! ESPECIALLY WITH *SALT WATER!* *HA! HA! HA! HA!*

HERE, HOOK! HERE'S THE FLOUR!

THERE YOU ARE, *CAP'N!* *EAT HEARTY!*

ALL RIGHT, NOW! SKEEVER AND I'LL START LOOKIN' FOR THE DIAMONDS! *KRANK!* YOU MAN THE WHEEL! PUT ABOUT FOR PORT ELIZABETH AND KEEP HER STEADY AS SHE GOES!

RIGHT!

SURE, HOOK! SURE!

NIGHT FALLS SILENTLY AROUND THE SMALL VESSEL, AND HOOK AND SKEEVER RETURN TO THE WHEEL...

ANY LUCK, HOOK?

NO! AND TO TOP IT OFF, THE WIND'S DYIN'! WE'RE LIABLE TO BE *BECALMED!*

3

WHAT IN BLAZES!??? *KRANK!* YOU STUPID KNUCKLEHEAD! I TOLD YOU TO KEEP HER *STEADY AS SHE GOES!*

WAIT A MINUTE, HOOK! I...I AIN'T NO GOOD AT NAVIGATING...

SAP! I OUGHTA BREAK YOU IN HALF! YOU BEEN SAILING IN *CIRCLES!*

MEANWHILE CAPTAIN CUTTER IS STILL DRIFTING IN THE LIFEBOAT. HE HAS BEEN UNCONSCIOUS, BUT NOW HIS HEAD CLEARS... AND VAGUE FORMS TAKE SHAPE...

MY...MY HEAD! WHERE..? I'M IN A LIFEBOAT! STRANGE...WHAT AM I DOING HERE? RIGHT UNDER THE STERN OF MY SHIP!

HMM...THE *SHARK'S* BECALMED! I HAVE TO GET BACK ABOARD! NO ONE'S GOING TO TAKE OVER MY SHIP WHILE *I* CAN HELP IT!

OH-OH! THERE'S KRANK! HOPE HE DOESN'T TURN AROUND!

...THIS OUGHT TO MAKE YOU PRETTY CRANKY, KRANK!

WHA...? *WHO'S THAT?* UGGH!

SPLASH!

4

HOOK! I HEARD A SPLASH!

SO DID I! C'MON! LET'S GO TOPSIDE! IF THAT FOOL KRANK HAS FOULED UP AGAIN, I'LL MURDER HIM!

KRANK? KRANK! WHERE ARE YOU? HE DOESN'T ANSWER, HOOK!

WE'LL LOOK FOR HIM! YOU TAKE THE STERN! I'LL SEARCH FOR'ARD!

SPLASH!

SKEEVER?... SKEEVER! WHAT HAPPENED!? ANSWER ME!

BLAST YOU, SKEEVER! IF YOU'RE PLAYIN' GAMES WITH ME, S'HELP ME, I'LL KILL YOU!

...C'MON, NOW! I...I WAS ONLY KIDDING! I WON'T HURT YOU... C'MON OUT... I...I...DON'T LIKE BEIN' ALONE! HEH...HEH...

YOU'RE NOT ALONE, HOOK!

SKEEVER?

5

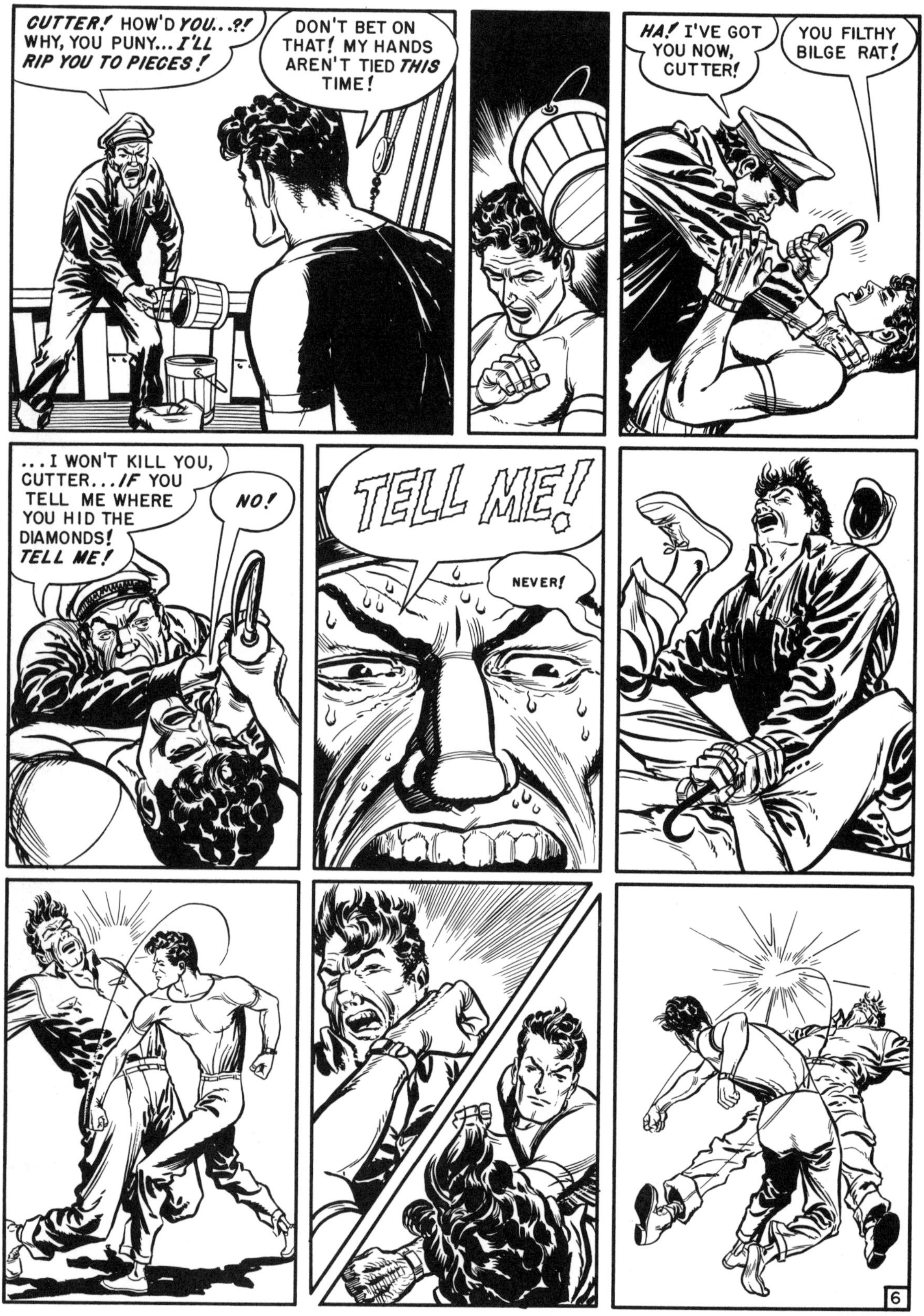
CUTTER! HOW'D YOU..?! WHY, YOU PUNY... I'LL RIP YOU TO PIECES!
DON'T BET ON THAT! MY HANDS AREN'T TIED THIS TIME!
HA! I'VE GOT YOU NOW, CUTTER!
YOU FILTHY BILGE RAT!
...I WON'T KILL YOU, CUTTER...IF YOU TELL ME WHERE YOU HID THE DIAMONDS! TELL ME!
NO!
TELL ME!
NEVER!
6

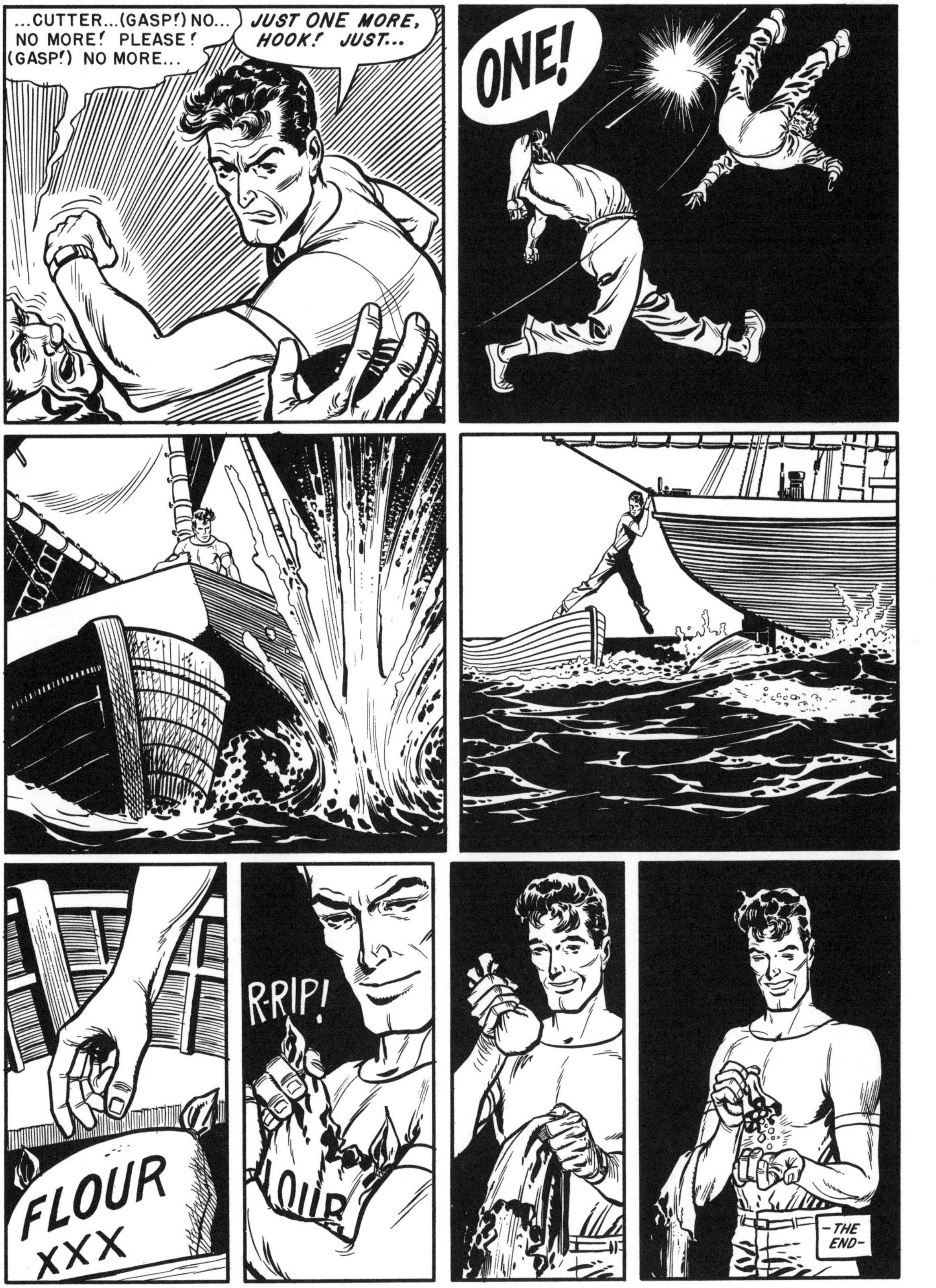
...CUTTER...(GASP!) NO... NO MORE! PLEASE! (GASP!) NO MORE...
JUST ONE MORE, HOOK! JUST...
ONE!
FLOUR XXX
R-RIP!
-THE END-

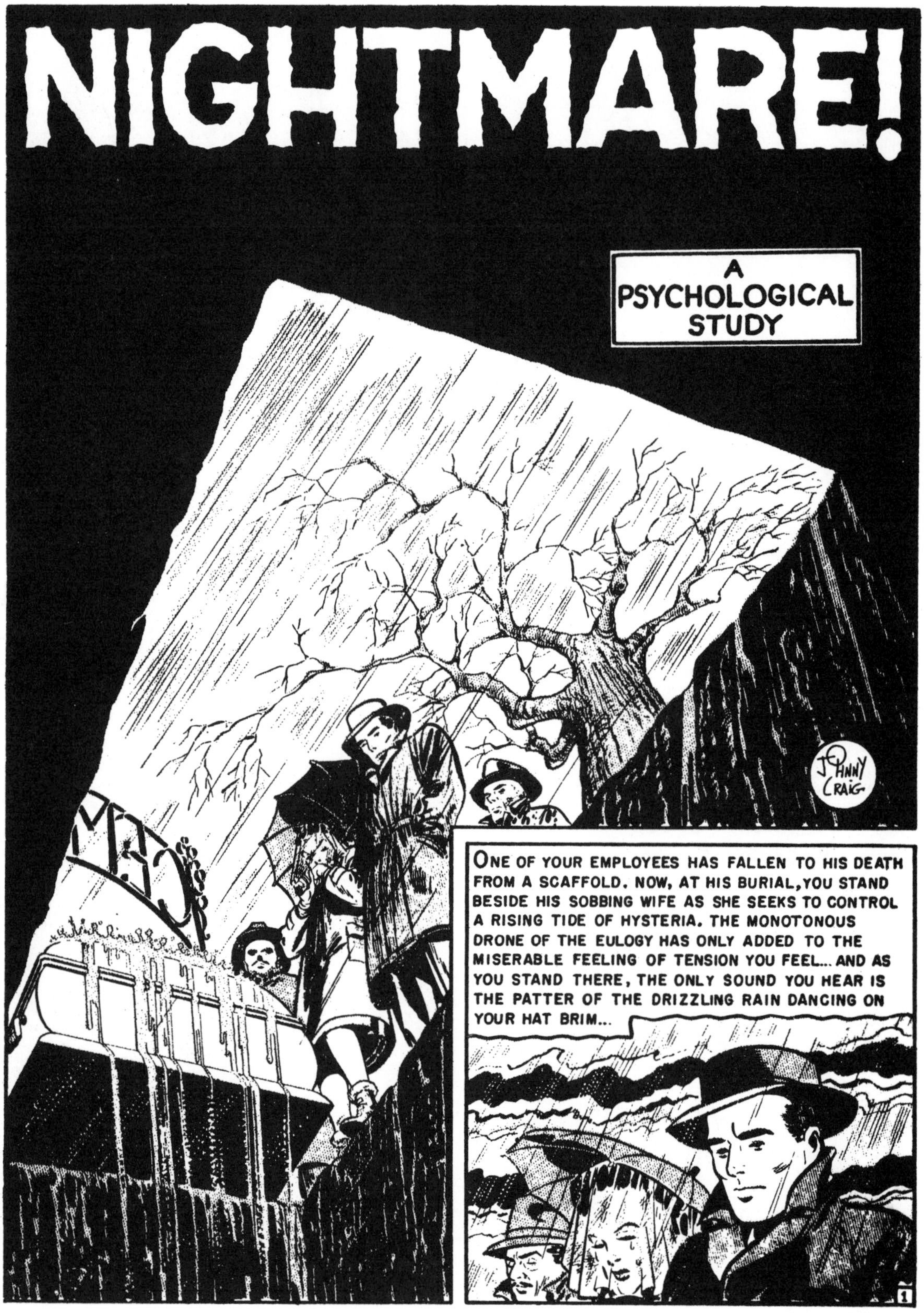
NIGHTMARE!
A PSYCHOLOGICAL STUDY
JOHNNY CRAIG
ONE OF YOUR EMPLOYEES HAS FALLEN TO HIS DEATH FROM A SCAFFOLD. NOW, AT HIS BURIAL, YOU STAND BESIDE HIS SOBBING WIFE AS SHE SEEKS TO CONTROL A RISING TIDE OF HYSTERIA. THE MONOTONOUS DRONE OF THE EULOGY HAS ONLY ADDED TO THE MISERABLE FEELING OF TENSION YOU FEEL... AND AS YOU STAND THERE, THE ONLY SOUND YOU HEAR IS THE PATTER OF THE DRIZZLING RAIN DANCING ON YOUR HAT BRIM...
1

UNTIL NOW THE WIDOW HAS BEEN SILENT AND MOTIONLESS... BUT AS THE PALL-BEARERS STEP FORWARD...

NO! STOP! DON'T LOWER THE CASKET! IT'S EMPTY! THE CASKET IS EMPTY!

GRAB HER! SHE'S HYSTERICAL!

YOU TRY TO QUIET THE WOMAN, BUT HAVE NO SUCCESS. FINALLY, TO APPEASE HER, THE CASKET IS OPENED...

GOOD HEAVENS! SHE WAS RIGHT! THE CASKET IS EMPTY!

EMPTY? BUT THAT'S IMPOSSIBLE!

HOW CAN WE HAVE A FUNERAL WITHOUT A CORPSE?

A FUNERAL HAS TO HAVE A BODY!

YES! WE MUST FIND ONE!

OF COURSE! WE MUST GET A BODY! BUT WHERE?

I DON'T CARE WHERE! I INSIST WE HAVE A BODY FOR MY POOR HUSBAND'S BURIAL!

WAIT.. WE HAVE A BODY! RIGHT HERE!

MY HUSBAND'S EMPLOYER! YES! EXCELLENT!

HE'LL MAKE A FINE BODY!

WHAT? SAY, WHAT IS THIS? ARE YOU ALL INSANE?

NO! STOP! FOR GOD'S SAKE, LET ME GO! STOP! PLEASE! YOU CAN'T BURY ME! I'M ALIVE!

HURRY! HURRY! PUSH HIM IN! PUSH HIM IN!

QUICK, NOW! CLOSE THE TOP DOWN! WE'LL HAVE TO NAIL HIM IN!

HA! HA! HA! HA! HA! HA! HA! HA! HA! HA! HA! HA!

LET ME HELP!

HELP! HEL...:.? WHA...WHAT? WHERE...OH...THANK HEAVEN! I'VE *BEEN DREAMING!* THOSE BLASTED *NIGHTMARES!* I'M ...I'M SHAKING LIKE A LEAF!

YOU ARE TOO FRIGHTENED TO SLEEP, SO YOU SIT IN A CHAIR AND READ...

CONFOUND IT...I'M SO EXHAUSTED! CAN'T KEEP MY EYES OPEN! I'D BETTER GET...YAWN-N-N...DRESSED AND TAKE A WALK!

LEAVING YOUR HOUSE, YOU ROAM THROUGH DESERTED STREETS TO THE OUTSKIRTS OF THE TOWN...

MISERABLE WEATHER! I WISH MORNING WERE HERE!...GETTING TO BE A NERVOUS...
WHAT'S THAT?

ABOVE THE HOWLING RAIN YOU THINK YOU HEAR A CRY FOR HELP! YOU AREN'T CERTAIN... SO YOU WAIT, STRAINING YOUR EARS TO LISTEN.. AND IT COMES AGAIN!

SOMEONE *IS* CALLING! IT'S COMING FROM OUT THERE IN THE FIELD SOMEWHERE!

YOU CRAWL THROUGH THE FENCE AND BEGIN TO SEARCH FOR WHOEVER HAS CALLED THE DRIVING RAIN BLINDS YOUR VISION AND YOU STRUGGLE TO KEEP WALKING, FOR THE MUDDY SLIME IS TREACH- EROUS... GRASPING...

BLAZES!... LIKE WALKING THROUGH A FIELD OF *GLUE!* (GASP) CAN'T...CAN'T LIFT MY FOOT! SO MUDDY...KEEP SINKING DEEPER..

DESPERATELY, YOU SUMMON ALL YOUR STRENGTH! YOU TRY TO FREE YOURSELF... AND THEN SUDDENLY... AS YOU SINK DEEPER, YOU REALIZE YOU HAVE STUM- BLED INTO...NOT A *MUD HOLE*...BUT A HUNGRY, SUCK- ING BOG OF *QUICKSAND!*

OH, LORD...HELP ME! I'VE GOT TO GET OUT OF THIS! IT'S JUST LIKE ALL MY *NIGHTMARES!* I'LL BE BURIED ALIVE!

PANIC-STRICKEN, YOU FLAIL YOUR ARMS, SCREAM- ING AS LOUD AS YOU CAN! TEARS RUN FROM YOUR EYES AND WAVES OF TERROR SHAKE YOUR SWEAT- COVERED BODY! YOU ARE INSANE WITH FEAR! THE QUICKSAND IS ABOVE YOUR CHEST, NOW...OVER YOUR CHIN! THEN COMES THE GRITTY, GAGGING SENSA- TION AS THE SAND FLOODS IN YOUR MOUTH... THE CHOKING SUFFOCATION AS IT CLOGS YOUR NOSTRILS.. AND THEN BURNING, EMPTY BLACKNESS...

3

 WHA..? WHY...*I'M ALIVE! I'M BACK IN MY ROOM!* I MUST HAVE FALLEN ASLEEP HERE IN THE CHAIR WHILE I WAS READING! IT WAS ONLY ANOTHER *NIGHTMARE!*

I...I CAN'T TAKE MUCH MORE OF THIS! IT'S DAYLIGHT NOW...I'LL GO VISIT A...A DOCTOR TODAY! I...I MUST HAVE HELP!

 AND SO, SEVERAL HOURS LATER, YOU ARE USHERED INTO THE PRIVATE OFFICE OF A FAMOUS PSYCHIATRIST...

YOUR NAME, AGE AND OCCUPATION, PLEASE...

MY NAME IS JOHN SEVERIN! I'M 28 YEARS OLD, AND I'M A CONSTRUCTION ENGINEER!

 ALL RIGHT, MR. SEVERIN! NOW WHAT SEEMS TO BE THE TROUBLE?

DR. FROYD...FOR *MONTHS* NOW I'VE BEEN HAVING HORRIBLE *NIGHTMARES!* I....I CAN'T GET RID OF THEM! THEY'RE SO *REAL*, THAT LATELY I'M NOT SURE WHEN I'M *AWAKE* OR WHEN I'M *ASLEEP!*

THEY ALL END THE SAME WAY! I'M ALWAYS BEING *BURIED ALIVE* IN ONE WAY OR ANOTHER! HONESTLY, DR. FROYD, I'M GOING TO PIECES! I'M AFRAID TO SLEEP AT NIGHT!

I SEE...SUPPOSE YOU LIE DOWN ON THIS COUCH AND TELL ME ABOUT ONE OF YOUR NIGHTMARES!

JUST RELAX, MR. SEVERIN! JUST RELAX!

OH-H-H...THIS COUCH FEELS GOOD! I'VE BEEN GETTING SO LITTLE SLEEP...(YAWN) I'M SO EXHAUSTED! WELL, DOCTOR, I REMEMBER ONE DREAM I HAD ABOUT FOUR NIGHTS AGO...

 "IN THIS DREAM I WAS WALKING A DIRT ROAD THAT WOUND ENDLESSLY BESIDE A CEMETERY. I THINK IT WAS RAINING...YES, IT WAS!...AND THE TOMBSTONES COVERED THE GROUND AS FAR AS THE EYE COULD SEE! SUDDENLY, I HEARD A VOICE CALLING MY NAME...

"I HURRIED THROUGH THE GRAVEYARD SEEKING THE SOURCE OF THE VOICE I HAD HEARD. ALL AT ONCE, I CAME UPON A MAUSOLEUM...ITS DOOR STOOD AJAR...

"SOMEHOW I KNEW THAT THE VOICE HAD COME FROM WITHIN. I ENTERED...I SAW A CASKET, ITS LID CLOSED... AND FROM INSIDE IT I HEARD THE VOICE CALLING MY NAME!

"I RUSHED TO THE CASKET...FLUNG OPEN THE TOP! AND THEN...

"A...A *THING* REACHED UP OUT OF THE COFFIN AND GRABBED ME! A SCREAM STRANGLED AND DIED IN MY THROAT AND BEFORE I KNEW IT...THIS *THING* HAD...HAD PULLED ME *INTO THE COFFIN!*

"THE LID SLAMMED SHUT! I FOUGHT FRANTICALLY TO OPEN IT, BUT...THE THING WRAPPED ITS ARMS ABOUT ME IN AN IRON GRASP AND HELD ME DOWN! *I BEGAN SCREAMING!*

"THE THING ONLY HELD ME TIGHTER! AS I FOUGHT AND STRUGGLED TO FREE MYSELF, I SENSED THAT THIS INHUMAN CREATURE WAS LAUGHING AT ME... FOR IT SEEMED THAT ITS MOUTH WAS TWISTED IN A WICKED GRIN! AFTER A WHILE I CEASED FIGHTING! MY BODY WENT LIMP...AND MY FACE RESTED ON THE FACE OF THE THING. I SOBBED QUIETLY IN DESPAIR...

"SOON EVERY BREATH WRACKED MY LUNGS WITH SEARING PAIN! I GASPED AND PANTED FOR AIR... *AIR!* BUT THE THING ONLY GRINNED INTO MY FACE AND HELD ME *TIGHTER!* AS I LAY THERE DYING, I COULD HEAR THE CRASHING OF THUNDER... AND MINGLED WITH IT I HEARD THE THING CHUCKLING QUIETLY TO ITSELF..."

5

AND THAT'S HOW IT ENDED, DR. FROYD! JUST LIKE *ALL* MY NIGHTMARES! I WAS *BURIED ALIVE!*

I SEE! WELL, MR. SEVERIN, I THINK I CAN READILY EXPLAIN THE CAUSE OF YOUR NIGHTMARES! IT'S QUITE SIMPLE!

YOU'RE *OVERWORKED*, MR. SEVERIN! AND YOUR DREAMS ARE NOTHING BUT SUBCONSCIOUS MANIFESTATIONS OF THIS FACT! IN OTHER WORDS, YOU FEEL YOU ARE SIMPLY "BURIED UNDER TOO MUCH *WORK!*"

DO YOU REALLY THINK SO, DOCTOR?

OF COURSE! IT'S NOTHING AT ALL TO WORRY ABOUT! GO AWAY... TAKE A VACATION!

I HOPE YOU'RE RIGHT, DOCTOR! I'LL ASK MY BOSS THIS AFTERNOON FOR A VACATION! I CERTAINLY COULD *USE* ONE!

GOOD! GOOD! A LITTLE REST, AND YOU'LL BE AS GOOD AS NEW! TAKE MY WORD FOR IT... I KNOW WHAT I'M TALKING ABOUT!

OKAY, DR. FROYD! YOU KNOW, I FEEL BETTER ALREADY!

AH, IT'S A BEAUTIFUL DAY! I'M GLAD I DECIDED TO VISIT DR. FROYD! I SHOULD HAVE GONE TO HIM A LONG TIME AGO!

I'LL SEE MR. HARRISON... ASK HIM TO LET ME HAVE MY SUMMER VACATION NOW! DO ME A WORLD OF GOOD! RIGHT NOW, THOUGH, I BETTER GET TO WORK... SEE HOW THAT BUILDING CONSTRUCTION IS COMING ALONG...

YOUR FIRM IS BUILDING A NUMBER OF OFFICE BUILDINGS, AND AS CONSTRUCTION ENGINEER, IT IS YOUR JOB TO SUPERVISE THE WORK...

HI, SEVERIN! WHERE YOU BEEN ALL MORNING?

HELLO, PAUL! I... AH ... I OVERSLEPT! SAY, WHY ISN'T ANYONE WORKING?

ARE YOU KIDDING? IT'S *LUNCH TIME!* I HAVEN'T EATEN YET! JOIN ME?

NO... NO, PAUL! THANKS, BUT I'VE ALREADY EATEN!

OKAY! I'LL SEE YOU LATER, IF YOU DON'T GO BACK TO THE OFFICE!

YEAH... SURE! SO LONG!

THE MEN HAVE BEEN READYING THE WOODEN FRAMES INTO WHICH THE CEMENT IS POURED TO FORM THE BUILDING'S FOUNDATION, WHEN THE CEMENT DRIES, THESE FORMS WILL BE REMOVED!

HMM... EVERYTHING'S ALL SET FOR THE CEMENT TO BE POURED IN! THAT'S GOOD! WE'RE RIGHT ON SCHEDULE!

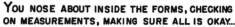

YOU NOSE ABOUT INSIDE THE FORMS, CHECKING ON MEASUREMENTS, MAKING SURE ALL IS OKAY...

HMM... SPECIFICATIONS ARE CORRECT! NICE, NEAT JOB, TOO... (YAWN-N) GOSH, BUT I'M SLEEPY!

WELL... LUNCH HOUR IS OVER! TIME TO GET BACK TO WORK... HEY!

WHAT'S THE MATTER WITH *YOU?*

THEY'RE GONNA POUR THE FOUNDATION FOR THAT SECTION OF THE BUILDING! AND MR. SEVERIN'S DOWN IN THE FORMS!

HOLY SMOKE! THEY DON'T SEE HIM! MR. SEVERIN! LOOK OUT!

THE MACHINERY DOWN THERE IS MAKING TOO MUCH NOISE! HE DIDN'T HEAR YOU! HEY! MR. SEVERIN! MR. SEVERIN! LOOK OUT!

MR. SEVERIN! MR. SEVERIN!

7

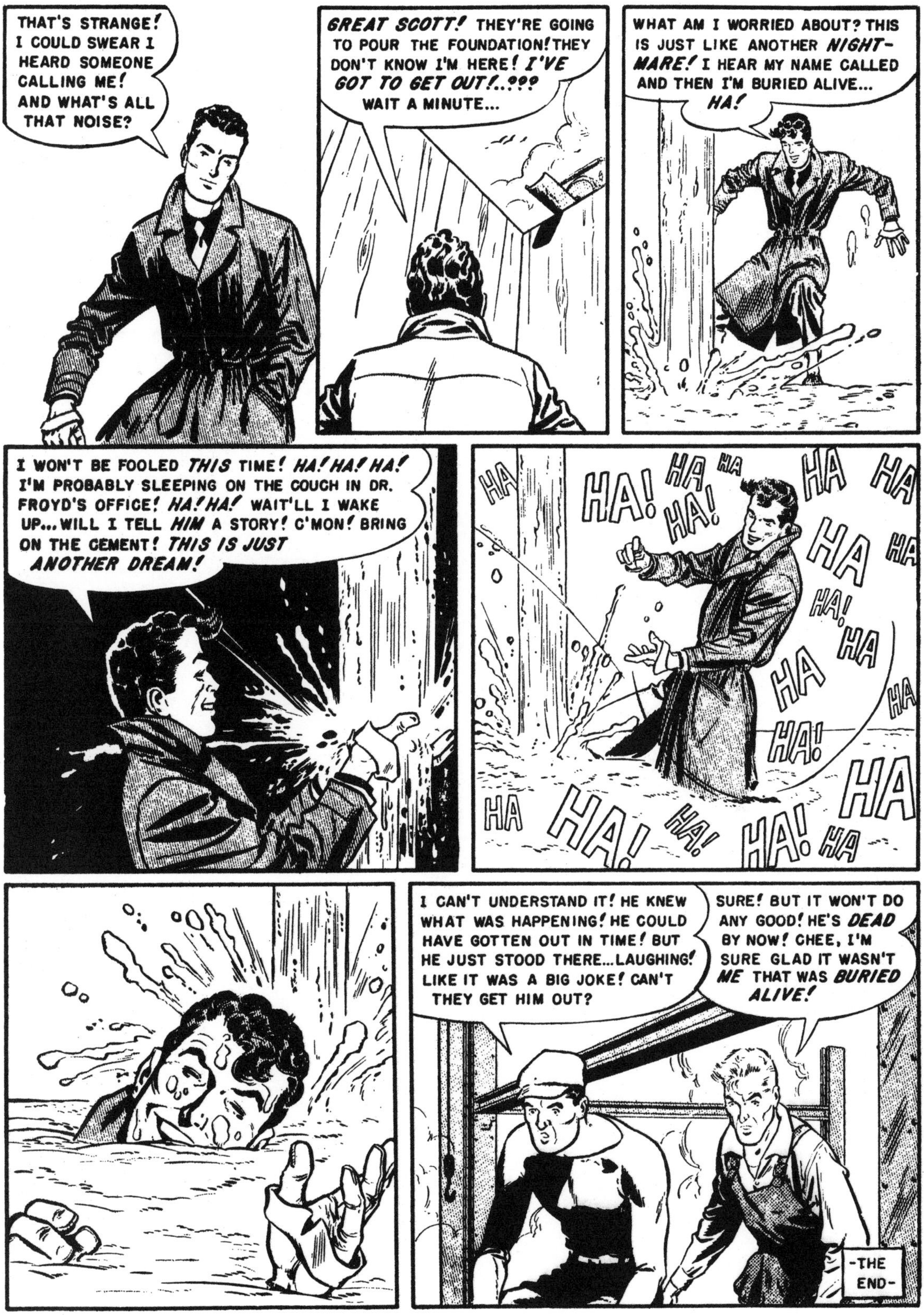
THAT'S STRANGE! I COULD SWEAR I HEARD SOMEONE CALLING ME! AND WHAT'S ALL THAT NOISE?
GREAT SCOTT! THEY'RE GOING TO POUR THE FOUNDATION! THEY DON'T KNOW I'M HERE! I'VE GOT TO GET OUT!..??? WAIT A MINUTE...
WHAT AM I WORRIED ABOUT? THIS IS JUST LIKE ANOTHER NIGHT-MARE! I HEAR MY NAME CALLED AND THEN I'M BURIED ALIVE... HA!
I WON'T BE FOOLED THIS TIME! HA! HA! HA! I'M PROBABLY SLEEPING ON THE COUCH IN DR. FROYD'S OFFICE! HA! HA! WAIT'LL I WAKE UP... WILL I TELL HIM A STORY! C'MON! BRING ON THE CEMENT! THIS IS JUST ANOTHER DREAM!
HA HA! HA HA! HA HA HA HA HA HA! HA HA HA HA HA! HA HA HA! HA! HA! HA HA
I CAN'T UNDERSTAND IT! HE KNEW WHAT WAS HAPPENING! HE COULD HAVE GOTTEN OUT IN TIME! BUT HE JUST STOOD THERE... LAUGHING! LIKE IT WAS A BIG JOKE! CAN'T THEY GET HIM OUT?
SURE! BUT IT WON'T DO ANY GOOD! HE'S DEAD BY NOW! CHEE, I'M SURE GLAD IT WASN'T ME THAT WAS BURIED ALIVE!
-THE END-

DEAD-RINGER
NO! NO! DON'T KILL ME! (SOB!) PLEASE! GIMME A CHANCE! LISTEN TO ME! LISTEN TO MY STORY!
JOHNNY CRAIG

I... I GUESS I WAS JUST BORN UNLUCKY! NEVER HAD A CHANCE TO MAKE ANYTHING OF MYSELF! I WAS POOR...FROM A POOR FAMILY... TOUGH NEIGHBORHOOD!

MOST OF THE OTHER GUYS I KNEW WERE ABLE TO RISE ABOVE THEIR ENVIRONMENT AND MAKE SOMETHING OF THEMSELVES...BUT ME... I DIDN'T HAVE THE GUTS! I CHOSE THE 'EASY' WAY!

GUNS BOUGHT AND SOLD

ONE NIGHT I KNOCKED OVER A GROCERY STORE! I HAD THE JOINT CASED...EVERYTHING WENT OFF SMOOTHLY...

IT WAS THE BIGGEST JOB I'D EVER PULLED! THE SHOP OWNER GAVE ME A LITTLE TROUBLE WHEN HE BARGED IN ON ME, BUT I TOOK CARE OF HIM AND LAMMED!

I WAS PRETTY SCARED AFTER IT WAS ALL OVER, AND I HOLED UP IN SOME CHEAP HOTEL TO HIDE OUT. THAT WAS HOW IT STARTED. I BOUGHT EVERY NEWSPAPER IN TOWN, THE NEXT DAY...

'GROCER ROBBED OF $243 LAST NIGHT, AND BEATEN BY UNKNOWN ASSAILANT!' *HAH! UNKNOWN!* GOOD! WAIT A MINUTE! WHAT'S *THIS!*

'MILLIONAIRE VICTIM OF AMNESIA! RESTING AT SANEVILLE SANITARIUM! CHARLES ROBERTS, WEALTHY BANKER...' *HOLY SMOKES! THIS PICTURE OF HIM! HE...*

eflector
MILLIONAIRE
VICTIM OF
AMNESIA!

...*HE LOOKS JUST LIKE ME!*

BOY! A MILLIONAIRE... A DEAD RINGER FOR ME! WHAT I WOULDN'T GIVE TO BE IN HIS PLACE... AMNESIA OR NOT! SAY-Y... WHY NOT?

WITH HIM HAVING AMNESIA, I KNOW AS MUCH ABOUT HIM AND HIS BACKGROUND AS HE DOES! I CAN EVEN KNOW MORE BY READING UP ON HIM! HMMM...

THE IDEA INTRIGUED ME! THE MORE I THOUGHT ABOUT IT, THE MORE I LIKED IT! BUT, TO TAKE THE PLACE OF MILLIONAIRE CHARLES ROBERTS WOULD MEAN KILLING HIM! WAS IT WORTH THE RISK?

THAT NIGHT I WENT TO SANEVILLE AND SNEAKED INSIDE THE SANITARIUM GROUNDS TO CASE THE PLACE.

BLAZES! HE DOES LOOK EXACTLY LIKE ME! LIKE WE WERE TWINS! WHAT A SET-UP!

IT TOOK SEVERAL NIGHTS TO PLAN THE CAPER...AND I NEEDED TIME TO DECIDE WHETHER OR NOT TO GO THROUGH WITH IT...

GOES TO BED AT TEN... NO ONE BOTHERS HIM TILL MORNING. GIVES ME PLENTY OF TIME! ROOM'S ON THE GROUND FLOOR...

I'D...I'D NEVER KILLED BEFORE! I WAS A LITTLE FRIGHTENED... BUT I WANTED TO TAKE HIS PLACE IN LIFE! ONE NIGHT I DECIDED TO MAKE MY MOVE...

I MADE MY LAST TRIP TO THE SANITARIUM. IT WAS AFTER MIDNIGHT WHEN I CLIMBED THE WALL AND CAUTIOUSLY EDGED UP TO HIS WINDOW...

I TREMBLED VIOLENTLY, AS SLOWLY...INCH BY INCH...I RAISED THE WINDOW. THE MINUTES SEEMED TO FLY PAST AND I WORRIED ABOUT WHETHER I WOULD HAVE ENOUGH TIME...

I CLIMBED INTO THE ROOM. I WAS BREATHING HEAVILY...IT SOUNDED LOUD ENOUGH TO WAKE THE DEAD! BUT THE FIGURE IN BED REMAINED MOTIONLESS.

I PULLED CHLOROFORM AND A RAG FROM MY POCKET...AND EDGED TOWARD THE BED. SLOWLY...SLOWLY, I MOVED...

THEN I WAS BESIDE HIM! MY HAND, A LEADEN WEIGHT, SOAKED THE RAG AND I HELD IT ABOVE HIS FACE...

I STOOD THERE WHILE THE FUMES OF CHLOROFORM FILLED THE ROOM...WHILE THE MILLIONAIRE, WITH EACH DEEP, STEADY BREATH, SUCKED IT INTO HIS LUNGS...

I...I DON'T KNOW HOW LONG IT TOOK. TIME WAS A CRAZILY MOVING THING THAT NIGHT. AFTER WHAT SEEMED AN ENDLESS NIGHTMARE, I LIFTED HIS BODY TO MY BACK AND TOTED HIM AWAY...

DEEP...DEEP INTO THE SURROUNDING WOODS OF THE SANITARIUM I CARRIED HIM, TO A PLACE I HAD CHOSEN PREVIOUSLY. TOOLS WERE THERE AND I SET TO WORK...DIGGING A MILLIONAIRE'S GRAVE!

I WORKED FEVERISHLY! DEEPER AND DEEPER I DUG INTO THE EARTH! I WANTED MILLIONAIRE CHARLES ROBERTS SO DEEP, THE WORLD WOULD *NEVER* FIND HIM!

THERE! (GASP!) THAT'S DEEP ENOUGH! NOW... TO THROW HIM IN!

I CHANGED CLOTHES WITH HIM AND DROPPED HIM INTO THE YAWNING PIT. HE LANDED WITH A MUFFLED *THUD* AND I PILED THE DIRT IN ON TOP OF HIM!

...GOT TO HURRY! HURRY! GOT TO HURRY!

I...I RACED MADLY BACK TO THE SANITARIUM AND SLIPPED INTO BED! TRACES OF CHLOROFORM STILL LINGERED, BUT THEY WOULD DISPERSE BY THE TIME MORNING CAME...

AN HOUR TO GO! AN HOUR TO GO! (GASP!) HAVE I MADE ANY MISTAKES? GOT TO THINK!

WOULD THEY KNOW I WASN'T THE *REAL* CHARLES ROBERTS? WOULD THEY DISCOVER WHAT I HAD DONE? WOULD THEY? *WOULD THEY?*

SOUNDS OF MOVEMENTS CAME FROM THE CORRIDOR OUTSIDE THE ROOM WHILE I WAITED... HARDLY DARING TO BREATHE... FOR THE CRUCIAL MOMENT TO ARRIVE. *SUDDENLY THE DOOR WAS FLUNG OPEN!*

WE STARED AT EACH OTHER...AND A MILLION GRUESOME THOUGHTS RACED THROUGH MY MIND ALL AT ONCE! WHY DIDN'T SHE *SAY* SOMETHING?

MORNING, MR. ROBERTS! DID I STARTLE YOU?

WH...ER, AH...YES...YES, YOU DID! GOOD...GOOD MORNING...

I HAD PASSED THE TEST! I ALMOST COLLAPSED WITH RELIEF! I WENT THROUGH THE ENTIRE DAY WITHOUT MISHAP. OH, I MADE A *FEW* BONERS, BUT NO ONE NOTICED ANYTHING WRONG. THAT NIGHT I DREAMED OF THE BEAUTIFUL FUTURE...

LITTLE BY LITTLE, I ACTED AS IF I WERE RECOVERING MY MEMORY! THEY FELL FOR IT LIKE A TON OF BRICKS!

YOUR IMPROVEMENT HAS BEEN AMAZING, MR. ROBERTS! YOU'RE ALMOST READY TO BE SENT HOME!

IT WASN'T LONG AFTER THAT I *WAS* SENT HOME!

WELL, TODAY'S THE BIG DAY, MR. ROBERTS! YOUR WIFE IS WAITING OUTSIDE TO TAKE YOU HOME!

MY... MY WIFE?

A FIT OF PANIC SEIZED ME! I HAD FORGOTTEN ABOUT HIS WIFE! WOULD *SHE* NOTICE ANYTHING? THERE WAS NOTHING I COULD DO... I *HAD* TO SEE HER!

... WONDERFUL TO SEE YOU UP AND AROUND AGAIN, CHARLES, DEAR!

IT'S... IT'S GOOD TO BE ABLE TO ... GO HOME, TERRY!

WE ARRIVED HOME SEVERAL HOURS LATER...

TERRY, DARLING, YOU'RE LATE!

SORRY, PAUL, SWEETHEART, BUT I JUST *HAD* TO BRING CHARLES HOME!

HEY!

WHAT... WHAT'S GOING ON HERE? WHO IS THIS GUY?

ARE YOU SERIOUS? THINK HARD, CHARLES... YOU ONLY MARRIED ME BECAUSE IT WOULD LOOK GOOD AS FAR AS YOUR BUSINESS WAS CONCERNED! *REMEMBER?*

ARE... ARE YOU CRAZY? YOU MEAN...

I MEAN THAT YOU AND I NEVER LOVED EACH OTHER TO BEGIN WITH! AND DON'T START PESTERING ME NOW JUST BECAUSE YOU DON'T REMEMBER! NOW, WHY NOT GO AWAY AND LEAVE US BE?

I WAS STUNNED! THE NEWSPAPERS HAD SAID SHE WAS A *DEVOTED* WIFE, BUT NOW I KNEW IT WAS ALL *AN ACT!* SHE *HATED* ME... AND PAUL DID TOO!

HMM... THIS MAY NOT BE AS NICE AS I THOUGHT! EVEN THE SERVANTS DISLIKE ME... I CAN TELL BY THE WAY THEY ACT!

6

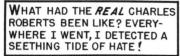

WHAT HAD THE *REAL* CHARLES ROBERTS BEEN LIKE? EVERY-WHERE I WENT, I DETECTED A SEETHING TIDE OF HATE!

THE DEVIL WITH THEM! I CAN HAVE ANYTHING I WANT! THE DEVIL WITH THEM ALL!

ONE DAY I DECIDED TO VISIT MY OFFICE. MY BUSINESS PARTNERS WERE THERE WHEN I ARRIVED...

WELL, GENTLEMEN! IT'S WONDERFUL TO BE BACK ON THE JOB! YES, SIR! LET ME TELL...

OH, SHUT UP, CHARLES! WE HAVE ENOUGH TROUBLES WITHOUT LISTENING TO YOU!

TROUBLES? WHA...WHAT? I... I DON'T UNDERSTAND!

YOU UNDERSTAND, ALL RIGHT, YOU CHEAP *LIAR!*

IT'S ALL *YOUR* FAULT! WE SHOULD NEVER HAVE TRUSTED YOU IN THE FIRST PLACE!

WE *FOUND OUT* HOW YOU'VE BEEN CHEATING INNOCENT PEOPLE OF THEIR LIFE'S SAVINGS BY POCKETING THE MONEY INSTEAD OF INVESTING IT FOR THEM!

YOU'RE LUCKY WE'RE NOT SENDING YOU TO *JAIL!*

WE'VE MADE GOOD EVERY CLAIM AGAINST US, CHARLES! AND WE USED *YOUR* CAPITAL TO DO IT!

YOU'RE *BROKE!* YOU HAVEN'T A RED CENT AND YOU'RE IN DEBT UP TO YOUR EARS!

WHAT HAD I STEPPED INTO? HERE I THOUGHT I WOULD BE SITTING ON *TOP OF THE WORLD*... AND NOW I WAS *WORSE* OFF THAN *BEFORE!* I LEFT THE OFFICE... BEGAN WALKING THE STREETS, WHEN...

DON'T MOVE, ROBERTS! I HAVE A GUN IN YOUR BACK!

WHA...WHAT'S GOING ON? WHAT DO YOU WANT?

THE CAR STANDING AT THE CURB... *GET IN!*

I SAT IN THE BACK SEAT, AN ARMED MAN ON EITHER SIDE, WHILE A THIRD DROVE US OUT OF THE CITY ALONG LONELY COUNTRY ROADS...

YOU DON'T KNOW WHO WE ARE ROBERTS, BUT OUR DAD COMMITTED SUICIDE BECAUSE YOU SWINDLED HIM OUT OF EVERY CENT HE OWNED! TONIGHT WE'RE GOING TO PAY YOU BACK...*IN FULL!*

GOOD LORD! THEY'RE GOING TO KILL ME! WHAT'LL I DO? I CAN'T TELL THEM WHO I REALLY AM! I'LL GET THE CHAIR FOR KILLING ROBERTS!

...BUT IF I DON'T TELL... I'LL DIE... RIGHT NOW!

THIS PLACE IS AS GOOD AS ANY, MIKE.

IF I TELL, MAYBE I'LL BE ABLE TO BEAT THE RAP! AT LEAST I'LL HAVE A CHANCE! (SOB!) I DON'T WANT TO DIE!

OKAY, ROBERTS. GET OUT...

LISTEN, FELLAS, YOU GOT THE WRONG GUY! I'M NOT THE ONE YOU WANT! LISTEN TO ME!

YOU GONNA DO IT, RALPH?

YEAH!

NO! NO! DON'T KILL ME! (SOB!) PLEASE! GIMME A CHANCE! YOU HEARD MY STORY! YOU BELIEVE ME, DON'TCHA?!

DON'TCHA?

BLAM!

HEY... AH... YOU BELIEVE ALL THAT STUFF HE TOLD US?

NAH! EVEN IF IT WAS TRUE... HE'S A DEAD-RINGER, NOW!

-THE END-

THE VAULT OF HORROR!

HA! HA! HA! WELL...YOU READERS MUST HAVE STOUT HEARTS TO CONTINUE COMING BACK FOR MORE OF MY GRUESOME TALES! THIS TIME I HAVE A *REAL SHOCKER* FOR YOU! A STORY THAT WILL SEND VIBRANT CHILLS OF TERROR THROUGH YOU, AND RACK YOUR BODY WITH ITS SUSPENSE! THIS YARN, FROM MY PRIVATE COLLECTION, IS CALLED...

WEREWOLF CONCERTO!

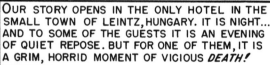

OUR STORY OPENS IN THE ONLY HOTEL IN THE SMALL TOWN OF LEINTZ, HUNGARY. IT IS NIGHT... AND TO SOME OF THE GUESTS IT IS AN EVENING OF QUIET REPOSE. BUT FOR ONE OF THEM, IT IS A GRIM, HORRID MOMENT OF VICIOUS *DEATH!*

YA-AAA-AGGH!

HORRIBLE! TORN TO SHREDS!

THIS IS THE THIRD TIME IT'S HAPPENED!

THE HOTEL MANAGER IS NAMED HUBERT ANTONE... A QUIET, NERVOUS INDIVIDUAL WHO IS NOTHING LESS THAN APPALLED AT THE HIDEOUS EVENT! BUT THEN...WHO WOULDN'T BE? HEH! HEH!

I'M CHECKING OUT! THREE DEATHS IN THREE MONTHS IS TOO MUCH!

WHAT KIND OF A HOTEL IS THIS, ANYWAY?

PLEASE! PLEASE... I BEG YOU!

I'M NOT GOING TO STAY IN THIS PLACE AND BE MURDERED!

NEITHER AM I!

BUT...BUT THE POLICE WILL CATCH THE KILLER!

BAH! THREE TIMES IT'S HAPPENED! ALL THE SAME WAY!

SURE! IT'S AWFUL! I'M GETTING OUT!

≡SIGH≡ ALL RIGHT, GENTLEMEN ... I CAN'T BLAME YOU!

YES...HEH, HEH! THREE MURDERS IN THREE MONTHS IS ENOUGH TO RUIN ANY HOTEL!

OH-H...THIS IS TERRIBLE! THE HOTEL IS GETTING A BAD REPUTATION! IF I DON'T DO SOMETHING SOON, I'LL BE RUINED!

BUT WHAT CAN I DO? WHAT? I...EH?.. WAIT! WHAT'S THIS?

2

'MADEMOISELLE MICHELINE... FAMED CONCERT PIANIST... TO GIVE CONCERTS IN BRAVDA!' *BRAVDA?* WHY, THAT'S NOT *FIVE MILES* FROM HERE! SAY-Y...THAT GIVES ME AN IDEA!

MADEMOISELLE MICHELINE? THIS IS HUBERT ANTONE, MANAGER OF THE FAMOUS VENETIAN GARDENS HOTEL IN LEINTZ! I WISH TO OFFER YOU MY FINEST HOTEL SUITE TO USE DURING YOUR ENGAGEMENT IN BRAVDA! I OFFER IT TO YOU... *FREE!*

YOU ARE TOO KIND, M'SIEU! I AM HAPPY TO ACCEPT!

HA! HA! WITH MADEMOISELLE MICHELINE AS MY GUEST, THE TOURISTS WILL *FIGHT* TO GAIN ENTRANCE! *HA! HA!* I'M A *GENIUS!*

YES, HUBERT WAS PROUD OF HIMSELF, AND THAT NIGHT HE SLEPT BLISSFULLY! HOWEVER, THE FOLLOWING AFTERNOON, A LARGE TRUCK PULLED TO A STOP IN FRONT OF THE HOTEL!

JUST A MOMENT! WHAT'S GOING ON HERE? I DIDN'T ORDER ANY PIANO! OUR SUITES ARE ALL COMPLETELY FURNISHED!

THIS IS MADEMOISELLE MICHELINE'S PERSONAL CONCERT PIANO! WHERE *SHE* GOES, *THIS* GOES, TOO!

MADEMOISELLE MICHELINE? PERSONAL PIANO? OH!... OH, OF COURSE! CERTAINLY! *CERTAINLY!* RIGHT THIS WAY!

THIS IS OUR FINEST SUITE! IT COVERS *ONE ENTIRE FLOOR!* I'LL HAVE *THIS* PIANO REMOVED SO YOU CAN SET *HERS* IN ITS PLACE! ER...ANY IDEA WHEN THE MADEMOISELLE WILL ARRIVE?

PROBABLY TODAY. SHE DOESN'T LET THIS PIANO OUT OF HER SIGHT FOR LONG!

3

64

HUBERT WAS *ECSTATIC* WITH JOY! HE WAITED ALL DAY IN ANXIOUS ANTICIPATION...BUT MADEMOISELLE MICHELINE DIDN'T ARRIVE! LATE THAT EVENING...

...HER CLOTHES AND PERSONAL BELONGINGS CAME, SIR, BUT NOT *HER!*

NOT YET, EH? PERHAPS SHE'S NOT COMING UNTIL TOMORROW!

... *WHAT THE DEVIL!* THAT...THAT GIRL STEPPING FROM THE ELEVATOR! *IT'S MADEMOISELLE MICHELINE!*

HOLY SMOKES! WHEN DID *SHE* GO UP?

MADEMOISELLE MICHELINE! IT'S AN HONOR TO HAVE YOU AS OUR GUEST! I MUST APOLOGIZE FOR NOT BEING ON HAND TO GREET YOU! AH...WE DIDN'T SEE YOU CHECK IN...

QUITE ALL RIGHT, M'SIEU. IT IS OF NO CONSEQUENCE. I SHALL BE OUT ALL EVENING. PLEASE SEE THAT NO ONE ENTERS MY ROOM!

IDIOT! YOU SAID SHE *DIDN'T* ARRIVE! WHY DIDN'T YOU *TELL* ME SHE WAS HERE?!

BUT...BUT SHE *DIDN'T* ARRIVE! I MEAN, SHE *DIDN'T* CHECK IN! SEE? THE REGISTER HASN'T BEEN SIGNED! MAYBE THE ELEVATOR BOY...

HONEST, MR. ANTONE! I'VE BEEN ON DUTY ALL DAY, AND I *SWEAR* I DIDN'T TAKE HER UP! SOMEBODY RANG THE *DOWN* BUZZER ON HER PRIVATE FLOOR...*AND THERE SHE WAS!*

HMPH! SLEEPING ON THE JOB, PROBABLY! I'VE NEVER BEEN SO EMBARRASSED!

HEH, HEH! WELL ANYWAY, FRIENDS, WEEKS PASSED AND THE HOTEL BEGAN TO PROSPER AGAIN! HUBERT WAS VERY HAPPY! BUT LOVELY MADEMOISELLE MICHELINE INTRIGUED HIM...

PUZZLING...CAN'T UNDERSTAND HER. NEVER SEE HER DURING THE DAY...SAYS SHE PRACTICES AT NIGHT! YET NO ONE HAS EVER *HEARD* HER PRACTICE! ...MAYBE SHE'S A *PHONEY?*

4

RIDICULOUS! TOO WELL KNOWN TO BE A PHONEY! NEVER SEEMS TO EAT...NOT IN THE *HOTEL*, ANYWAY! STRANGE GIRL...CAN'T FIGURE HER... MUMBLE... *mumble...*

YES, EVERYTHING WAS FINE! GUESTS CONTINUED TO ARRIVE AND THE FUTURE LOOKED BRIGHT. IT SEEMED THAT PEOPLE HAD FORGOTTEN ABOUT THE GORY MURDERS...UNTIL ONE NIGHT...

...A CROUCHED, FURTIVE FIGURE PROWLED THROUGH THE HOTEL HALLS AND QUIETLY ENTERED ONE OF THE ROOMS...

?

AAA-AGGH-HHH!

HEH, HEH, HEH! YEP, IT HAPPENED AGAIN! THE SAME WAY AS THE OTHERS... WITH THE VICTIM BRUTALLY TORN AND RIPPED TO PIECES! AND WHAT A COMMOTION *THAT* CAUSED! IN NO TIME AT ALL, GUESTS AND EMPLOYEES STREAMED FROM THE HOTEL!

I'M NOT STAYING HERE ANY LONGER! THE POLICE SAY A *WEREWOLF* IS WHAT KILLED THOSE PEOPLE!

YEAH! I WON'T STAY IN THIS PLACE EITHER!

I'M GOING, TOO!

...I WOULDN'T BE FOUND *DEAD* IN THIS JOINT!

5

66

MY WIFE AND I ARE CHECKING OUT! IF THERE'S A *WEREWOLF* AROUND, *WE'LL* VACATION ELSEWHERE!

I...I UNDERSTAND, SIR...

EVERYONE'S GONE! *EVERYONE!* EVEN ALL MY EMPLOYEES HAVE LEFT! I'M...I'M *RUINED!*

POOR HUBERT! BUT WHAT COULD HE EXPECT? NOT MANY PEOPLE APPRECIATE BEING *MURDERED!* HEH, HEH! WELL, AS BEFORE, WEEKS PASSED, AND HUBERT WAS ALONE IN THE HOTEL... EXCEPT FOR *ONE OTHER* PERSON!

MADEMOISELLE MICHELINE! IT IS SO *GOOD* OF YOU TO REMAIN! I AM SORRY I CANNOT GIVE YOU BETTER SERVICE, BUT...

DO NOT APOLOGIZE, M'SIEU! I KNOW YOU CANNOT GET ANYONE TO WORK HERE. THEY ARE ALL *AFRAID!*

YES! YES! YOU'RE RIGHT! YOU'RE SO UNDERSTANDING! SHALL I TAKE YOU TO YOUR SUITE?

NO, THANK YOU, M'SIEU. I HAVE LEARNED TO OPERATE THE ELEVATOR MYSELF! GOOD NIGHT!

ACH! I'M A NERVOUS WRECK! WISH I COULD GET A DECENT NIGHT'S REST! I...I... FEEL SO *STRANGE* ALL OF A SUDDEN...

FEEL LIKE... LIKE...OH, NO! NOT AGAIN... I...I CAN'T FIGHT IT! I HAVE TO GIVE IN...HAVE TO...

6

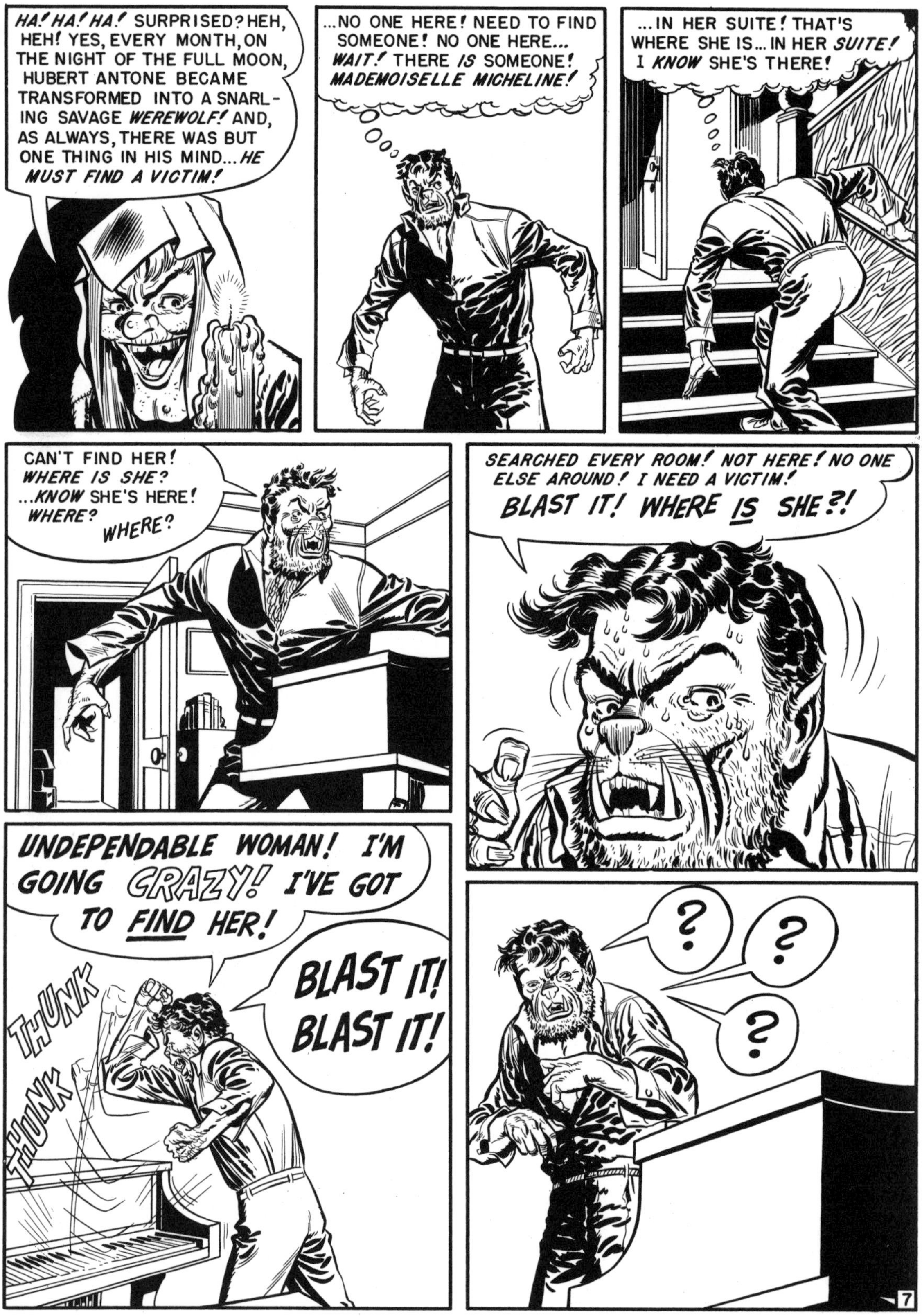
HA! HA! HA! SURPRISED? HEH, HEH! YES, EVERY MONTH, ON THE NIGHT OF THE FULL MOON, HUBERT ANTONE BECAME TRANSFORMED INTO A SNARLING SAVAGE WEREWOLF! AND, AS ALWAYS, THERE WAS BUT ONE THING IN HIS MIND... HE MUST FIND A VICTIM!
...NO ONE HERE! NEED TO FIND SOMEONE! NO ONE HERE... WAIT! THERE IS SOMEONE! MADEMOISELLE MICHELINE!
...IN HER SUITE! THAT'S WHERE SHE IS... IN HER SUITE! I KNOW SHE'S THERE!
CAN'T FIND HER! WHERE IS SHE? ...KNOW SHE'S HERE! WHERE? WHERE?
SEARCHED EVERY ROOM! NOT HERE! NO ONE ELSE AROUND! I NEED A VICTIM! BLAST IT! WHERE IS SHE?!
UNDEPENDABLE WOMAN! I'M GOING CRAZY! I'VE GOT TO FIND HER!
BLAST IT! BLAST IT!
THUNK
THUNK
?
?
?
7

WHAT THE DEVIL??? HER PIANO...IT DIDN'T MAKE ANY NOISE WHEN I HIT THE KEYS! ???

...SOMETHING COCKEYED... NO MUSIC!

CLUNK!

CLUNK-CLUNK!

WHAT THE...? NO STRINGS IN IT! NO STRINGS! ONLY...ONLY DIRT!

DIRT! WHY IN THE WORLD WOULD SHE KEEP DIRT IN HER PIANO...UNLESS... UNLESS...

GOOD LORD! I KNOW WHY! AND I KNOW WHY NO ONE EVER HEARD HER PRACTICE... AND WHY SHE NEVER EATS!

OF COURSE! IT'S ALL CLEAR NOW! THAT'S WHY NO ONE SEES HER DURING THE DAY... ONLY AT NIGHT! BECAUSE... BECAUSE SHE SLEEPS ALL DAY...HERE IN THIS PIANO! SHE'S...SHE'S A...

VAMPIRE!

-THE END-

HEH, HEH, HEH! NOW THERE WAS A STIRRING FINALE THAT I THOUGHT WAS IN GOOD TASTE! MADEMOISELLE MICHELINE REALLY ENDED HER SOLO WITH A HOT LICK, DIDN'T SHE? WELL, AFTER THAT, YOU CAN BE SURE NO ONE WAS BOTHERED BY WEREWOLVES! HOW-EVER THEY DID HAVE SOME RUN-INS WITH A VAMPIRE! HEH! HEH! BUT READ ON, FRIENDS! THERE ARE MORE CHILLS AWAITING YOU!

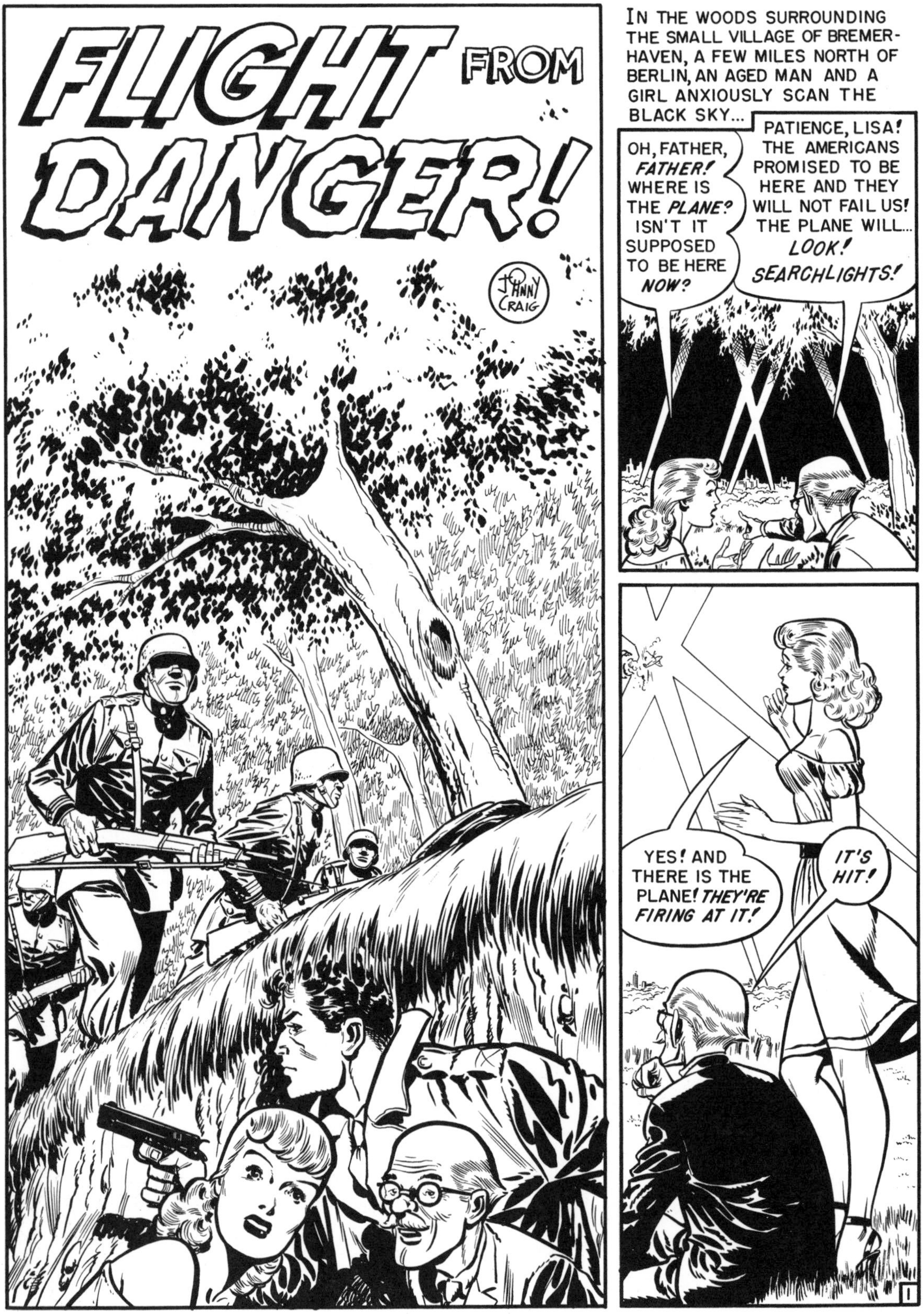
FLIGHT FROM DANGER!
JOHNNY CRAIG
IN THE WOODS SURROUNDING THE SMALL VILLAGE OF BREMERHAVEN, A FEW MILES NORTH OF BERLIN, AN AGED MAN AND A GIRL ANXIOUSLY SCAN THE BLACK SKY...
OH, FATHER, FATHER! WHERE IS THE PLANE? ISN'T IT SUPPOSED TO BE HERE NOW?
PATIENCE, LISA! THE AMERICANS PROMISED TO BE HERE AND THEY WILL NOT FAIL US! THE PLANE WILL... LOOK! SEARCHLIGHTS!
YES! AND THERE IS THE PLANE! THEY'RE FIRING AT IT!
IT'S HIT!
1

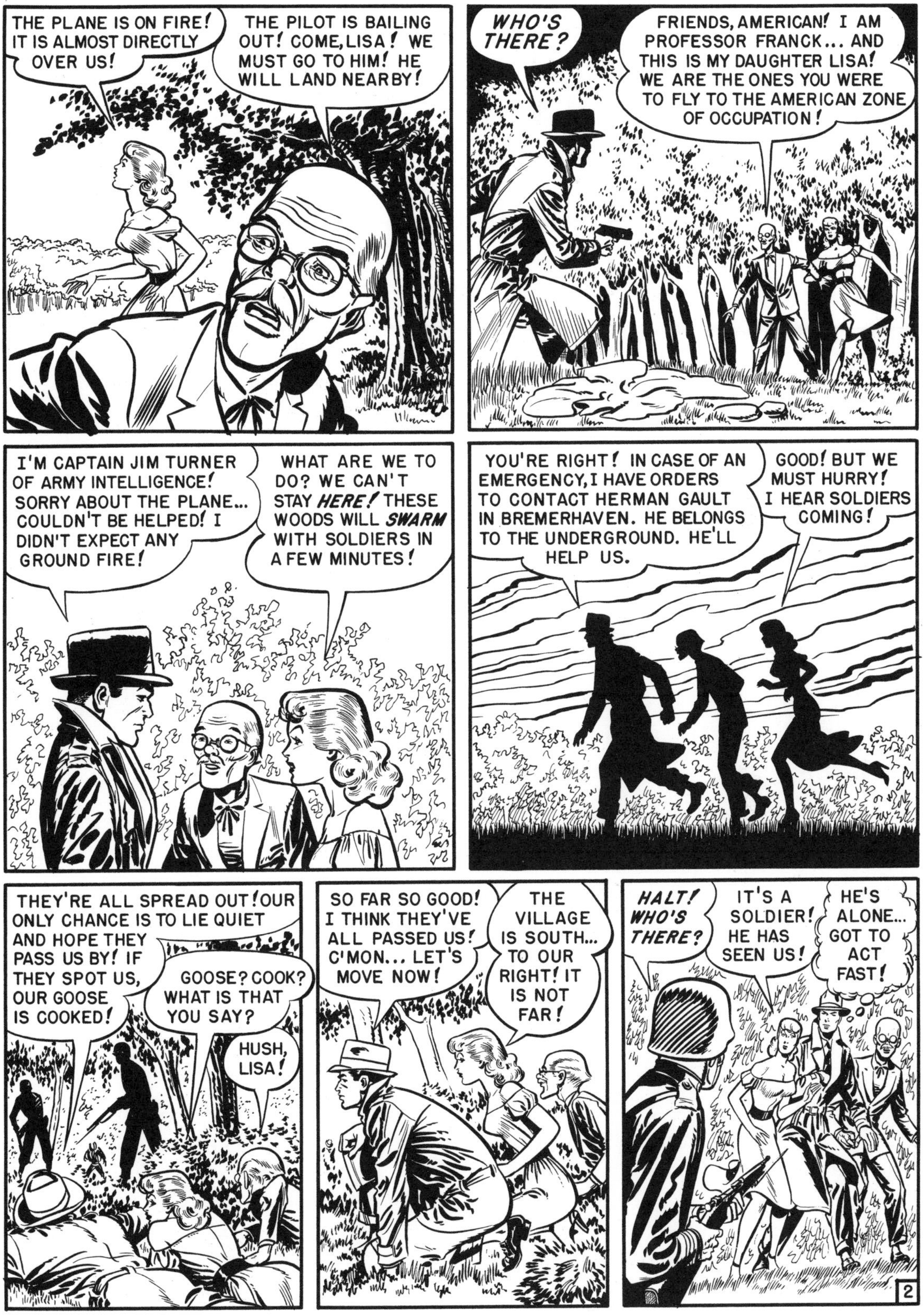
THE PLANE IS ON FIRE! IT IS ALMOST DIRECTLY OVER US!
THE PILOT IS BAILING OUT! COME, LISA! WE MUST GO TO HIM! HE WILL LAND NEARBY!
WHO'S THERE?
FRIENDS, AMERICAN! I AM PROFESSOR FRANCK... AND THIS IS MY DAUGHTER LISA! WE ARE THE ONES YOU WERE TO FLY TO THE AMERICAN ZONE OF OCCUPATION!
I'M CAPTAIN JIM TURNER OF ARMY INTELLIGENCE! SORRY ABOUT THE PLANE... COULDN'T BE HELPED! I DIDN'T EXPECT ANY GROUND FIRE!
WHAT ARE WE TO DO? WE CAN'T STAY HERE! THESE WOODS WILL SWARM WITH SOLDIERS IN A FEW MINUTES!
YOU'RE RIGHT! IN CASE OF AN EMERGENCY, I HAVE ORDERS TO CONTACT HERMAN GAULT IN BREMERHAVEN. HE BELONGS TO THE UNDERGROUND. HE'LL HELP US.
GOOD! BUT WE MUST HURRY! I HEAR SOLDIERS COMING!
THEY'RE ALL SPREAD OUT! OUR ONLY CHANCE IS TO LIE QUIET AND HOPE THEY PASS US BY! IF THEY SPOT US, OUR GOOSE IS COOKED!
GOOSE? COOK? WHAT IS THAT YOU SAY?
HUSH, LISA!
SO FAR SO GOOD! I THINK THEY'VE ALL PASSED US! C'MON... LET'S MOVE NOW!
THE VILLAGE IS SOUTH... TO OUR RIGHT! IT IS NOT FAR!
HALT! WHO'S THERE?
IT'S A SOLDIER! HE HAS SEEN US!
HE'S ALONE... GOT TO ACT FAST!
2

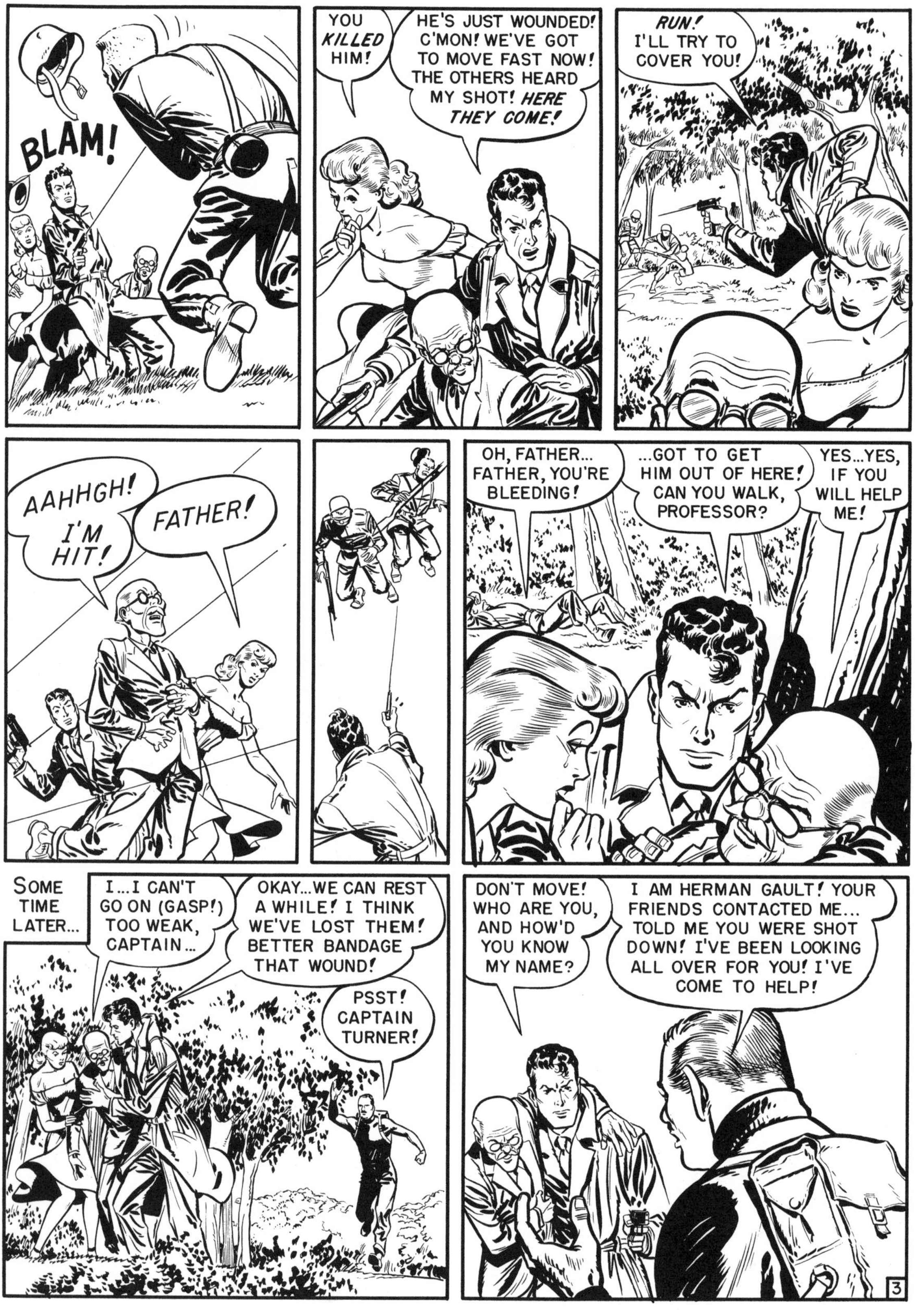
BLAM!
YOU KILLED HIM!
HE'S JUST WOUNDED! C'MON! WE'VE GOT TO MOVE FAST NOW! THE OTHERS HEARD MY SHOT! HERE THEY COME!
RUN! I'LL TRY TO COVER YOU!
AAHHGH! I'M HIT!
FATHER!
OH, FATHER... FATHER, YOU'RE BLEEDING!
...GOT TO GET HIM OUT OF HERE! CAN YOU WALK, PROFESSOR?
YES...YES, IF YOU WILL HELP ME!
SOME TIME LATER...
I...I CAN'T GO ON (GASP!) TOO WEAK, CAPTAIN...
OKAY...WE CAN REST A WHILE! I THINK WE'VE LOST THEM! BETTER BANDAGE THAT WOUND!
PSST! CAPTAIN TURNER!
DON'T MOVE! WHO ARE YOU, AND HOW'D YOU KNOW MY NAME?
I AM HERMAN GAULT! YOUR FRIENDS CONTACTED ME... TOLD ME YOU WERE SHOT DOWN! I'VE BEEN LOOKING ALL OVER FOR YOU! I'VE COME TO HELP!
3

I BROUGHT A FIRST-AID KIT! HERE, MISS... DRESS YOUR FATHER'S WOUND!

WE'LL ACCEPT THE KIT, BUT THIS GUN STAYS WHERE IT IS UNTIL YOU GIVE THE PASSWORD!

OF COURSE! THE PASSWORD IS "TOP HAT"!

CHECK!

THE WOUND IS BANDAGED, CAPTAIN!

COME, WE GO TO MY HOUSE! IT IS VERY NEAR!

GOOD. I'LL CARRY THE PROFESSOR!

A SHORT WHILE LATER...

I'VE CONTACTED YOUR FRIENDS. ANOTHER PLANE WILL BE SENT!

IT BETTER COME QUICK! OUR PROFESSOR IS SINKING FAST.

CAPTAIN...

LISA...YOUR FATHER! HE'S...HE'S NOT...?

YES... HE IS DEAD!

I'M...I'M SORRY, LISA. I GUESS IT'S ALL MY FAULT!

DON'T BLAME YOURSELF, CAPTAIN! IT WAS NOT YOUR FAULT! WELL... HE IS DEAD! BUT HE WANTED THE UNITED STATES TO HAVE THE HYDROGEN BOMB HE DEVELOPED... AND THEY SHALL HAVE IT!

BUT... BUT HOW?

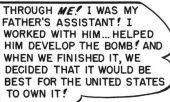

THROUGH ME! I WAS MY FATHER'S ASSISTANT! I WORKED WITH HIM... HELPED HIM DEVELOP THE BOMB! AND WHEN WE FINISHED IT, WE DECIDED THAT IT WOULD BE BEST FOR THE UNITED STATES TO OWN IT!

WE TRIED TO ESCAPE TO THE AMERICAN ZONE IN BERLIN, BUT COULDN'T MAKE IT! THEN THE UNDERGROUND CONTACTED YOUR FRIENDS... AND YOU WERE SENT TO HELP US!

LISA, LISA...

CAPTAIN! SOLDIERS ARE SEARCHING ALL THE HOUSES FOR YOU! THEY WILL BE HERE ANY MINUTE! YOU MUST LEAVE!

4

Later, atop a grassy hill, Lisa's father is buried...

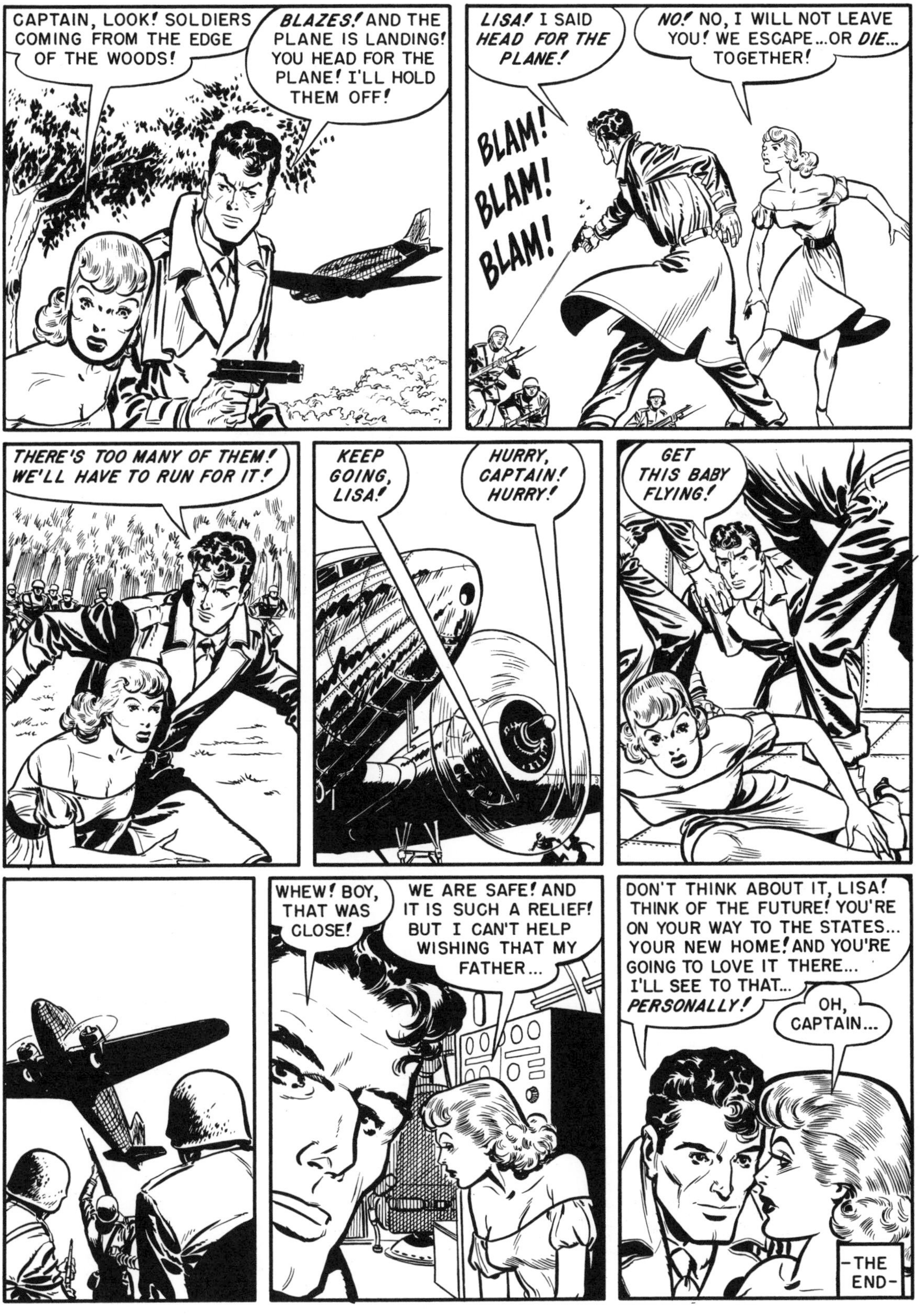
CAPTAIN, LOOK! SOLDIERS COMING FROM THE EDGE OF THE WOODS!
BLAZES! AND THE PLANE IS LANDING! YOU HEAD FOR THE PLANE! I'LL HOLD THEM OFF!
LISA! I SAID HEAD FOR THE PLANE!
NO! NO, I WILL NOT LEAVE YOU! WE ESCAPE...OR DIE... TOGETHER!
BLAM! BLAM! BLAM!
THERE'S TOO MANY OF THEM! WE'LL HAVE TO RUN FOR IT!
KEEP GOING, LISA!
HURRY, CAPTAIN! HURRY!
GET THIS BABY FLYING!
WHEW! BOY, THAT WAS CLOSE!
WE ARE SAFE! AND IT IS SUCH A RELIEF! BUT I CAN'T HELP WISHING THAT MY FATHER...
DON'T THINK ABOUT IT, LISA! THINK OF THE FUTURE! YOU'RE ON YOUR WAY TO THE STATES... YOUR NEW HOME! AND YOU'RE GOING TO LOVE IT THERE... I'LL SEE TO THAT... PERSONALLY!
OH, CAPTAIN...
-THE END-

POISON!

THE MOURNERS IN THE CEMETERY WERE SILENT EXCEPT FOR THE MUFFLED SOBS THAT OCCASIONALLY INTERRUPTED THE WHISPERS OF THE DRIZZLING RAIN. I STOOD AT THE HEAD OF THE GROUP WITH ELSA, MY HOUSEKEEPER, AT MY SIDE. WE WERE ATTENDING THE FUNERAL OF MY WIFE!

THE MINISTER BEGAN HIS EULOGY... AND WE STOOD THERE AS THE SOAKING RAIN SEEPED THROUGH OUR CLOTHES AND CHILLED US TO THE BONE. IT WAS DIFFICULT TO TAKE MY EYES FROM THE CASKET...

I LOOKED AT ELSA. HER HEAD WAS BOWED AND SHE GRIPPED MY ARM TIGHTLY. A SINGLE TEAR ROLLED DOWN HER FACE... OR WAS IT A RAINDROP?

I SHIVERED FROM THE COLD. THE EULOGY WAS FINISHED NOW...AND AS THE CASKET WAS LOWERED INTO THE YAWNING GRAVE, I COULD HARDLY KEEP FROM...SMILING!

YES, MY FACE WAS A MASK, BUT DEEP INSIDE I ROARED WITH LAUGHTER! WHY SHOULDN'T I? IT WAS OVER NOW. I COULD LAUGH NOW. I HAD KILLED MY WIFE WITH *POISON*...HAD COMMITTED THE PERFECT MURDER...AND NO ONE KNEW! *NO ONE KNEW!*

ELSA AND I DROVE HOME IN SILENCE. ONCE THERE, I WENT DIRECTLY TO MY LIQUOR CABINET AND POURED US BOTH A DRINK...

HERE, ELSA, DRINK THIS! IT'LL HELP SETTLE YOUR NERVES. FUNERALS ARE SO...SO *UPSETTING!*

THANK YOU, MR. BOLES!

I GLANCED IN THE MIRROR AND LET A TRACE OF A SMILE CROSS MY FACE AS I DRANK A SILENT TOAST TO MYSELF. I'D HAVE TO BE MORE CAREFUL. ELSA SHOULDN'T SUSPECT THAT I WAS ANYTHING BUT HEARTBROKEN BY MY WIFE'S DEATH...

...A TERRIBLE THING! MARGARET WAS SUCH A *GOOD* WIFE! I...I DID EVERYTHING I COULD. YOU *KNOW* ALL THE THINGS I DID FOR HER!

YES, MR. BOLES. ...I KNOW *EVERYTHING* YOU DID!

THANKS FOR THE DRINK, MR. BOLES! IT HELPED A LOT!

2

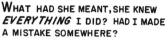

WHAT HAD SHE MEANT, SHE KNEW *EVERYTHING* I DID? HAD I MADE A MISTAKE SOMEWHERE?

RIDICULOUS! HOW COULD SHE *POSSIBLY* KNOW? HEH! JUST MY NERVES ACTING UP...

I FELT CERTAIN I WAS SAFE. BUT NONETHELESS I STAYED IN THE STUDY UNTIL DINNER...

I HOPE YOU'RE NOT THINKING OF...AH... LEAVING, NOW THAT MARGARET... ISN'T HERE!

OH, NO... BUT I *AM* THINKING ABOUT WRITING A BOOK!

WRITING A BOOK? I DIDN'T KNOW YOU WANTED TO WRITE! WHAT TYPE OF BOOK WILL IT BE?

A *MURDER* MYSTERY!

FEAR RAN THROUGH ME LIKE A HIGH-VOLTAGE CURRENT! THE TONE OF HER VOICE WHEN SHE SAID IT... THE LOOK IN HER EYES...

MR. BOLES...YOU HAVEN'T FINISHED EATING!

I... I'M NOT HUNGRY!

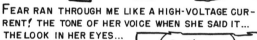

SHAKING UNCONTROLLABLY, I RAN TO THE STUDY AND POURED MYSELF A DRINK...

SHE *DOES* KNOW! BUT *HOW?* HOW *COULD* SHE KNOW?

NO...WAIT! I'M...I'M LETTING MY NERVES RUN AWAY WITH ME. I STILL CAN'T BE *POSITIVE!*

I HAD TO BE *CERTAIN!* I RETURNED TO THE TABLE. ELSA WAS SITTING THERE, DRINKING HER COFFEE AS IF NOTHING HAD HAPPENED!

THAT...THAT BOOK YOU'RE GOING TO WRITE. WHAT'S THE PLOT ABOUT?

OH, THAT! WELL, IT'S ABOUT A MAN WHO MURDERS HIS WIFE...WITH *POISON!*

I SAT ROOTED TO THE CHAIR AS SHE RELATED THE PLOT OF HER 'BOOK', FOLLOWING IN EXACT DETAIL THE METHOD IN WHICH I HAD KILLED MY WIFE! THERE WERE NO DOUBTS NOW. SHE *KNEW! ELSA KNEW I MURDERED MY WIFE!*

...AND THAT'S THE STORY, MR. BOLES. DON'T YOU THINK IT SOUNDS... *TRUE TO LIFE?*

3

WE STARED AT EACH OTHER, MY THOUGHTS RACING MADLY! IF SHE KNEW I KILLED MARGARET, WHY HADN'T SHE TOLD THE POLICE? WHAT WAS SHE UP TO?

...INCIDENTALLY, MR. BOLES... DON'T YOU THINK I SHOULD RECEIVE A RAISE IN PAY? ...A *LARGE* RAISE?

SO *THAT* WAS IT! *BLACKMAIL!* SHE WANTED MONEY IN RETURN FOR HER *SILENCE!* AND I WAS HELPLESS TO DO ANYTHING ABOUT IT...

YOU HAVEN'T ANSWERED MY QUESTION, MR. BOLES!

WHAT? OH...YES! YES. I'LL SEE THAT YOU GET A RAISE!

THAT WAS THE BEGINNING... A RAISE IN SALARY. BUT IT DIDN'T STOP THERE...

MY ROOM LOOKS TERRIBLE! DON'T YOU THINK IT SHOULD BE REDECORATED, MR. BOLES?

OF COURSE, ELSA...IF *YOU* THINK SO!

IT WENT ON AND ON... AND I COULDN'T STOP HER! THERE WAS NOTHING I COULD DO!

IT'S GETTING SO *COLD* OUT, NOW. I CERTAINLY COULD USE A NEW COAT, MR. BOLES... A *MINK* COAT!

IT'S SO TIRING TO USE BUSES AND SUBWAYS, MR. BOLES! I *WISH* I HAD A BRAND-NEW SHINY CAR!

AS LONG AS I GAVE HER WHAT SHE WANTED, I WAS SAFE! BUT IF IT KEPT UP LONG ENOUGH, I'D GO *BROKE!* AND WHAT WOULD KEEP HER FROM TALKING *THEN?*

THIS CAN'T GO ON ANY LONGER. I'VE GOT TO PUT AN END TO IT! AND THERE'S ONLY ONE WAY... *ELSA MUST DIE!*

YES, ELSA HAD TO *DIE!* IT WAS THE ONLY WAY I WOULD BE *COMPLETELY* SAFE! BUT EVEN IN THAT I FOUND HER PREPARED...

...NO, I'M NOT AFRAID ANYTHING WILL HAPPEN TO ME! I HAVE PLENTY OF...'INSURANCE'!

OH?

YES, I HAVE *LOADS* OF...ER... '*INSURANCE*'! ALL IN A LETTER TUCKED AWAY IN MY SAFETY-DEPOSIT VAULT...*TO BE OPENED ONLY IN THE EVENT OF MY DEATH!*

...THINKS SHE'S PRETTY SMART! WELL, I'LL SHOW HER... *I'LL* SHOW HER! THERE'S MORE THAN *ONE* WAY TO SKIN A CAT!

I CAN'T KILL HER! THAT LETTER IN HER VAULT TELLS ALL ABOUT HOW I MURDERED MARGARET! BUT MAYBE... SAY... *I HAVE IT!*

I...ER...I THINK I'LL GO FOR A DRIVE, ELSA! I WANT TO GET SOME CIGARETTES!

CERTAINLY, MR. BOLES! TONIGHT'S MY NIGHT OFF, SO I MAY NOT BE HERE WHEN YOU RETURN!

HER NIGHT OFF... JUST WHAT I WANTED! I DROVE ACROSS TOWN AND BOUGHT MORE OF THE SAME POISON WITH WHICH I HAD KILLED MY WIFE. BY THE TIME I GOT BACK, THE ENTIRE PLAN WAS COMPLETE IN MY MIND.

ELSA? *ELSA!* YOU HERE?

I SEARCHED THE HOUSE TO MAKE SURE SHE WAS GONE, AND THEN WENT TO THE LIQUOR CABINET BEHIND THE BAR...

SHE'LL NEVER GET WISE TO *THIS!* WHEN THE TIME COMES, I'LL TAKE JUST ENOUGH OF THIS POISON TO MAKE ME SICK. THEN I'LL SAY *SHE* TRIED TO POISON *ME!*

WHEN I HAVE HER ARRESTED, SHE'LL BRING OUT THAT LETTER SHE HAS IN HER VAULT, INCRIMINATING ME! AND WHEN THE COPS FIND MY *WIFE* WAS POISONED, I'LL CLAIM THAT ELSA MURDERED *HER* TOO!

DANGER POISON

5

I'LL MAKE SURE THE COPS FIND THE POISON IN *HER* ROOM! EVEN IF SHE DOESN'T GO TO JAIL, THERE'LL BE ENOUGH AGAINST HER TO DISPROVE ANYTHING IN THAT LETTER, AND THAT'S THE MAIN IDEA!

THERE! THERE'S ENOUGH POISON IN EVERY ONE OF THESE WHISKEY BOTTLES TO *KILL* A MAN WITH JUST ONE...SMALL...HEY! I...FEEL...DIZZY...

...NOT ENOUGH SLEEP...HAVEN'T BEEN EATING WELL...LOST A LOT OF WEIGHT! OVER-TIRED! I...I OUGHT TO BE IN BED...

I WENT TO BED BUT I COULDN'T SLEEP. A STORM WAS RAGING OUTSIDE AND I LISTENED TO THE HOWLING WIND AND DRIVING RAIN...UNTIL ELSA RETURNED...

ELSA...I'M NOT FEELING WELL! WILL YOU CALL THE DOCTOR AND ASK HIM TO COME OVER?

CERTAINLY, MR. BOLES!

HELLO? HELLO, OPERATOR? OPERATOR? *OPERATOR!* HANG IT ALL! THE LINE'S *DEAD!*

THE STORM MUST HAVE DOWNED THE TELEPHONE LINES...THE WIRE'S DEAD!

OH...THAT'S TOO BAD! WELL, I GUESS IT CAN WAIT UNTIL TOMORROW!

SUDDENLY I HAD AN IDEA! TONIGHT WAS PERFECT FOR MY PLAN. HER NIGHT OFF TO GIVE HERSELF AN 'ALIBI'...TELEPHONE OUT OF ORDER...*PERFECT!*

ON SECOND THOUGHT, ELSA, I *DO* FEEL VERY SICK! DO YOU THINK YOU COULD WALK TO THE DOCTOR'S HOUSE TO GET HIM?

...BUT IT'S SUCH A *TERRIBLE STORM!* I...OH, ALL RIGHT! YOU *DO* LOOK PRETTY BAD...

6

POISON!

SHE'S GONE! FINE! EVERYTHING'S WORKING OUT *FINE!* NOW TO GET THE POISON!

AH...JUST A LITTLE BIT NOW... DON'T WANT TO OVERDO IT! JUST ENOUGH TO MAKE ME SICK. JUST ENOUGH TO SHOW TRACES OF IT IN MY SYSTEM!

I SWALLOWED THE POISON. IN A SHORT WHILE I FELT ITS EFFECTS. I WAITED FOR ELSA TO RETURN WITH THE DOCTOR, PRAYING THAT THEY WOULD HURRY! BUT TIME PASSED AND THEY DIDN'T ARRIVE...

I BEGAN TO HAVE MISGIVINGS! SUPPOSE ELSA HAD GONE TO THE POLICE INSTEAD? THE HOURS WENT BY AND I WAS NEARLY GOING *CRAZY* WITH FEAR!

MY BRAIN REELED AND THE FLOOR SWAYED BENEATH ME! NEEDLES OF PAIN STABBED MY BODY... I TREMBLED VIOLENTLY...

WHERE ARE THEY? *WHERE ARE THEY?* WHY DON'T THEY COME?

HEAR NOISES! ALL KINDS OF NOISES! NOISES *POUNDING* IN MY *HEAD!* WHY DON'T THEY STOP! STOP IT!

STOP IT!

...MAYBE THEY'RE DOWNSTAIRS NOW, TRYING TO GET IN. MAYBE THEY CAN'T GET IN...YES, THAT'S IT...

7

THEY CAN'T GET IN...CAN'T GET IN! *I'LL* LET THEM IN! *I'LL* GO DOWN AND LET THEM IN!

OHH-H-H...MY...MY LEG! IT'S...IT'S BROKEN! *BROKEN!* THE PAIN! I...I CAN'T STAND THE *PAIN!* CAN'T MOVE...CAN'T...

MY LEG HAD BEEN SNAPPED BY MY FALL! I LAY THERE, MOTIONLESS, FOR A LONG TIME...GASPING FOR EVERY BREATH...THE AGONY WRACKING MY BODY. THEN I SLIPPED OFF INTO THE ABYSMAL DEPTHS OF DARKNESS...

FINALLY THE BLACKNESS BEGAN TO CLEAR. I COULD DISCERN VAGUE SHADOWS...AND I HEARD VOICES AS IF FROM FAR AWAY. SOMETHING BURNED MY MOUTH AND THROAT.

WILL HE BE ALL RIGHT?

HAD A NASTY FALL...PRETTY BAD SHAPE, BUT HE'LL BE OKAY!

THE VOICES WERE NEARER NOW AND THE SHADOWS BEGAN TO CLEAR. IT WAS ELSA...ELSA AND *THE DOCTOR!* THANK HEAVEN HE HAD COME! *I HAD BEEN SAVED!*

HE'S COMING OUT OF IT NOW, ATTABOY...YOU'RE ALL RIGHT, NOW, MR. BOLES!

I WAS ALL RIGHT. BUT...SOMEHOW I *WASN'T* ALL RIGHT! THE PAIN I FELT BEFORE WAS NOTHING WHEN COMPARED WITH THE PAIN I FELT *NOW!* AND IT WAS CREEPING THROUGH MY WHOLE BODY...BURNING, CONVULSING ME! IT WAS GETTING *WORSE AND WORSE! WHAT WAS WRONG!?*

I WAS WORRIED FOR AWHILE, MR. BOLES...HAD A TOUGH TIME BRINGING YOU AROUND! *IT TOOK TWO WHOLE TUMBLERS OF YOUR WHISKEY TO FIX YOU UP!*

THE END

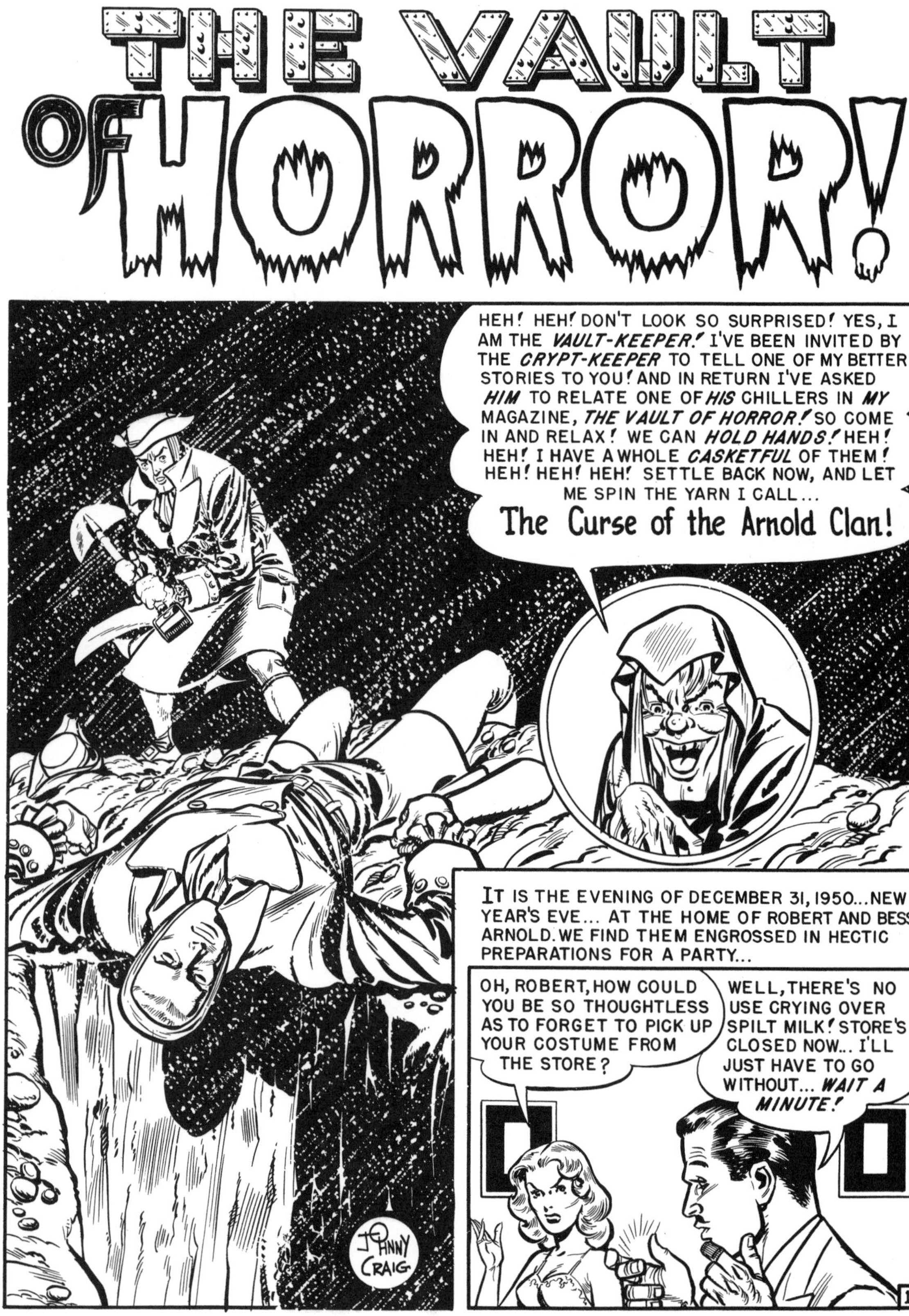
THE VAULT OF HORROR!
HEH! HEH! DON'T LOOK SO SURPRISED! YES, I AM THE VAULT-KEEPER! I'VE BEEN INVITED BY THE CRYPT-KEEPER TO TELL ONE OF MY BETTER STORIES TO YOU! AND IN RETURN I'VE ASKED HIM TO RELATE ONE OF HIS CHILLERS IN MY MAGAZINE, THE VAULT OF HORROR! SO COME IN AND RELAX! WE CAN HOLD HANDS! HEH! HEH! I HAVE A WHOLE CASKETFUL OF THEM! HEH! HEH! HEH! SETTLE BACK NOW, AND LET ME SPIN THE YARN I CALL...
The Curse of the Arnold Clan!
JOHNNY CRAIG
IT IS THE EVENING OF DECEMBER 31, 1950... NEW YEAR'S EVE... AT THE HOME OF ROBERT AND BESS ARNOLD. WE FIND THEM ENGROSSED IN HECTIC PREPARATIONS FOR A PARTY...
OH, ROBERT, HOW COULD YOU BE SO THOUGHTLESS AS TO FORGET TO PICK UP YOUR COSTUME FROM THE STORE?
WELL, THERE'S NO USE CRYING OVER SPILT MILK! STORE'S CLOSED NOW... I'LL JUST HAVE TO GO WITHOUT... WAIT A MINUTE!
1

UP IN THE ATTIC! THERE'S *LOTS* OF OLD CLOTHES UP THERE! CLOTHES WORN BY MY ANCESTORS *GENERATIONS* AGO! I'LL RUN UP AND HAVE A LOOK!

WELL, I HOPE YOU FIND *SOMETHING!* AND HURRY, DEAR... IT'S GETTING LATE!

...HAVEN'T BEEN UP HERE SINCE I WAS A KID! CONFOUND IT! I'M *CERTAIN* THOSE OLD CLOTHES WERE IN *ONE* OF THESE TRUNKS! MAYBE THAT ONE OVER THERE IN THE CORNER!

AH! HERE'S WHAT I WAS LOOKING FOR! HOPE THEY FIT! DON'T WANT TO... SAY, WHAT'S THIS? AN OLD *BOOK!*

'THE CURSE OF THE ARNOLD CLAN!' HMPF! NEVER SAW *THIS* BEFORE! A BOOK TELLING ALL ABOUT MY ANCESTORS! WRITTEN IN 1903... ALMOST FIFTY YEARS AGO! WONDER WHAT IT SAYS...

"1750—the first of the Arnolds, Jeremiah, lies in his death-bed with his two sons, Jason and George, at his side..."

MY SONS... I SHALL SOON BE OF ANOTHER WORLD. I LEAVE A WILL STATING THAT MY WEALTH IS TO BE DIVIDED BETWEEN THEE BOTH ON JANUARY 1ST, 1751! USE THE MONEY WISELY!

"But one son, Jason Arnold, brooded and sulked as New Year's Day moved closer... ever closer..."

I SHALL *NOT* SHARE FATHER'S WEALTH WITH GEORGE! I AM OLDER THAN HE... *I SHOULD HAVE IT ALL!* I WILL *NOT* BE DONE OUT OF IT!

"And by New Year's Eve, Jason had decided!"

JASON! 'TIS *NEW YEAR'S EVE!* WHY DO YE BRING ME OUT HERE IN THIS WILDS? *WHY?*

PATIENCE, GEORGE! I HAVE SOMETHING TO SHOW THEE!

2

THERE, GEORGE! THERE, BEFORE THEE, IS WHAT I HAVE BROUGHT THEE TO SEE!

JASON! BE YE DAFT? ON SUCH A FREEZING EVE, YE BRING ME HERE TO GAZE AT A MERE HOLE IN THE EARTH?

'TIS NO MERE HOLE IN THE EARTH, GEORGE! *'TIS THY GRAVE IT BE!!*

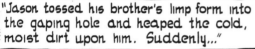

"Jason tossed his brother's limp form into the gaping hole and heaped the cold, moist dirt upon him. Suddenly..."

JASON...

WHA..? 'TIS GEORGE! CALLING TO ME FROM HIS GRAVE!

JASON! I *CURSE* THEE, JASON! I CURSE THEE AND THY DESCENDANTS! *EVERY FIFTY YEARS, ON NEW YEAR'S EVE; THE ELDEST OF THY DESCENDANTS SHALL BE BURIED ALIVE!!* THIS BE MY *CURSE*, BROTHER JASON!

"In a fearful state, Jason finished his work and returned home. He received the entire inheritance...but he lived in fear..."

...GOING CRAZY! CAN'T FORGET GEORGE'S *CURSE!* IF I BE ALIVE IN FIFTY YEARS, I WILL BE THE ELDEST ARNOLD! MAYHAP IF I GIVE HIM A DECENT BURIAL, THE CURSE WILL NOT OCCUR!

"And so it was that with the Spring thaw, George's body was 'found' and later laid to rest in a mausoleum..."

HERE, MY BROTHER! I BURY THEE WITH THY TRUSTY MUSKET AND POWDER-HORN IN THE HOPE THAT NOW AT LAST YOU WILL SET MY MIND AT REST!

"But Jason found no peace. He squandered all his wealth trying to find happiness, and on New Year's Eve, fifty years later, while cowering in his cellar, his house collapsed...and Jason was buried alive!"

HEH, HEH, HEH! QUITE A TREASURY OF INFORMATION, EH? WHAT WOULD *YOU* DO IF *YOU* WERE READING THAT BOOK, AND IT WAS ABOUT *YOUR* FAMILY? HEH! OF COURSE...*YOU'D READ ON!* AND THAT'S JUST WHAT ROBERT ARNOLD DID!

"The first curse of the Arnold clan had come to pass!"

"Jason Arnold had died in 1800, and for the next fifty years all was well...until New Year's Eve, 1850..."

THE ARNOLD CURSE SHAN'T WORK ON *ME!* I'VE LIVED IN THIS WILDERNESS FOR YEARS... ALL *ALONE!* I'LL NOT BE BURIED UNDER A FALLING HOUSE OR ANY SUCH THING!

"No, there were no buildings or people by which Albert Arnold could be harmed. Nothing, except..."

WHA..? *QUICKSAND!* I'M TRAPPED IN A BOG OF QUICK-SAND! *HELP! HELP!* I'LL BE *BURIED ALIVE!*

"And for the second time, the curse of the Arnold clan had taken it's toll!"

"It was the same in 1900. On New Year's Eve, William Arnold, while working the night shift in a coal mine, was trapped in a shaft cave-in!"

HMPF! THAT'S ALL THERE IS! LET'S SEE... LAST TIME WAS IN 1900. THEN THE NEXT TIME WILL BE NEW YEAR'S EVE, 1950...*GOOD GOSH!* THAT'S *TONIGHT!* AND *I'M* THE *OLDEST LIVING ARNOLD!*

HA! WHY, IT'S *RIDICULOUS!* THOSE DEATHS WERE ONLY A LOT OF FREAK *ACCIDENTS!* HA! WHAT NONSENSE! NOTHING'S GOING TO HAPPEN TO *ME!*

I FOUND A HONEY OF A COLONIAL COSTUME, DEAR! I'LL BE READY IN A FEW MINUTES!

PLEASE HURRY, ROBERT. WE'RE LATE NOW!

HEH! WELL, ROBERT AND BESS WENT TO THE PARTY. THEY HAD A GAY TIME LAUGHING, DRINKING, DANCING! AND THEN THE HOST MADE AN ANNOUNCEMENT...

HA! HA! THAT'S RIGHT, FOLKS, A *SCAVENGER HUNT!* EVERYONE WILL DRAW A TICKET, AND THE FIRST PERSON TO BRING BACK WHATEVER'S WRITTEN ON THEIR TICKET GETS A *PRIZE!* C'MON!

OH, GOODNESS! I HAVE TO BRING BACK A *MOOSE HEAD!*

GOSH! I HAVE TO FIND AN OLD MUSKET AND A POWDER-HORN! WHERE THE DEVIL WILL I ... HEY-Y-Y...

MY ANCESTOR, GEORGE ARNOLD, WAS *BURIED* WITH A MUSKET AND POWDER-HORN! HM-M-M... AND THE CEMETERY ISN'T *FAR* FROM HERE, EITHER...

5

...CEMETERY IS JUST AHEAD! I'LL HAVE THAT MUSKET AND POWDER-HORN BEFORE THE OTHERS EVEN *START!*

I'LL HAVE TO SNEAK IN. THE CARETAKER WOULD NEVER LET ME IN *THIS* TIME OF NIGHT, ESPECIALLY IN *THIS* GET-UP!

THERE'S THE MAUSOLEUM OVER THERE! BOY! THIS PLACE IS *WEIRD!* HOPE THIS DOESN'T TAKE LONG!

I'M IN LUCK! THIS DOOR IS SO OLD, THE LOCK HAS JUST ABOUT RUSTED AWAY! I COULD HAVE OPENED IT WITH A HAIRPIN!

AH! HERE IT IS! THE LAST RESTING PLACE OF GEORGE ARNOLD!

GEORGE ARNOLD

... MUSKET AND POWDER-HORN SHOULD BE INSIDE! *UNH!* THIS... THIS SLAB IS... SURE *HEAVY!*

WHEW! BOY! THAT WAS A *JOB!* UGH! WHAT A SMELL! HERE'S THE MUSKET AND... *WHAT'S THAT?*

BLAZES! THE CARETAKER'S COMING TO MAKE HIS ROUNDS! I CAN'T LET HIM FIND ME *HERE!* *WHAT'LL I DO?*

6

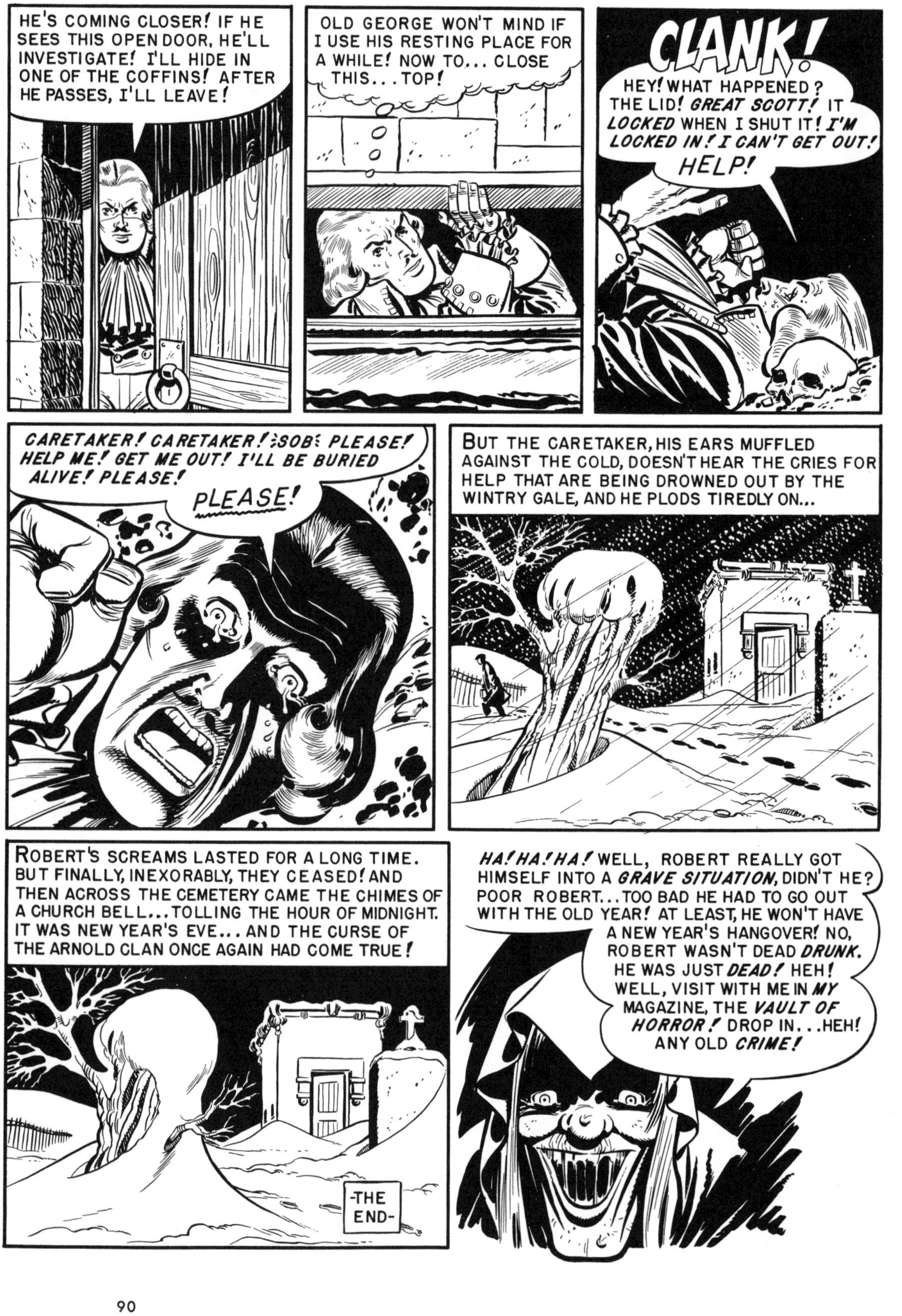
HE'S COMING CLOSER! IF HE SEES THIS OPEN DOOR, HE'LL INVESTIGATE! I'LL HIDE IN ONE OF THE COFFINS! AFTER HE PASSES, I'LL LEAVE!
OLD GEORGE WON'T MIND IF I USE HIS RESTING PLACE FOR A WHILE! NOW TO... CLOSE THIS... TOP!
CLANK!
HEY! WHAT HAPPENED? THE LID! GREAT SCOTT! IT LOCKED WHEN I SHUT IT! I'M LOCKED IN! I CAN'T GET OUT! HELP!
CARETAKER! CARETAKER! SOB PLEASE! HELP ME! GET ME OUT! I'LL BE BURIED ALIVE! PLEASE!
PLEASE!
BUT THE CARETAKER, HIS EARS MUFFLED AGAINST THE COLD, DOESN'T HEAR THE CRIES FOR HELP THAT ARE BEING DROWNED OUT BY THE WINTRY GALE, AND HE PLODS TIREDLY ON...
ROBERT'S SCREAMS LASTED FOR A LONG TIME. BUT FINALLY, INEXORABLY, THEY CEASED! AND THEN ACROSS THE CEMETERY CAME THE CHIMES OF A CHURCH BELL... TOLLING THE HOUR OF MIDNIGHT. IT WAS NEW YEAR'S EVE... AND THE CURSE OF THE ARNOLD CLAN ONCE AGAIN HAD COME TRUE!
-THE END-
HA! HA! HA! WELL, ROBERT REALLY GOT HIMSELF INTO A GRAVE SITUATION, DIDN'T HE? POOR ROBERT... TOO BAD HE HAD TO GO OUT WITH THE OLD YEAR! AT LEAST, HE WON'T HAVE A NEW YEAR'S HANGOVER! NO, ROBERT WASN'T DEAD DRUNK. HE WAS JUST DEAD! HEH! WELL, VISIT WITH ME IN MY MAGAZINE, THE VAULT OF HORROR! DROP IN... HEH! ANY OLD CRIME!

THE VAULT OF HORROR!

HEH, HEH, HEH! IT'S NICE TO SEE SO MANY OF YOU READERS BACK AGAIN FOR ANOTHER GRUESOME STORY! WELL, *THIS* TALE TAKES PLACE IN MERRY OLD ENGLAND... HEH, HEH! ONLY THINGS AREN'T AT ALL *MERRY* IN *THIS* YARN! TSK! TSK! DON'T LOOK SO *FRIGHTENED!* I HAVEN'T EVEN *BEGUN* TO RELATE THE *BLOOD-CURDLER* I CALL...

TERROR ON THE MOORS!

ALONG THE BUMPY, GUTTED ROAD THAT WINDS THROUGH THE BARREN ENGLISH MOORS, A LONE CAR CAUTIOUSLY MADE ITS WAY... TRYING DESPERATELY TO FIND SAFE PASSAGE THROUGH THE DENSE, IMPENETRABLE FOG. BEHIND THE WHEEL SAT JIM RYAN, AN AMERICAN TOURIST...

BLAST THIS FOG! CAN'T SEE A THING! I'VE GONE OFF THE ROAD FOUR TIMES! IT'S IMPOSSIBLE TO GO ANY FURTHER! DON'T EVEN KNOW WHERE I *AM*, ANYMORE!

HMM...THIS GATE LOOKS LIKE THE ENTRANCE TO AN ESTATE. GOOD THING I STOPPED WHEN I DID! MAYBE THEY'LL PUT ME UP FOR THE NIGHT...

JIM RYAN FOUND HIS WAY TO AN ANCIENT, DECREPIT HOUSE. THE DOOR WAS OPENED TO HIS KNOCKS, AND AN AGED, BENT BUTLER USHERED HIM INTO THE PRESENCE OF ANDREW CLYMORE...

...AND WITH THE ROAD SO DANGEROUS BECAUSE OF THE FOG, MR. CLYMORE, I THOUGHT PERHAPS...

OF COURSE, MR. RYAN...

WE HAVEN'T HAD A GUEST IN OVER THIRTY YEARS! EVERS AND I LIVE HERE ALONE! HOWEVER, WE SHALL BE GLAD TO HAVE YOU SPEND THE NIGHT...

DINNER IS SERVED, MR. CLYMORE...

...YES, MR. RYAN, I AM AN OLD MAN WITH NOT MUCH TIME LEFT! ANOTHER HEART ATTACK WILL MEAN THE END...

I'M VERY SORRY TO HEAR THAT, MR. CLYMORE!

SUDDENLY, FROM OUT OF THE DARK RECESSES OF THE HOUSE, CAME A SHRILL, PIERCING, UNEARTHLY SCREAM...

GREAT SCOTT! WHAT WAS THAT?

I HEARD NOTHING, MR. RYAN. WHAT SEEMS TO BE THE MATTER?

YOU...YOU DIDN'T HEAR THAT...THAT... OH...I'M...IT MUST HAVE BEEN MY IMAGINATION...

I'M ... I'M SORRY, MR. CLYMORE! I'M VERY TIRED... ON EDGE, I GUESS...

OF COURSE! IF YOU'VE FINISHED EATING, I'LL SHOW YOU TO YOUR ROOM!

BY CANDLELIGHT, MR. CLYMORE SLOWLY LED THE WAY TO THE GUEST ROOM. EVERS WAS COMING DOWN THE STAIRS, HOLDING A LARGE, CLOTH-COVERED PLATTER...

GOOD-NIGHT, MR. RYAN. I TRUST YOU SLEEP WELL!

THANK YOU, EVERS. GOOD NIGHT!

EVERS HAD PAUSED FOR ONLY A MOMENT... BUT IT WAS LONG ENOUGH FOR JIM RYAN TO SMELL THE UNGODLY ODOR THAT CAME FROM THE COVERED PLATTER. IT WAS A STRONG, NAUSEATING SMELL... LIKE THE STENCH OF DECAYED ROTTED *FLESH!*

...WHAT AN IMMENSE DOOR! AND THOSE STRANGE WHIMPERING SOUNDS FROM BEHIND IT...

HERE IS YOUR ROOM, MR. RYAN!

JIM FELL ASLEEP QUICKLY! BUT SOME HOURS LATER...

BLAZES! THOSE HORRIBLE SHRIEKS! COMING FROM ACROSS THE HALL! *WHAT'S GOING ON OVER THERE?*

...SOUNDS LIKE AN *ANIMAL*... GROWLING AND SNARLING! AND YET... IT SOUNDS ALMOST *HUMAN!* WHATEVER'S IN THERE IS MAKING A TERRIFIC RACKET!

...SEEMS TO BE SCRATCHING... DIGGING FOR SOMETHING! AND IT'S POUNDING ON THE WALL... ON THE WALL BETWEEN *THIS* ROOM AND MR. CLYMORE'S!

93

...STRANGE... I *THINK* I HEAR MOANS FROM INSIDE MR. CLYMORE'S ROOM! BUT I... I CAN'T BE SURE! *CONFOUND IT!* I HOPE HE'S ALL RIGHT!

UNNERVED, JIM RYAN RETURNED TO BED! HE SLEPT LITTLE, AND WAS FULLY DRESSED WHEN THERE WAS A FURIOUS POUNDING ON HIS DOOR THE NEXT MORNING. THE NOISE FROM ACROSS THE HALL HAD CEASED...

EVERS! WHAT'S THE MATTER?

MR. RYAN! HE'S DEAD! MR. CLYMORE IS *DEAD!* A HEART ATTACK DURING THE NIGHT! PLEASE COME!

HE'S DEAD ALL RIGHT! LOOKS LIKE HE WAS *FRIGHTENED* TO DEATH!

A LONG TIME AGO HE MADE ME PROMISE TO *CREMATE* HIS BODY WHEN HE DIED, MR. RYAN. I HATE TO ASK YOU THIS... BUT I AM OLD! I... I CAN'T DO IT ALONE...

I... I UNDERSTAND, EVERS! YOU WANT ME TO BUILD THE FUNERAL PYRE! OKAY, I'LL DO IT... AS SOON AS IT STOPS RAINING!

RAINING? OH... I... I HADN'T NOTICED! YES... I GUESS WE'LL JUST HAVE TO *WAIT!*

YOU LOOK FRIGHTENED, EVERS! ANYTHING WRONG?

WRONG? NO... I ONLY PRAY THE RAIN STOPS *SOON!* IT *MUST* STOP SOON! IT *MUST!*

THE DAY PASSED SLOWLY. THE HOURS DRIFTED BY AND THE TORRENTS OF RAIN CONTINUED!

IT'S GETTING DARK, EVERS! MAYBE WE CAN CREMATE HIS CORPSE TOMORROW! WHY NOT GO TAKE A NAP?

NO! NO, I CAN'T LEAVE HIM *NOW!* IT'S... GETTING DARK!

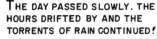

4

SUDDENLY, FROM THE MYSTERIOUS ROOM NEXT DOOR, CAME THE SOUNDS OF MOVEMENT. FIRST, LOW GROWLS AND SNARLS...AND THEN THE SCRATCHING, CLAWING SOUNDS OF CONCENTRATED DIGGING...

SNARL-L-L CRUN-NCH! SCRATCH!

NOTHING WAS SAID! THE BUTLER STIFFENED...HIS FACE A GHOSTLY PALLOR...AND BEADS OF SWEAT STOOD OUT ON HIS BROW. HE WAS IN DEATHLY FEAR, BUT HE REMAINED BY THE BED, STARING FIXEDLY AT THE WALL FROM WHICH THE SOUNDS CAME! WITH EACH HOUR, THE TENSION MOUNTED...

GROW-WLLL-L SCRATCH! SCRATCH!

THE RAIN'S STOPPED, EVERS. IT'S LATE... BUT MAYBE I CAN BUILD THE FUNERAL PYRE NOW...IF YOU WANT ME TO!

NO! NO, DON'T GO!

SCRATCH! SCRUN-NCH!

THIS PLACE IS DRIVING ME NUTS! WHAT'S GOING ON HERE, ANYWAY?!

...ALL RIGHT, MR. RYAN! IT'S ...IT'S NOT FAIR TO KEEP IT FROM YOU ANY LONGER! I'LL TELL YOU THE STORY...

SCRATCH SCRATCH SCRATCH

'IT BEGAN A LONG TIME AGO! MR. CLYMORE'S WIFE WAS A VICTIM OF CATALEPSY! WHENEVER SHE TOOK A FIT, SHE'D BE AS IF DEAD FOR HOURS. YOU'VE HEARD OF SUCH CASES?'

'FINALLY A FIT SEIZED HER FROM WHICH SHE DID NOT AWAKEN! DAYS PASSED! SHE WAS PRONOUNCED DEAD...AND WAS BURIED IN THE FAMILY CRYPT BEHIND THIS HOUSE...'

'THE FOLLOWING NIGHT, MR. CLYMORE HEARD MOANS COMING FROM THE MAUSOLEUM. HE RUSHED IN AND RIPPED OPEN HIS WIFE'S COFFIN! SHE WAS ALIVE! BUT SHE WAS IN A STATE OF VERY SEVERE SHOCK!'

5

SHE NEVER FULLY RECOVERED FROM THAT EXPER-IENCE, MR. RYAN! A YEAR LATER, THEY HAD THEIR FIRST AND ONLY CHILD! IT WAS THEN THAT MRS. CLYMORE *REALLY* DIED... THAT TIME THERE WAS NO MISTAKE!

'THE CHILD WAS A *REVOLTING MONSTROSITY!* NO ONE WAS ALLOWED TO SEE IT... NOT EVEN MY-SELF! MR. CLYMORE WITHDREW FROM THE WORLD...'

'HE DISCHARGED THE HOUSEHOLD STAFF, AND CARED FOR THE CREA-TURE IN SECLUSION. AS IT GREW OLDER, IT BECAME VICIOUS... AND THEN HE PUT IT IN THAT ROOM AND HAD THAT DOOR BUILT TO HOLD IT. WE DESTROYED THE KEY...'

SEVERAL MONTHS AGO, THE MON-STER UNDERWENT A HORRIBLE MENTAL CHANGE! *IT WOULD EAT ONLY DEAD FLESH! IT HAD BECOME A GHOUL!*

TOGETHER WE HAVE KEPT IT ALIVE BY FEEDING IT DECAYED CORPSES FROM THE MAUSOLEUM. BUT NOW... NOW THE BEAST IS DIGGING THROUGH THE WALL! *HE'S TRYING TO GET OUT!*

GOOD LORD!

IT WILL SOON SUCCEED! YOU CAN TELL BY THE SOUNDS! ANY TIME NOW IT WILL BURST THROUGH! IF NOT TONIGHT, *TOMORROW NIGHT!* I CAN'T STAND IT MUCH LONGER!

EVERS! GET HOLD OF YOURSELF! *LISTEN TO ME!* ARE THERE ANY WEAPONS WE CAN USE?

YES...(SOB)... IN THE BUREAU! TWO... TWO PISTOLS... *LOOK! THE WALL! IT'S BREAKING OPEN!*

CRUNCH!

JIM RYAN RACED TO THE BUREAU AND SEARCHED FRANTICALLY UNTIL HE FOUND THE PISTOLS...

⊙W!!!XW! FLINTLOCKS!

HURRY! A GUN! GIVE ME A GUN! IT'S OUT! LOOK AT IT! LOOK AT IT!

RYAN WHIRLED AND STARED AT THE MOST HIDEOUS BEING HE HAD EVER SEEN! IT WAS BEYOND DESCRIPTION... BEYOND THE MOST FANTASTIC APPARITION IN HIS WILDEST NIGHTMARE! EVERS SNATCHED A GUN FROM HIS HAND AND FIRED BLINDLY...

BLAM!

THE MONSTER WAS UPON THE LITTLE BUTLER IN AN INSTANT. THEY WENT DOWN IN A TUMBLED MASS OF THRASHING LEGS AND FRENZIED, TERRIFIED SCREAMS. JIM RAISED HIS GUN, TOOK COOL DELIBERATE AIM, AND SQUEEZED THE TRIGGER!

THE PISTOL HAD MISFIRED! IT WAS TOO LATE TO FIRE AGAIN, FOR THE INHUMAN THING SLITHERED ACROSS THE FLOOR AND, WITH A MIGHTY PUSH OF ITS HUGE ARMS, LEAPED UPON HIM!

CLICK!

JIM FELL BACKWARDS TRYING TO DODGE THE HURTLING FORM, AND HIS HEAD STRUCK THE WALL SHARPLY. THE ROOM REELED! VAGUE VISIONS SWAM BEFORE HIM... THE BEAST, CROUCHED OVER THE BODY ON THE BED... CANDLES SETTING FIRE TO THE RUG... THEN BLACKNESS...

HE REGAINED HIS SENSES IN A FEW MOMENTS. SMOKE FILLED HIS NOSTRILS, AND THE CRACKLE OF FLAMES, HIS EARS. HE SAW THE MONSTER FLITTING WILDLY ABOUT THE CORPSE... SNATCHING AT ITS FACE REPEATEDLY WITH JAGGED TEETH...

7

THE FLAMES RACED MADLY ABOUT THE ROOM! CHOKING FROM THE ACRID FUMES, JIM CRAWLED TO THE SIDE OF THE BUTLER!

EVERS! EVERS!

...WHY...HE... HE'S DEAD!

HE TURNED JUST IN TIME TO SEE THE HORRID CREATURE, AFIRE, LEAP FROM THE BED AND, SCREAMING FRANTICALLY, SCURRY BACK INTO THE HOLE IN THE WALL. THROUGH THE FLAMES LICKING THE BEDCLOTHES. JIM STARED IN HORROR AT THE MUTILATED REMAINS OF MR. CLYMORE...

GOOD LORD! THAT... THAT THING WAS... FEASTING ON...ON ITS FATHER!

SUDDENLY RYAN NOTICED BURNING EMBERS FALLING FROM THE CEILING! WITH A THUNDEROUS ROAR THE ROOF COLLAPSED, JUST AS HE DARTED THROUGH THE BLAZING DOORWAY...

LUNGS ACHING AND EYES SMARTING FROM THE PUNGENT SMOKE, HE STUMBLED DOWN THE STAIRS AND OUT OF THE HOUSE...THE MONSTER'S FRIGHTFUL, SOUL-SEARING SCREECHES OF AGONY RINGING IN HIS EARS...

AS JIM WATCHED DAZEDLY, THE ROARING FLAMES ENVELOPED THE HOUSE AND RAZED IT TO THE GROUND... A MASS OF SMOKING RUBBLE! THE PITIFUL SHRIEKS GREW WEAKER AND WEAKER... UNTIL HE HEARD THEM NO MORE!

FOR A LONG WHILE AFTER THE LAST EMBER HAD DIED, HE DID NOT MOVE ...BUT FINALLY HE STUMBLED TO HIS CAR, SLID BEHIND THE WHEEL AND SLOWLY DROVE AWAY. HE LOOKED BACK SEVERAL TIMES...UNTIL THE SMOKING REMAINS OF THE HOUSE WERE SWALLOWED BY THE FOG AND DISAPPEARED FROM VIEW...

—THE END—

HEH, HEH! PLEASANT? I HOPE THE TALE LEFT YOU WITH A WARM FEELING... AND THAT IT STIMULATED YOUR...HEH... YOUR APPETITE! OH, BY THE WAY... DON'T FEEL SORRY FOR THE MONSTER! AFTER ALL, HE DIED WITH A HOT MEAL IN HIS TUMMY... MOOR OR LESS! HEH! HEH! HEH! NOW READ ON...

THE VAULT OF HORROR!

HEH, HEH! AN INCREASE IN THE POPULATION OF A GREAT CITY'S TEEMING MILLIONS IS OF GREAT IMPORTANCE TO THE STATISTICIAN... BUT TO THE SANITATION DEPT. IT MEANS ONLY THAT MUCH MORE GARBAGE TO COLLECT...

THE CITY HAS A HUGE, EFFICIENT SYSTEM FOR THE REMOVAL OF TRASH, AND ONE OF ITS MOST RESPECTED ASSETS IS ITS FLEET OF STREAMLINED TRUCKS!

THESE PROUD VEHICLES COVER EVERY PART OF THE METROPOLIS, AND THERE ARE BUT FEW ITEMS THAT CANNOT BE CRUSHED, BROKEN AND HACKED TO BITS BY THEIR GLEAMING, WHIRLING BLADES...

KA-CHOMP! CAR-RUNCH!

HAVING EATEN THEIR FILL OF GARBAGE, THEY AT ONCE TRAVEL TO THE CITY DUMP AND PURR CONTENTEDLY WHILE THEY DISCHARGE THEIR CARGO.

HERE IS WHERE EVERY BIT OF THE CITY'S COLLECTED WASTE IS BROUGHT. AND IT IS HERE, IN THIS SCAVENGERS' PARADISE, THAT ONE MAY FIND...

...ALMOST ANYTHING!

HEH, HEH! QUITE A *SHOCKING* THING TO FIND, ISN'T IT? NATURALLY, THE MAN ALMOST *FAINTED* UPON VIEWING HIS HORRID DISCOVERY! BUT HE RACED MADLY TO INFORM THE POLICE... *AFTER* HE HAD REMOVED THE RING AND STUFFED IT INTO HIS POCKET, OF COURSE! HOW, YOU MAY ASK, DID THE HAND HAPPEN TO BE LYING IN THE CITY DUMP? HEH! HEH! WELL, THERIN LIES OUR STORY! IT'S A *GRIPPING* TALE AND I CALL IT...

SEEDS of DEATH!

GHOST STORIES

LET'S GO BACK IN TIME TO WHERE OUR STORY *REALLY* BEGAN... TO A SMALL FARM ON THE OUTSKIRTS OF THE LARGE CITY.

ON THIS PARTICULAR FARM LIVED THE OWNER, BASIL WOODS... HIS WIFE CONNIE...

...AND A HIRED HAND NAMED CLIFF!

OH, CLIFF... CLIFF! HE'S SO *CRUEL!*

CONNIE, DARLING, IF HE HITS YOU AGAIN... SO HELP ME, I THINK I'LL *KILL* HIM!

HMPF! THE FOOLS! THEY THINK I DON'T *KNOW* THEY'RE IN LOVE! THEY THINK I'VE BEEN *BLIND* TO WHAT'S GOING ON BEHIND MY BACK!

NO MAN CAN TAKE MY WIFE FROM ME AND *LIVE!* I'LL FIX THE DIRTY HOME-WRECKER WHEN THE TIME COMES!

HEH, HEH! WELL, THAT'S THE SITUATION, DEAR READERS... THE *ETERNAL TRIANGLE!* TIME PASSED... AND BASIL WAITED PATIENTLY, UNTIL ONE DAY...

CLIFF, WHILE YOU'RE IN TOWN TODAY, WOULD YOU BUY ME SOME *GARDENIA SEEDS?* I WANT TO PLANT THEM IN THE GARDEN!

SURE, MRS. WOODS!

HE'LL BE IN THE CITY ALL DAY... WON'T BE BACK TILL LATE TONIGHT! AND HE'LL PROBABLY TAKE THE SHORT-CUT 'CROSS THE FIELD TO THE HOUSE... HMM-M...

... AND SO, LATE THAT NIGHT...

'EVENING, CLIFF! DID YOU GET MY WIFE'S GARDENIA SEEDS?

EH? OH... HI, MR. WOODS! YES, I HAVE THEM RIGHT HERE!

HERE THEY ARE! WANT TO TAKE A LOOK?

THWUNK!

⸘GASP!⸘ THERE... IT'S DONE! NOW TO BURY HIM... ⸘GASP!⸘... HEE, HEE! IN TIME TO COME, HIS BODY'LL MAKE FINE FERTILIZER FOR THIS FIELD! ⸘GASP!⸘

3

HEH, HEH! YES, THE DEED WAS DONE! NOW BASIL WOODS FELT CERTAIN HIS WIFE WOULD SOON FORGET HER SILLY LOVE AFFAIR. THE NEXT MORNING...

I CAN'T UNDERSTAND IT! CLIFF HASN'T RETURNED FROM THE CITY YET! I HOPE HE'S ALL RIGHT!

CLIFF HASN'T RETURNED? TCH, TCH!

HA, HA! SHE'S WORRIED! BUT AS THE DAYS PASS, SHE'LL FORGET HIM... SHE'LL FORGET!

WELL, THE DAYS DID PASS BUT CONNIE DIDN'T FORGET! AND ONE EVENING AS BASIL RETURNED FROM THE FIELDS...

CONNIE? CONNIE! TARNATION! WHERE IS THAT WOMAN? WHA... A NOTE!

Basil

Basil—
Forgive me. I have gone to the city to search for Cliff. I simply can't stand worrying about him any longer. I must find him.
Connie

THAT BLASTED NO-GOOD! I'LL TEACH HER TO RUN OFF LIKE THIS! I'LL GO TO THE CITY AND DRAG HER BACK BY THE HAIR OF HER HEAD!

4

GOODBYE, MY CHILD. I'M SORRY I COULDN'T BE OF ANY HELP, BUT I HAVEN'T SEEN MY SON FOR QUITE SOME TIME!

THANK YOU... GOODBYE...

BASIL!

YAS, IT'S ME! DIDJA THINK IT WAS GONNA BE YOUR PRECIOUS CLIFF?

BASIL, PLEASE! DON'T HIT ME!

HIT YOU! WHY, I'LL BEAT YOUR STUPID HEAD IN! I'LL TEACH YOU TO RUN OFF!

DON'T TOUCH ME!

YOU AND YOUR PRECIOUS CLIFF! WELL, YOU'LL NEVER SEE HIM AGAIN!

YOU STAY AWAY FROM ME! DON'T TOUCH ME!

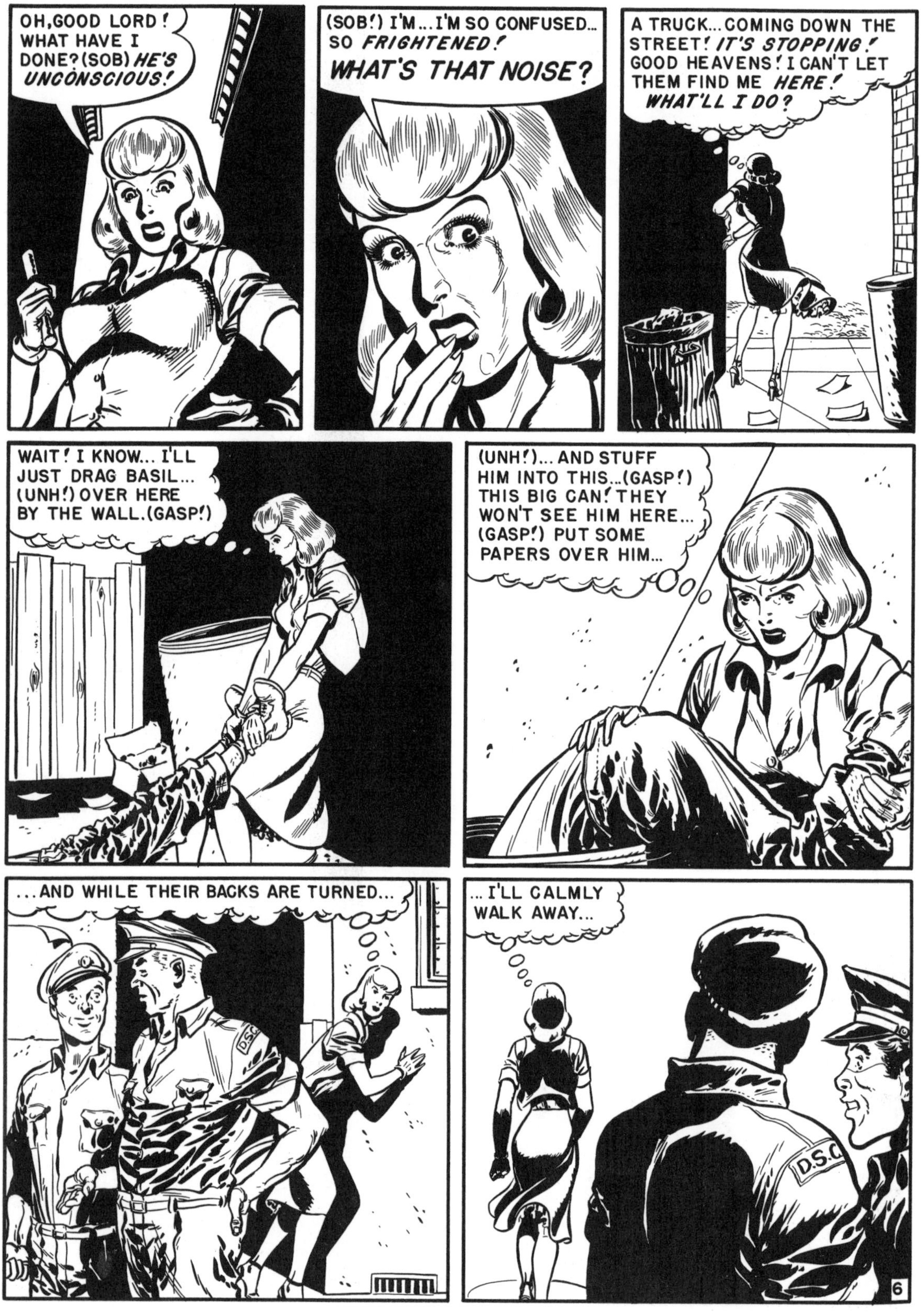
OH, GOOD LORD! WHAT HAVE I DONE? (SOB) HE'S UNCONSCIOUS!
(SOB!) I'M...I'M SO CONFUSED... SO FRIGHTENED! WHAT'S THAT NOISE?
A TRUCK...COMING DOWN THE STREET! IT'S STOPPING! GOOD HEAVENS! I CAN'T LET THEM FIND ME HERE! WHAT'LL I DO?
WAIT! I KNOW... I'LL JUST DRAG BASIL... (UNH!) OVER HERE BY THE WALL. (GASP!)
(UNH!)... AND STUFF HIM INTO THIS...(GASP!) THIS BIG CAN! THEY WON'T SEE HIM HERE... (GASP!) PUT SOME PAPERS OVER HIM...
...AND WHILE THEIR BACKS ARE TURNED...
D.S.C.
...I'LL CALMLY WALK AWAY...
D.S.C.
6

HEH! NATURALLY, CONNIE WAS UNAWARE OF HER HUSBAND'S FATE, AND FOR THE NEXT FEW WEEKS, SHE SEARCHED THE CITY IN VAIN... FOR CLIFF...

FINALLY, SHE RETURNED TO THE FARM. SAD AND WEARY, SHE TROD THE SHORT-CUT ACROSS THE FIELD TOWARD THE HOUSE. SUDDENLY, SHE STOPPED... HER EYES WIDENED!

SHE STOOD TRANSFIXED IN HORROR! BEFORE HER, NOT TEN FEET FROM WHERE SHE STOOD, WAS A MOUND OF *GARDENIAS!* ALL AT ONCE, THERE CAME THE SHOCKING REALIZATION THAT AT LAST SHE HAD FOUND... HER PRECIOUS CLIFF...

BACKLASH!

I HAVE IT! I HAVE IT! WHAT AN IDEA! AT LAST I'LL BE A SUCCESS!

1

HA! HA! IT'S WONDERFUL! THE GREATEST PLOT FOR A MYSTERY STORY EVER CONCEIVED! AND IT'S FOOLPROOF!

FOR *YEARS* MYSTERY WRITERS HAVE BEEN SEARCHING FOR A *LOGICAL, WORKABLE* METHOD BY WHICH A CRIME COULD BE COMMITTED BEHIND THE *LOCKED DOORS* OF A *SEALED ROOM!* AND *I'VE FOUND* IT!

IT'S ALMOST TOO GOOD TO BE *TRUE!* I'VE DEVISED A WAY TO ENTER A LOCKED ROOM... AND TO *EXIT* FROM IT, *LEAVING ALL DOORS AND WINDOWS LOCKED AND BOLTED FROM THE INSIDE!*

WHY, IT'S A WAY TO COMMIT THE *PERFECT CRIME!* THIS STORY WILL SELL LIKE WILD-FIRE! LET'S SEE, NOW... WHAT SHOULD I CALL IT? HOW SHOULD I BEGIN?...

FOR THREE DAYS AND NIGHTS, DAVE WILTON POUNDS HIS TYPE-WRITER KEYS AS IF HIS VERY LIFE DEPENDS ON IT. FINALLY, THE STORY IS FINISHED AND IN THE MAILBOX...

AH! IN A FEW DAYS, I'LL PROBABLY FIND A BIG, FAT, JUICY CHECK IN THE MAIL!

CURB YOUR DOG

INSTEAD OF AN EXPECTED CHECK, DAVE FINDS...

A REJECTION SLIP! BUT... BUT... WHY, MY ENVELOPE WASN'T EVEN OPENED! THEY DIDN'T EVEN READ MY STORY!

WELL, THAT'S *THEIR* HARD LUCK! I'LL JUST SEND IT TO *ANOTHER* PUBLISHING HOUSE!

2

AND DAVE *DOES* MAIL IT TO ANOTHER PUBLISHER! A FEW DAYS LATER...

'SORRY. NOT ACCEPTING ANY UNSOLICITED MATERIAL AT THIS TIME!'

BAH!

THEY DIDN'T READ IT, EITHER! *THE FOOLS!* WHY WON'T THEY GIVE ME A CHANCE?

I'LL KEEP SENDING IT OUT! *SOMEONE* WILL READ IT... AND THEN MY WORRIES WILL BE OVER...

THE WEEKS PASS AND STILL DAVE'S STORY KEEPS RETURNING... UNOPENED, UNREAD... FROM EVERY PUBLISHER HE SENDS IT TO...

FIVE! FIVE TIMES IT'S COME BACK! THEY WON'T EVEN *READ* IT! *WHAT'S THE MATTER?* (SOB)

(SOB) I'LL... I'LL TRY *ONCE* MORE! THE *HARNOLD PUBLISHING HOUSE* MIGHT... MIGHT (SOB) OH, WHAT'S THE USE? *THEY'LL* PROBABLY REJECT IT, TOO!

MYSTERY PLOTS

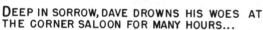

DEEP IN SORROW, DAVE DROWNS HIS WOES AT THE CORNER SALOON FOR MANY HOURS...

STINKIN' PUBLISHERS! WON'T EVEN GIMME A CHANCE! WON'T EVEN *READ* MY STUFF! HERE I AM WITH A STORY ABOUT A *PERFECT CRIME*, AND...

? *PERFECT CRIME?*

Harnold Publishing House
42 Grand Square
Metropolis

OF COURSE! WHY DIDN'T I THINK OF THIS BEFORE? I DON'T *NEED* THOSE... THOSE *MISERLY*, PUNK PUBLISHERS! *I KNOW HOW TO COMMIT THE PERFECT CRIME!*

3

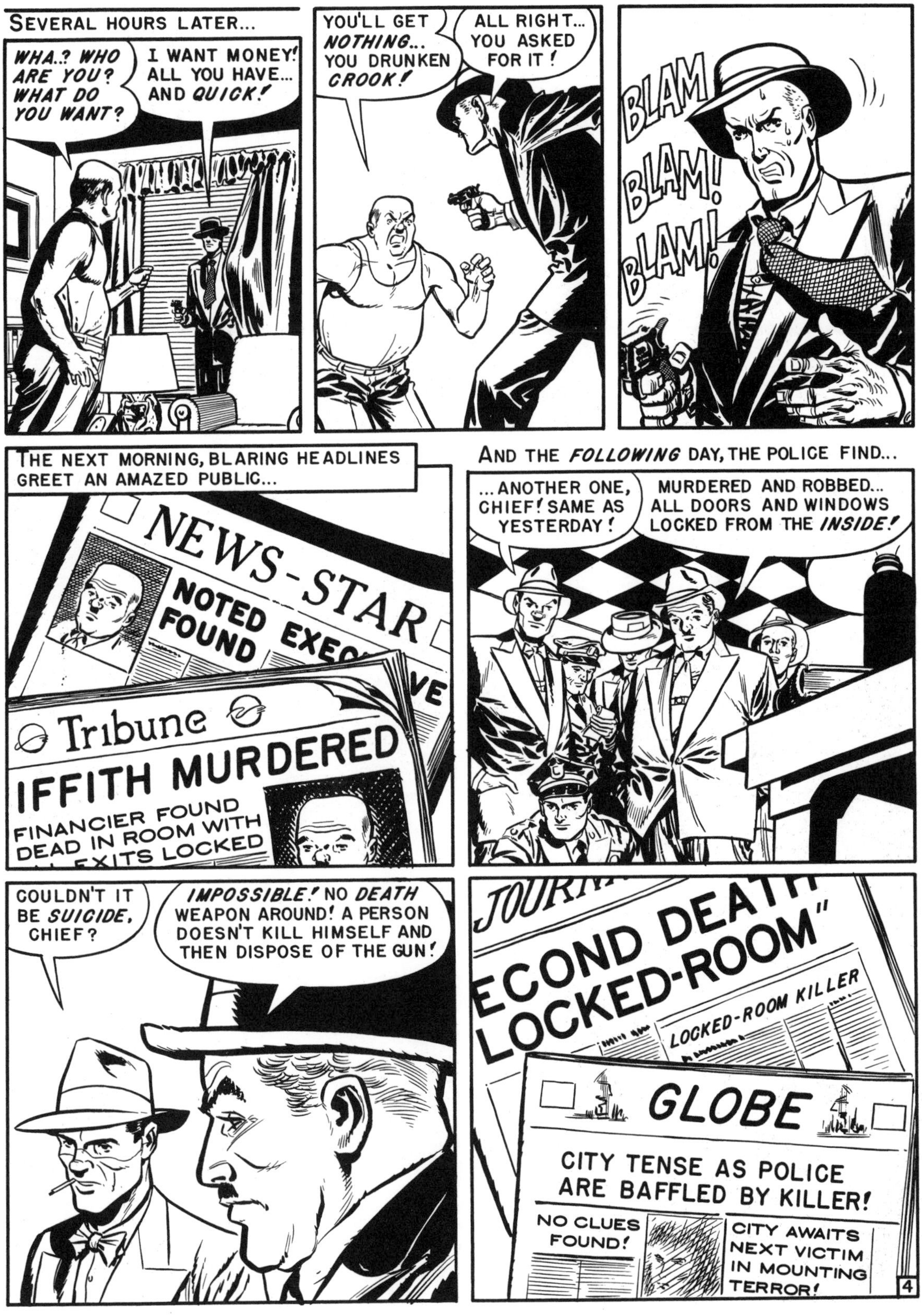
SEVERAL HOURS LATER...
WHA..? WHO ARE YOU? WHAT DO YOU WANT?
I WANT MONEY! ALL YOU HAVE... AND QUICK!
YOU'LL GET NOTHING... YOU DRUNKEN CROOK!
ALL RIGHT... YOU ASKED FOR IT!
BLAM
BLAM!
BLAM!
THE NEXT MORNING, BLARING HEADLINES GREET AN AMAZED PUBLIC...
NEWS-STAR
NOTED EXEC
FOUND
VE
Tribune
IFFITH MURDERED
FINANCIER FOUND DEAD IN ROOM WITH
EXITS LOCKED
AND THE FOLLOWING DAY, THE POLICE FIND...
...ANOTHER ONE, CHIEF! SAME AS YESTERDAY!
MURDERED AND ROBBED... ALL DOORS AND WINDOWS LOCKED FROM THE INSIDE!
COULDN'T IT BE SUICIDE, CHIEF?
IMPOSSIBLE! NO DEATH WEAPON AROUND! A PERSON DOESN'T KILL HIMSELF AND THEN DISPOSE OF THE GUN!
JOURN
ECOND DEATH
LOCKED-ROOM"
LOCKED-ROOM KILLER
GLOBE
CITY TENSE AS POLICE ARE BAFFLED BY KILLER!
NO CLUES FOUND!
CITY AWAITS NEXT VICTIM IN MOUNTING TERROR!
4

A CITY HELD IN THE GRIP OF *FEAR*...

DON'T WORRY, HONEY! I PUT *TEN DIFFERENT LOCKS* ON THE DOOR! THAT KILLER COULD *NEVER* GET IN NOW!

AN ENTIRE CITY QUAKING IN HORROR WITH EACH PASSING NIGHT...

IT'S TIME FOR *ME* TO STAND GUARD, DEAR! BETTER GET SOME SLEEP!

...A CITY TREMBLING WITH THE QUESTION..."WHO'S NEXT?"

AND FROM IT ALL THERE RISES A HERO TO COME FORTH AND ISSUE A CHALLENGE...A HERO NAMED *MATTHEW KEE*... *LOCKSMITH!*

...I'M NOT AFRAID! THAT KILLER WILL NEVER GET INTO *THIS* HOUSE!

...I'VE DESIGNED AND BUILT *SPECIAL LOCKS*... *COMBINATION LOCKS*... *TIME LOCKS*... AND I'VE INSTALLED THEM HERE IN MY HOME!

I *DARE* THAT MURDERER TO TRY TO GET IN *MY* HOUSE!

A HERO STANDING FACE TO FACE WITH DEATH! AND NEXT MORNING MATTHEW KEE IS...A *DEAD* HERO...

DAILY MAIL

KEE KILLED!

LOCKSMITH VICTIM OF LOCKED-ROOM

HERO FOUND DEAD! ALL EXITS LOCKED FROM THE INSIDE!

M. KEE

GEORGE! WHAT HAPPENED TO ALL THE LOCKS ON THE DOOR?

...*THEY'RE* NOT GOING TO DO US ANY GOOD! I TRADED THEM IN FOR A *REVOLVER!*

BOY! HAVE YOU SEEN THE LATEST ABOUT THE LOCKED-ROOM KILLER?

YEH! AIN'T IT AWFUL? ME AN' THE WIFE ARE A-SCARED TO STAY HOME NIGHTS!

THE COPS DON'T KNOW IF THEY'RE COMIN' OR GOIN'!

YOU OUGHTA SEE MY OFFICE! EVERYBODY'S TOO AFRAID TO SLEEP AT *NIGHT*, SO WE ALL SNOOZE ALL DAY AT WORK! *NOTHIN'* GETS DONE!

FOR ONCE IN YOUR LIFE YOU'RE LUCKY THAT YOU'RE *MARRIED*! I LIVE *ALL ALONE*!

YEH! WELL, IT CAN'T LAST *FOREVER*! THE COPS WILL CATCH UP WITH TH' KILLER!

?

?

HO HA HA HA HO HO HA HA! HA! HO HA HA HA! HA! HO HA HA HO HA

HA! HA! WHAT A LAUGH! THE COPS WILL *NEVER* GET *ME!* AND EVEN IF THEY DO, THEY'LL HAVE TO *PROVE* HOW I GOT *IN* AND *OUT* OF THOSE LOCKED ROOMS!

AHH-HRR! THE WHOLE THING IS *COCKEYED!* I SIT HERE ALL DAY, DRINKING AWAY THE MONEY I'VE *MURDERED* FOR!

IT'S ALL WRONG! I'M A *WRITER*, NOT A *KILLER!* IT'S ALL WRONG! *AHHR!* BETTER GO HOME...GET SOME SLEEP...

6

THE NEXT NIGHT...
WHOOSH! I FEEL AWFUL! BETTER DRINK SOME BLACK COFFEE!

...MUST'VE SLEPT ALL DAY! SAY, WHAT'S THAT OVER THERE UNDER THE DOOR? LOOKS LIKE AN ENVELOPE...

WHY...IT'S MY STORY! SENT BACK FROM THE HARNOLD PUBLISHING HOUSE! BUT... IT'S BEEN OPENED THIS TIME! THEY READ IT!

? SAY, THAT'S NOT GOOD! WHOEVER READ MY STORY AT HARNOLD'S KNOWS I'M THE LOCKED-ROOM KILLER!

WAIT A MINUTE... I'M ALL CONFUSED!

I MUST HAVE MAILED THIS STORY TO HARNOLD'S WHILE I WAS DRUNK! WHOEVER OPENED AND READ MY STORY MUST HAVE CONNECTED THE NEWSPAPER HEADLINES WITH ME...

...YET THIS RETURN LETTER TO ME IS POSTMARKED SEVERAL DAYS AGO! I DON'T GET IT AT ALL!

EH? SAY... WHAT'S THIS? YESTERDAY'S PAPER!

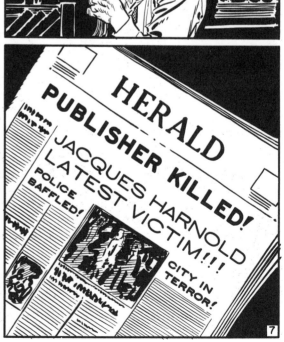
HERALD
PUBLISHER KILLED!
JACQUES HARNOLD LATEST VICTIM!!!
POLICE BAFFLED!
CITY IN TERROR!

7

GREAT SCOTT! THIS EXPLAINS EVERYTHING! HARNOLD WAS MURDERED THE DAY BEFORE YESTERDAY... A LOCKED-ROOM VICTIM! BUT I DIDN'T KILL HIM!

IT'S SIMPLE NOW! WHOEVER READ MY STORY IS HARNOLD'S MURDERER! THAT'S WHY THE POLICE WEREN'T TOLD ABOUT ME!

HARNOLD'S MURDERER COULDN'T TELL THE POLICE THAT I'M THE REAL LOCKED-ROOM KILLER WITHOUT ENDANGERING HIMSELF!

...BUT NOW HE KNOWS WHO I AM! AND THAT'S DANGEROUS FOR ME! THEY MIGHT BE ABLE TO PIN HARNOLD'S DEATH ON ME TOO, IN SOME WAY... IF THE COPS FOUND OUT ABOUT MY STORY...

THEY'D NEVER BELIEVE ANYTHING I SAY...HMM...COME TO THINK OF IT, I'M JUST AS DANGEROUS TO HARNOLD'S MURDERER... AS HE IS TO ME! HMM...

I'D BETTER GET RID OF HIM, JUST TO BE SAFE!! THAT IS...

...THAT IS, IF HE DOESN'T GET THE SAME IDEA! BLAZES! HE CAN COMMIT A LOCKED-ROOM MURDER TOO! HE MIGHT BE PLANNING TO KILL ME RIGHT NOW!

EXACTLY!

-THE END-

THE VAULT OF HORROR!

HEH, HEH! IT'S SO NICE TO SEE YOUR EAGER FACES *LEERING* AT ME AGAIN, IN *EXPECTATION!* WELL, YOU WON'T BE DISAPPOINTED, I ASSURE YOU! FROM MY PRIVATE COLLECTION OF *HAIR-RAISERS*, I'VE SELECTED *THIS* STORY FOR YOUR...HEH...*ENJOYMENT!* I CALL IT...

VOODOO DEATH!

HEH! EVER READ *TRAVEL FOLDERS*? YOU KNOW...THOSE PAMPHLETS THAT TELL ABOUT ALL THE GLORIOUS WONDERS AND BEAUTIES OF THE WEST INDIES! PALM TREES... MOONLIGHT ON THE OCEAN...ETC....ETC.! *HEH! HEH! HEH!* ...STRANGE, ISN'T IT, THAT THEY NEVER MENTION *OTHER* INTERESTING SIGHTS, SIGHTS THAT TOURISTS ARE *NOT* TO SEE? SIGHTS LIKE... A *VOODOO RITUAL*?

HURRY UP, JAY...WE'RE ALMOST THERE!

CONFOUND IT, BILL! I DON'T LIKE THIS ONE BIT! ALMOST WISH WE'D NEVER COME TO *HAITI!*

HAITI!...ISLAND OF BEAUTY...SERENITY! HAITI!...ISLAND OF LEGENDS...MYSTERY!

JAY! THERE! LOOK! WE'RE JUST IN TIME!

FOR PETE'S SAKE, BILL, SHUT UP... OR THEY'LL HEAR US!

BILL, LET'S GET OUT OF HERE! IF THOSE NATIVES CATCH US WATCHING THEIR RITUAL, THEY'LL...

I KNOW! I KNOW! KEEP QUIET, WILL YOU?

WHAT ARE THEY DOING?

A NATIVE WAS SHOT TO DEATH IN TOWN TODAY! THEY'RE WORKING OVER HIM NOW!

As THEY WATCH THE DANCERS' FRENZY, THE HIGH PRIESTESS PLACES A DOLL BESIDE THE STILL FORM OF THE CORPSE...

THE *VOODOO DRUMS* BEAT LOUDER AND THE HIGH PRIESTESS BENDS OVER THE BODY! THE NATIVES CLOSE IN AROUND HER, BLOCKING HER FROM VIEW...

WHAT'S SHE DOING?

I DON'T KNOW! I CAN'T SEE HER!

MINUTES LATER, THE CHANTING, SCREAMING NATIVES WITHDRAW...LEAVING THE PRIESTESS STANDING OVER THE BODY AND THE DOLL! NOW THERE IS AN EXPECTANT SILENCE...

...AND THEN, THE DEAD NATIVE *STIRS!* HIS EYES OPEN, GLASSY AND EMPTY... *AND HE RISES!* THE DOLL STANDS UPRIGHT...*AND THEN DARTS AWAY INTO THE JUNGLE!*

BILL! THE DOLL! THE... THE DEAD MAN! HE'S ALIVE!! HE...THE...

SHUT UP, YOU X@!!$?@ FOOL! THEY'LL HEAR YOU!

2

IT'S TOO LATE! THEY'VE SEEN US! **RUN!**

BILL! THEY'VE CAUGHT ME! HELP! BILL! COME BACK! DON'T LEAVE ME!

HEH! BILL RACES MADLY BACK TO THE HOTEL AND ANXIOUSLY PACES THE FLOOR IN TERROR! AS DAWN BREAKS, AND JAY FAILS TO APPEAR, HE BEGINS FRAN- TICALLY TO PACK HIS VALISE! SUD- DENLY, THE DOOR OPENS...

JAY!

JAY! THANK HEAVEN YOU'RE OKAY! I...I WAS WORRIED SICK OVER YOU! BUT YOU'RE ALL RIGHT...YOU ESCAPED!

...VOODOO DOLL... ZOMBIE...

YOU'RE EXHAUSTED! BUT A GOOD NIGHT'S REST WILL FIX YOU UP! YOU LIE DOWN... AS SOON AS I FINISH PACKING OUR THINGS, WE'RE LEAVING THIS ISLAND! WE'RE GOING HOME!

THE TWO FRIENDS LEAVE FOR NEW YORK ON THE NEXT BOAT. TWO DAYS OF COMPLETE REST HAVE APPARENTLY SETTLED JAY'S NERVES ...AND THE FRIGHTFUL ORDEAL IN HAITI IS ALMOST FORGOTTEN BY THEM BOTH! BUT ONE NIGHT WHEN BILL ENTERS HIS STATEROOM...

WHA..? WHAT'S THAT ON MY BUNK??

A...A VOODOO DOLL!

THE NATIVES SENT A DOLL AFTER ME! IT'S STARTING TO MOVE! GOT TO GET RID OF IT!...THE PORTHOLE!

JAY! JAY!

COME HERE, QUICK!

BILL! WHAT'S THE MATTER?!

JAY! A *VOODOO DOLL!*... ON MY BUNK! IT...IT *MOVED!*

VOODOO DOLL? BILL, ARE YOU CERTAIN?

YES! YES! I THREW IT OUT THE PORTHOLE! THE NATIVES SENT IT AFTER ME! IT...*IT HAD A LONG NEEDLE IN ITS HANDS!*

YOU MUST HAVE BEEN SEEING THINGS, BILL! YOUR EYES ARE PLAYING TRICKS!

YOU...YOU THINK SO? MAYBE...MAYBE YOU'RE RIGHT! IT CERTAINLY IS *FANTASTIC* ENOUGH...

BILL IS COMPLETELY UNNERVED...BUT BY THE TIME THEY REACH NEW YORK, HE IS CERTAIN THE WICKED *VOODOO DOLL* HAS BEEN DESTROYED! HEH, HEH! ONE NIGHT THERE IS A KNOCK ON THE DOOR OF THE APARTMENT HE SHARES WITH JAY...

YES?

WHY...THAT'S ODD! NO ONE HERE... JUST A PACKAGE!

4

...STRANGE...NO RETURN ADDRESS...NO POSTAGE...WONDER WHAT'S IN IT...

CURIOUS, BILL HASTILY RIPS THE PACKAGE OPEN! AND THEN HIS HANDS TREMBLE...HIS MOUTH DROPS WIDE AS HE STARES AT THE CONTENTS...

THE...THE VOODOO DOLL!

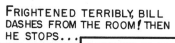

FRIGHTENED TERRIBLY, BILL DASHES FROM THE ROOM! THEN HE STOPS...

I THREW IT IN THE FIRE! THE FLAMES WILL DESTROY IT! BUT...MAYBE...

...IT CAME BACK WHEN I THREW IT OUT THE PORTHOLE! IT CAN MOVE! IT MIGHT GET AWAY! I...I'D BETTER GO BACK...BETTER MAKE SURE!

...THERE'S THE BOX...THE PACKAGE...BUT WHERE'S THE DOLL?

IT'S GONE!

GONE! SOMEWHERE IN THIS ROOM! HIDING...WAITING TO POUNCE ON ME! WAITING TO STAB ME WITH THAT...THAT NEEDLE! HELP! HELP!

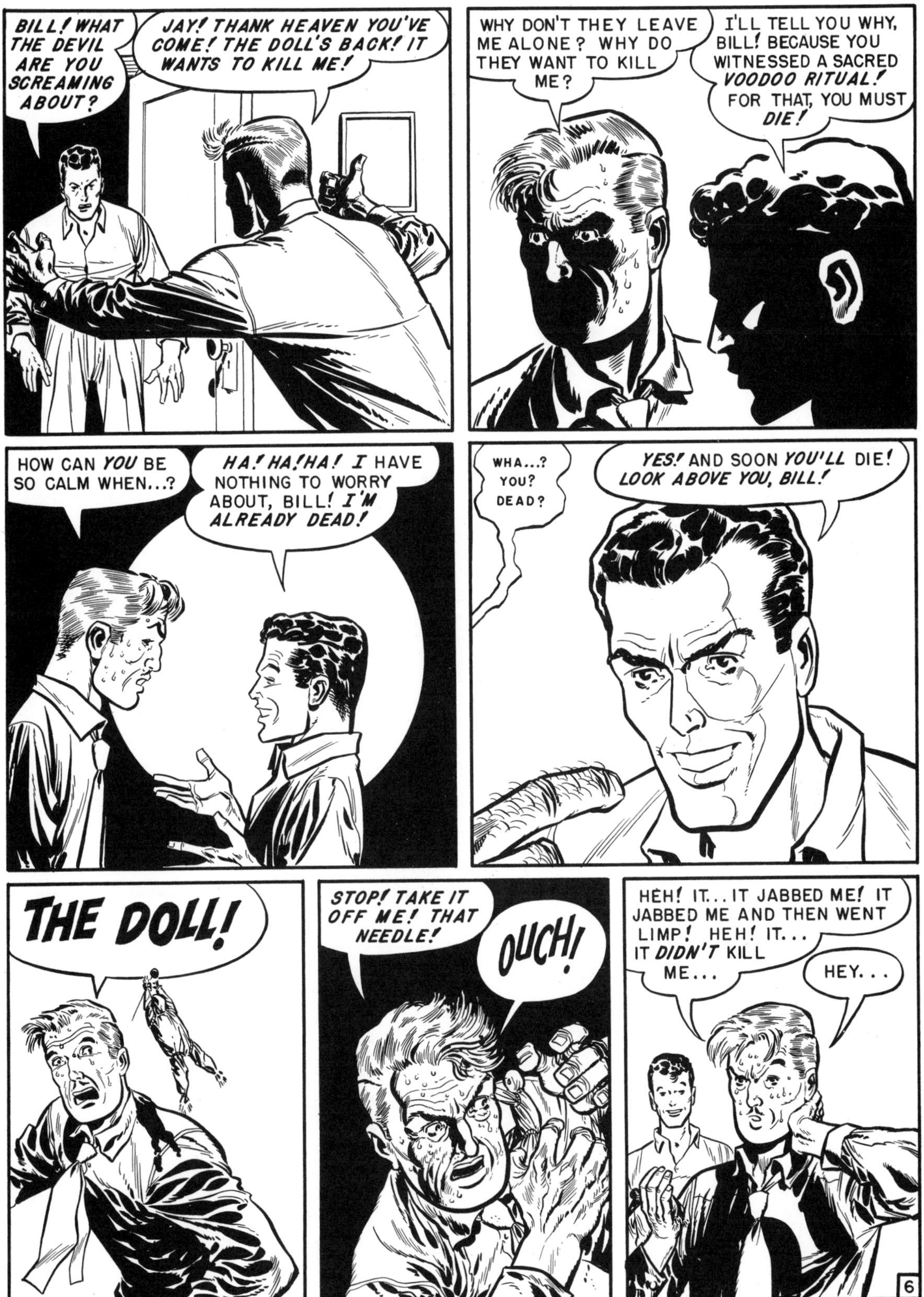
BILL! WHAT THE DEVIL ARE YOU SCREAMING ABOUT?
JAY! THANK HEAVEN YOU'VE COME! THE DOLL'S BACK! IT WANTS TO KILL ME!
WHY DON'T THEY LEAVE ME ALONE? WHY DO THEY WANT TO KILL ME?
I'LL TELL YOU WHY, BILL! BECAUSE YOU WITNESSED A SACRED VOODOO RITUAL! FOR THAT, YOU MUST DIE!
HOW CAN YOU BE SO CALM WHEN...?
HA! HA!HA! I HAVE NOTHING TO WORRY ABOUT, BILL! I'M ALREADY DEAD!
WHA...? YOU? DEAD?
YES! AND SOON YOU'LL DIE! LOOK ABOVE YOU, BILL!
THE DOLL!
STOP! TAKE IT OFF ME! THAT NEEDLE!
OUCH!
HEH! IT... IT JABBED ME! IT JABBED ME AND THEN WENT LIMP! HEH! IT... IT DIDN'T KILL ME...
HEY...
6

MY...MY *NECK!* GETTING NUMB... *HURTS!*

YES! THE NEEDLE WAS *POISONED!* SOON YOUR WHOLE *BODY* WILL *HURT!* THEN YOU'LL BE *DEAD*...AS *I* AM DEAD!

YES, I'M *DEAD!* THE NATIVES *KILLED* ME THAT NIGHT! THEY KILLED ME AND BROUGHT ME BACK TO *LIFE*...LIKE THEY DID TO THAT DEAD NATIVE! THEY *SENT* ME TO YOU WITH THAT *VOODOO DOLL* TO PUNISH *YOU!* THE DOLL HAS DONE ITS JOB!.. AND WHEN YOU DIE *I* WILL CEASE TO *EXIST* ALSO! *I'M A ZOMBIE!*

YOU'RE DEAD! AND I'LL BE DEAD (GASP) IN A MOMENT! (GASP) THIS DOLL! IT... IT KILLED ME! THIS WICKED, VICIOUS VOODOO DOLL!

R-RI-I-P

I'LL DESTROY IT!... RIP IT TO SHREDS! RIP IT! (GASP) *TEAR IT!—?*

WHA... WHAT'S THIS?

BILL'S RAGE SUDDENLY CEASES! A SCREAM STRANGLES IN HIS THROAT AS HE STARES DOWN AT WHAT HIS HAND HOLDS...

GOOD LORD! IT'S A... HEART! A HUMAN HEART!

YES, BILL! THAT'S HOW THEY GAVE IT *LIFE!* THEY GAVE THE DOLL A HEART!

MY HEART!

—THE END—

HEH! HEH! HEH! SUCH JOY! NOW WASN'T THAT *HEART-RENDING?* OF COURSE, JAY *COULD* HAVE TOLD BILL WHAT HAD HAPPENED, BUT I GUESS HE JUST *DIDN'T HAVE THE HEART!* WELL, BILL GOT THE *POINT*, HEH! HEH...IN THE *CUTTING* CLIMAX TO THIS *THROBBING* TALE! I HOPE I'LL BE SEEING YOU IN MY *OWN* MAGAZINE, *THE VAULT OF HORROR!* UNTIL THEN, FIENDS... BE OF *STOUT HEART*... HEH, HEH, HEH!

THE VAULT OF HORROR!

WELL, WELL, WELL... THREE HOLES IN THE GROUND AND ALL THAT SORT OF ROT! I HAVE A *DILLY* OF A STORY FOR YOU THIS TIME, FRIENDS, FULL OF PASSION, GRIEF... AND *HATE!* HEH, HEH! SO RELAX FOR A WHILE... *IF YOU DARE*...AND READ THE TALE I CALL...

SINK-HOLE!

SIX MONTHS, SHE REFLECTED. SIX LONG, WEARY MONTHS...THE LONGEST, MOST MISERABLE MONTHS OF HER LIFE! SHE WAS LOOKING OUT THE WINDOW OF THE RAMSHACKLE FARM-HOUSE AT A CLOUD OF DUST FAR DOWN THE ROAD, AND SHE LET HER THOUGHTS DRIFT BACK... BACK TO THE BEGINNING...

TWO YEARS AGO SHE HAD JOINED A 'LONELY-HEARTS PEN-PALS CLUB! THAT WAS WHERE (BY MAIL) SHE HAD MET ALDOUS BARSTOW...

OH, HE SENT A PICTURE THIS TIME! HE'S NICE LOOKING! AND HIS LETTERS SOUND SO WARM...SO TENDER!

A YEAR OF CORRESPONDENCE HAD FOLLOWED. THE SPELL OF LONELINESS HAD BEEN BROKEN BY THE LETTERS FROM YOUNG, SYMPATHETIC ALDOUS.

HEAVENS! HE WANTS ME TO MARRY HIM AND LIVE ON HIS FARM...HIS BEAU-TIFUL, COUNTRY FARM!

SHE HAD ACCEPTED HAPPILY, AND SEVERAL DAYS LATER HAD STEPPED FROM THE TRAIN... FACE TO FACE WITH ALDOUS!

YOU'RE ALDOUS? BUT THE PICTURE YOU SENT...I MEAN, IN THE PICTURE YOU...YOU LOOK...

YOUNGER? WHY, SURE! THAT SNAPSHOT WAS TAKEN MORE'N FIFTEEN YEARS AGO! I WAS GOING TO HAVE A MORE RECENT ONE MADE, BUT THEY COST MONEY!

...OF COURSE...

IT HADN'T REALLY MATTERED TO HER THEN, SHE REMEMBERED. ALTHOUGH HE WAS NO LONGER YOUNG, SHE HAD STIFLED HER MISGIVINGS AS THEY BOUNCED ALONG THE DUSTY ROAD TO THE FARM...

THE 'BEAUTIFUL COUNTRY FARM' TURNED OUT TO BE A GROUP OF DILAPIDATED BUILDINGS SQUATTING ON THE PARCHED, SUNBAKED EARTH. IT WAS A TERRIFIC SHOCK TO HER. SHE COULD HARDLY STEP FROM THE FLIVVER...

IT WASN'T ONLY THE LOOK OF THE PLACE, IT WAS THE FEEL OF IT! SHE STARED DAZEDLY AT THE DINGY, CLAPBOARD FRAME OF HER NEW HOME AND SHUDDERED. IT FELT EMPTY! IT SEEMED LIKE A PLACE WHERE NO ONE LIVED!

ALDOUS! IT... IT'S...LOVELY!

...PREACHER'S WAITING INSIDE! CEREMONY SHOULD NOT TAKE MORE'N A FEW MIN-UTES! YOU BRING THE BAGS!

2

AND SO THEY HAD BEEN MARRIED! SHE HAD SENSED IT WOULDN'T WORK OUT, AND HAD BEEN RIGHT! NOW, SIX MONTHS LATER, SHE WATCHED THE SMALL DUST CLOUD MOVE CLOSER... AND TRIED TO HOLD BACK HER TEARS...

...PROBABLY MR. FARNSWORTH, THE GOVERNMENT HEALTH INSPECTOR...

...OLD FUDDY-DUDDY FARNSWORTH! SHE DISLIKED THE PRYING OLD FOOL, BUT HE WAS SOMEONE TO TALK TO! AS THE CAR DREW NEARER, SHE SAW THAT IT *WASN'T* FARNSWORTH! SHE HURRIED OUTSIDE AS THE CAR PULLED INTO THE YARD...

'MORNING! I'M *RICK HUDSON*, THE NEW HEALTH INSPECTOR! I'M TAKING OVER MR. FARNSWORTH'S JOB! ARE YOU MRS. BARSTOW?

WHY...WHY, YES! I'M MRS. BARSTOW! I'M *VERY* GLAD TO MEET YOU, MR. HUDSON. COME! I'LL... I'LL SHOW YOU AROUND...

SHE COULDN'T HAVE BEEN MORE PLEASANTLY SURPRISED! HER FACE FLUSHED...HER BODY TINGLED AT THE NEARNESS OF HIM AS HE CHECKED THE FARM'S SANITARY CONDITIONS...

I...I HOPE EVERYTHING IS ALL RIGHT, MR. HUDSON!

EVERYTHING'S FINE, MRS. BARSTOW!

SHE LIKED THIS MAN WHO HAD SUDDENLY ENLIVENED HER DRAB LIFE. SHE LIKED HIM MORE THAN WAS GOOD FOR A MARRIED GIRL...

WOULDN'T YOU RATHER CALL ME... *SHIRLEY?*

I GUESS SO! YOU CAN CALL ME RICK!

FINALLY HE HAD TO LEAVE, AND SHE FOUND HERSELF TRYING DESPERATELY TO KEEP HIM FROM GOING...

...BUT WOULDN'T YOU LIKE TO HAVE SOME COFFEE? I...

MAYBE NEXT TIME, SHIRLEY! SO LONG!

SHE STOOD THERE LONG AFTER THE CAR HAD DISAPPEARED... UNTIL THE NOISY SPUTTERINGS OF ALDOUS' TRACTOR BURST HER THOUGHTS LIKE A PIN TOUCHED TO A BALLOON...

HEAVENS! ALDOUS WILL WANT HIS LUNCH! I DIDN'T REALIZE IT WAS SO LATE!

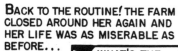

BACK TO THE ROUTINE! THE FARM CLOSED AROUND HER AGAIN AND HER LIFE WAS AS MISERABLE AS BEFORE...

ALDOUS, I...I'D LIKE TO HAVE A NEW DRESS... *PLEASE*...

WHAT'S THE MATTER WITH THE ONE YOU GOT ON?

WHY... NOTHING! I JUST THOUGHT...

YOU THOUGHT WRONG! THINK I'M *MADE* OF MONEY? WHEN YOU *NEED* A DRESS, YOU'LL GET ONE! NOT BEFORE!

SHE FOUGHT TO CONTROL A FLOOD OF TEARS, BUT IT WAS IMPOSSIBLE...

THE MEAN, STINGY, OLD SKINFLINT! I HATE HIM! (SOB) *HATE* HIM!

HE NEVER WANTED A *WIFE!* HE ONLY WANTED SOMEONE TO COOK, TO SEW, TO *SLAVE* FOR HIM! IT WAS CHEAPER FOR HIM TO MARRY ME THAN TO PAY A HOUSEKEEPER! (SOB!)

...I WISH I COULD GO AWAY...*LEAVE* THIS PLACE! BUT I CAN'T! I HAVE NO MONEY...CLOTHES! (SOB) AND WHERE COULD I GO? WHAT WOULD I DO? I'LL *NEVER* BE ABLE TO FREE MYSELF FROM HIM!

THE ONLY THING THAT MADE LIFE BEARABLE FOR HER IN THE MONTHS THAT FOLLOWED, WERE RICK'S VISITS. SHE WAS IN LOVE WITH HIM...

RICK...YOU'VE FINISHED INSPECTING THE FARM. CAN'T...CAN'T YOU STAY A WHILE? MUST YOU GO?

I'M SURPRISED AT YOU, SHIRLEY! WHAT WOULD ALDOUS SAY IF HE HEARD YOU TALK LIKE THAT?

ALDOUS! THAT WAS THE TROUBLE! SHE WAS CERTAIN RICK CARED FOR HER, AND THAT THE ONLY THING THAT KEPT HIM FROM SHOWING IT...WAS THE FACT THAT SHE WAS *MARRIED!*

ALDOUS! HOW I *DETEST* HIM! HE'S RUINED MY LIFE! I WISH HE'D *DIE!*

4

AT THAT MOMENT ALDOUS CAME IN FROM THE FIELDS...

⊙⌐!!⨯⨯⌐! NEARLY GOT MYSELF *KILLED!* THOSE DANGED *SINK HOLES!*

? SINK HOLES? WHAT'S A *SINK HOLE?*

THEY'RE CAUSED BY UNDER-GROUND RIVERS! THE RIVER KEEPS EATIN' AWAY THE SOIL UNTIL THE TOP GROUND JUST CAVES IN!

OH!

...I WAS DRIVIN' THE TRACTOR CROSS THE FIELD TO THE HOUSE WHEN THE GROUND JUST OPENED UP NOT TEN FEET IN FRONT OF ME!...STOPPED JUST IN TIME!

OH...

DANGED SINK HOLES! *PRACTICALLY BOTTOMLESS!* IF I'D FALLEN IN THERE, YOU'D *NEVER* HAVE FOUND ME!

OH?

THE ENTIRE PLAN STRUCK HER WITH SHOCKING FORCE! HERE WAS HER ONE AND ONLY CHANCE FOR FREEDOM... FOR HAPPINESS! AND SHE WAS IN NO MOOD TO LET IT SLIP BY...

KLANG!

SHE DRAGGED THE UNCONSCIOUS ALDOUS FROM THE HOUSE...AND WITH GREAT EFFORT, LIFTED HIM ONTO THE TRACTOR. OVERHEAD, THE DARK SKY RUMBLED OMINOUSLY AS IF IN REPROACH...

HAVE TO HURRY! HE... HE'LL WAKE UP... SOON! (GASP!)

INTERCONTINENTAL DIESEL

SILENTLY, SHE THANKED ALDOUS FOR HAVING MADE HER LEARN TO WORK THE TRACTOR! NOW, WHEN HER FUTURE...HER LIFE... DEPENDED ON IT, SHE WAS ABLE TO SEND THE MACHINE LURCHING ACROSS THE FIELDS...

5

DROPLETS OF RAIN PLUNGED FROM THE SKY INTO THE EARTH! THE WIND ROSE, WHIPPING HER HAIR! SHE REACHED THE SINK HOLE...

...IT'S BIG! *BIG!* PLENTY BIG ENOUGH FOR THE TRACTOR, TOO!

SHE RACED BACK TO THE TRACTOR AND PROPPED ALDOUS IN ITS SEAT! FRANTICALLY, SHE HEADED THE TRACTOR TOWARD THE GAPING HOLE, WAITED... *AND THEN LEAPED CLEAR!*

SPRAWLED ON THE GROUND, SHE WATCHED SPELLBOUND AS THE TRACTOR TEETERED ON THE EDGE OF THE PIT... AND THEN TOPPLED INTO OBLIVION...

THERE WAS AN INVESTIGATION BUT IT DISCLOSED NOTHING...

YOU'LL NEVER FIND A BODY DOWN *THERE!* PROBABLY CARRIED AWAY BY THAT UNDERGROUND RIVER! NO SIGN OF THE TRACTOR, EITHER!

...AND THEN THERE WAS THE INQUEST...

...BECAUSE THE BODY OF THE DECEASED HAS NOT BEEN FOUND, THE VERDICT IS 'DEATH BY ACCIDENT, DUE TO THE CAUSES OF NATURE!'

...AND THEN SHE WAS FREE! SHE KNEW RICK WOULD SOON COME TO HER, AND SHE STROLLED ABOUT THE FARM WHILE SHE WAITED. IT WAS THE SAME UGLY, EMPTY-FEELING FARM... STILL THE PLACE WHERE, IT SEEMED, NO ONE LIVED!

RICK CAME... AND SHIRLEY RAN HAPPILY TO HIM...

I... I HEARD ABOUT ALDOUS, SHIRLEY! I'M SORRY!

DON'T BE SORRY, RICK, BE *GLAD!* HE WAS MEAN... *CRUEL!* HE STOOD BETWEEN US, BUT NOW WE'RE FREE, RICK! *FREE!*

WE DON'T HAVE TO BE AFRAID TO SHOW OUR FEELINGS ANYMORE, RICK DARLING! TELL ME! TELL ME ALL THE THINGS YOU'VE BEEN WANTING TO TELL ME!

WHAT ARE YOU TALKING ABOUT? I CAME TO SAY "GOOD-BYE"!

"GOOD-BYE?"

SURE! JOE FARNSWORTH'S COMING BACK TO TAKE OVER MY JOB! I'M BEING SENT TO ANOTHER STATE!

ANOTHER STATE?! YOU'LL... YOU'LL TAKE ME WITH YOU, WON'T YOU, RICK? FOR HEAVEN'S SAKE, DON'T LEAVE ME HERE! SAY YOU'LL TAKE ME WITH YOU!

ARE YOU KIDDING?

LOOK, SHIRLEY...YOU'RE A NICE KID, BUT I CAN'T TAKE YOU WITH ME! I'VE BEEN HAPPILY MARRIED FOR YEARS! I GOT A WIFE AND TWO KIDS!

RICK!

RICK...

SHE NEVER SAW OR HEARD FROM RICK AGAIN. SHE REMAINED, LASHED TO THE DESOLATE FARM, WHILE THE WEEKS PASSED INTO MONTHS... AND ONE DAY, AS SHE WENT TO DRAW WATER FROM THE WELL...

...CHILLY OUT HERE... BETTER PULL THE BUCKET UP AND HURRY INSIDE!

SHE WOUND THE HANDLE, DRAWING THE BUCKET UPWARD! ONCE...TWICE... THEN, SUDDENLY IT STOPPED!

UNGH! WON'T COME UP ANY FURTHER! SOMETHING... SOMETHING'S HOLDING IT BACK!

7

SHE PITTED ALL HER STRENGTH TO THE TASK OF RAISING THE BUCKET, BUT IT WAS NO USE! THE HANDLE WAS WRENCHED FROM HER GRIP!

THE BUCKET'S GOING *DOWN!* SOMETHING'S PULLING IT BACK *DOWN!*

THE ROPE UNCOILED TO ITS FULL LENGTH, AND THEN IT SNAPPED TAUT! IT SWAYED AND JERKED...

IT'S...IT'S AS IF SOMETHING... IS *CLIMBING UP!*

ROOTED TO THE SPOT, SHE STARED IN HORROR AS FIRST ONE HAND SLID OVER THE WELL'S WALL...AND THEN ANOTHER...

SHE WAS PETRIFIED! THE INCREDULOUSLY HORRIBLE THING GRASPED HER ARM WITH A SLIMY, MOLTED HAND AND PULLED HER CLOSE TO ITS SOAKING BODY! SHE FOUGHT HYSTERICALLY...BUT THE SLOPPING, MAGGOT-COVERED LIMBS LOCKED HER IN A DEATH GRIP...AND DRAGGED HER INTO THE DEPTHS!

THE HOLLOW ECHOES OF HER SCREAMS CEASED ABRUPTLY, AND A CLOAK OF UTTER SILENCE SEEMED TO SETTLE OVER THE EMPTY FARM! NOW IT TRULY WAS...A PLACE WHERE NO ONE LIVED!

-THE END-

HEH! HEH! HEH! *WELL*-DONE! *WELL*-DONE! IF SHIRLEY HADN'T GONE TO THE WELL, SHE MIGHT NOT HAVE *KICKED THE BUCKET!* OF COURSE, YOU REALIZE NOW THAT THE UNDERGROUND RIVER FROM THE SINK HOLE WAS THE WATER THAT FED THE WELL! HEH! I'LL BET ALDOUS EXPERIENCED A *SINKING* FEELING WHEN HE WENT TO HIS DEATH! OH, WELL... AS THE SAYING GOES,"HOW YA GONNA KEEP 'EM DOWN ON THE FARM AFTER THEY'VE SEEN DEAD ALDOUS?" *HEH! HEH! HEH!*

THE SEWER!

AH! THERE WAS HEADROOM HERE...ROOM FOR HIM TO STAND UPRIGHT, TO REST! HE SLUMPED AGAINST THE SLIME-COVERED WALL, CLOSED HIS EYES AND GULPED GREAT MASSES OF AIR. A SMILE FLICKED ACROSS HIS FACE, FOR HE KNEW THINGS WOULD BE ALL RIGHT NOW! ALL HE HAD TO DO WAS WAIT FOR THE WATER TO SUBSIDE AND THEN HE COULD ESCAPE!

NOW WAS THE TIME TO THINK, TO PLAN HIS NEXT MOVE... AND TO DO THAT HE HAD TO REACH BACK THROUGH HIS JUMBLED THOUGHTS TO THE BEGINNING OF THE WHOLE COCKEYED EPISODE...

IT BEGAN AT A PARTY GIVEN BY JOHN AND IRENE GOLDEN. HE WELL REMEMBERED DANCING WITH HER...

WHAT'S BOTHERING YOU, IRENE?

THE USUAL THING, HARRY!

THE "USUAL THING" HAD BEEN HER HUSBAND, MATINEE IDOL JOHN GOLDEN, SURROUNDED BY LOVELY YOUNG FEMALES...

MR. GOLDEN, I JUST THINK YOU'RE SO WONDERFUL!

Y'DO, EH? HA! SO DO I! HA! HA! WHASH YOUR NAME, SWEETHEART?

I HATE HIM WHEN HE'S LIKE THAT, HARRY! YOU'RE HIS BUSINESS MANAGER! YOU MADE HIM THE SUCCESS HE IS TODAY!

WE BOTH KNOW THAT, BUT... SAY, HAVEN'T YOU HAD ENOUGH TO DRINK TONIGHT?

NOT YET, I HAVEN'T! OH, HARRY, I COULD KILL HIM WHEN HE MAKES SUCH A... A FOOL OF HIMSELF! IF JOHN WERE ONLY MORE TENDER TO ME! MORE... MORE CONSIDERATE! MORE LIKE... OH, I DON'T KNOW!

MORE LIKE ME, YOU MEAN?

HARRY HAD HEARD HER TALK LIKE THAT OFTEN! BUT THAT NIGHT THERE WAS SOMETHING IN HER VOICE THAT WAS NEVER THERE BEFORE, AND IT PLEASED HIM GREATLY... FOR HARRY WAS DESPERATELY IN LOVE WITH IRENE GOLDEN!

...MORE LIKE YOU, HARRY? WHY, NOW THAT YOU MENTION IT... I GUESS THAT'S JUST WHAT I MEAN!

THAT'S WHAT I THOUGHT YOU MEANT! COME HERE...

OH, HARRY... I... I... THINK I'M IN LOVE WITH YOU...

IRENE...

2

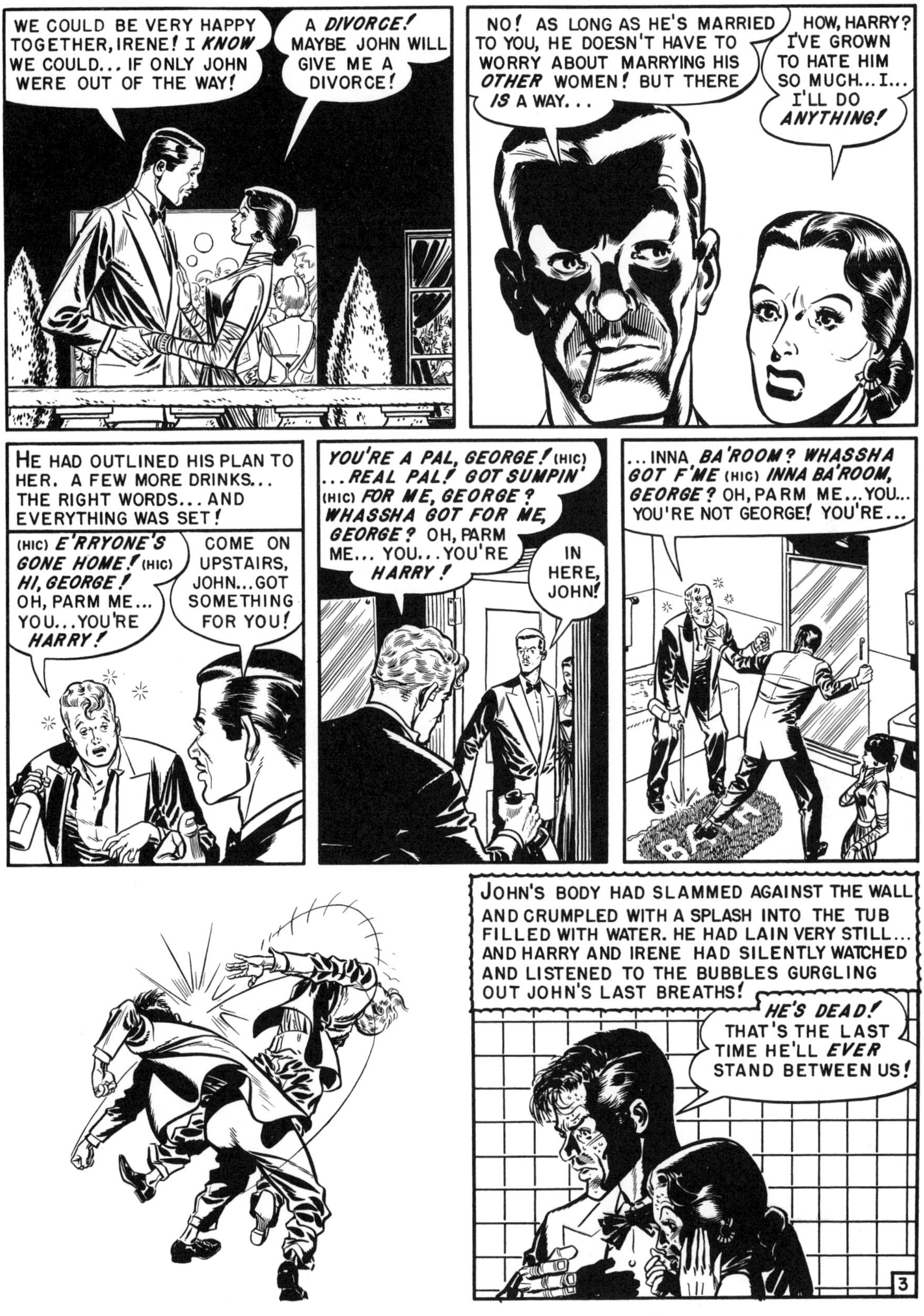
WE COULD BE VERY HAPPY TOGETHER, IRENE! I KNOW WE COULD... IF ONLY JOHN WERE OUT OF THE WAY!
A DIVORCE! MAYBE JOHN WILL GIVE ME A DIVORCE!
NO! AS LONG AS HE'S MARRIED TO YOU, HE DOESN'T HAVE TO WORRY ABOUT MARRYING HIS OTHER WOMEN! BUT THERE IS A WAY...
HOW, HARRY? I'VE GROWN TO HATE HIM SO MUCH... I... I'LL DO ANYTHING!
HE HAD OUTLINED HIS PLAN TO HER. A FEW MORE DRINKS... THE RIGHT WORDS... AND EVERYTHING WAS SET!
(HIC) E'RRYONE'S GONE HOME! (HIC) HI, GEORGE! OH, PARM ME... YOU... YOU'RE HARRY!
COME ON UPSTAIRS, JOHN... GOT SOMETHING FOR YOU!
YOU'RE A PAL, GEORGE! (HIC) ...REAL PAL! GOT SUMPIN' (HIC) FOR ME, GEORGE? WHASSHA GOT FOR ME, GEORGE? OH, PARM ME... YOU... YOU'RE HARRY!
IN HERE, JOHN!
...INNA BA'ROOM? WHASSHA GOT F'ME (HIC) INNA BA'ROOM, GEORGE? OH, PARM ME... YOU... YOU'RE NOT GEORGE! YOU'RE...
JOHN'S BODY HAD SLAMMED AGAINST THE WALL AND CRUMPLED WITH A SPLASH INTO THE TUB FILLED WITH WATER. HE HAD LAIN VERY STILL... AND HARRY AND IRENE HAD SILENTLY WATCHED AND LISTENED TO THE BUBBLES GURGLING OUT JOHN'S LAST BREATHS!
HE'S DEAD! THAT'S THE LAST TIME HE'LL EVER STAND BETWEEN US!
3

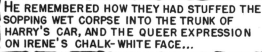

He remembered how they had stuffed the sopping wet corpse into the trunk of Harry's car, and the queer expression on Irene's chalk-white face...

WHAT...WHAT WILL WE DO WITH HIM?

I...I DON'T KNOW! THROW HIM DOWN A SEWER, I GUESS! YEAH, *THAT'S* IT! *A SEWER!*

They had found a sewer in a deserted section, and Harry had pried it open... it was then that the rain had begun...

HURRY UP...DON'T WANT TO BE SEEN!

DON'T...DON'T HURT HIM...

HURT HIM? ...CAN'T HURT HIM NOW! HE'S DEAD!

DEAD?

DEAD?!

GOOD GOD, HE'S DEAD! WE'VE MURDERED HIM! WHAT HAVE WE DONE?!

WHA..?

YOU LITTLE IDIOT! WHAT'S THE MATTER WITH YOU?

WE'VE KILLED HIM! I MUST HAVE BEEN INSANE TO LET YOU TALK ME INTO THIS! GOD, FORGIVE ME! WE'VE MURDERED HIM! MURDERED HIM!

COME BACK HERE!

LEAVE ME ALONE! I HATE YOU! I MUST HAVE BEEN CRAZY TO THINK I COULD LOVE A MURDERER! YOU MURDERED MY HUSBAND!

4

CAN'T FOLLOW HER! HAVE TO GET RID OF THE BODY! SHE'LL BE ALL RIGHT...PROBABLY GO HOME! I'LL MEET HER THERE... SOON AS I FINISH WITH JOHN!

BUT SHE HADN'T RETURNED HOME! HE DIDN'T KNOW *WHERE* SHE HAD GONE... AND FEARING FOR HIS SAFETY, HE HAD DRIVEN THE STREETS TILL DAWN. HE BOUGHT A NEWSPAPER...

AH! HERE IT IS! *GOOD LORD!* SHE WENT TO THE *POLICE!* BUT SHE HASN'T TALKED! THEY THINK SHE'S INSANE... UNDER OBSERVATION...

HE HAD READ THE DETAILS! SHE HAD SUFFERED A GREAT SHOCK... HAD GONE TO THE POLICE BABBLING LIKE A LUNATIC ABOUT *MURDER!*

WAIT! THEY'RE HOPING THAT SHE'LL COME TO HER SENSES...THAT THE SHOCK WILL *WEAR OFF!* HMM... IF SHE TALKS... BUT *MAYBE* I CAN KEEP HER QUIET! THEY DON'T KNOW JOHN'S DEAD...

A PLAN HAD FORMED ITSELF IN HIS MIND. HE HAD GONE HOME... SHAVED, CHANGED HIS CLOTHES. IT WOULD BE RISKY...

... ONLY THING TO DO! IF I CAN GET ALONE WITH HER, I'LL SHUT HER UP FOR GOOD!

HARRY HAD GONE TO THE POLICE. THEY HAD QUESTIONED HIM FOR HOURS BUT FINALLY IT WAS OVER! HE HAD MADE HIS BID THEN...

...BUT CAN'T I SEE HER JUST FOR A *MOMENT?*

SORRY. SHE'S VIOLENT, YOU KNOW...UNDER TWENTY-FOUR HOUR GUARD! NO VISITORS!

PLEASE! I *MUST* SEE HER! I'M...I'M *WORRIED* ABOUT HER! I'LL ONLY BE A MINUTE...

SORRY. WE'LL TAKE GOOD CARE OF HER! YOU GO HOME... WE'LL LET YOU KNOW IF ANYTHING DEVELOPS!

IT HADN'T WORKED! AND AFTER DRIVING THROUGH THE TORRENTS OF RAIN FOR MANY HOURS, HE HAD RETURNED HOME...

YOU HARRY MARKS? WE WANT TO TALK TO YOU!

DETECTIVES!

HEY! COME BACK HERE!

THEN THE CHASE HAD BEGUN! UP ONE STREET... DOWN ANOTHER! THROUGH ALLEYS AND OVER BACK FENCES! BUT THEY WERE EVERYWHERE...

SHE TALKED! THE @W!!XXM@! FOOL *TALKED!* COPS ARE *ALL* OVER!

THEY'RE *AFTER* ME, ALL RIGHT! THE WHOLE NEIGHBORHOOD'S *FULL* OF THEM! THEY'RE *EVERYWHERE,* LOOKING FOR ME! IRENE MUST HAVE TOLD THEM *EVERYTHING!* LAST TIME I'LL EVER TRUST A WOMAN!

@W!!xx! *RAIN!* STREETS ARE FLOODED! RIVER MUST HAVE OVERFLOWED ITS BANKS! *HEY!* THEY'RE COMING THIS WAY! I'LL CUT THROUGH THIS ALLEY!

WHA...? IT'S A *DEAD END!* WHAT'LL I DO?... CAN'T GO BACK... THEY'LL SPOT ME SURE! WAIT! THIS *SEWER!*

...SHOULD HAVE THOUGHT OF THIS BEFORE! LET THEM LOOK FOR ME UP THERE! I'LL SLIP RIGHT BY THEM... BY MOVING *UNDERNEATH* THEM!

6

134

THE WATER HADN'T BEEN DEEP AT FIRST, BUT AS HE PLODDED THROUGH THE STENCH-RIDDEN SEWER, THE WATER FROM THE STREETS ABOVE GRADUALLY BEGAN TO FILL THE TUNNEL...

...CAN'T STAND UP! NOT ENOUGH ROOM! (GASP)...KEEP MATCHES DRY! WATER'S UP TO MY CHEST!

HE HAD ALMOST BECOME PANICKY, AND HAD SHED HIS COAT AND JACKET BECAUSE THEY HAD HELD HIM BACK! THE WATER HAD RISEN HIGHER...UP TO HIS NECK...

TOO LATE TO TURN BACK! (GASP!) NEVER MAKE IT...WATER'S TOO HIGH... RISING TOO FAST!

THEN HE HAD REACHED THE PLACE WHERE HE NOW STOOD! THERE WAS ROOM TO STAND...AND TO BREATHE! HE SIMPLY HAD TO WAIT FOR THE WATER TO LOWER...AND HE COULD BE SAFE!

(GASP!) CAN'T GO ANY FURTHER! WATER'S RUSH-ING OUT THROUGH THAT SMALL PIPE! (GASP!) BETTER KEEP AWAY FROM IT...TERRIFIC SUCTION! (GASP!)

AND HE HAD RESTED! NOW HE OPENED HIS EYES, AND SAW WITH RELIEF THAT THE WATER WAS NO HIGHER! HE CHUCKLED. HE'D GET OUT OF THIS YET! SUDDENLY...

WHAT THE..? SOMETHING...SOMETHING IN THE WATER BUMPED AGAINST ME! I'LL STRIKE A MATCH...

HIS NUMBED FINGERS FUMBLED CLUMSILY! HE STRUCK THE MATCH THREE TIMES BEFORE IT FLARED...ITS LIGHT REVEALING HIS DISCOVERY...

JOHN!

HARRY BACKED FRANTICALLY AWAY FROM THE FLOATING, BLOATED CORPSE! THEN, REALIZA-TION AND FEAR STRUCK HIM...

HE'S BEING DRAWN INTO THE SMALL PIPE! HE'LL BLOCK THE WATER'S ONLY OUTLET!

7

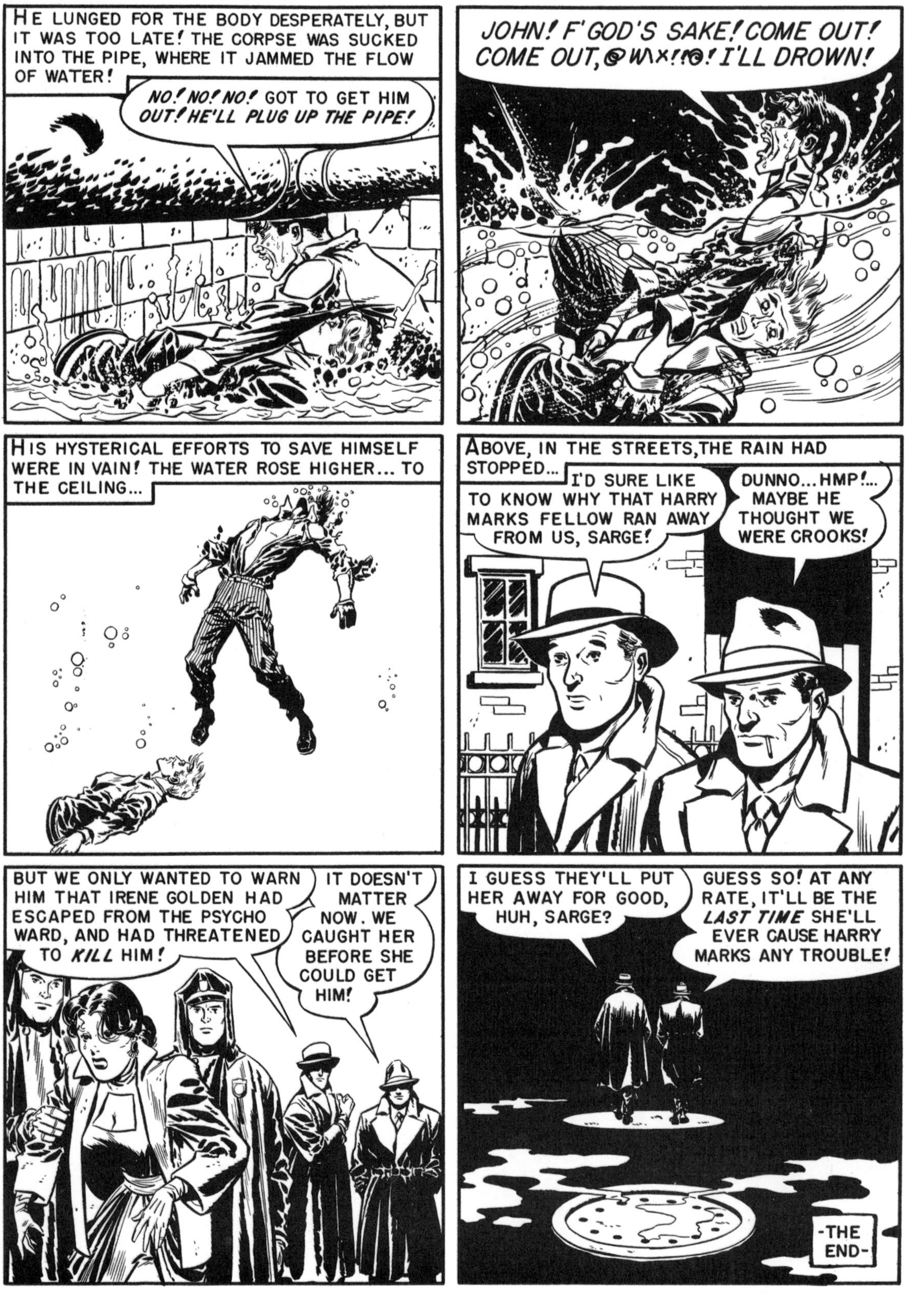
HE LUNGED FOR THE BODY DESPERATELY, BUT IT WAS TOO LATE! THE CORPSE WAS SUCKED INTO THE PIPE, WHERE IT JAMMED THE FLOW OF WATER!
NO! NO! NO! GOT TO GET HIM OUT! HE'LL PLUG UP THE PIPE!
JOHN! F'GOD'S SAKE! COME OUT! COME OUT, @W\X!!@! I'LL DROWN!
HIS HYSTERICAL EFFORTS TO SAVE HIMSELF WERE IN VAIN! THE WATER ROSE HIGHER... TO THE CEILING...
ABOVE, IN THE STREETS, THE RAIN HAD STOPPED...
I'D SURE LIKE TO KNOW WHY THAT HARRY MARKS FELLOW RAN AWAY FROM US, SARGE!
DUNNO... HMP!... MAYBE HE THOUGHT WE WERE CROOKS!
BUT WE ONLY WANTED TO WARN HIM THAT IRENE GOLDEN HAD ESCAPED FROM THE PSYCHO WARD, AND HAD THREATENED TO KILL HIM!
IT DOESN'T MATTER NOW. WE CAUGHT HER BEFORE SHE COULD GET HIM!
I GUESS THEY'LL PUT HER AWAY FOR GOOD, HUH, SARGE?
GUESS SO! AT ANY RATE, IT'LL BE THE LAST TIME SHE'LL EVER CAUSE HARRY MARKS ANY TROUBLE!
-THE END-

THE VAULT OF HORROR!

HELLO, AGAIN, YOU LITTLE MONSTERS! I GUESS YOU'VE BEEN EXPECTANTLY WAITING FOR THIS LATEST TALE FROM MY PRIVATE COLLECTION OF HORROR STORIES! WELL, HEH, HEH... I WON'T DISAPPOINT YOU! THIS TIME I'LL TELL YOU A TRULY *REVOLTING* YARN, SO GET A STRONG HOLD ON YOUR STOMACH! HEH! I CALL IT...

MIDNIGHT SNACK!

SCENE: THE HOME OF DUNCAN REYNOLDS! TIME: MIDNIGHT!

MIDNIGHT! BRR-R! THESE HORROR STORIES (YAWN-N) CERTAINLY GIVE A PERSON GOOSE PIMPLES!

...OUGHT TO GO TO BED! (YAWN-N-N) FEEL TIRED! BUT MAYBE I BETTER HAVE A SNACK FIRST! DIDN'T REALIZE I WAS SO HUNGRY! (YAWN!)

HEY! WHAT THE? HOW THE DEVIL DID I GET HERE? LAST THING I REMEMBER, I... OH, WHAT'S THE DIFFERENCE? I WANT TO BE HERE! SOMETHING TELLS ME I SHOULD BE HERE!

BOY! I'M SO HUNGRY, MY STOMACH HURTS! I BETTER GET SOME FOOD!

HEH, HEH! DUNCAN SURVEYS THE DESERTED STREET, AND ON THE CORNER HE SEES...

A RESTAURANT! I'M IN LUCK! I HOPE IT'S STILL OPEN FOR BUSINESS!

AH! IT IS OPEN!

YES, SIR? WHAT'LL IT BE?

...LET'S SEE! I'LL HAVE... ER... I'LL...

SNIFF! SNIFF!

UGH! WHAT A SICKENING ODOR!

...SIZZLING HAMBURGERS THAT... THAT BACON FRYING! I'M... I'M *SO HUNGRY!* SO HUNGRY, AND YET... THE SMELL OF FOOD COOKING MAKES ME *ILL!*

WELL, MISTER, WHAT'LL IT BE?

...CAN'T UNDERSTAND IT! THAT COOKED MEAT IS... MAKING ME *NAUSEOUS!*

HEH! HEH! POOR DUNCAN! HE WANTS SO MUCH TO EAT *SOMETHING*... ONLY HE DOESN'T KNOW WHAT IT *IS* THAT HE *WANTS!* ANYWAY, HE STUMBLES OUT INTO THE STREET AND SPENDS SEVERAL MINUTES THERE, REGAINING HIS COMPOSURE...

...EVERYTHING SEEMS SO *COCKEYED* TONIGHT! I... I *OUGHT* TO GO *HOME*, BUT SOMETHING... SOMETHING WON'T LET ME! I... CAN'T CONTROL MYSELF...

(GLA-ACK!) JUST THE *THOUGHT* OF THAT *COOKED* FOOD SICKENS ME! *UGH!*... NEVER HAPPENED TO ME *BEFORE!* HMPF! LAST TIME I'LL EVER GO INTO *THAT* RESTAUR...

...GEE! I... I FEEL ...DIZZY! AWFULLY DIZZY! FEEL LIKE I'M... GOING TO PASS OUT...

3

BLACKNESS CLOUDS HIS EYES AND MIND! HE FEELS HIMSELF FLOATING IN A WHIRLING VOID... AND THEN, SUDDENLY, IT IS OVER...

WHAT TH...? A CEMETERY! HOW DID I GET HERE..? WHERE'S THE RESTAURANT? AND THIS SHOVEL! HOW DID I GET THIS SHOVEL?

AGAINST HIS WILL, HE ENTERS THE CEMETERY AND GOES FROM ONE GRAVE TO ANOTHER...

WHAT AM I DOING? WHAT AM I LOOKING FOR? HAVE I GONE CRAZY? WAIT! THIS GRAVE! A RECENT ONE!

NOW I KNOW WHY I HAVE THIS SHOVEL! BECAUSE I HAVE TO DIG UP THIS... THIS GRAVE! THIS BRAND NEW GRAVE!

BEWILDERED, AND DRIVEN BY A FURY HE CANNOT RESIST, DUNCAN AGAIN AND AGAIN DIGS DEEPER INTO THE EARTH!

FINALLY, THE COFFIN IS BARED, THE LID RAISED...

AH! HERE IT IS! HERE IS WHAT I'VE BEEN SEARCHING FOR ALL EVENING!

SUDDENLY, A SPARK OF REALIZATION SEEPS INTO HIS CONCIOUSNESS... A REALIZATION OF WHAT HE IS ABOUT TO DO!

GOOD LORD! I...I MUST BE INSANE! WANTING TO...TO...NO! NO! DON'T LET ME DO IT!

OH, PLEASE! PLEASE! DON'T MAKE ME DO IT! BUT...BUT I...HAVE TO... SOMETHING'S FORCING ME TO...OH-H... I...I FEEL...DIZZY AGAIN...

HEH, HEH! AGAIN THE EMPTY TERRIFYING BLACK-NESS SURROUNDS HIM, AND WHEN HE REGAINS CONSCIOUSNESS...

WHA...WHAT? MUST HAVE PASSED OUT AGAIN! I...I FEEL SO STRANGE! I...*GOOD LORD! THE...THE CORPSE! WHAT HAVE I DONE?!*

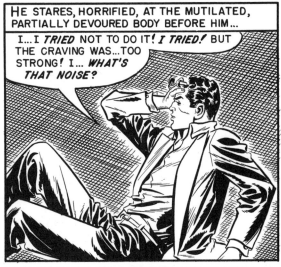

HE STARES, HORRIFIED, AT THE MUTILATED, PARTIALLY DEVOURED BODY BEFORE HIM...

I...I *TRIED* NOT TO DO IT! *I TRIED!* BUT THE CRAVING WAS...TOO STRONG! I... *WHAT'S THAT NOISE?*

PEOPLE! A CROWD OF PEOPLE... WITH *TORCHES!* THEY'RE AFTER ME... COMING THIS WAY!

THEY WANT TO TAKE AWAY MY FOOD! BUT I WON'T LET THEM! I'LL RUN AWAY WITH IT!

THEY'VE *SEEN* ME!...HAVE TO RUN *FASTER!* I'LL HIDE MY FOOD! MUSTN'T LET THEM *CATCH* ME!

TIRING UNDER THE CORPSE'S WEIGHT AS HE DODGES AND WEAVES THROUGH THE GRAVEYARD, DUNCAN SUDDENLY TRIPS...AND *FALLS!*

AN ETERNITY SEEMS TO PASS, BUT FINALLY HIS ARM QUIVERS...HIS EYES FLICKER AND OPEN...

WHY...*I'M BACK HOME!* WHERE...WHERE'S THE GRAVEYARD...THE *CORPSE?* OH...I...I GET IT NOW! HUH! I'VE BEEN HERE ALL THE TIME! MUST HAVE FALLEN ASLEEP! *I'VE ONLY BEEN DREAMING!*

5

WHOOSH! WHAT A NIGHTMARE THAT WAS! DREAMING I WAS A GHOUL! UGH! HOW FANTASTIC! LAST TIME I'LL EVER READ HORROR STORIES BEFORE GOING TO BED!

SAY, IT'S LATE! MUST HAVE DOZED FOR SEVERAL HOURS! HO-HUM, GUESS I'LL FIX SOME COFFEE AND HIT THE SACK!

NOW THAT I THINK ABOUT THAT DREAM I HAVE TO LAUGH! NEVER THOUGHT HORROR TALES WOULD AFFECT... SAY... WHAT THE...?

CLICK!

THAT'S STRANGE! WHAT ARE ALL THE SHELVES AND FOOD FROM THE REFRIGERATOR DOING ON THE TABLE? I DON'T REMEMBER PUTTING THEM THERE!

SALMON

CHEESE

Perplexed, DUNCAN OPENS THE REFRIGERATOR DOOR... AND OUT TUMBLES A PARTIALLY EATEN CORPSE!

Stunned BY HIS DISCOVERY, HE STARES AT THE GRUESOME SIGHT AND SUDDENLY HE REALIZES...

THIS CORPSE! IT'S THE ONE IN MY DREAM! ONLY... ONLY NOW I KNOW IT... IT WASN'T A DREAM! IT WAS TRUE! I ACTUALLY DID WHAT I THOUGHT I DREAMED! I... I'M... I'M A GHOUL!

—THE END—

HEH! HEH! HEH! THE MORAL OF THIS TALE IS: 'HE WHO EATS AND RUNS AWAY, WILL LIVE TO EAT ANOTHER DAY!' HEH! ISN'T THAT SILLY? WHO EVER HEARD OF EATING A DAY! DUNCAN CERTAINLY WOULDN'T! IT'S TOO BAD HE TRIPPED AND FELL IN THE CEMETERY... BUT THAT'S WHAT HAPPENS WHEN YOU CARRY AROUND TOO MUCH DEAD WEIGHT! HEH! HEH! HEH! AND NOW, I'LL TURN YOU BACK TO MY FELLOW GhouLunatic, THE CRYPT-KEEPER!

THE VAULT OF HORROR!

HEH, HEH! WELCOME TO THE *VAULT OF HORROR!* ONCE AGAIN I HAVE A CHILLING STORY TO SOOTHE YOUR PALPITATING HEARTS! IT'S FROM MY PRIVATE COLLECTION AND TAKES PLACE IN THE *DEEP SOUTH!* I THINK YOU'LL LIKE IT! I CALL THIS LITTLE SPINE-TINGLER...

SOUTHERN HOSPITALITY!

ABNER SCANLON WAS A GIGOLO! BECAUSE HE SO DISLIKED WORK...AND SINCE HE WAS SO HANDSOME...HE PREYED ON RICH WOMEN, AND USED HIS WILES TO SLYLY DRAW MONEY FROM THEM...

GOOD THING I LEFT NEW YORK. I COULD'VE MARRIED THAT DAME, BUT SHE WAS *TOO* OLD... EVEN FOR *ME!*

POSING AS A WEALTHY NEW YORK PUBLISHER, HE TRAVELED TO GEORGIA...AND THERE, BECAUSE HIS FUNDS WERE LOW, HE MARRIED A YOUNG GIRL FROM ONE OF THE SOUTH'S RICHEST CLANS.

AH! I'M SET FOR LIFE! BEAUTIFUL...AND *RICH!* I SURE CAN PICK 'EM!

HEH! ABNER DIDN'T PAT HIMSELF ON THE BACK FOR LONG. HIS WIFE WAS BEAUTIFUL...BUT NEITHER SHE NOR HER FAMILY HAD A *DIME!*

BROKE?! *BROKE?!* WHAT DO YOU MEAN, YOU'RE *BROKE?*

BUT, DARLING, WITH ALL *YOUR* MONEY, I DIDN'T THINK...

MY MONEY?! *I* DON'T HAVE ANY *MONEY!* I THOUGHT *YOU* HAD MONEY!

WHAT DOES IT MATTER, IF WE LOVE ONE ANOTHER?

STUPID! *STUPID! STUPID! I* DON'T *LOVE* YOU! I ONLY MARRIED YOU BECAUSE I THOUGHT YOU WERE *RICH!*

ABNER!

YOU *TRICKED* ME! *TRICKED ME!* OH, WHAT A *SAP* I AM!

ABNER, PLEASE DON'T TALK LIKE THAT!

OUR PLANTATION HAS BEEN LOSING MONEY FOR *YEARS!* BUT MY FAMILY IS A PART OF THE SOUTH'S HERITAGE! *WE'RE A PROUD FAMILY!* AND WE WERE BROUGHT UP TO BE PROUD OF OUR BIRTHRIGHT, AND TO *DEFEND* IT! THAT'S WHY WE PRETEND TO BE WEALTHY WHEN WE ARE REALLY...

BAH! YOU TRICKED ME!

OH, FATHER... AUNT MARTHA... HE DOESN'T *LOVE* ME! HE ONLY...

THERE, THERE, CLAUDIA, CHILD... DON'T FRET!

AH NEVAH YET MET A YANKEE WHO WAHN'T A *CAD!*

HEH, HEH! THAT WAS A SAD DAY FOR ABNER, BUT THINGS SOON QUIETED DOWN. CLAUDIA'S FATHER AND AUNT NEVER SO MUCH AS BREATHED ANOTHER SOUTHERN-FRIED WORD ABOUT THE INCIDENT. INSTEAD, THEIR LIVES SEEMED TO BE CONCERNED MOSTLY WITH THE GRAND AND GLORIOUS PAST OF THEIR ANCESTORS...

HE WAS SUCH A *GREAT* MAN, WASN'T HE, MARTHA?

(SIGH) YES...

EH? WHO?

WHY...SEBASTIAN CORNELIUS JACKSON! CLAUDIA'S GREAT-GRANDFATHER! HE WAS ONE OF THE GREATEST HEROES OF THE *CIVIL WAR!*

OH...YOU MEAN OLD POKER FACE?

OLD POKER FACE!? WHY, SUH, YOUAH EYES ARE GAZIN' UPON ONE OF THE MOST *FAMOUS* MEN IN AMERICAN *HISTORY!* A MOAH *UPRIGHT* AND *COURAGEOUS* MAN NEVAH *LIVED!* WHY, HE *BUILT* THIS VERY PLANTATION WE LIVE ON!

OH...OKAY...

IT WAS *HE* WHO SAVED THIS FINE HOUSE FROM THE RAVAGES OF THE *UNION* ARMY, AND WE ARE ETERNALLY GRATEFUL FOR THE BENEFITS WE DERIVED FROM HIS *VISION*... HIS *STRENGTH* AND *WISDOM!* HE HAS BEEN A MODEL TO US... ALWAYS READY TO DEFEND THE *HONOR* AND *RESPECTABILITY* OF OUR NAME!

OKAY, OKAY!

A *GENTLEMAN*, SUH! AND ONE OF THE MOST BRILLIANT GENERALS IN THE WAR! HE BEGAN A FINE TRADITION AND HE UPHELD THE DIGNITY AND *HONOR* OF THAT TRADITION TILL THE DAY HE *DIED!* MAY HE REST IN PEACE!

OKAY! OKAY! I *SAID* OKAY!

YES! AND NOW WE WHO ARE LEFT MUST *MAINTAIN* THE HONOR AND NOBILITY OF THAT GRAND TRADITION, AND MUST *NEVER* BESMIRCH THE JACKSON NAME, EVEN IF IT MEANS *DEATH!*

OKAY! OKAY! OKAY!

3

ABNER WAS VERY UNSATISFIED WITH HIS LOT. HE HADN'T MARRIED TO HELP DEFEND THE JACKSON HONOR...HE HAD WED FOR *MONEY!* AND HE SOON FOUND AN EASY WAY OF GETTING IT!

CLAUDIA! THE ANTIQUE VASE! IT'S MISSING!

HMMM...I THINK I CAN GIVE YOU ABOUT THIRTY DOLLARS ON THIS...

AHHH! IT'S WORTH MORE...BUT IT'S A DEAL!

AND THEN IT WAS THE GAY LIFE FOR ABNER SCANLON...

NIGHTCLUBS, BARS, RESTAURANTS, WINE, WOMEN, SONG...AND HE LOVED EVERY PRECIOUS MINUTE!

BUT SOON HIS MONEY WAS GONE, AND IT WAS BACK TO THE PLANTATION, AND...

YOU!

YOU, SUH, ARE A CAD!

OH, ABNER! ABNER, WHY DID YOU DO IT?

...WHASHA MATTER? I WANNA HAVE A GOOD TIME! NEED MONEY... THASH ALL! HOCKED A CRUMMY OL' VASE! WHASHA DIF?

OH, THE SHAME OF IT! PAWNING AN HEIRLOOM THAT WAS HANDED DOWN FROM *GRANDFATHER!*

...AND CAROUSING ABOUT THE TOWN! *DRINKING!* YOU, SUH, HAVE DISGRACED THE NAME OF JACKSON!

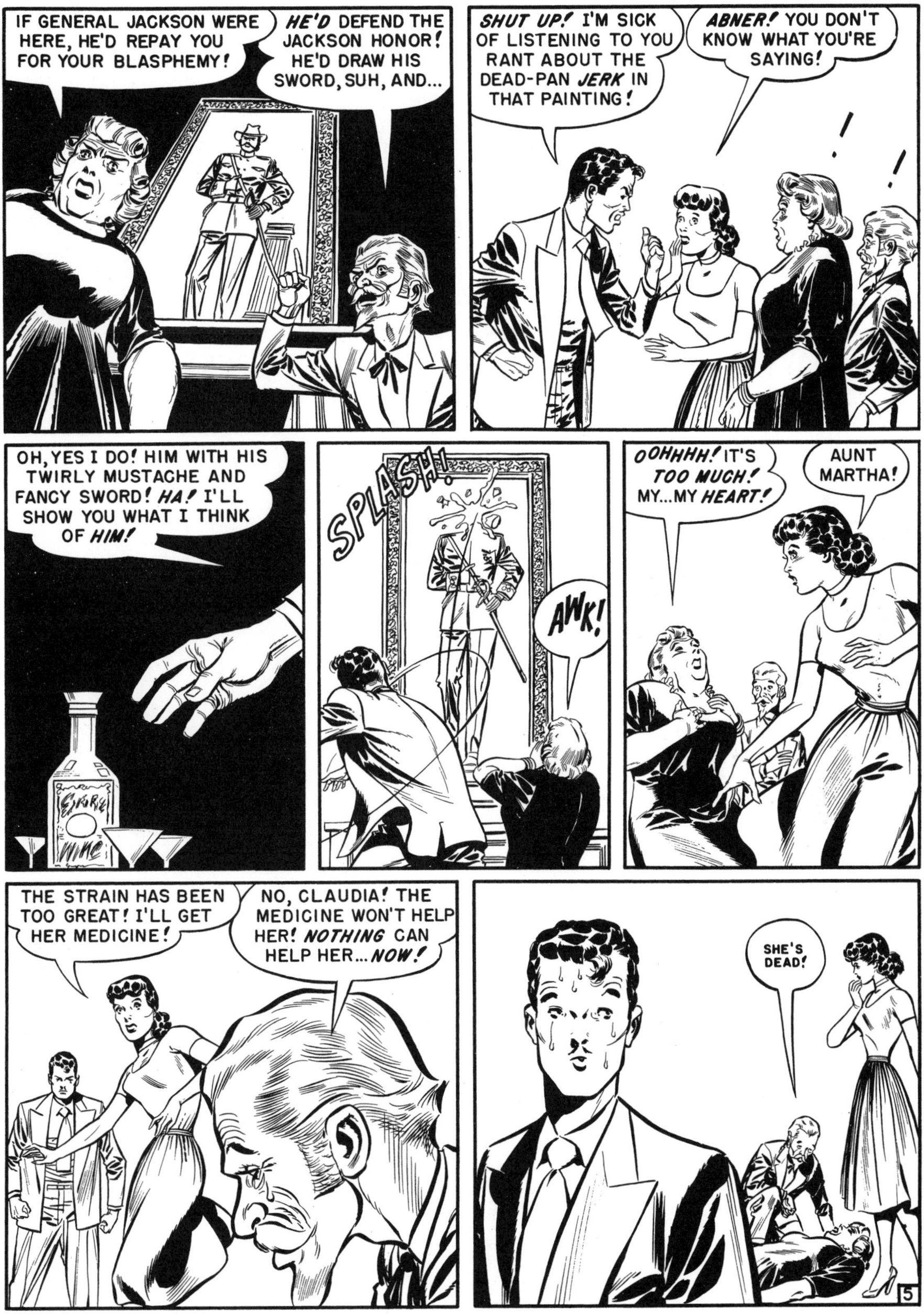
IF GENERAL JACKSON WERE HERE, HE'D REPAY YOU FOR YOUR BLASPHEMY!
HE'D DEFEND THE JACKSON HONOR! HE'D DRAW HIS SWORD, SUH, AND...
SHUT UP! I'M SICK OF LISTENING TO YOU RANT ABOUT THE DEAD-PAN JERK IN THAT PAINTING!
ABNER! YOU DON'T KNOW WHAT YOU'RE SAYING!
! !
OH, YES I DO! HIM WITH HIS TWIRLY MUSTACHE AND FANCY SWORD! HA! I'LL SHOW YOU WHAT I THINK OF HIM!
SPLASH!
AWK!
OOHHHH! IT'S TOO MUCH! MY...MY HEART!
AUNT MARTHA!
THE STRAIN HAS BEEN TOO GREAT! I'LL GET HER MEDICINE!
NO, CLAUDIA! THE MEDICINE WON'T HELP HER! NOTHING CAN HELP HER... NOW!
SHE'S DEAD!
5

HEH, HEH, HEH! WELL, AUNT MARTHA'S FUNERAL WAS A QUIET AFFAIR. CLAUDIA AND HER FATHER SAID NOTHING ABOUT WHAT HAD CAUSED AUNT MARTHA'S DEATH TO SAFEGUARD THE JACKSON REPUTATION! THEN SOME DAYS LATER...

ABNUH! WHAT ARE YOU DOING?

NOTHING, NOTHING! MIND YOUR OWN BUSINESS!

JUMPIN' JEHOSOPHAT! THAT'S THE FRAME FROM GRANDFATHER'S PICTURE! THE PAINTING OF HIM IS GONE FROM THE WALL!

SO WHAT?! SO WHAT?! I SHOVED THE PAINTING UP IN THE ATTIC, AND I'M GOING TO SELL THIS FRAME! SO WHAT?!

THIS TIME, SUH, YOU HAVE GONE TOO FAR! IF GRANDFATHER WERE HERE, HE'D DEFEND HIS HONOR... AND I, IN HIS STEAD, MUST DO LIKEWISE! SUH! I CHALLENGE YOU TO A DUEL!

SLAP!

CRACK

?

...LUVVA PETE! THE OLD GUY'S DEAD!

6

YOU...YOU'VE *KILLED* HIM!

SHUT UP! IF YOU TELL ONE WORD ABOUT WHAT HAPPENED, *YOU'LL* DIE TOO! BESIDES... THE *SCANDAL* WOULD *RUIN* THE FAMILY'S HONOR!

FEARING FOR HER SAFETY, AND AWARE OF THE DANGER TO THE JACKSON REPUTATION, CLAUDIA REMAINED SILENT. AFTER THE BURIAL, ABNER'S OUTLOOK BRIGHTENED...

ABNER? WHERE ARE YOU GOING?

TO THE ATTIC! THERE'S A LOT OF THINGS UP THERE THAT I CAN SELL! *HA! HA!* AND NO ONE CAN STOP ME!

AH! LET'S SEE! OH! THERE'S THE PAINTING OF OLD "SOUR-PUSS JACKSON"! HIM AND HIS FANCY SWORD! FMPFF! BET IT WAS NEVER OUT OF ITS SHEATH!

WONDER WHAT I SHOULD SELL FIRST! THERE'S A *LOT* OF ANTIQUES HERE THAT OUGHT TO BRING A GOOD PRICE...

SAY...

I THINK I'LL SELL THIS WHOLE PLANTATION! *YEAH!* WHO CAN STOP ME? OUGHT TO GET QUITE A WAD FOR THIS DUMP! HMMM...

SURE! AFTER I COLLECT ON THIS PLACE, I'LL GET A QUICK DIVORCE, AND THEN... *EH?* WHAT'S THAT NOISE?

WHA...?

ALONE IN HER ROOM, CLAUDIA SUDDENLY STIFFENED AS AN AGONIZING SCREAM PIERCED THE MORBID STILLNESS OF THE HOUSE...

HEAVENS! THAT SCREAM CAME FROM THE ATTIC!

7

149

QUICKLY, SHE FLASHED THE LIGHT AROUND THE ATTIC UNTIL IT CAME TO REST ON THE PAINTING. SHE STEPPED BACK, STUNNED... FOR GENERAL SEBASTIAN CORNELIUS JACKSON SEEMED TO BE SMILING... AND *HIS SWORD WAS GONE!* THE SCABBARD IN THE PAINTING WAS NOW... *EMPTY!*

THE END-

THE VAULT OF HORROR!

PFAH! NOW THAT YOU'VE FINISHED THAT WISHY-WASHY POT OF GOOK THE *OLD WITCH* BREWED FOR YOU, I'M SURE YOU'LL WELCOME A *REAL* HORRIFYING TALE! AND THAT'S JUST WHAT I HAVE PREPARED FOR YOU! SO GET READY, FRIENDS... BECAUSE THIS *NERVE-CRACKING* STORY FROM MY PRIVATE LIBRARY TAKES US TO *IRELAND*, AND GIVES US AN OPPORTUNITY TO HEAR THE TERRIFYING WAIL OF... **THE HOWLING BANSHEE!**

THROUGH THE BLANKET OF FOG THAT ENVELOPED THE LITTLE VILLAGE OF KILDARE IN IRELAND, THE SOUND OF FOOTSTEPS HERALDED THE APPROACH OF THE STRANGER TO THE COTTAGE DOOR...

KNOCK KNOCK!

GOOD EVENING! I'M PAT BRADY... FROM AMERICA! ARE YOU....?

WELL! COME IN, LAD! COME IN! 'TIS LONG THAT WE'VE WAITED FOR YE!

YOU MUST BE TIM O'SHEA... MY FATHER'S FRIEND! YOU RECEIVED MY CABLEGRAM?

AYE! AYE! AND 'TIS GLAD I AM THAT YE'LL BE STAYIN' WITH US! COME, SIT DOWN, LAD!

I KNEW YIR PARENTS WELL, PATRICK! 'TIS SAD THAT THEY DIED WHEN YE WAS SUCH A WEE TOT!

YES! I GREW UP IN AN ORPHANAGE UNTIL I WAS OLD ENOUGH TO GET A JOB!

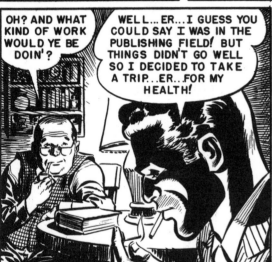

OH? AND WHAT KIND OF WORK WOULD YE BE DOIN'?

WELL...ER...I GUESS YOU COULD SAY I WAS IN THE PUBLISHING FIELD! BUT THINGS DIDN'T GO WELL SO I DECIDED TO TAKE A TRIP...ER...FOR MY HEALTH!

HEH! HEH! PAT WASN'T ACTUALLY *LYING*, MIND YOU... BUT HE DID *STRETCH* THE TRUTH A BIT! YOU SEE, IN NEW YORK HE HAD BEEN A *BOOKIE* FOR A HUGE GAMBLING SYNDICATE

FATHER?

OH... NOREEN! COME HERE, CHILD! I WANT YE TE MEET PAT BRADY... THE LAD FROM AMERICA! PATRICK... THIS IS ME DAUGHTER...

HELLO, NOREEN...

T...TOP O' THE EVENIN' TO YE... PATRICK...

WELL, THAT WAS HOW PAT BRADY ARRIVED IN IRELAND, AND HOW HE MET NOREEN. THEY FELL IN LOVE QUICKLY, AND AS TIME PASSED, PAT GREW TO LIKE HIS NEW LIFE...

OH, PATRICK...'TIS SO FOINE YOU'RE DOIN' IN FATHER'S OFFICE...

I KNOW, HONEY. SOON, MAYBE WE WILL BE ABLE TO GET MARRIED!

2

YES, PAT WAS A HAPPY MAN! THE PEACEFUL CONTENTMENT HE FELT WAS SUCH A WONDERFUL CHANGE FROM THE HECTIC, FRIGHTENED LIFE HE'D LED JUST A SHORT WHILE BEFORE! HEH! BUT HIS HAPPINESS WAS SHORT-LIVED...

PARDON ME! GOT A MATCH?

EH?... OH, SURE!

NICK! ERNIE!

HI YA, KID!

YEH! HI YA! LONG TIME NO SEE!

WHAT DO YOU GUYS WANT? WHAT ARE YOU DOING HERE?

...BOSS SENT US, KID. TOOK US A WHILE TO FIND YOU. TH' BOSS WANTS US TO PAY YOU OFF, KID.

YEH! BUT GOOD!

NO! I DIDN'T SQUEAL TO THE COPS! IT WAS SOMEONE ELSE! I DIDN'T DO IT!

...BOSS THINKS YA DID. HE DON'T LIKE PUNKS THAT CROSS HIM AND THEN COP A BREEZE.

YEH!

...BUT... YOU WOULDN'T DO IT HERE! NOT NOW! THERE'S... TOO MANY PEOPLE...

I KNOW, KID, I KNOW. NOT HERE... NOT NOW... BUT SOMETIME...SOMEWHERE. TH' BOSS WANTS US T' PAY YOU OFF, KID.

YEH! BUT GOOD!

3

FROM THAT MOMENT ON, PAT WAS A DIFFERENT MAN. FEAR CROWDED HIS EVERY HOUR, AND DEATH FOLLOWED HIS EVERY STEP! ONE EVENING...

NOREEN, I...I WANT TO TELL YOU SOMETHING... ABOUT MY PAST...

SURE, AND 'TIS WILLING I AM TE LISTEN... *WAIT!* *WHAT'S THAT?*

WHAT? WHAT DID YOU HEAR?

THE BANSHEE! 'TIS THE WAIL OF THE *BANSHEE* I HEAR! TH' SAINTS PRESARVE US. 'TIS OUR FAMILY BANSHEE FOR-TELLIN' THE DEATH OF AN O'SHEA!

NONSENSE! THERE'S NO SUCH THING!

'TIS *WRONG* YOU ARE, PAT! I CAN *HEAR* IT...WAILIN' AND A-HOWLING! PATRICK! 'TIS *FRIGHTENED* I AM!

CUT IT OUT! IF *YOU* CAN HEAR THAT BANSHEE, THEN WHY DON'T *I*?

YOU'RE NOT MY *KIN*, PATRICK. ONLY CERTAIN FAMILIES HAVE BANSHEES, AND 'TIS ONLY THEIR KIN WHO ARE ABLE TO *HEAR* IT!

...I DON'T HEAR IT, NOW...

YOU NEVER *DID* HEAR IT! *THERE'S NO SUCH THING, I TELL YOU!* YOUR IMAGINATION'S PLAYING *TRICKS* ON YOU!

I HAVE ENOUGH WORRIES WITHOUT YOU TALKING LIKE CRAZY ABOUT A *BANSHEE!*

...BUT, PATRICK! I CAN SEE THAT YE DON'T UNDERSTAND, BUT 'TIS TRUE, 'TIS *TRUE!*

I'VE HEARD IT *BEFORE!* THE LAST TIME I HEARD IT WAS JUST BEFORE ME MATHER DIED! OH, MY PATRICK!

NUTS! I TELL YOU THERE'S *NO SUCH THING!*

IN THE DAYS THAT FOLLOWED, PAT BRADY LED A HECTIC LIFE...

THWOK!

RAT-A-TAT TAT-TAT

AND WHENEVER HE FELT SAFE IN THE ARMS OF NOREEN...

IN A FEW MORE DAYS WE'LL BE MARRIED, SWEETHEART! HAPPY?

SURE AND YE KNOW I AM... WAIT! I HEAR THE BANSHEE!

FOR PETE'S SAKE, ARE YOU GOING TO START THAT AGAIN?

BUT PATRICK! I HEAR IT! 'TIS WARNING ME THAT AN O'SHEA WILL DIE!

ME FATHER'S OLD, PATRICK! AND HE'S NOT BEEN WELL! I WORRY!

STOP TALKING LIKE THAT! THERE'S NO SUCH THING, YOU HEAR? NO SUCH THING!

AND ALONE, IN THE QUIET OF HIS ROOM HE SAT, GUN IN HAND, SWEATING...STARTING AT EVEN THE SLIGHTEST SOUND...WAITING FOR WHAT HE THOUGHT WAS INEVITABLE...

...ANOTHER NIGHT WITHOUT SLEEP! NICK AND ERNIE ARE GOING TO COME FOR ME SOONER OR LATER... WHAT ARE THEY WAITING FOR?

5

HEH! HEH! BY THE TIME PAT'S WEDDING DAY ARRIVED, HE WAS A NERVOUS WRECK! I'VE SEEN JITTERY BRIDEGROOMS, BUT HE WAS WORSE THAN ANY! HE WAS SURE NICK AND ERNIE WOULD BE MEAN ENOUGH TO FINISH THEIR JOB BEFORE THE DAY WAS OVER...

...BUT *NOTHING* HAPPENED!

WHAT A HONEYMOON! I'M SO ON EDGE I CAN'T STAY PUT!

AYE! AND I, TOO, AM THE SAME!

THIS WAITING IS DRIVING ME *CRAZY!* IF IT LASTS MUCH LONGER, I'LL *CRACK!*

YOU'RE ON EDGE? WHAT'VE *YOU* GOT TO BE JITTERY ABOUT?

'TIS THE BANSHEE OI'M THINKIN' OF!

BANSHEE! BANSHEE! YOU AND YOUR COCK-EYED *BANSHEE!* YOU LITTLE *IDIOT!* DON'T YOU KNOW MY *LIFE* IS IN DANGER? *WAIT!* I HEARD A NOISE!

WHAT IS IT? YOU LOOK SO *FRIGHTENED!*

IT'S NICK AND ERNIE! THEY'VE COME TO *KILL* ME! THEY'RE OUTSIDE THE HOUSE! I...I *HEARD* THEM!

WELL, I'M *READY* FOR THEM! I'VE BEEN *WAITING* FOR THIS! I'LL GO *MEET* THEM! *I'LL BLOW THEIR BRAINS OUT!*

PATRICK! DON'T GO! PLEASE! *WAIT!*

OUT INTO THE SILENT DARKNESS WENT PAT. MOVING QUIETLY THROUGH THE FOLIAGE, HE LISTENED INTENTLY FOR ANY SOUND...

...BLASTED *FOG!* CAN'T SEE A *THING!*..WHA...?

BEHIND ME! SOMEONE'S MOVING UP *BEHIND* ME!

6

BLAM! BLAM! BLAM! BLAM!

NOREEN!

SHE'S DEAD! I KILLED HER! THE BANSHEE WAS RIGHT! IT DID WARN HER THAT AN O'SHEA WOULD DIE! WHA...?

THAT SCREAM! IT'S THE BANSHEE! IT'S HOWLING FOR ME! I MARRIED AN O'SHEA! I'M PART OF THE FAMILY NOW! THAT'S WHY I CAN HEAR IT NOW!

AAOOWWWOOOO

NICK! AND ERNIE! THEY'RE GOING TO KILL ME! THE BANSHEE'S WARNING ME!

...AND EVEN IF THEY DON'T KILL ME, I'LL BE HUNG FOR MURDERING NOREEN! (SOB) EITHER WAY, I'M DONE FOR! THERE'S NO USE FIGHTING IT! (SOB) THERE'S NO WAY OUT FOR ME!

THE END..

HEH! HEH! I THINK THAT STORY WAS A HOWLING SUCCESS, DON'T YOU? WAIL, WHAT ARE YOU GONNA DO? THE O'SHEA BANSHEE CERTAINLY CALLED THAT SHOT! POOR NOREEN! SHE DIDN'T HAVE MUCH OF A MARRIAGE! JUST A SHORT SHRIEK-END! WELL, I'LL BE LURKING FOR YOU IN MY OWN MAGAZINE, THE VAULT OF HORROR! COME VISIT WITH ME, EH? HEH! HEH! HEH!

IF YOU HAVEN'T AS YET RE-CEIVED PHOTOS OF THE THREE GHOULUNATICS, READ THE OLD WITCH'S NICHE IN THIS ISSUE...

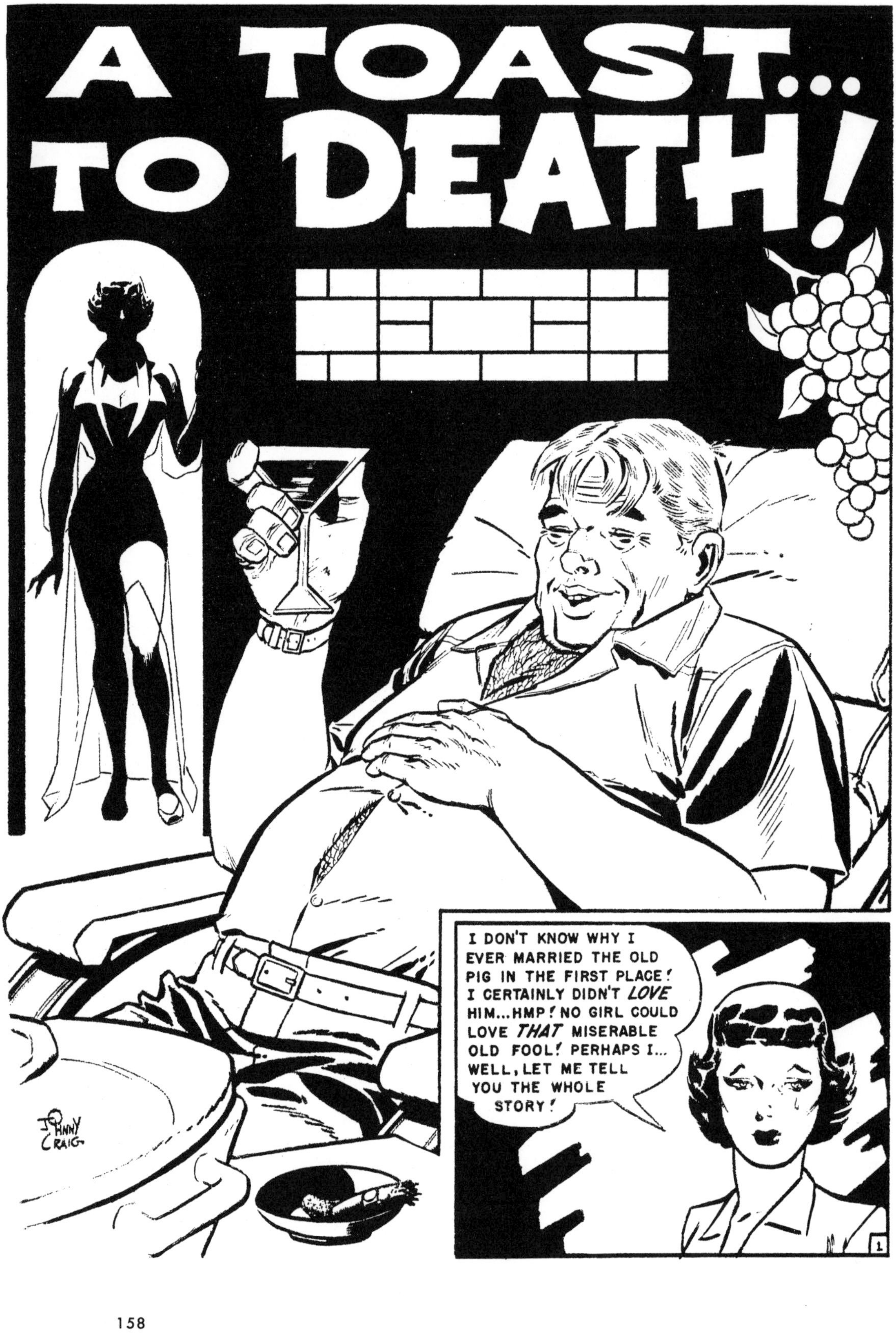
A TOAST... TO DEATH!
JOHNNY CRAIG
I DON'T KNOW WHY I EVER MARRIED THE OLD PIG IN THE FIRST PLACE! I CERTAINLY DIDN'T *LOVE* HIM...HMP! NO GIRL COULD LOVE *THAT* MISERABLE OLD FOOL! PERHAPS I... WELL, LET ME TELL YOU THE WHOLE STORY!
1

'I FIRST MET HIM IN 'FRISCO' WHEN I WAS NINETEEN. HE WAS A VINTNER, AND HAD JUST SOLD A BIG SHIP-MENT OF WINE. WE HAD LOTS OF GOOD TIMES...'

HAVING FUN, SHERRY?

YEAH! C'MON, LET'S DANCE!

'HE SPENT PLENTY OF DOUGH, AND I GUESS I EXPECTED IT TO BE LIKE THAT EVEN AFTER I MARRIED HIM.'

WE'VE BEEN MARRIED FOUR MONTHS! YOU HAVEN'T TAKEN ME OUT ONCE!

I CAN'T HELP IT! THE GRAPES KEEP ME BUSY!

'BUT IT REALLY WASN'T BAD. I LOLLED AROUND IN THE SUN, AND TOOK LIFE EASY...'

'YES, IT HAD BEEN NICE AT FIRST... BUT DOING NOTHING SOON BECAME VERY BORING...'

...BUT ALPHONSE, I WANT TO HAVE FUN! CAN'T WE GO OUT TONIGHT?

SORRY, SHERRY, BUT THE GRAPES NEED ALL MY ATTENTION! YOU UNDER-STAND!

'IT WOULD HAVE BEEN ALL RIGHT IF THE HUGE ACRES OF VINEYARDS REQUIRED HIS SPECIAL ATTENTION... BUT HE LEFT THAT TO HIS HIRED WORKERS! WHAT HE CONCERNED HIMSELF WITH WAS A STINKIN' VINE THAT GREW JUST OUTSIDE THE HOUSE... HIS SPECIAL BABY!'

ARE YOU GOING TO SIT OUT HERE ALL NIGHT?

BUT, SHERRY! I'VE RECEIVED FROST WARNINGS! I HAVE TO SEE THAT THE SMUDGE POTS KEEP MY GRAPES WARM!

'IT WAS FROM THIS SPECIAL VINE THAT HE MADE HIS FINEST WINE... WHICH HE KEPT IN A SMALL CASK. IT WAS DELICIOUS... BUT I WOULD NEVER ADMIT IT!'

AHH-H-H! SUCH BOUQUET! SUCH FRAGRANCE! ISN'T IT SIMPLY SUPERB?

PHOOEY!

2

'I SOON BEGAN TO HATE ALPHONSE FOR THE ATTENTION HE LAVISHED ON THE GRAPES! AND WITH NOTHING TO DO, I HAD PLENTY OF TIME TO THINK ABOUT IT...' HE *NEVER* PAYS ANY ATTENTION TO *ME!* ALL HE CARES ABOUT IS HIS SPECIAL *WINE!* *I HATE HIM!*

I OUGHT TO *LEAVE* HIM... BUT WHY SHOULD *I* GIVE UP THIS LUXURY? EVERYTHING WOULD BE FINE... IF ONLY ALPHONSE WERE OUT OF THE WAY...

HMMM...

'I SOON WAS GIVEN A PERFECT CHANCE TO RID MYSELF OF HIM. HE HAD TO TRAVEL TO ITALY ON BUSINESS, AND ON THE EVE OF HIS DEPARTURE I WAS WELL PREPARED...'

THIS BOTTLE OF *CYANIDE* WILL FIX HIM!

A TOAST... TO A SUCCESSFUL TRIP... DARLING!

AWK! MY... MY THROAT! I'M... I'M BURNING UP! SHERRY! YOU... YOU POISONED ME!

HELP! HELP ME! SHERRY! I'M DYING! HELP ME! *OOH-HH-HH...*

MURDER STORIES!

'I WAS UNNATURALLY CALM. QUICKLY, I BEGAN DRAGGING HIM OVER TO THE WINDOW...'

UNGH!...WEIGHS A TON...FAT *PIG!* I'M *GLAD* HE'S *DEAD!*

'I OPENED THE WINDOW! WITH A SUPREME EFFORT, I LIFTED HIM TO THE SILL, AND PUSHED HIM OUT...'

THERE! NOW TO GET OUTSIDE!

'THAT HAD BEEN THE EASIEST WAY TO GET HIM OUTSIDE...AND HE HADN'T DROPPED FAR...'

...NOW I'LL JUST DRAG HIM OVER HERE TO THE SPECIAL... ...*UNGH*... GRAPEVINE...

'I WORKED ALL THAT NIGHT... DIGGING A GRAVE FOR HIS BODY.'

...(PANT) LOVES HIS GRAPES, DOES HE? (PANT) I'LL SEE THAT HE'LL BE WITH THEM (PANT) *FOREVER!*

'BY DAYBREAK, THE JOB WAS COMPLETED.' *THERE!* EVERY-THING IS BURIED! HIS BODY... LUGGAGE...*EVERYTHING!* BURIED WITH HIS PRECIOUS *GRAPES!*

'NO ONE NOTICED ANYTHING SUSPICIOUS. AS FAR AS ANYONE KNEW, ALPHONSE WAS AWAY...ON BUSINESS!'

HA! HA! HA! THIS IS GOING TO BE PERFECT! IN A FEW DAYS I'LL START WRITING THE LETTERS!

'I WROTE LETTERS TO MY HUSBAND IN ITALY... AND WHEN I RECEIVED THEM ALL BACK, I CALLED THE *POLICE!*'

YES, INSPECTOR, I'M *WORRIED!* ALPHONSE SHOULD BE IN ITALY, BUT ALL MY MAIL HAS COME BACK UNOPENED! COULD YOU INVESTIGATE FOR ME?

'AND INVESTIGATE THEY *DID!* I SPENT MANY TRYING WEEKS THEN, BUT IT ALL BLEW OVER!'

WE KNOW YOUR HUSBAND NEVER LEFT THE COUNTRY, BUT AS YET WE HAVEN'T BEEN ABLE TO LOCATE HIM! HE'S JUST *DISAPPEARED!*

BUT INSPECTOR! WHAT WILL I DO?

... LOOKS LIKE HE'S DESERTED YOU! HAPPENS OFTEN! JUST HAVE TO WAIT AND SEE! HE MAY COME BACK!

OH ... I SEE! THANK YOU!

'WHEN THE INSPECTOR HAD GONE, I LAUGHED! I *ROARED* WITH LAUGHTER, AND THE JOY OF KNOWING I WAS SAFE!'

WHAT A WONDERFUL FEELING! THE POLICE DON'T SUSPECT A THING!

'FROM THEN ON, I KNEW ALL I HAD TO DO WAS WAIT! BUT I ENJOYED MYSELF TOO ...'

THE FOREMAN TAKES CARE OF ALL THE WORK TO BE DONE, AND THE BUSINESS RUNS ITSELF! IN SEVEN YEARS I'LL BE *LEGALLY* FREE FROM ALPHONSE!

'SEVERAL YEARS PASSED ... AND ONE DAY WHILE MY NEW SWIMMING POOL WAS BEING COMPLETED...'

HMM... I JUST NOTICED! THE SPECIAL GRAPEVINE WHERE ALPHONSE IS BURIED HASN'T BEEN CULTIVATED!

... I HAVEN'T GONE NEAR IT IN YEARS! JUST TO BE ON THE SAFE SIDE I THINK I'LL ASK THE FOREMAN ABOUT IT! I DON'T WANT TO TAKE ANY CHANCES ON AROUSING *ANYONE'S* SUSPICIONS!

...WHY, CERTAINLY, MA'AM! I'LL BE GLAD TO SEND ONE OF MY MEN OVER TO HELP YOU!

THANK YOU...

5

'THE NEXT MORNING, AS I FINISHED BREAKFAST, I HEARD A KNOCK ON THE DOOR. I OPENED IT...'

OH...

MORNING, MA'AM! MY NAME IS JACK THOMPSON! THE FOREMAN SENT ME OVER... SAID YOU HAD SOME SPECIAL WORK FOR ME!

MY HEART BEAT LIKE THUNDER IN MY BREAST AT THE SIGHT OF THIS YOUNG, HANDSOME GOD. I CLUTCHED MY ROBE TIGHTER ABOUT ME...'

WORK? OH! OH, YES! ER...WELL, I'LL BE WITH YOU IN A MOMENT! I HAVE TO DRESS!

FINE, MA'AM! I'LL WAIT!

I FELT LIKE A SCHOOL GIRL AS I STOOD BY, WATCHING JACK PICK THE GRAPES... AND WHEN HE TURNED TO SPEAK TO ME, I TREMBLED WITH EXCITEMENT...

...THIS ENOUGH GRAPES, MA'AM?

YES! YES... JACK! THAT'S ENOUGH!

NEVER HAD I EXPERIENCED SUCH A FEELING! AND IN THE DAYS THAT FOLLOWED, WHILE HE PROCESSED THE WINE, I FOUND THAT I DIDN'T WANT TO BE AWAY FROM HIM!'

'HE WAS YOUNGER THAN I, BUT I KNEW HE WAS ATTRACTED TO ME! WHEN THE WINE HAD BEEN MADE, WE STORED IT IN THE WINE CELLAR...'

...GUESS I WON'T BE SEEING YOU AGAIN, MA'AM!

OH...ER...YES, YOU WILL! I... I HAVE MORE THINGS FOR YOU TO DO!

'I GRASPED THE FLIMSIEST EXCUSES TO KEEP HIM WITH ME, AND AS TIME PASSED WE REALIZED WE LOVED ONE ANOTHER...'

OH, SHERRY... SHERRY, MY DARLING! I WANT YOU SO!

JACK...

FOR THE FIRST TIME IN MY LIFE I WAS TRULY, DEEPLY IN LOVE! IT WAS EXCITING... AND YET IT MADE ME FEEL COMFORTABLE AND SECURE...'

WHEN CAN WE BE MARRIED, SHERRY?

WE MUST WAIT, JACK! I'M NOT LEGALLY FREE TO MARRY UNTIL SEVEN YEARS AFTER MY HUSBAND'S...ER...DISAPPEARANCE! HAVE PATIENCE.

6

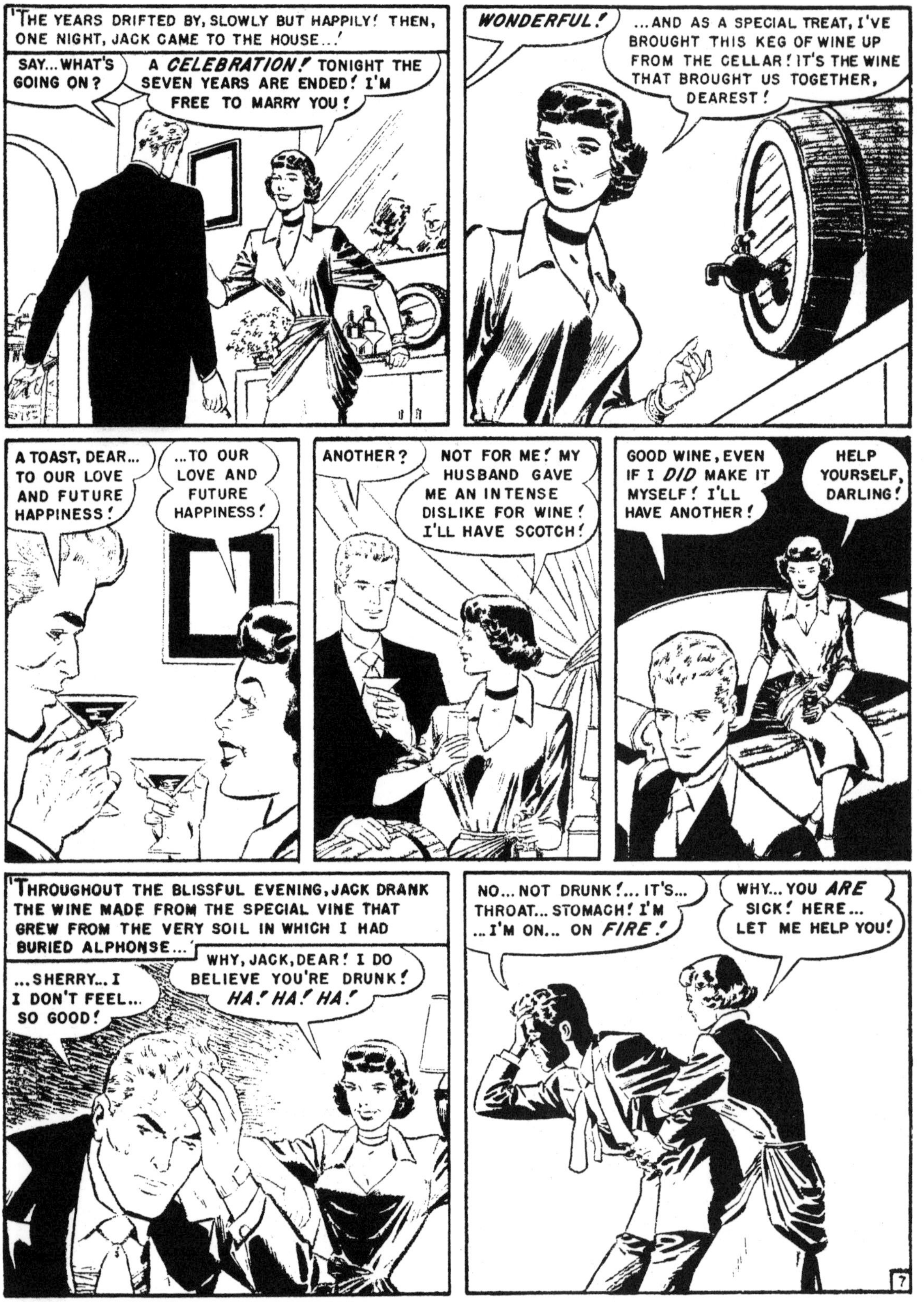
'THE YEARS DRIFTED BY, SLOWLY BUT HAPPILY! THEN, ONE NIGHT, JACK CAME TO THE HOUSE...'
SAY...WHAT'S GOING ON?
A CELEBRATION! TONIGHT THE SEVEN YEARS ARE ENDED! I'M FREE TO MARRY YOU!
WONDERFUL!
...AND AS A SPECIAL TREAT, I'VE BROUGHT THIS KEG OF WINE UP FROM THE CELLAR! IT'S THE WINE THAT BROUGHT US TOGETHER, DEAREST!
A TOAST, DEAR... TO OUR LOVE AND FUTURE HAPPINESS!
...TO OUR LOVE AND FUTURE HAPPINESS!
ANOTHER?
NOT FOR ME! MY HUSBAND GAVE ME AN INTENSE DISLIKE FOR WINE! I'LL HAVE SCOTCH!
GOOD WINE, EVEN IF I DID MAKE IT MYSELF! I'LL HAVE ANOTHER!
HELP YOURSELF, DARLING!
'THROUGHOUT THE BLISSFUL EVENING, JACK DRANK THE WINE MADE FROM THE SPECIAL VINE THAT GREW FROM THE VERY SOIL IN WHICH I HAD BURIED ALPHONSE...'
...SHERRY...I I DON'T FEEL... SO GOOD!
WHY, JACK, DEAR! I DO BELIEVE YOU'RE DRUNK! HA! HA! HA!
NO...NOT DRUNK!... IT'S... THROAT... STOMACH! I'M ...I'M ON... ON FIRE!
WHY... YOU ARE SICK! HERE... LET ME HELP YOU!
7

...LEMMEE...LEMMEE OPEN MY COLLAR! FEEL SO...SO *SICK!* MY STOMACH! *OOOHH-H!*

OH, JACK, DEAR!

THE PAIN! I'M BURNING *UP!* SHERRY! *HELP ME!* SHERRY... (GASP!) SHERRY...

JACK!

'I KNELT THERE IN DISBELIEF! JACK WAS *DEAD!* THEN SUDDENLY, I RUSHED TO THE PHONE...'

OPERATOR! *OPERATOR,* GET ME A DOCTOR! PLEASE! HELP ME! SOMEONE HELP ME!

THE DOCTOR SAID JACK HAD BEEN *POISONED*... WITH *CYANIDE!* I COULDN'T FIGURE IT AT FIRST, BUT THEN I REALIZED WHAT HAD HAPPENED! I HAD GIVEN ALPHONSE SUCH A LARGE AMOUNT OF POISON THAT WHEN HE WAS BURIED, THE GRAPEVINE ABSORBED IT THROUGH THE SOIL!

WE MADE WINE FROM THOSE POISONED GRAPES, AND WHEN JACK *DRANK* IT... WELL! ANYWAY, I COULDN'T EXPLAIN *WITHOUT CONFESSING I'D KILLED ALPHONSE*...SO THEY HAD ME! THE TRIAL WAS SHORT... I WAS FOUND GUILTY OF *FIRST DEGREE MURDER!*

SO HERE I AM! THEY'RE COMING FOR ME! I CAN HEAR THEM WALKING DOWN THE CORRIDOR! THEY'LL TAKE ME TO THE *GAS CHAMBER!* HMPF! DO YOU KNOW WHAT KIND OF GAS THEY USE? *CYANIDE!* THAT'S THE SAME STUFF THAT *I* USED TO KILL ALPHONSE! ISN'T THAT A *LAUGH?*

THE END

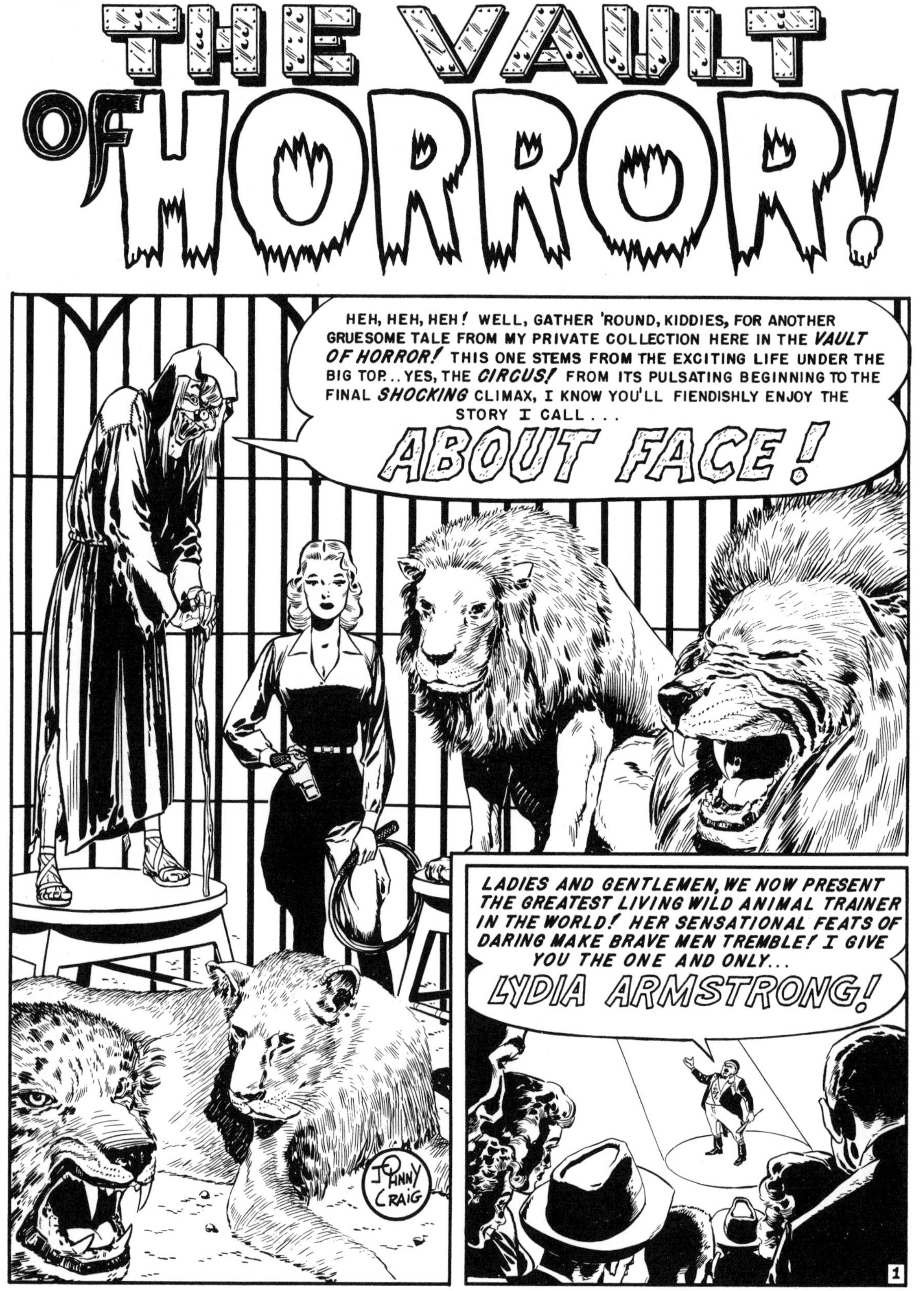
THE VAULT OF HORROR!
HEH, HEH, HEH! WELL, GATHER 'ROUND, KIDDIES, FOR ANOTHER GRUESOME TALE FROM MY PRIVATE COLLECTION HERE IN THE VAULT OF HORROR! THIS ONE STEMS FROM THE EXCITING LIFE UNDER THE BIG TOP... YES, THE CIRCUS! FROM ITS PULSATING BEGINNING TO THE FINAL SHOCKING CLIMAX, I KNOW YOU'LL FIENDISHLY ENJOY THE STORY I CALL...
ABOUT FACE!
JOHNNY CRAIG
LADIES AND GENTLEMEN, WE NOW PRESENT THE GREATEST LIVING WILD ANIMAL TRAINER IN THE WORLD! HER SENSATIONAL FEATS OF DARING MAKE BRAVE MEN TREMBLE! I GIVE YOU THE ONE AND ONLY...
LYDIA ARMSTRONG!
1

LYDIA ARMSTRONG! "BEAUTY" AND "BRAVERY" WERE SYNONOMOUS WITH HER NAME...AND THE AUDIENCE SAT SPELLBOUND AS SHE PUT THE BIG CATS THROUGH THEIR PACES!

C'MON, BOY, UP! *UP!* ATTA BOY! EASY, NOW...EASY...

SHE RISKED DEATH AGAIN AND AGAIN WHILE SHE PERFORMED...AND SHE CLIMAXED HER ACT BY LYING FLAT ON HER BACK, UNARMED, WITH HER HANDS BENEATH HER...

C'MON, KING...OVER HERE. C'MON, NOW... EASY, BOY...EASY...

SLOWLY, THE HUGE BEAST DID HER BIDDING! HE STOOD OVER HER SUPPLE FORM...THEN BENT HIS SHAGGY HEAD. AT HER COMMAND, HIS MOUTH OPENED...

THEN, WHILE THE AUDIENCE GASPED, SHE LET THE LION'S JAW CLOSE ABOUT HER FACE!

THE CROWD'S THUNDEROUS APPLAUSE ROLLED THROUGH THE BIG TOP LIKE THUNDER! LYDIA ARMSTRONG TOOK SEVERAL BOWS...

...THOSE WHO SAW THE SLEEK BLACK PANTHER CROUCH TO SPRING...AND WHO CRIED OUT IN WARNING ...COULD NOT BE HEARD ABOVE THE TUMULTUOUS OVATION! THE BEAUTEOUS LYDIA TURNED...*TOO LATE!*

OVER AND OVER THEY ROLLED IN THE CENTER OF THE CAGE AS THE PANTHER CLAWED HER BODY AND TORE VICIOUSLY AT HER FACE! BAREHANDED, LYDIA FOUGHT VALIANTLY...

2

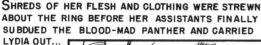

SHREDS OF HER FLESH AND CLOTHING WERE STREWN ABOUT THE RING BEFORE HER ASSISTANTS FINALLY SUBDUED THE BLOOD-MAD PANTHER AND CARRIED LYDIA OUT...

THEY RUSHED HER TO THE HOSPITAL... BUT THERE WAS LITTLE THE SURGEONS COULD DO!

SHE'S BEEN TERRIBLY RIPPED AND TORN!

... LUCKY IF SHE LIVES!

... HER FACE! HOW... HOW *HORRIBLE!*

HEH! HEH! WELL, LYDIA LIVED! THEY HAD PATCHED HER *BODY* UP TILL IT WAS GOOD AS NEW... BUT THERE WAS NOTHING THEY COULD DO TO FIX HER *FACE!* SHE WORE A BLACK VEIL TO HIDE THE HIDEOUS SIGHT... AND SHE BROODED DEEPLY! HEH! HEH!

STOP! DON'T YOU *DARE* TAKE A PICTURE OF ME! *GO AWAY! LEAVE ME ALONE!*

OUCH! OKAY, MISS ARMSTRONG! OKAY!

LYDIA ARMSTRONG RETIRED FROM THE WORLD! HER MAID AND CHAUFFEUR WERE THE ONLY PEOPLE SHE SAW...

NO ONE'S EVER SEEN HER FACE! POOR THING! SHE'S SO WEALTHY... AND YET SO LONELY!

IS THAT SO?

YES... THE WORLD FORGETS SO SOON! IT MUST BE AWFUL TO BE IN HER POSITION... I FEEL SO SORRY FOR HER!

I THINK SHE'S CRACKED UP! HAVE YOU SEEN THE KIND OF BOOKS SHE'S COLLECTING?

BEHIND LOCKED DOORS, LYDIA PORED OVER STACKS OF ANCIENT BOOKS WRITTEN IN A STRANGE LANGUAGE ABOUT *WITCHCRAFT!*

... IT MUST BE IN ONE OF THESE BOOKS! IT *MUST* BE! I HOPE I'M TRANSLATING CORRECTLY!

WITCHCRAFT

LORE

3

LATE INTO THE NIGHT SHE READ, AND OFTEN TILL THE NEXT MORNING...

IT'S NOT HERE! MAYBE THAT NEW SET OF BOOKS WILL HAVE WHAT I'M LOOKING FOR!

WHEN SHE WASN'T COOPED UP IN HER ROOM, HER CHAUFFEUR WOULD DRIVE HER THROUGH THE SUR- ROUNDING COUNTRYSIDE...

BEAUTIFUL DAY, ISN'T IT, MISS ARMSTRONG?

YES...BEAUTIFUL! NOT UGLY...NOT LIKE MY FACE!

YOU SHOULDN'T TALK LIKE THAT, MISS ARMSTRONG! GOOD LOOKS AREN'T EVERYTHING! NOBODY LIKES TO EAT A ROTTEN APPLE JUST BECAUSE THE SKIN IS PRETTY! IT'S WHAT'S INSIDE THAT COUNTS!

YOU...YOU SOUND LIKE YOU MEAN THAT...STEVE!

I DO MEAN IT! TO ME, YOUR FACE DOESN'T MEAN A THING! I LIKE YOU AND WORK FOR YOU BECAUSE YOU... WELL, BECAUSE YOU'RE A WONDERFUL GIRL!

YOU... YOU'RE JUST SAYING THAT! I DON'T BELIEVE YOU!

YOU DON'T? ALL RIGHT,... THEN I'LL PROVE IT!

TO HER SURPRISE, STEVE PULLED TO THE SIDE OF THE ROAD AND PARKED...

WHA... WHY DID YOU STOP? WHAT ARE YOU GOING TO DO?

I'M JUST GOING TO PROVE TO YOU THAT I MEANT ALL THOSE THINGS I SAID! C'MERE!

AFTER THAT, THEY WENT DRIVING MORE OFTEN! AND LYDIA FOUND HERSELF DEVOTING LESS AND LESS TIME TO THE READING OF WITCHCRAFT BOOKS!

HE'S BEEN *WONDERFUL!* HE'S GIVEN ME AN ENTIRELY NEW FUTURE TO LOOK FORWARD TO!

HEH, HEH! YES, LYDIA VERY QUICKLY FELL IN LOVE WITH STEVE! THE MONTHS PASSED...

BUT STEVE! HOW CAN YOU EXPECT ME TO BELIEVE YOU *LOVE* ME? YOU'VE NEVER *SEEN* MY *FACE!*

CAN'T YOU UNDERSTAND? I DON'T CARE *WHAT* YOU LOOK LIKE! I LOVE YOU FOR WHAT YOU *ARE!*

...IF YOU MEAN THAT, STEVE, THEN YOU WON'T MIND PROVING IT TO ME, WILL YOU?

EH? OH, OF COURSE NOT!

GOOD! I HOPE YOU'VE BEEN HONEST WITH ME... AS WELL AS *YOURSELF... BECAUSE I'M GOING TO REMOVE MY VEIL!*

WHAT???

THIS WAS A SURPRISE! STEVE NEVER EXPECTED *THIS* TO HAPPEN. BUT HE READIED HIMSELF! WITH TREMBLING HANDS LYDIA TOOK THE VEIL FROM HER FACE!

EVERY FIBRE AND MUSCLE IN STEVE'S BODY SHUD-DERED AT THE TWISTED, GHASTLY SIGHT THAT HAD BEEN BARED TO HIS EYES... AND ONLY HIS IRON WILL KEPT HIM FROM FAINTING...

THEY STARED AT ONE ANOTHER FOR LONG, AGONIZING MINUTES! DROPLETS OF SWEAT FORMED ON HIS BROW AS STEVE STRAINED TO KEEP HIS COUNTENANCE PAS-SIVE! THEN SUDDENLY LYDIA FLUNG HERSELF INTO HIS ARMS, SOBBING HYSTERICALLY FOR JOY!

OH, STEVE! STEVE, MY DARLING!

IN LYDIA'S EYES, STEVE HAD PROVEN HIS LOVE FOR HER, AND SHE WAS VERY HAPPY. THEN ONE NIGHT SHE FINALLY FOUND WHAT SHE HAD BEEN SEARCHING FOR IN HER MANY BOOKS...

HERE IT IS! BUT...NOW THAT I KNOW STEVE LOVES ME, IT DOESN'T SEEM SO IMPORTANT!

THROUGH LONG WEARY HOURS SHE READ AND TRANSLATED THE WEIRD CRYPTIC PASSAGES...AND WHEN SHE HAD FINALLY FINISHED...

BRR...JUST AS WELL THAT IT'S *NOT* IMPORTANT! I HAVEN'T THE NERVE FOR *THIS!*

LYDIA THRUST THE BOOKS ASIDE AND FORGOT ABOUT THEM! SHE AND STEVE WERE TOGETHER ALWAYS... BUT ONE DAY, SEVERAL MONTHS LATER, SHE NOTICED A CHANGE IN STEVE! AND IT WORRIED HER!

IS ANYTHING WRONG, DEAR? YOU SEEM SO THOUGHTFUL AND QUIET LATELY!

IT'S NOTHING, LYDIA! I... I'VE JUST BEEN THINKING ABOUT MY FUTURE! I'VE BEEN WANTING TO SET MYSELF UP IN BUSINESS, BUT...WELL...

YOU SEE, DARLING... I WANT TO EARN ENOUGH MONEY SO YOU WON'T FEEL THAT *YOU* ARE SUPPORTING *ME!* I WANT YOU TO BE PROUD OF ME... ONLY IT TAKES MONEY TO GET STARTED!

I KNOW, STEVE! HOW MUCH WILL YOU NEED?

OH...A LOT! I DON'T KNOW EXACTLY! WHY?

I HAVE *PLENTY* OF MONEY! WHY NOT LET ME START YOU IN BUSINESS? YOU CAN PAY ME BACK LATER!

6

171

OH, NO, LYDIA! BESIDES, I...

I DON'T WANT TO HEAR ANOTHER WORD! IN FACT, I'LL CALL MY LAWYERS TODAY AND AUTHORIZE THEM TO GIVE YOU *POWER OF ATTORNEY!*

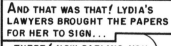

AND THAT WAS THAT! LYDIA'S LAWYERS BROUGHT THE PAPERS FOR HER TO SIGN...

THERE! NOW, DARLING, YOU ARE IN COMPLETE CONTROL OF *ALL MY WEALTH!*

SEVERAL DAYS LATER, SHE RECEIVED A LETTER...

WHY...IT'S FROM *STEVE!* AND IT'S POSTMARKED *'FLORIDA'!* HE'S *LEFT ME!* HE'S TAKEN ALL MY MONEY AND *LEFT* ME!

TEARFULLY, SHE READ THE LETTER! CRUEL, VILE WORDS SHE ALWAYS FEARED HEARING ABOUT HER FACE SPRANG AT HER FROM ALMOST EVERY LINE... DERISIVE, SCORNFUL...

HE ONLY WANTED MY MONEY! (SOB!) OH, HOW COULD HE BE SO WICKED? (SOB!)

I'LL FIX HIM! I'LL SHOW HIM! *AH!* HERE'S THAT WITCHCRAFT BOOK! IF THIS WORKS, HE'LL BE SORRY FOR THE REST OF HIS LIFE!

ACCORDING TO THE BOOK, I'LL NEED TWO POR- TRAITS! ONE OF MYSELF AS I LOOKED BEFORE THE ACCIDENT... AND ONE OF STEVE! I GUESS THESE PHOTOGRAPHS WILL DO!

FOLLOWING DIRECTIONS, SHE FILLED A HUGE CAULDRON WITH WEIRD LIQUIDS, AND HEATED IT TILL IT BUBBLED WITH INTENSE FURY...

THERE! EVERYTHING'S READY! THIS *HAS* TO WORK! IT *HAS* TO!

7

THEN SHE TOOK BOTH PHOTOS AND DIPPED THEM INTO THE SEETHING BREW...

FERVENTLY WHISPERING A BLACK INCANTATION, SHE WAITED A SPECIFIC LENGTH OF TIME...

...AND THEN WITHDREW THE PHOTOGRAPHS!

WHY! *THEY'RE BLANK!* AND THE CAULDRON HAS CEASED TO BOIL!

DID IT WORK? *I MUST SEE! A MIRROR!* OH, I'M SO NERVOUS I CAN HARDLY TAKE OFF MY VEIL!

BREATHLESSLY SHE YANKED THE COVERING FROM HER FACE! A STARTLED GASP ESCAPED FROM HER TWITCHING LIPS...

IT WORKED! OH, I'M BEAUTIFUL AGAIN! THANK HEAVENS! OH, THANK HEAVENS!

AND IN FLORIDA...

AAAGGH-HH-H! STEVE! YOUR *FACE!*

HEH, HEH! I BET STEVE'S NEW GIRL FRIEND WAS SURPRISED! BUT IN A WAY HE *WAS* A BIT *TWO-FACED*, WASN'T HE? YOU MIGHT THINK THAT LYDIA ACTED A LITTLE *CATTY* ABOUT THE WHOLE AFFAIR, BUT AFTER ALL, SHE'D LIVED WITH *CATS* FOR YEARS! WHEN SHE GOT HER BEAUTY BACK, SHE WAS PRETTY AS A *PICTURE!* BUT IF YOU THINK *SHE* USED TO BE UGLY, WAIT'LL YOU SEE *MY* PICTURE! YES, A *REAL PHOTOGRAPH...* AND YOU CAN FIND OUT HOW TO GET IT JUST BY READING *THE VAULT KEEPER'S CORNER* IN THIS ISSUE! HEH! 'BYE FOR NOW!

HATCHET-KILLER!

THE SLEEPING SUBURB OF WESTFALLS LIES HUDDLED UNDER A DRENCHING TORRENT OF RAIN... HUSHED... TENSE... EXPECTANTLY AWAITING THE LIGHT OF DAY THAT IS BUT A FEW HOURS HENCE. PEOPLE RESTLESSLY TOSS AND TURN IN THEIR BEDS, AND THE RAINDROPS SOUND LIKE A MILLION SOFTLY FALLING FOOTSTEPS THAT HERALD THE APPROACH OF DEATH!

A BOLT OF LIGHTNING FLASHES THROUGH THE BLACK SKY, AND THE FOLLOWING CLAP OF THUNDER MOMENTARILY DROWNS THE RAIN'S WHISPERINGS. THEN ALL IS STILL AGAIN...AND THE SHROUD OF FEAR SETTLES ONCE MORE...

WHAT MAKES AN ENTIRE COMMUNITY DREAD THE OMINOUS NIGHT? WHAT IS IT THAT CAUSES A MAN TO LEAP FROM HIS BED UPON HEARING A STRANGE NOISE AND PEER ANXIOUSLY THROUGH THE RAIN-STREAKED WINDOW PANE?

THE ANSWER LIES IN THE RAIN-SWEPT STREET, IN THE HEADLINES OF A SOPPING, THREE-DAY-OLD NEWSPAPER...

AN UNKNOWN, MANIACAL KILLER! *THAT* IS THE REASON FOR THE TENSION...THE FEAR... THE MANY DREAMS...

TRIBUNE
ET-KILLER
IKES AGAIN

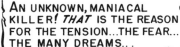

NO! NO! NO!

NO!
OH...

HEY, HONEY! WAKE UP! YOU'VE BEEN HAVING A *NIGHTMARE!*

OH, TOM! THANK GOODNESS YOU WOKE ME! I WAS HAVING A *TERRIBLE* DREAM ABOUT THAT AWFUL *HATCHET-KILLER!*

WELL, YOU'RE ALL RIGHT NOW! YOU SHOULDN'T THINK ABOUT IT SO MUCH!

I CAN'T HELP IT! THREE PERSONS HAVE BEEN KILLED! THERE'S NO TELLING *WHO'LL* BE NEXT! I'M... I'M *FRIGHTENED!*

NOW, DON'T WORRY! THE POLICE WILL CATCH THE KILLER!

2

I'LL HAVE TO BE LEAVING FOR WORK SOON...DON'T WANT TO MISS THE TRAIN! HILDA COMING TODAY?

THE PART-TIME MAID? YES, I... OH, THERE'S THE DOORBELL...

HELLO, HILDA! WE WERE WONDERING IF YOU WERE COMING THIS WEEK!

TERRIBLE DAY OUTSIDE! BUT A GOOD DAY TO STAY *INSIDE* AND CLEAN!

I'M GLAD YOU *DID* COME! YOU CAN KEEP MY WIFE COMPANY WHILE I'M GONE!

IS THERE SOMETHING THE MATTER, MRS. NORTH?

IT'S THOSE HATCHET KILLINGS! THEY MAKE ME NERVOUS! I'M AFRAID TO BE ALONE!

WELL, DON'T YOU FRET ABOUT THAT! NO ONE'S GOING TO HURT YOU!

TIME FOR ME TO SHOVE OFF, HONEY! I'LL HAVE TO FINISH SOME WORK AT THE OFFICE, SO I WON'T BE HOME TILL LATE TONIGHT!

ALL RIGHT, DEAR! GOODBYE!

OH, THE WEATHER IS SIMPLY *AWFUL!* AND I WAS SUPPOSED TO GO SHOPPING WITH FLORA HUTCHINSON!

FLORA HUTCH... WHY, MRS. NORTH! HAVEN'T YOU READ TODAY'S PAPER? *THE HUTCHINSONS ARE DEAD!*

DEAD? WHY, HILDA...WHAT DO YOU MEAN?

THE *HATCHET-KILLER,* MRS. NORTH! KILLED THEM BOTH WHILE THEY SLEPT! THEY WERE *HACKED TO PIECES!* HERE...READ IT!

3

OH, HILDA! THIS IS HORRIBLE!

Star NEWS

WO KILLED IN SLEEP

HUTCHINSONS OF HATCHET-

HATCHET KILLINGS TOTAL 5!

WE WERE SO CLOSE! I KNEW THEM BOTH SO WELL! THAT MAKES FIVE THAT ARE DEAD! OH, WHERE WILL IT END?

SOMETIMES I THINK THE MURDERER IS TOO SMART TO BE CAUGHT!

HILDA, YOU KNEW THE HUTCHINSONS, DIDN'T YOU?

YES! MATTER OF FACT I WORKED FOR THEM JUST YESTERDAY!

...AND THEY WERE KILLED LAST NIGHT! THE KILLER MUST BE INSANE! A FIEND!

PERHAPS!

THE DAY PASSES SLOWLY AND THE RAIN STORM INCREASES IN FURY WHILE MRS. NORTH BUSIES HERSELF WITH HOUSE CLEANING TO KEEP HER MIND OFF THE HATCHET-KILLER!

OHH...WHAT A DAY! HMM! SIX O'CLOCK! WHILE HILDA'S UPSTAIRS, I'LL TURN ON THE TELEVISION... GET THE NEWS!

...AS FOR THE POLICE, THEY CLAIM THE HATCHET-KILLER COULD BE EITHER A MAN OR WOMAN, BUT MUST BE OF CONSIDERABLE SIZE AND STRENGTH AS EVIDENCED BY THE VIOLENCE OF THE...

TSK, TSK...

4

...LAST NIGHT'S DOUBLE MURDER HAS FURNISHED THE POLICE WITH A CLUE! A WHITE SCARF WAS FOUND AT THE SCENE OF THE CRIME AND...

OH! I HEAR HILDA COMING DOWNSTAIRS...

CLICK!

...STILL WORRYING ABOUT THE HATCHET-KILLER, MRS. NORTH?

WELL... A LITTLE, HILDA! I DO WISH THE POLICE WOULD CATCH WHOEVER IT IS!

OH, THE KILLER IS SMART, ALL RIGHT...BUT IT WAS A BIG MISTAKE TO LEAVE THAT WHITE SCARF WHERE...

HOW DID YOU KNOW ABOUT THAT?

WHY...MRS. NORTH, I... I...ER...

I HEARD IT ON TELEVISION JUST A MINUTE AGO! HOW DID YOU KNOW ABOUT IT?

I...I HEARD IT ON THE RADIO IN YOUR BEDROOM!

...OH! I'M SORRY, HILDA! I DIDN'T MEAN TO...

SHE SEEMED SO GUILTY! BUT...IT'S NOT POSSIBLE SHE COULD BE THE KILLER! YET...SHE IS VERY STRONG! OH, I WISH TOM WERE HERE!

HILDA... I THINK WE'VE DONE ENOUGH FOR TODAY! YOU CAN GO HOME...IF YOU WISH!

OH, BUT I'M NOT GOING, MRS. NORTH! I WOULDN'T THINK OF LEAVING YOU ALONE!

5

YOU'RE... YOU'RE *NOT* GOING?

NO! YOUR HUSBAND WON'T BE HOME TILL LATE... AND THE STORM IS SO BAD... I'LL STAY!

MRS. NORTH IS FRIGHTENED... AND AS THE EVENING HOURS WEAR ON, HER SUSPICIONS OF HILDA MULTIPLY!

HATCHET-KILLER?

IF TOM DOESN'T COME HOME SOON, I'LL GO TO PIECES... I KNOW I WILL! HILDA WORKED FOR THE HUTCHINSONS... SHE COULD'VE WORKED FOR THE OTHERS THAT WERE...

?

HILDA! WHAT ARE YOU DOING WITH THAT HATCHET?

WHY, MRS. NORTH... I WAS JUST GOING TO CHOP SOME WOOD FOR THE FIRE!

OH, LORD...LORD, HELP ME! I...I CAN'T STAND MUCH MORE OF THIS! THIS *WAITING*...THIS NOT *KNOWING*...IT'S DRIVING ME *CRAZY!* TOM! I'LL...I'LL CALL TOM...(SOB) ASK HIM TO COME HOME!

...HELLO? HELLO, OPERATOR!... OPERATOR! WHY... THE PHONE'S DEAD!

GOOD LORD!

SHE MUST'VE CUT THE LINE! SHE...SHE WANTS TO KILL ME! THAT'S WHY SHE STAYED LATE TONIGHT! SHE KNEW TOM WAS WORKING LATE! HILDA'S GOING TO KILL ME! HILDA'S THE HATCHET-KILLER!

6

SHE CAN'T WAIT MUCH LONGER! SHE'LL TRY TO KILL ME SOON! BUT I'LL BE READY FOR HER! I'LL KEEP THIS KITCHEN KNIFE!

IF ONLY TOM WERE HERE! I CAN'T PHONE THE POLICE... AND NO NEIGHBORS LIVE NEAR ENOUGH! SHE'D BUTCHER ME BEFORE I REACHED THE DOOR! OH, TOM... HURRY HOME... *PLEASE!*

OH... HERE SHE COMES! GOD, MAKE HER *WAIT!* (SOB) WHA... WHY... SHE'S LOOKING FOR SOMETHING! WHAT COULD SHE DO...

OH, MY GOD!

THE HATCHET! LYING ON THE TABLE! SHE SEES IT!... SHE'S MOVING TOWARD IT!

...MRS. NORTH...

STAY AWAY! STAY AWAY OR I'LL KILL YOU! DON'T COME NEAR ME!

STOP YELLING, MRS. NORTH! AND GIVE ME THAT KNIFE... YOU...

I WARN YOU! STAY AWAY FROM ME! STAY BACK!

7

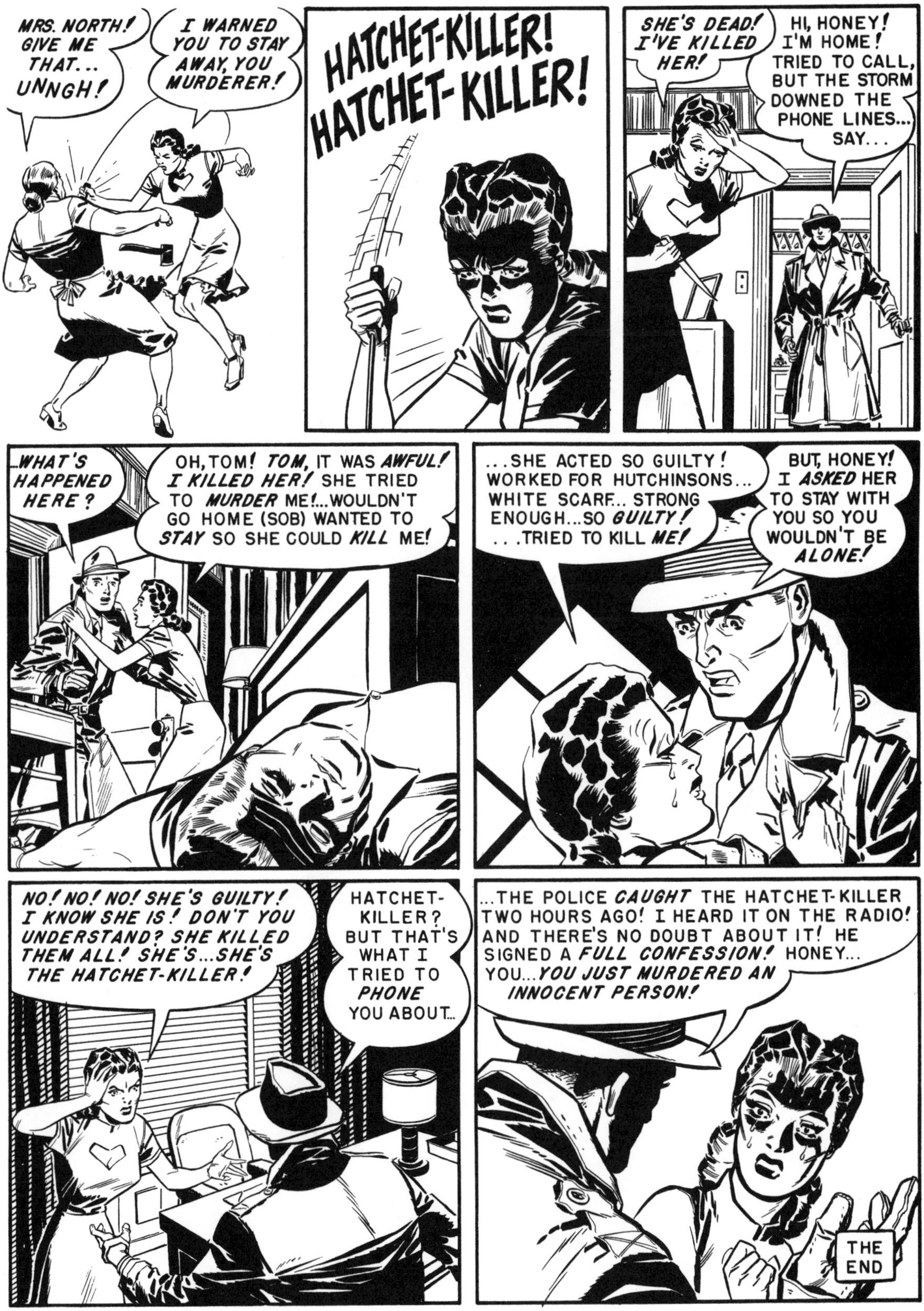
MRS. NORTH! GIVE ME THAT... UNNGH!
I WARNED YOU TO STAY AWAY, YOU MURDERER!
HATCHET-KILLER! HATCHET-KILLER!
SHE'S DEAD! I'VE KILLED HER!
HI, HONEY! I'M HOME! TRIED TO CALL, BUT THE STORM DOWNED THE PHONE LINES... SAY...
...WHAT'S HAPPENED HERE?
OH, TOM! TOM, IT WAS AWFUL! I KILLED HER! SHE TRIED TO MURDER ME!...WOULDN'T GO HOME (SOB) WANTED TO STAY SO SHE COULD KILL ME!
...SHE ACTED SO GUILTY! WORKED FOR HUTCHINSONS... WHITE SCARF... STRONG ENOUGH...SO GUILTY! ...TRIED TO KILL ME!
BUT, HONEY! I ASKED HER TO STAY WITH YOU SO YOU WOULDN'T BE ALONE!
NO! NO! NO! SHE'S GUILTY! I KNOW SHE IS! DON'T YOU UNDERSTAND? SHE KILLED THEM ALL! SHE'S...SHE'S THE HATCHET-KILLER!
HATCHET-KILLER? BUT THAT'S WHAT I TRIED TO PHONE YOU ABOUT...
...THE POLICE CAUGHT THE HATCHET-KILLER TWO HOURS AGO! I HEARD IT ON THE RADIO! AND THERE'S NO DOUBT ABOUT IT! HE SIGNED A FULL CONFESSION! HONEY... YOU...YOU JUST MURDERED AN INNOCENT PERSON!
THE END

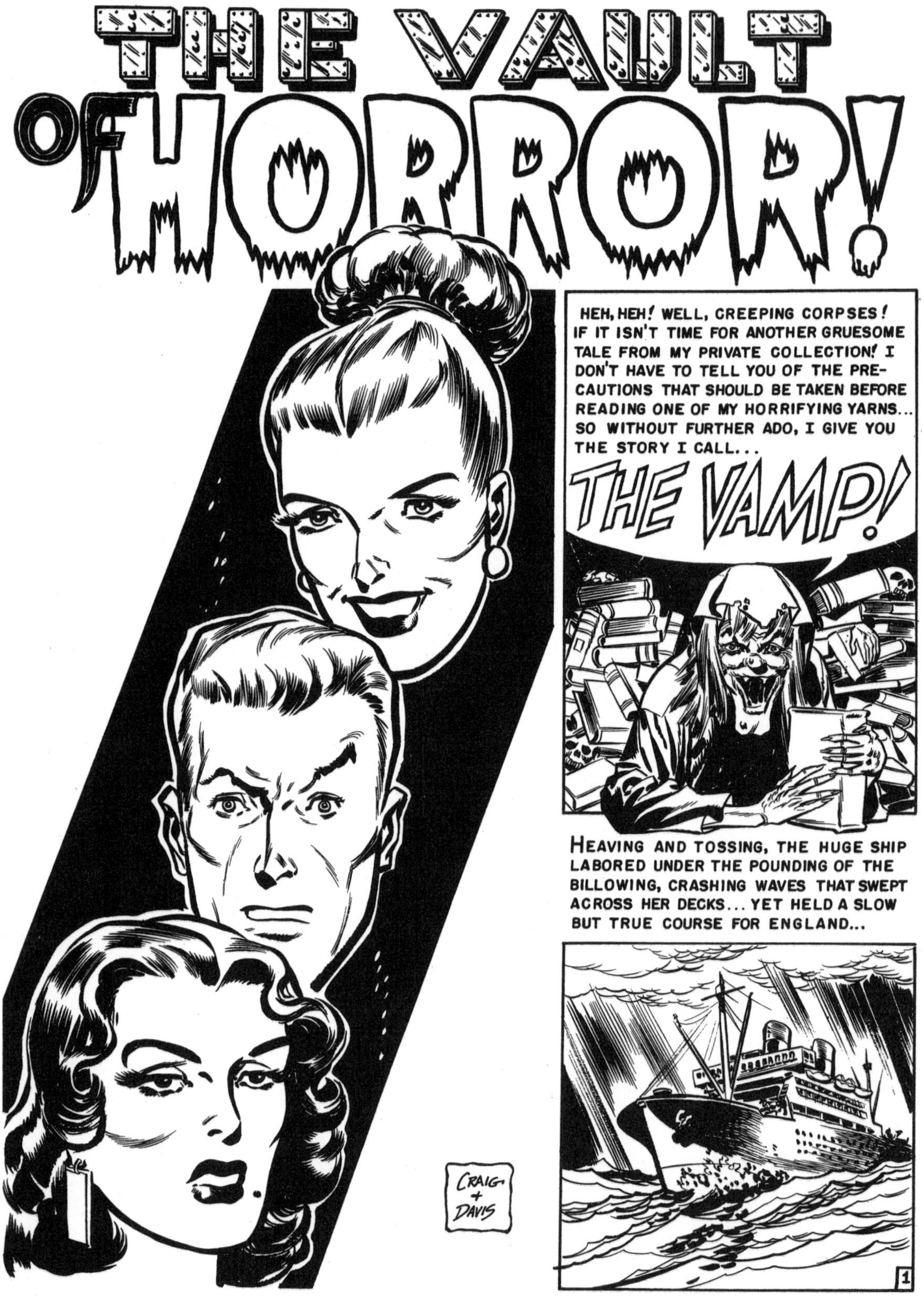
THE VAULT OF HORROR!
HEH, HEH! WELL, CREEPING CORPSES! IF IT ISN'T TIME FOR ANOTHER GRUESOME TALE FROM MY PRIVATE COLLECTION! I DON'T HAVE TO TELL YOU OF THE PRECAUTIONS THAT SHOULD BE TAKEN BEFORE READING ONE OF MY HORRIFYING YARNS... SO WITHOUT FURTHER ADO, I GIVE YOU THE STORY I CALL...
THE VAMP!
HEAVING AND TOSSING, THE HUGE SHIP LABORED UNDER THE POUNDING OF THE BILLOWING, CRASHING WAVES THAT SWEPT ACROSS HER DECKS... YET HELD A SLOW BUT TRUE COURSE FOR ENGLAND...
CRAIG + DAVIS
1

NESTLED COMFORTABLY IN THEIR CABIN, ARTHUR LANG AND HIS WIFE, DEENA, HAPPILY PORED OVER TRAVEL FOLDERS OF THE EUROPEAN CONTINENT...

ISN'T IT *WONDERFUL*, ARTHUR? IT'S JUST LIKE A SECOND HONEYMOON!

ONE WHOLE MONTH! BOY, ARE WE GOING TO HAVE A *TIME*!

SEVERAL DAYS LATER, THEIR SHIP DOCKED IN ENGLAND...

WHY, I CAN'T BELIEVE IT! IT'S NOT FOGGY AT ALL!

HA, HA! NOT *EVERY* DAY IS RAINY AND FOGGY, DEENA! THE SUN SHINES HERE TOO!

DURING THE TWO WEEKS THAT FOLLOWED, ARTHUR AND DEENA LIVED LIFE TO THE HILT... LONDON, PARIS, GENEVA, VIENNA, MILAN, ROME...

AND FINALLY ONE NIGHT, TIRED BUT HAPPY, THEY CHECKED INTO A HOTEL IN BUDAPEST, *HUNGARY!*

OH, I'M JUST *EXHAUSTED!* I'M GOING STRAIGHT TO BED!

NOT ME! I THINK I'LL TAKE A WALK BEFORE I TURN IN!

WELL, IF I'M ASLEEP WHEN YOU GET BACK, DON'T DISTURB ME! I THINK I COULD SLEEP FOR A WEEK!

OKAY, HONEY! PLEASANT DREAMS!

EERIE SHADOWS FELL ACROSS THE STREETS, AS ARTHUR WALKED THROUGH THE CHILLY, DAMP HUNGARIAN NIGHT...

I'VE COME A LONG WAY...BEEN WALKING LONGER THAN I THOUGHT...

...GUESS I'D BETTER START BACK TO THE HOTEL! MAYBE DEENA'S... SAY! WHAT'S THAT NOISE? SOUNDS LIKE SOMEONE RUNNING THIS WAY!

A GIRL!

HELP! OH, HELP PLEASE! A DEAD MAN...DOWN THERE!

A DEAD MAN? WE BETTER CALL THE POLICE!

NO! THEY WILL BE HERE SOON ENOUGH! IF YOU OR I ARE FOUND HERE, WE WILL BE IN GREAT TROUBLE! WE MUST LEAVE!

BUT...BUT WHY? WE HAVEN'T DONE ANYTHING! AT LEAST...

THERE HAVE BEEN A SERIES OF MURDERS OF LATE! THE POLICE HAVE REACHED THE POINT WHERE THEY WILL PROSECUTE ANYONE!

LISTEN! POLICE SIRENS!

YOU SEE? OH, PLEASE! YOU MUST BELIEVE AND TRUST ME! QUICKLY! THIS WAY!

ARTHUR HUMBLY FOLLOWED THE RAVISHING, DARK-HAIRED BEAUTY THROUGH NUMEROUS STREETS AND ALLEYS UNTIL FINALLY...

WE ARE SAFE NOW! I LIVE NEAR HERE... WILL YOU TAKE ME HOME?

WHY...WHY, YES! I'D BE DELIGHTED TO!

FOR A LONG WHILE THEY STOOD IN THE SHADOWS TALKING QUIETLY...INTIMATELY! ARTHUR'S HEAD REELED WITH THE SMELL OF HER EXOTIC PERFUME, THE CLOSENESS OF THEIR BODIES...

GEORGETTE...IT'S GETTING LATE! I MEAN...I DON'T WANT TO GO, BUT... MY WIFE...

I KNOW, ARTHUR! ...YOUR WIFE!

YOU'RE...YOU'RE THE MOST BEAUTIFUL WOMAN I'VE EVER MET! I...I ALMOST WISH THAT I WASN'T MARRIED! I MEAN, YOU SEEM TO CAST A SPELL OVER ME! GEORGETTE...

YES, ARTHUR?

GEORGETTE...

HEH, HEH! ARTHUR RETURNED TO THE HOTEL AND SNEAKED INTO BED! HE SLEPT FITFULLY, FOR A TANTALIZING VISION OF GEORGETTE PLAGUED HIS THOUGHTS. THE NEXT DAY, ARTHUR FOUND IT DIFFICULT TO KEEP HIS MIND FROM WANDERING...UNTIL HE SAW THE MORNING NEWSPAPER... HEH, HEH!

WHAT TIME DID YOU GET IN LAST NIGHT, ARTHUR?

VAMPIRE KILLING? I DIDN'T KNOW THERE *WERE* SUCH THINGS!

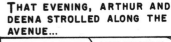

ARTHUR! I ASKED YOU A QUESTION!

HUH? *OH!* ER...A SHORT WHILE AFTER *YOU* WENT TO BED!

THAT EVENING, ARTHUR AND DEENA STROLLED ALONG THE AVENUE...

QUITE A LARGE CITY, ISN'T IT, DEENA?

NOT NEARLY AS LARGE AS... OH, ARTHUR! LOOK! OVER THERE!

SOMETHING MUST HAVE HAPPENED!

YEAH! A CROWD'S GATHER-ING! C'MON! LET'S TAKE A LOOK!

SUBWAY-WISE, ARTHUR AND HIS WIFE EASILY ELBOWED THEIR WAY TO THE FRONT OF THE CROWD...AND STARED DOWN AT THE LIFELESS BODY OF A YOUNG HUNGARIAN GIRL...

ARTHUR! SHE... *SHE'S DEAD!*

APPREHENSIVELY, ARTHUR'S EYES SEARCHED THE FACES OF THE PEOPLE AROUND HIM. A MOMENT PASSED BEFORE HE REALIZED THAT ONE WAS STARING DIRECTLY BACK AT HIM... *GEORGETTE!*

THEY LOOKED AT ONE ANOTHER FOR LONG MINUTES... AND THEN, SUDDENLY, SHE WAS GONE! ARTHUR TOOK HIS WIFE BACK TO THE HOTEL...

OOOOH... WHAT A *HORRIBLE* SIGHT! I HOPE I DON'T HAVE NIGHTMARES!

WELL, ER...DEENA, I'M GOING TO RUN DOWNSTAIRS FOR A FEW MINUTES...NEED SOME *FRESH AIR!*

A SHORT WHILE LATER ARTHUR WAS IN GEORGETTE'S ARMS...

BUT... GEORGETTE! I'M *MARRIED!* I...I...

DON'T THINK ABOUT IT, ARTHUR! NOW YOU BELONG TO *ME!*

BUT IT'S NOT RIGHT! IT'S...

I DON'T CARE! I LOVE YOU... AND *I WON'T LET ANYONE ELSE HAVE YOU!* YOU'RE MINE!

BUT...BUT IF SHE KNEW...

FORGET ABOUT HER! JUST... JUST KISS ME... LOVE ME...

IT WAS ALMOST DAWN WHEN ARTHUR TIREDLY AND SHAMEFACEDLY ENTERED THE HOTEL ROOM. HIS CONSCIENCE HAD FINALLY WON ITS BATTLE... AND HE WAS READY TO TELL EVERYTHING...

ARTHUR! WHERE HAVE YOU BEEN? I'VE BEEN SICK WITH *WORRY!*

DEENA...DEENA...I HAVE SOMETHING TO TELL YOU!

ARTHUR SLUMPED ON THE BED AND TOLD DEENA THE WHOLE, SORDID TRUTH.

...AND THAT'S IT, HONEY! SHE SAYS SHE WON'T GIVE ME UP...WON'T LET YOU HAVE ME!

I SEE! YOU...YOU MUST BE TIRED, DEAR. WHY DON'T YOU GO TO SLEEP?

THAT NIGHT, ARTHUR STRODE THE STREETS TO GEORGETTE'S HOUSE, DEEP IN THOUGHT...

I'LL TELL HER I CAN'T SEE HER ANYMORE! I DON'T *LOVE* HER...IT WAS JUST A *VACATION ROMANCE!* AN INFATUATION... *HEY!* WHAT'S GOING ON UP AHEAD THERE?

SOMEONE PULLED THAT MAN INTO THE ALLEY! *LISTEN TO HIS SCREAMS!* I'VE GOT TO HELP HIM!

RACING INTO THE ALLEY, ARTHUR SAW A SINISTER FIGURE HUDDLED OVER THE MAN ON THE GROUND...

HEY, YOU! STOP!

WHA...?

GEORGETTE.

YOU...KILLED HIM! YOU'RE A VAMPIRE! A FILTHY, BLOODTHIRSTY VAMPIRE! I HATE YOU! I DESPISE YOU! YOU DISGUST ME!

NO! ARTHUR, LISTEN TO ME!

LEAVE ME ALONE! GET OUT OF MY WAY! I NEVER WANT TO SEE YOU AGAIN!

ARTHUR! COME BACK! I WON'T LET YOU GO! I'LL KILL YOU BEFORE I'LL LET YOU GO BACK TO HER!

WHAP

LATER, ARTHUR BREATHLESSLY ENTERED THE HOTEL ROOM AND HURRIEDLY BEGAN PACKING. HIS WIFE WAS STRANGELY ABSENT...

...NARROW ESCAPE! I'M JUST A DUMB FOOL! WHEN DEENA COMES BACK WE'LL HOP A PLANE...

BUT HOURS PASSED BEFORE DEENA FINALLY RETURNED...

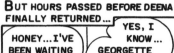

HONEY...I'VE BEEN WAITING FOR YOU!

YES, I KNOW... GEORGETTE SAID YOU WOULD BE!

GEORGETTE? YOU'VE BEEN TO SEE GEORGETTE?

YES! I WENT TO ASK HER TO GIVE YOU UP...BUT WE QUARRELED!

IS THAT WHY YOU LOOK SO...SO PALE? WHAT...WHAT HAPPENED?

WE ARGUED...AND THEN SHE ATTACKED ME! I KNOW SHE BIT ME...

...SEE? HERE? HERE ON THE NECK! I GUESS I PASSED OUT THEN!

ON THE NECK? GOOD LORD! NO WONDER YOU'RE SO PALE! SHE'S DRAINED YOU OF YOUR BLOOD! SHE...SHE'S TURNED YOU INTO A... A ...

VAMPIRE!

- THE END -

HEH, HEH, HEH! THAT'S THE KIND OF STORY I LIKE TO TELL ... EVERYBODY GETS IT ... IN THE NECK! BUT GEORGETTE KEPT HER WORD, DIDN'T SHE? SHE COULDN'T KILL ARTHUR HERSELF...SO SHE FIXED IT SO DEENA WOULD DO THE JOB! WE ALL KNOW THAT A VAMPIRE'S VICTIM BECOMES A VAMPIRE TOO! THAT'S REALLY GETTING RID OF TWO BATS WITH ONE STONE, EH? WELL... NOW I'LL TURN YOU BACK TO THE OLD WITCH... ANOTHER OLD BAT! YOU'LL FIND HER COLUMN BRIMMING OVER WITH INFO INCLUDING THE METHOD FOR OBTAINING ACTUAL PHOTOS OF YOUR THREE GHOULUNATICS!

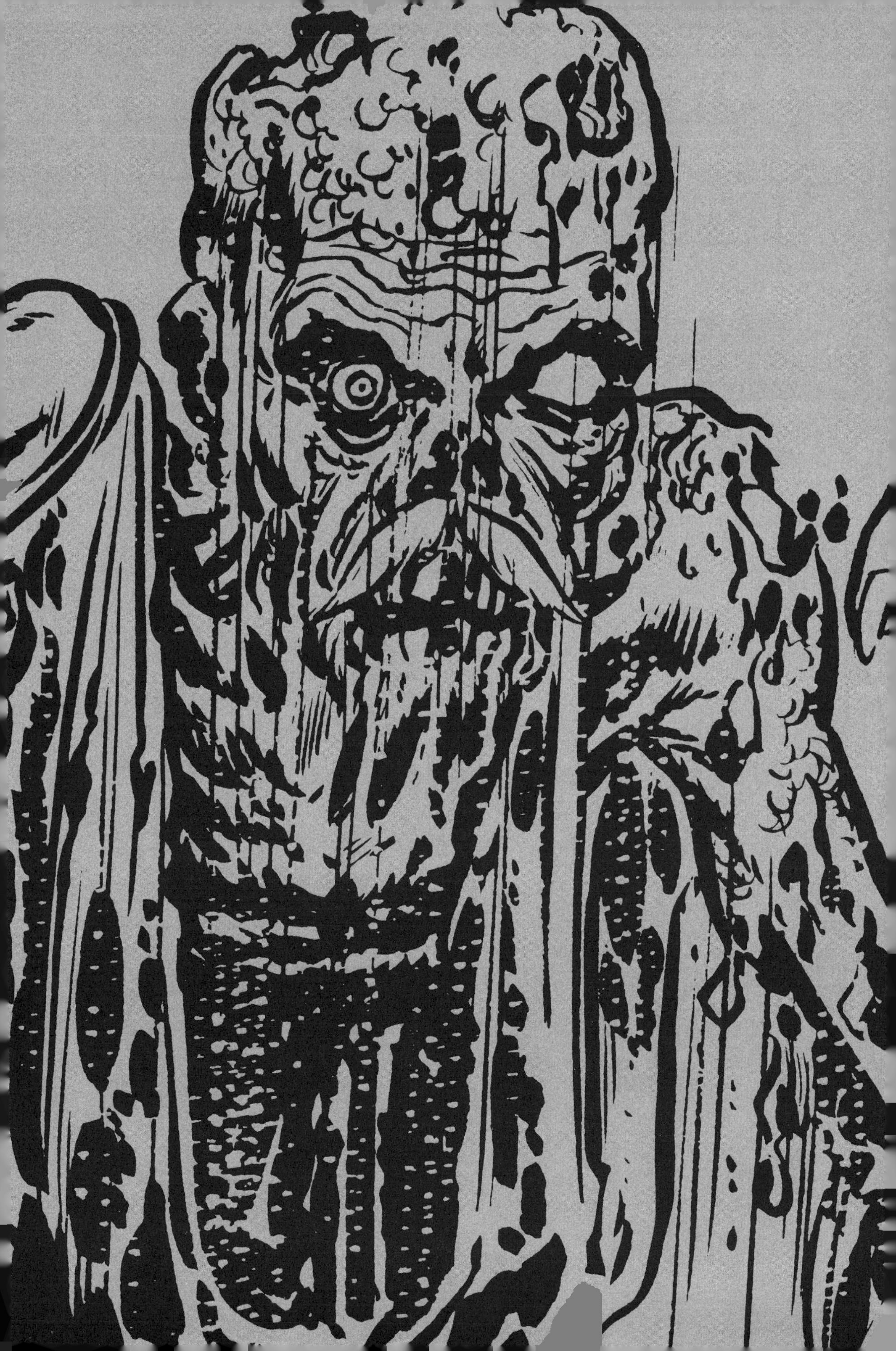

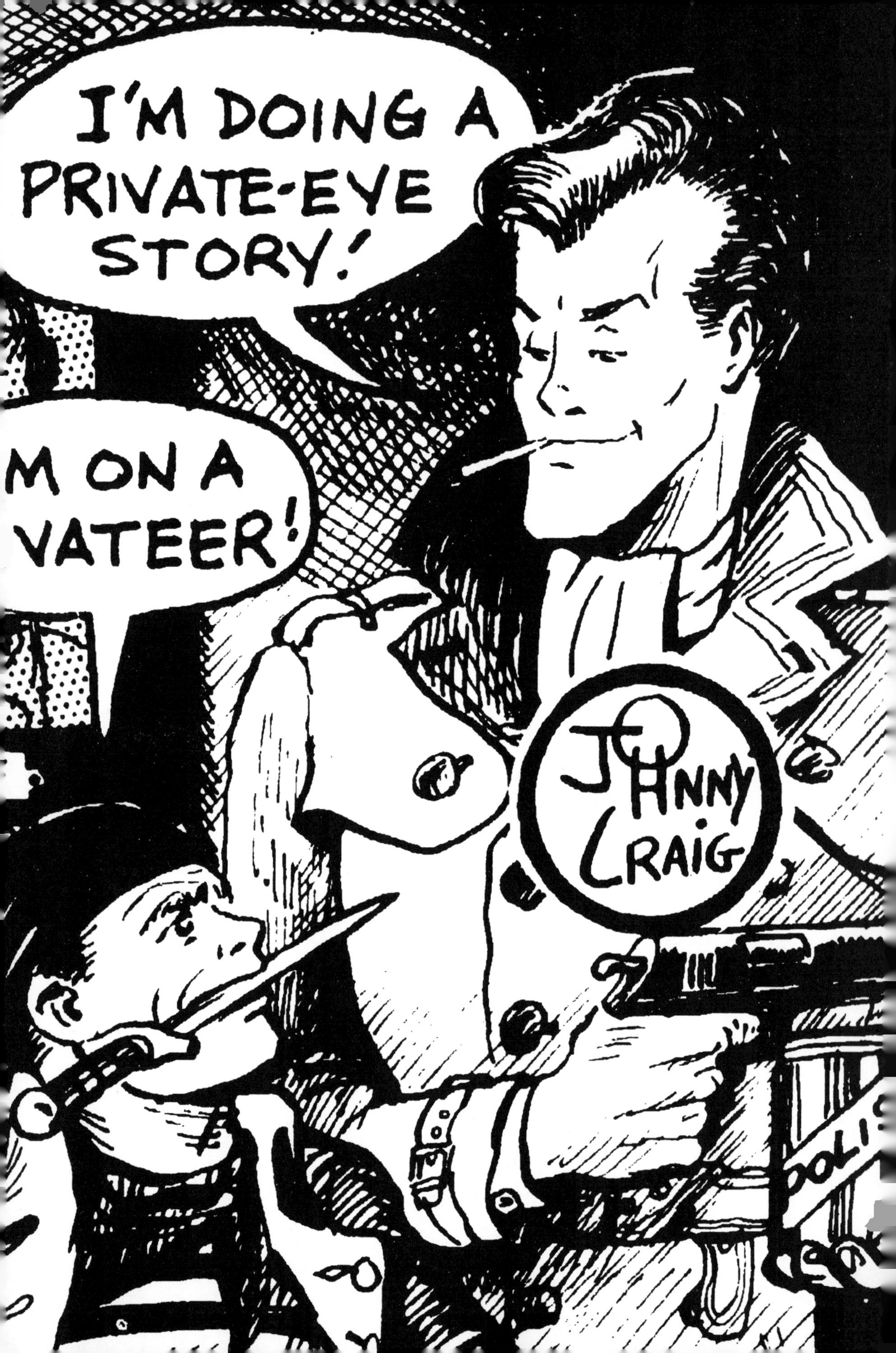
I'M DOING A PRIVATE-EYE STORY!
M ON A VATEER!
JOHNNY CRAIG

JOHNNY CRAIG

"Really great and so neat. ... I used to tell him that maybe that's why you're slow — every time you use something, you clean it. A nice person ... a gentleman right down the line."

— Marie Severin

If hard-boiled crime novelist James M. Cain had been a cartoonist, chances are he would have drawn like Johnny Craig, EC's master of genteel horror and nerve-jangling suspense.

It's safe to say that Craig was not one of the fastest artists in the EC stable. He was known for his slow, meticulous approach to drawing, and yet his total output of pages is larger than many realize. The stories in this volume represent only about a quarter of his work for EC.

As he noted in 1970, in an interview with Roger Hill in *Squa Tront* #4, "I was supposed to do at least three stories a month. I was lucky if I did one." Still, Craig's meticulousness paid off with his well-written and superbly drawn stories and his striking, sometimes notorious, covers.

He was EC's longest-serving artist, having started when the company was still known as Educational Comics and run by Bill Gaines's father, M.C. Gaines (known variously as "Charlie" or "Max"). He stayed with the company to the end of its comic book days and on through the short-lived Picto-Fiction period. He also served as editor for the last six issues of *Vault of Horror* and all five issues of the New Direction title, *Extra* (for which he also drew the covers).

When the Picto-Fiction magazines folded in 1956, Craig tried freelancing but found comics work harder and harder to come by. He left the field in the late 1950s. For a number of years, Craig concentrated on advertising illustration and art direction. He eventually returned to comics, first in 1964 for American Comics Group, then in 1966, working under the pseudonym Jay Taycee (derived from his initials), for Warren's black-and-white horror magazines, *Eerie* and *Creepy* (which provided a welcoming environment for several EC alumni).

Eventually, Craig wound up penciling and inking for DC and Marvel on characters such as Hawkman and Iron Man, but his slow, meticulous approach to producing comic art left his editors fuming. Additionally, his work was tampered with to make it conform to house styles, so he finally left the comics field entirely around 1980.

OPPOSITE: A Marie Severin caricature of Reed Crandall (left) and Johnny Craig (right). Detail from one of several "Thank you for your note" fliers that were sent to EC letter writers. This one is circa 1954.

Given the remarkable skill Craig developed as a comic book artist and painter, he had surprisingly little formal art training. He studied at the Art Students League, but he learned on the job from an early age. Born April 25, 1926, in Pleasantville, New York and raised in New York City, John Thomas Alexis Craig entered the comics business in 1940 at the age of 14, working part-time for artist Harry Lampert. Lampert, who co-created and drew the first adventure of The Flash in *Flash Comics* #1 (January 1940) from All-American Comics, also worked on The King; Red, White and Blue; and The Atom before joining the Army later that year. (All-American Comics was owned and managed by M.C. Gaines in partnership with DC owner Harry Donenfeld.)

For one dollar a week, Craig did Lampert's filing, ruled and lettered his pages, and ran errands while Lampert was producing The King. After Lampert's departure to serve Uncle Sam, Craig went to work for legendary editor Sheldon Mayer at the All-American offices at 225 Lafayette Street in Manhattan, still part-time, but now working as a staff artist, doing paste-ups, corrections, lettering, and other production tasks. He worked there until 1944, when he joined the Merchant Marine. He later joined the Army and was sent to Germany, where he was wounded.

In 1946, he returned to civilian life in the U.S. and promptly wed Antoinette ("Toni") Picciallo. He briefly freelanced for companies such as Fox, Lev Gleason, and Magazine Enterprises. Then he went back to work for M.C. Gaines, not at All-American (which Gaines had sold his share of to DC during the war) but at Gaines's new comics company, Educational Comics. The original EC produced uplifting (but deadly dull) fare like *Picture Stories From the Bible* and *Picture Stories From Science*, along with kiddy comics like *Land of the Lost* and *Tiny Tot Comics*.

This time, however, Craig wasn't working in the production department — he was drawing covers and stories for comics such as *Blackstone the Magician Detective Fights Crime* (certainly a contender for "longest comic book title of all time") and *Moon Girl and the Prince* (Moon Girl, with art by Sheldon Moldoff, was Gaines's attempt to create another Wonder Woman).

Craig had only been working for EC as an artist for a few months when, in 1947, Gaines was killed in a boating accident. Gaines's son William ("Bill"), who had aspirations to become a chemistry teacher, reluctantly took over the company at the insistence of his mother, Jessie Gaines, who, on the advice of friends, refused to close down her late husband's heretofore unprofitable comics venture. After Max Gaines's death, his business manager Sol Cohen realized that EC was going down the tubes, so one of Cohen's first moves was to stop publishing new *Picture Stories* titles, and to change EC's name to Entertaining Comics. Then he killed off the kiddy titles and tried his hand at coming up with some crime, Western, and romance comics that might actually sell.

At first, Bill Gaines, who was somewhat estranged from his father and didn't really care about the comics business, did little with the company beyond coming in occasionally to sign checks. But after a few months of reading some comics, he became interested in the business and tried to make EC a going concern.

Under Bill Gaines, Johnny Craig gamely shifted over to drawing Western covers and stories for *Saddle Justice* and *Gunfighter*, and crime covers and stories for *War Against Crime* and *Crime Patrol*. (He drew all 11 covers for *War Against Crime* and all 10 for *Crime Patrol*.) He and Al Feldstein collaborated a few times as "F.C. Aljohn," including the cover and lead story for *Modern Love* #2.

That slate of early EC me-too genre titles (there was also *Saddle Romances* and *A Moon ... A Girl ... Romance*) didn't exactly set the comics world on fire, but it did give Craig steady work, and his art got better and better.

Early in 1950, after Sheldon Moldoff presented Bill Gaines with a horror comic prototype (and after a handful of horror stories in *War Against Crime* and *Crime Patrol* sparked an uptick in reader interest), Gaines decided to stop copying existing trends and try something new. (Moldoff thought he had a deal with Gaines but was never compensated for his idea. The stories Moldoff drew for his prototype did see print in various EC titles later on.)

Craig drew the very first EC horror covers (*Crime Patrol* #16 and *War Against Crime* #11, both February-March 1950), though he did not draw the first appearance of the Vault-Keeper, who was to become his signature character. The Vault-Keeper's first few tryout appearances were written and drawn by Al Feldstein in the final two issues of those crime titles. With the first issue of *Vault of Horror* (confusingly designated "#12," dated April-May 1950), Johnny Craig became the regular artist for the Vault-Keeper.

That year, EC dropped all of its old titles and began publishing its "New Trend" titles, beginning with *The Crypt of Terror* (soon renamed *Tales From The Crypt*) and *The Vault of Horror*. *Weird Science* and *Weird Fantasy* followed, then *Haunt of Fear*, *Crime SuspenStories*, and *Two-Fisted Tales*. The EC lineup was expanded through 1954 with the addition of *Frontline Combat*, *Shock SuspenStories*, *Mad*, *Panic*, and *Piracy*, later to be followed by the "New Direction" and "Picto-Fiction" titles.

Even though he was in on Gaines's and Feldstein's early brainstorming sessions, Johnny Craig modestly declined any credit for helping to create EC's horror comics, though he did draw one of the earliest horror stories in comics, "Zombie Terror!," which ran in EC's *Moon Girl* #5, Fall 1948 (not in this volume). "I seem to recall being quite pleased with the idea of coming out with a new line of material that we felt would sell very well, that would be interesting to both write and draw. I was pleased, but I don't think I had much to do with the actual decision," Craig noted in that 1970 *Squa Tront* interview.

Although hardly the grisliest of the EC contributors (Jack Davis and Graham Ingels vied for that honor), Craig nonetheless became

notorious to the non-comics reading public when one of his covers, showing a ghastly close-up of a hanged man's face (*Crime SuspenStories* #20) was reprinted in Frederic Wertham's *Seduction of the Innocent*, with the caustic caption: "The cover of a children's comic book."

Even more notoriously, another Craig cover was singled out on live television, April 21, 1954, during the Senate Subcommittee on Juvenile Delinquency hearings as a prime example of bad taste. Senator Estes Kefauver (D-Tennessee), displayed a copy of the current issue of *Crime SuspenStories* (#22, May 1954) to Bill Gaines during the hearings, and asked pointedly, "This seems to be a man with a bloody ax holding a woman's head up, which has been severed from her body. Do you think that's in good taste?"

Gaines replied that he thought it was, "for the cover of a horror comic," then went on to

dig his grave deeper. "A cover in bad taste, for example, might be defined as holding her head a little higher so that blood could be seen dripping from it and moving the body a little further over so that the neck of the body could be seen to be bloody."

Kefauver noted, "You've got blood coming out of her mouth." Gaines responded, "A little."

What Gaines was describing in such lurid detail, unbeknownst to the senators and the television audience, was, in fact, the exact cover that Craig had originally drawn — "blood dripping from neck," as Gaines recalled it to Rich Hauser in a 1969 interview. "You could see the bottom of the severed neck and blood was dripping out. To Craig, I said, 'Johnny, move the cover up so the bottom of the page cuts this whole thing off and there isn't any [blood].'" Gaines had actually had Craig tone it down!

Craig was also responsible for a Christmas-themed *Vault* cover that still retains its power to shock, more than 60 years after it was published. *Vault of Horror #35* shows a suburban housewife recoiling in horror from the sight of her Christmas present beneath the tree: a coffin. Behind her, her murderous husband stands poised to decapitate her with an ax. Another grisly Craig cover, *Vault of Horror #30*, showed a severed arm hanging from a subway car strap while passengers in the background gape at it in shock.

So, despite Wallace Wood's ironic comment that Craig drew "the cleanest horror stories you ever saw," Craig certainly earned his stripes at EC, with his graphically striking covers and stories and his intelligently written scripts in *Vault of Horror*. He drew all 29 covers for *Vault of Horror* (making him the only artist to draw all the covers for the complete run of a New Trend title), drew all the lead stories except for two, and edited its final six issues. He also made a strong impression on EC fans with his taut suspense yarns in most issues of *Crime SuspenStories*. He drew 21 of that title's first 22 covers, some of which (as noted above) are as grisly as anything featured on the covers of EC's horror titles.

Among his other artistic trademarks were Craig's slinky, Caniff-esque *femmes fatales* and his distinctive manner of rendering sweat drops on his characters' faces. Craig's stories in the five issues of *Extra* (which he also edited), his covers for the five-issue run of *M.D.*, and his illustrations in EC's Picto-Fiction titles are among his finest work for the company, demonstrating a mature flowering of his talent for dynamic storytelling and excellent writing. One of his *Extra* stories, "Dateline Algiers" (not in this volume), even prefigured the Picto-Fiction style of storytelling with an innovative mix of text and illustrations.

Al Williamson, who worked alongside Craig at EC, felt he was one of the best and most underrated artists. Williamson, as quoted in *The Art of Al Williamson*, summed it up this way: "Johnny Craig should have gotten much more recognition at EC because his stuff was really good ... he wrote good stories and drew them well, and knew how to entertain you."

In subsequent years, Craig's reputation as a skilled draftsman and wordsmith has only grown as his EC work has been more widely disseminated, and more fans have seen the EC cover recreations he was painting for collectors until the end of his life.

Johnny Craig passed away September 13, 2001. He was survived by his wife, Toni (who died in 2006), and his sons, John Jr. and Steven. Craig was inducted posthumously into the Will Eisner Comic Book Hall Of Fame in 2005. He left behind a personal reputation as a kind, gentlemanly soul beloved by family, colleagues, his small army of fans — and a professional reputation as one of the finest draftsmen and writers ever employed in the comics business.

S.C. "STEVE" RINGGENBERG has been an EC Comics fan since his early teens and has had the good fortune to interview many EC contributors, including publisher William Gaines, editors Al Feldstein and Harvey Kurtzman, artists John Severin, George Evans, Jack Davis, Jack Kamen, Al Williamson, Angelo Torres, Frank Frazetta, Sheldon Moldoff, and color editor Marie Severin. He has written comics scripts for DC, Marvel, Bongo, *Heavy Metal*, Red Circle, and Americomics. He has written six young adult novels and co-authored *Al Williamson: Hidden Lands*.

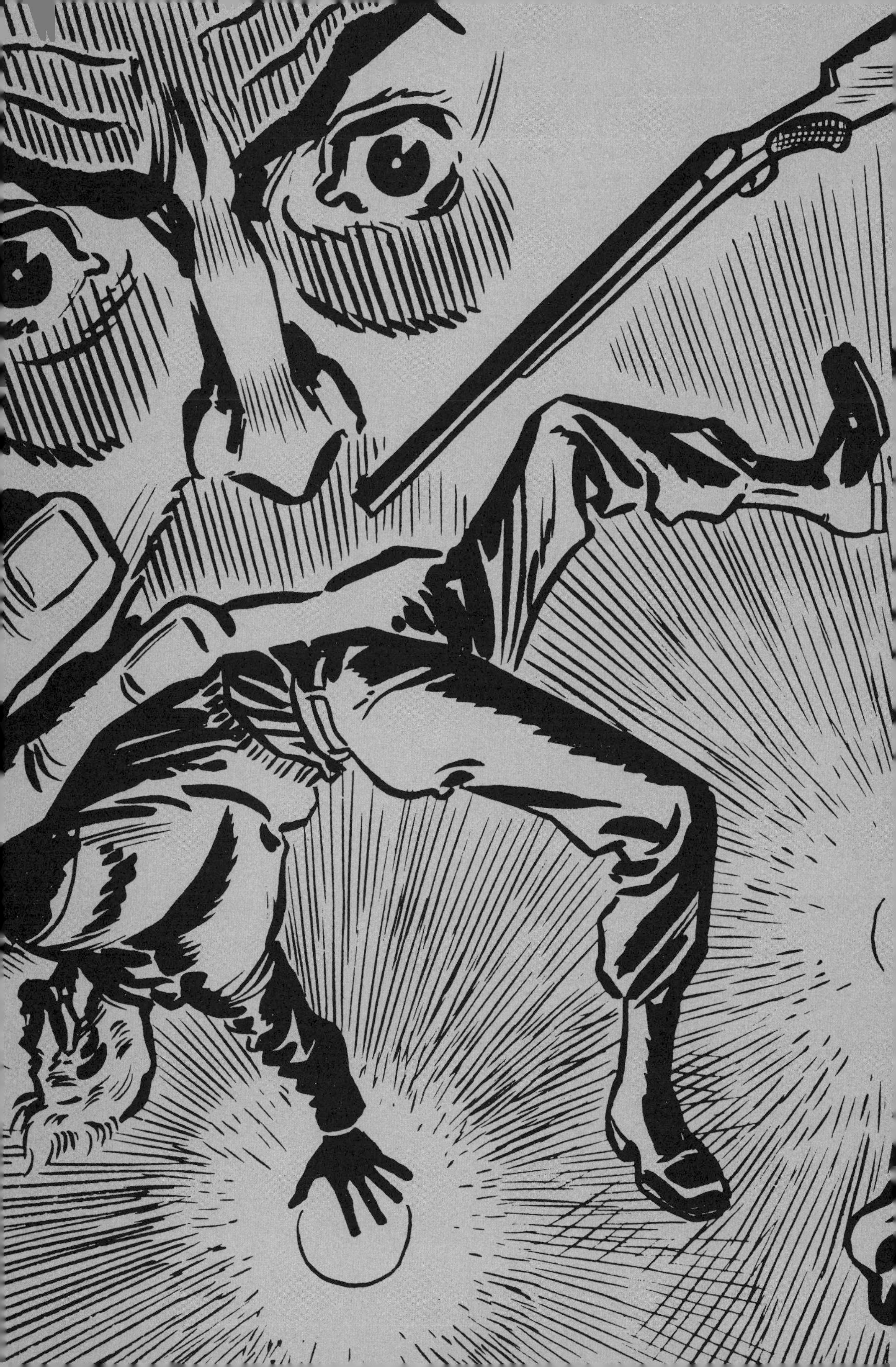

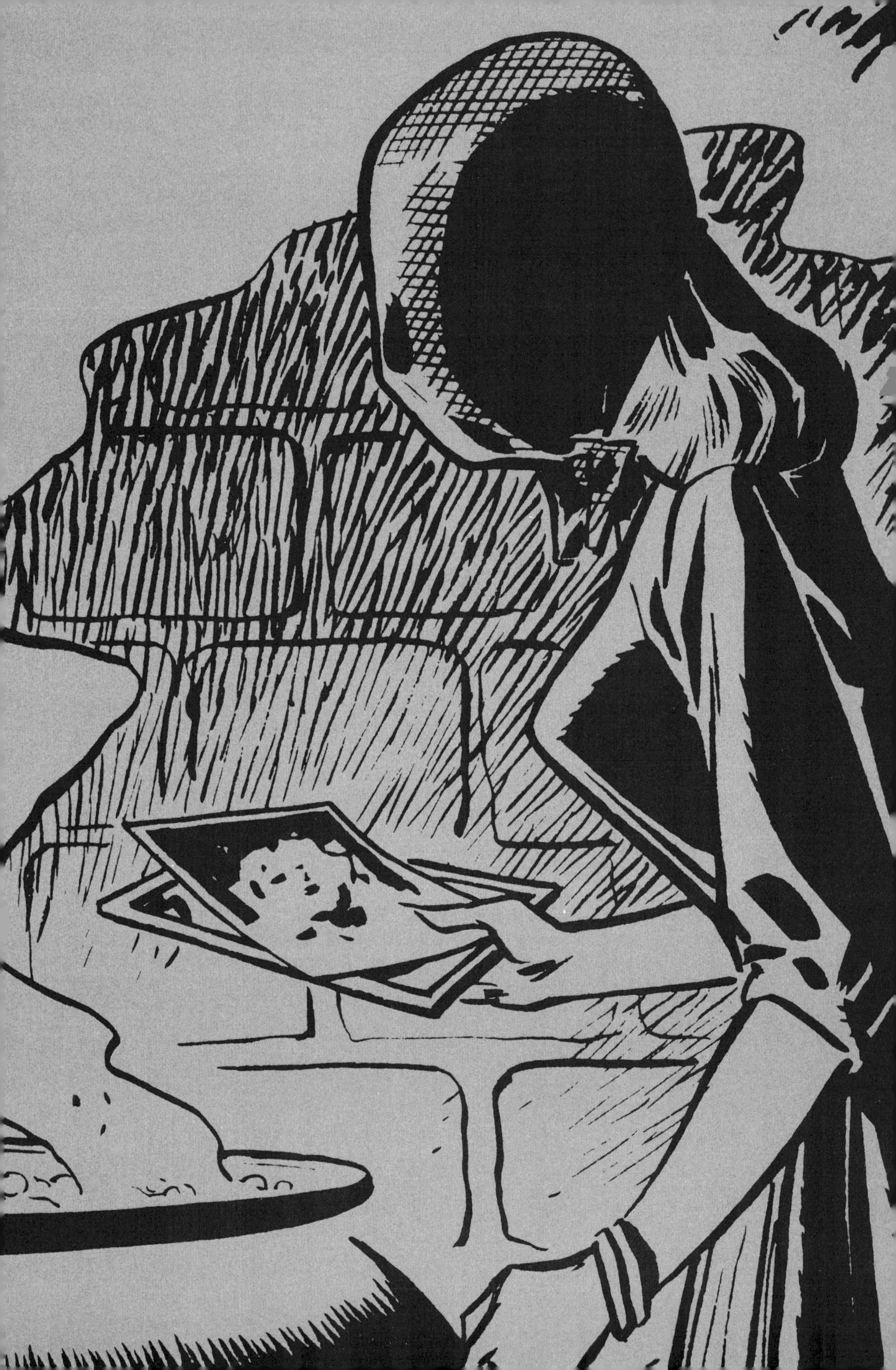

TED WHITE

CRIME, HORROR, TERROR, GORE, DEPRAVITY, DISRESPECT FOR ESTABLISHED AUTHORITY —AND SCIENCE FICTION, TOO!

THE UPS AND DOWNS OF EC COMICS

M.C. Gaines was both a practical man, credited with inventing the comic book as we know it (although comic strips had been reprinted in book form for more than two decades prior to his 1933 *Funnies on Parade*), and a visionary.

In the late 1930s, he formed a partnership with the owners of Detective Comics, Inc. (subsequently best known as DC Comics) and began publishing a series of superhero titles: *All-American Comics* (which featured the Green Lantern), *Flash Comics* (the Flash), *Sensation Comics* (Wonder Woman), *All-Star Comics* (The Justice Society of America), and *Comic Cavalcade* (a fatter 15¢ anthology of his superheroes).

But these were conventional commercial comic books of their day and, in essence, copies of DC's *Action Comics* (Superman), *Detective Comics* (Batman), and *World's Finest* (15¢ anthology), identical in formatting. Although successful, none (except, perhaps Wonder Woman's titles) matched the success of DC's Superman and Batman titles. All were published under the DC imprint, and the children who read them probably saw little difference among them.

These comics were forthrightly aimed at kids — theoretically an 8-year-old. Although comics were hugely popular and widely read by World War II and Korean War GIs, the fiction was maintained throughout the 1950s that the average comic book reader was still only 8 years old.

From their inception, comic books were looked down upon by much of American society. They cost only 10¢ and were often thrown away after reading. Many teachers regarded comic book reading as a detriment to genuine literacy. The theory was that kids who read comic books would never go on to read "real" literature — they would demand pictures with their prose.

Gaines thought that the comic book medium could be much more than just throwaway entertainment and he set out to prove it, first with *Picture Stories From the Bible*. It was earnestly done and intended to be educational rather than entertaining. Despite the best intentions of Gaines and his editors, writers, and artist (Don Cameron), it was pretty dull going for a comic book. But Gaines believed in it and pushed it.

Other matters were transpiring behind the scenes, and Gaines parted ways with DC in 1945, selling them all his titles except *Picture Stories From the Bible*.

Gaines began a new publishing imprint for his *Picture Stories* comics — Educational Comics, or "EC." In addition to *Picture Stories From the Bible*, he published *Picture Stories From American History*, *Picture Stories From Science*, and *Pictures Stories From World History*.

These were clearly intended to be sold in or through schools, and to be used with appropriate curricula. They were an idealistic venture, akin to *Classics Illustrated*, designed to prove that the lowly comic book could attain loftier goals of enlightenment.

But, like *Classics Illustrated*, they made no dent on academia. To teachers and other figures of authority over children, they were still "just comic books," and dismissed out of hand. And to the kids — their putative audience — they were dull stuff, lacking the excitement and panache of any superhero comic. They were not a commercial success.

When Gaines had left DC to found EC, he took one DC employee with him to be his business manager — Sol Cohen, whose first job as a teenager had been for DC, checking Manhattan comic book racks for sales movement during Superman's launch in 1938. Cohen had worked his way up through sales and distribution (DC and Independent News, an increasingly important distributor, had interlinking ownership), and he had a promising career at DC. But when Gaines asked Cohen to join him in his fledgling new company, Cohen accepted.

This proved to be a significant move for a reason no one anticipated. Because in 1947, M.C. Gaines and a friend, Sam Irwin, lost their lives in a boating accident on Lake Placid in New York. Gaines's final act was to save the life of his friend's 8-year-old son by throwing the boy to safety.

Gaines's son, William M. Gaines, inherited the company. But Bill was distant from his father, didn't care for comics, and was attending New York University with plans to become a chemistry teacher. Although entreated by his mother to take over the reins at EC, Bill was reluctant and for the first year did little but show up at the office periodically to sign checks.

Into this vacuum stepped Sol Cohen, EC's business manager. As he told me, years later, "the company was going down the toilet. The *Picture Stories* comics weren't selling and neither were the kiddy comics. I had to do something just to save my job."

His first act was to change "Educational Comics" to "Entertaining Comics."

"'Educational' was a word no comic-buying kid wanted to see. It was a kiss of death on any comic book," he told me.

His second act was to dump the *Picture Stories* titles and change the kiddy titles to crime, romance, and Western titles. (Due to postal regulations concerning second class mailing privileges — crucial for distribution purposes — it was financially wiser to change titles, continuing the previous numbering, than to drop one title and start a new one.)

1947 was a decisive turning point, although most of Cohen's changes occurred in 1948. In the late summer of 1947, *Moon Girl and the Prince* was launched. Moon Girl appears to have been a Wonder Woman copy. It went through two title changes before becoming *A Moon, A Girl, Romance*.

By then Bill Gaines was the editor. In early 1948, EC launched *War Against Crime!*

By 1949, Bill Gaines had become interested in comics. Sol Cohen moved on (to Avon Books) and Bill fully took over the company. He began bringing in the artists and editor/writers who would become known for their subsequent EC work.

Al Feldstein was brought in as a romance artist, although his first work for EC was for the Western title *Saddle Justice* in 1948.

Johnny Craig may have preceded Feldstein with work in the first *Gunfighter*, which also used Graham Ingels.

Harry Harrison and Wallace Wood (as collaborators) made their first appearance at EC in two Western titles that appeared at the end of 1949,

Gunfighter and *Saddle Romances*. (Harrison had appeared solo in a previous issue of the latter.)

The evolution of EC from 1947 to 1950 is one full of hints of the forthcoming "New Trend" titles. But New Trend fans may not find a lot to like in the earlier comics from EC. The quality was spotty, and there was not yet any focus on a unique style or approach to comics.

1950 was the year it all came together for EC. That spring saw the transformation of *War Against Crime!* into *The Vault of Horror*, *Crime Patrol* into *The Crypt of Terror* (later to become *Tales From the Crypt*), and *Gunfighter* into *The Haunt of Fear*, thus successfully establishing EC's horror-title trio.

The same month *Haunt of Fear* made its debut so did two science fiction titles, *Weird Science* (with #12, previously *Saddle Romances*), and *Weird Fantasy* (with #13, previously *A Moon, A Girl, Romance*).

In the fall of 1950, *Two-Fisted Tales* made its debut, taking over the numbering of *Haunt of Fear*, so its first issue was designated #18. This was done to satisfy — or dodge — those postal regulations. *Haunt of Fear* itself continued, renumbered, with #4. It confused the fans but made the business office happy. *Crime SuspenStories* premiered about the same time (starting with #1), thus setting in place EC's basic New Trend stable of titles.

Two-Fisted Tales was Harvey Kurtzman's first title, and it brought a sense of realism, irony, and anti-romance to war stories. *Frontline Combat* would join it half a year later.

Crime SuspenStories was Johnny Craig's title (as was, to a lesser degree, *Vault of Horror*; Al Feldstein was the overall SF and horror editor).

By 1951 the classic EC lineup was almost in place, lacking only *Shock SuspenStories* (1952) and *Mad* (1952).

The first half of the 1950s was EC's glory time — for better and for worse. For us comics fans, it was the best of times — crowned by superlative art and provocative stories — while for those who watched sternly over us, tut-tutting, it was the worst of times, a triumph of gore and disgust.

EC's basic "crime" was that its comics were not edited for that 8-year-old kid. They aimed higher, at a somewhat older, more mature audience.

(13-year-olds, perhaps — I was 13 when I discovered ECs, and I had by then mostly given up on other comics.)

The naysayers won, in the short-term. There were state and federal inquiries (inquisitions?), local comic book bonfires, and ultimately *Seduction of the Innocent* and the Comics Code. The New Trend comics were shelved in favor of a "New Direction" and new titles — horror and crime conspicuous by their absence.

But the tide had turned against EC. Its competitors wanted it put out of business (and many claim the Comics Code Authority was formed for that purpose).

In 1956 Bill Gaines gave up a losing fight and folded all his titles except *Mad* — which outlived him and survives wrapped in its decades-old formula to this day.

However, in the long term, EC has survived. There have been countless reprints of the comics themselves, as both comic books and as hardcover books. There have been TV shows and movies based on *Tales From the Crypt*. And now there are these ongoing collections from Fantagraphics, showcasing for the first time the individual artists whose works personified EC.

Theirs was a magical time — a time when young, ambitious artists decided for themselves to take comic book art to heights never previously dreamed of, heights that equaled the best work of the greatest of the newspaper strip artists of the 20th century.

Some of them went on to major successes in commercial art — book covers, movie posters, *TV Guide* covers — while others lived and eventually died in poverty.

No one told them then that what they were doing was a waste of time and ambition. We are all better off for their accomplishments, and we celebrate their work here.

TED WHITE *has been a comics fan for most of his life and, with Larry Stark, Bhob Stewart, and Fred von Bernewitz, was a seminal EC fan in the early 1950s. He has been a (still-quoted) jazz critic, a science fiction writer and editor, and a radio deejay. He wrote the Captain America novel* The Great Gold Steal *in 1966 and edited* Heavy Metal *in 1980.*

TITLES IN THIS SERIES

Corpse On The Imjin And Other Stories (Harvey Kurtzman)
Came The Dawn And Other Stories (Wallace Wood)
50 Girls 50 And Other Stories (Al Williamson)
'Tain't The Meat ... It's The Humanity And Other Stories (Jack Davis)
Fall Guy For Murder And Other Stories (Johnny Craig)
Child Of Tomorrow And Other Stories (Al Feldstein)
Sucker Bait And Other Stories (Graham Ingels)
Zero Hour And Other Stories (Jack Kamen)
Judgment Day And Other Stories (Joe Orlando)
Bomb Run And Other Stories (John Severin)
Aces High (George Evans)
Spawn Of Mars And Other Stories (Wallace Wood)
Grave Business And Other Stories (Graham Ingels)
Forty Whacks And Other Stories (Jack Kamen)
The High Cost of Dying And Other Stories (Reed Crandall)
The Living Mummy And Other Stories (Jack Davis)
Voodoo Vengeance And Other Stories (Johnny Craig)

COMING SOON

The Million-Year Picnic And Other Stories (Will Elder)

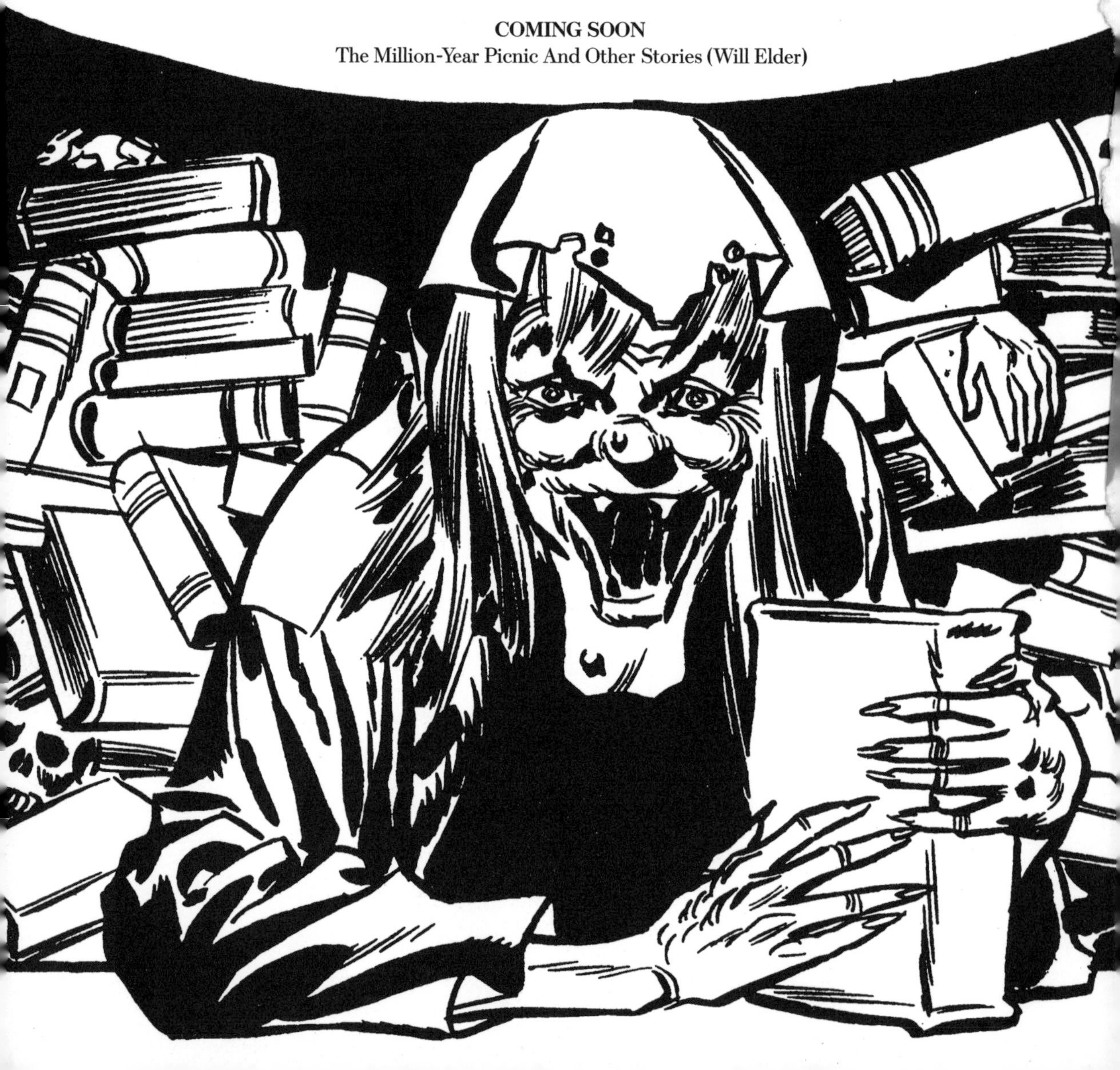